THE VINTNER'S LUCK

Elizabeth Knox

VICTORIA UNIVERSITY PRESS

VICTORIA UNIVERSITY PRESS
Victoria University of Wellington
PO Box 600 Wellington
http://www.vup.vuw.ac.nz

© Elizabeth Knox 1998

ISBN 0 86473 342 9

First published 1998
Reprinted 1998 (twice), 1999 (twice)

Printed by GP Print Ltd, Wellington

Could a stone escape from the laws of gravity? Impossible.
Impossible for evil to form an alliance with good.

Comte de Lautréamont

1808 Vin bourru *(new wine)*

A week after midsummer, when the festival fires were cold, and decent people were in bed an hour after sunset, not lying dry-mouthed in dark rooms at midday, a young man named Sobran Jodeau stole two of the freshly bottled wines to baptise the first real sorrow of his life. Though the festival was past, everything was singing, frogs making chamber music in the cistern near the house, and dark grasshoppers among the vines. Sobran stepped out of his path to crush one insect, watched its shiny limbs flicker then finally contract, and sat by the corpse as it stilled. The young man glanced at his shadow on the ground. It was substantial. With the moon just off full and the soil sandy, all shadows were sharp and faithful.

Sobran slid the blade of his knife between the bottleneck and cork, and slowly eased it free. He took a swig of the *friand*, tasted fruit and freshness, a flavour that turned briefly and looked back over its shoulder at the summer before last, but didn't pause, even to shade its eyes. The wine turned thus for the first few mouthfuls, then seemed simply 'a beverage', as Father Lesy would say, the spinsterish priest from whom Sobran and his brother, Léon, had their letters. The wine's now pure chemical power poured from Sobran's gut into his blood. He felt miserable, over-ripe, well past any easy relief.

Céleste was the daughter of a poor widow. She worked for Sobran's mother's aunt, fetched between the kitchen and parlour, was quicker than the crippled maid, yet was 'dear': 'Run upstairs, *dear...*'. Céleste kept the old lady company, sat with her hands *just so*, idle and attentive, while Aunt Agnès talked and wound yarn. At sixteen Sobran might have been ready to fall in love with her – now, at eighteen, it seemed his body had rushed between them. When he looked at Céleste's mouth, her shawled breasts, the pink fingertips of her hand curled over the top of the embroidery frame as she sat stitching a hunting-scene fire-screen, Sobran's prick would puff up

1

like a loaf left to prove, and curve in his breeches as tense as a bent
bow. Like his friend, Baptiste, Sobran began to go unconfessed for
months. His brother Léon looked at him with distaste and envy,
their mother shrugged, sighed, seemed to give him up. Then Sobran
told his father he meant to marry Céleste – and his father refused
him permission.

The elder Jodeau was angry with his wife's family. Why, he
wanted to know, hadn't his son been told? The girl didn't exactly set
snares, but she was fully conscious of her charms. Sobran was
informed that Céleste's father had died mad – was quite mad for
years, never spoke, but would bark like a dog. Then at midsummer
an uncle, in his cups, put a tender arm around Sobran's shoulder and
said don't – don't go near her, he could see how it was, but *that* cunt
was more a pit than most, a pit with slippery sides. 'Mark my
words.'

At the service after midsummer, in a church full of grey faces,
queasiness, and little contrition, Céleste had looked at Sobran, and
seemed to know he knew – not that he'd either asked or promised
anything – but her stare was full of scorn, and seemed to say, 'Some
lover *you* are.' Sobran had wanted to weep, and wanted, suddenly,
not to overcome Céleste, to mount a marital assault, but to
surrender *himself.* And, wanting, he ached all over. When Céleste
spoke to him after the service there was ice in her mouth. And when,
in his great-aunt's parlour, she handed him a glass of Malaga, she
seemed to curse him with her toast – '*Your health*' – as though it was
his health that stood between them.

Sobran got up off the ground and began to climb towards the
ridge. The vineyard, Clos Jodeau, comprised two slopes of a hill that
lay in the crooked arm of a road which led through the village of
Aluze and on past Château Vully on the banks of the river Saône. At
the river the road met with a greater road, which ran north to
Beaune. When the two slopes of Clos Jodeau were harvested, the
grapes of the slope that turned a little to the south were pressed at
Jodeau, and the wine stored in the family's small cellar. The
remainder of the harvested grapes were sold to Château Vully. The
wine of Clos Jodeau was distinctive and interesting, and lasted
rather better than the château's.

On the ridge that divided the slopes grew a row of five cherry trees. It was for these that Sobran made, for their shelter, and an outlook. Inside his shirt and sitting on his belt, the second bottle bumped against his ribs. He watched his feet; and the moon behind, over the house, pushed his crumbling shadow up the slope before him.

Last Sunday he had left Aunt Agnès's door before his family, only to go around the back to look in the door to the kitchen, where he knew Céleste had taken refuge. The door stood open. She was stooped over a sieve and pail as the cook poured soured milk into a cheese cloth to catch the curds. Céleste gathered the corners of the cloth and lifted it, dripping whey. She wrung it over the bucket. Then she saw Sobran, gave the cloth another twist and came to the door with the fresh cheese dripping on the flags and on to her apron. Her hands, slick with whey and speckled with grainy curds, didn't pause – as she looked and spoke one hand gripped and the other twisted. She told him he must find himself a wife. In her eyes he saw fury that thickened their black, her irises so dark the whites seemed to stand up around them like, in an old pan, enamel around spots worn through to iron. His desire took flight, fled but didn't disperse. Sobran knew then that he wanted forgiveness and compassion – *her* forgiveness and compassion, and that nothing else would do.

Sobran paused to drink, drank the bottle off and dropped it. He was at the cherry trees; the rolling bottle scattered some fallen fruit, some sunken and furred with dusty white mould. The air smelled sweet, of fresh and fermenting cherries and, oddly strong here, far from the well, a scent of cool fresh water. The moonlight was so bright that the landscape had colour still.

Someone had set a statue down on the ridge. Sobran blinked and swayed. For a second he saw what he *knew* – gilt, paint and varnish, the sculpted labial eyes of a church statue. Then he swooned while still walking forward, and the angel stood quickly to catch him.

Sobran fell against a warm, firm pillow of muscle. He lay braced by a wing, pure sinew and bone under a cushion of feathers, complicated and accommodating against his side, hip, leg, the pinions split around his ankle. The angel was breathing steadily, and smelled of snow. Sobran's terror was so great that he was calm, a serenity like that a missionary priest had reported having felt when he found himself briefly in the jaws of a lion. There was an interval of warm silence; then Sobran saw that the moon was higher and felt that his pulse and the angel's were walking apace.

Sobran looked up.

The angel's youth and beauty were a mask, superficial, and all that Sobran could see. And there was a mask on the mask, of watchful patience. The angel had waited some time to be looked at, after all. Its expression was open and full of curiosity. 'You slept for a while,' the angel said, then added, 'No, not a faint – you were properly asleep.'

Sobran wasn't afraid any more. This angel had been sent to him, obviously, not for comfort, but counsel, surely. Yet if Sobran confided nothing, and received no advice, the way he felt – enfolded, weak, warm in an embrace itself as invigorating as the air immediately over a wild sea – that alone seemed sufficient for now and for ever.

'I can sit,' Sobran said, and the angel set him upright. He felt the callused palms and soft wings brace, then release him. Then very slowly, as though knowing it might frighten, the angel raised his wings up and forward – they weren't as white as his skin, or the creamy silk he wore – and settled himself, the wings crossed before him on the ground, so that only his shoulders, head and neck were visible. When the angel released him, the world came back: Sobran heard the grasshoppers, and a dog bark down the valley at the house of Baptiste Kalmann, his friend. He recognised the dog's voice – Baptiste's favourite, the loyal Aimée.

Sobran told the angel about his love troubles, spoke briefly and economically, as though he paid for the privilege of a hearing. He told of his love, his parent's prohibition, and Céleste's father's madness. He said nothing offensive, nothing about his body.

The angel was thoughtful. He looked off into the shadow at the base of a vine where, following his gaze, Sobran saw the second bottle lay. He stretched for it, wiped the grit from its sides and offered it to the angel, who took it, covered the cork with his palm and, with no apparent use of force, drew it forth. The angel tilted the bottle to his mouth and tasted. Sobran watched the throat move, and light catch or come into a mark on the angel's side, on his ribs, right under his raised arm – a twisted shape – a scar or tattoo like two

4

interlocked words, one of which flushed briefly with a colour like light through the flank of a raised wave.

'A young wine,' the angel said. 'Reserve a bottle and we can drink it together when it's old.' He handed the bottle back. When Sobran put it to his mouth he felt the bottle neck, warm and wet. Again he tasted the wine's quick backward look, its spice – flirtation and not love.

'Was he mad, her father?' The angel asked.

Sobran licked his fingers, touched his own brow and made a hot stove hiss, as his grandmother had used to. 'Barked like a dog.'

'At the moon, or at people he didn't like?'

Sobran blinked, then laughed and the angel laughed with him – a dry, pretty laugh. 'I'd look into that further if I were you,' the angel said.

'This business of tainted blood,' Sobran said. 'There are so many stories of gulled brides and bridegrooms. Men or women who watch their own good corrupt and ail in their children.' He offered the wine again. The angel held up a refusing hand.

'It's too young, I know,' Sobran apologised.

'Do you suppose I live only on thousand-year eggs?'

Sobran looked puzzled, and the angel explained. 'In Szechuan, China, they bury eggs in ash – for a long while – then eat them, ash-coloured eggs.'

'A thousand years?'

The angel laughed. 'Do you think people could lay by, or wait so long to consume, or even *remember* where they had stored, *anything*, after a thousand years, whether appetising, precious, or lethal?'

The young man blushed, thinking that the angel was hinting at the Host, the thousand-year blessing which hadn't passed Sobran's lips for five Sundays now. 'Forgive me,' Sobran said.

'The wine?'

'I haven't received communion for five weeks.'

The angel said, flatly, 'Oh.' He thought a little, then got up, wrapped one arm about the trunk of the cherry tree and, with his other hand, hauled down a limb. The branch stooped till its leaves brushed Sobran's hair. The man picked some fruit, three on one stem, and the angel let the limb up again gently, his strength direct and dexterous. He sat, resettled his wings.

5

Sobran ate, his tongue separating the stones from sweet flesh and rolling them clean.

The angel said, 'You don't really know what Céleste knows, or what she thinks. You should just let her talk to you. Speak plainly, then simply listen. If the laws by which I have to live were numbered, that would be my first.'

A small crack opened in Sobran's self-absorption, his infantile certainty that the night was there to nourish and the angel to guide and comfort *him*. He said, 'Your first law would be our first commandment.'

'All angels love God,' the angel said, 'and have no other. He is our north. Adrift on the dark waters still we face Him. He made us – but He is love, not law.' The angel drew breath to say something further, but stopped, breath caught and lips parted. The wind got up and brushed the cherry trees, turned some of the angel's top feathers up to show paler down. The angel's eyes moved and changed, so that for a moment, Sobran expected to see the small green flames he often caught in the eyes of the farm cats.

Baptiste's Aimée was barking again, as if at a persistent prowling fox. Sobran thought of foxes, then that God was listening, that His ear was inclined to the hillside.

The angel stood abruptly – a soldier surprised by an officer jumping up to give a salute. Sobran flinched as another gust pressed the trees. The angel said, 'On this night next year I will toast your marriage.' Then the wind rose up in a whirling column, semi-solid with leaves, twigs and dust. The whirlwind reared, snakelike, and swallowed the angel so that Sobran saw the figure turning, face wrapped in his black hair and white clothes wrung hard against his body. The angel's wings snapped open, a slack sail suddenly fully fed, then angel and whirlwind were a league away and above, a dark blur in the clear sky. The wind dropped. Leaves, earth, twigs, and a few black-tipped, fawn feathers, sprinkled down over the northern slope of the vineyard.

The following day Sobran collected those feathers, and tied two by dark yarn to the topside of the rafters above his bed. The third, eighteen inches long, he put to use as a quill. Although it wouldn't trim down, it made a fine enough line. At the kitchen table, surrounded by his family, but in secret, since all but his brother were unlettered, Sobran wrote to Céleste. He dipped, watched the ink penetrate the feather's long chamber of air, wrote Céleste's name, then of his clumsiness and their consequent misunderstanding. He paused to wonder at his spelling, and ran the plume through his mouth, tasting fresh snow, which made his mouth tender as he dipped once more and wrote to beg a meeting.

1809 **Vin de coucher** *(nuptial wine)*

After midnight, with the bottle unopened beside him, Sobran lay on his back on top of the ridge and looked at the sky. High cloud formed an even film from horizon to horizon, through which the full moon showed, hugely haloed in rose, steely blue and bronze. It was the kind of moon that made his mother cross herself. But to Sobran it was simply a spectacle. He was happy and relaxed, his shirt open to air his skin and his arms under his head. He was sated. He had gone to bed early, made love, then got up and washed – it wouldn't do to meet an angel while glazed in places with love's juices, like an egg-white coated Michaelmas bun. But the satisfaction wouldn't wash away. Sobran smiled, slit his eyes and showed his throat to that airy wheel of moon-halo – a happy, animal homage.

There was a creak, like the rigging on a ship, a variable whistling, and the angel dropped down beside him, breathing hard. Sobran sat up and they grinned at each other. The angel's hair was stiff with frost, and sheets of watery ice were sliding off his steaming wings. He brushed at them with one hand, dripped, panted, laughed, explained that he'd been flying high and then handed Sobran a square, dark glass bottle. Xynisteri, he said, a white wine from Cyprus. Sobran should drink it with his wife. Then he added, soberly, 'I'm confident that you have a wife.'

Sobran began to unwrap the two glasses he had brought, set them on the ground, uncorked his own bottle and poured. 'This is our nuptial wine, a gift from the château, who take our own Jodeau South as table wine. We have the same pinot noir grapes, of course, and this slope is better, but their cellars are old and large.' He offered a glass to the angel. The red was robbed of its colour in the moonlight, the wine dark, semi-opaque, with a white shield, it seemed, laid on its surface. The angel took his glass and made his toast – 'To you' not 'May God bless you.'

Sobran said that, after the angel had counselled him, his love for Céleste had pained him less. 'Your talk drew its poison – taught me faith and patience and constancy.' He nearly said 'continence', but that was all part of thoughts he had to conceal, modestly, as a woman must cover her head in church. Besides, it wasn't entirely true. It was Sobran's incontinence that had finally decided his suit. When, in the first rain of late summer he had walked Céleste just yards off their path – they were walking home from his sister's – he had bent her against a forked sapling, raised her skirts and penetrated her petticoats. She skipped a month, and he married her.

'We are drinking to my daughter as well – to Sabine – to a wedding and a christening,' Sobran said, then blushed. 'Yes, quick work.'

'Conclusive.'

'No. Maybe next year a son.'

They were quiet for a time, then Sobran began to talk about Clos Jodeau, his future share in his father's vineyard, and how he was in charge of Baptiste Kalmann's vines too, while his friend was away with the army. 'And that is my excuse for tonight – seeing after some of Baptiste's business. The vines of Clos Kalmann are in a pretty poor state, and *have* had me up at all hours.' Sobran looked at the middle window on the upper floor of the house. 'When I can be sure Céleste will sleep soundly in my absence, I'll bring a lamp,' he said.

'Next year, you mean?' The angel smiled.

Sobran blushed. He felt the blush move into his hair and sweat start. He swallowed, then asked, 'Will you come?'

'Yes.'

'Though,' Sobran said, 'reading Baptiste's letters I have thought I might follow the Emperor too.'

'So you're not promising to be here next year. But *I* must promise.'

'These are times of great change,' Sobran said – but how could he explain to an unearthly being this local momentousness? He added, 'For all France.'

'I didn't know you thought of France,' the angel said. 'That's unusual in a Burgundian.'

'All right – I'll be here,' Sobran promised.

'One night each year, for the rest of your life,' the angel said. 'Or is that inconvenient?'

Sobran was flattered, but could immediately see problems. 'I might travel.'

The angel shrugged.

'A lifetime – so much to promise.'

'You've already promised your lifetime.'

It was like speaking to a tricky priest. And vows made in marriage were unexceptional – tenderness, vigilance, fidelity, hard work, all seemed easier to pledge than the same night every year. 'Is it bad luck to fail you?' Sobran asked.

'I'm not trying to sell you a sick pig, Sobran.'

Sobran was offended. 'If I bargain like a peasant, it's because I am one.'

The angel considered and, like a young girl, picked up a lock of his own hair and bit its end – Sobran heard it rustle between his teeth. After a moment the angel spat the hair out and said, 'I know nothing about luck. I'm not offering rewards or punishments, so don't promise. Just come.'

Sobran said he would. He forgot to be cautious or courteous and was simply moved.

The angel held out his glass and Sobran refilled it. 'Tell me about Céleste, and Sabine, and Léon, your brother who is with the priests, and Baptiste Kalmann, and what you think of this Emperor,' the angel said.

1810 Vigneron *(a vine-grower who may, or may not, be working for himself)*

Sobran brought the angel his discontent, a savour to their talk, a refinement, like a paper screw of salt for a lunch to be eaten out-of-doors, at the edge of a half-harvested meadow. The angel could solve this or salve that – Sobran's quarrels with his father, or his brother Léon, Céleste's odd moods, or the likelihood of a less promising harvest. Sobran felt that he was being kind, *and* thinking of the future – the blessing of this bond, that would last, surely, if the angel felt Sobran required his advice.

Sobran had, till then, only one friend he drank with. Try as he might, his inexperience, or his previous experience, caused some awkwardness in his handling of the angel. The procedures of their acquaintance were so different from those of his friendship with Baptiste Kalmann. His meetings with the angel were formal, respectful, as tamely satisfying as a pantry full of fresh preserves. The angel's attention was gratifying. But when Sobran listened to himself talking he was reminded of his father speaking to the Comte de Valday. Some weathervane in his father's talk always twitching a little to keep pointing true to the Comte's interest. Sobran heard a similar attentiveness in his own voice, and found himself a little resentful of the angel.

Céleste shook Sobran and he found his eyes had opened to follow a meteor of lamplight under the door. He heard footsteps on the stairs.

'It's your father. He knocked,' Céleste said.

Little Sabine heaved over in her sleep. Her feet came free of the covers and banged against the bars of the crib. Sobran got up, felt for her – yes, he'd heard right – tucked the covers around her and began to dress.

Outside a horse stamped and harness clinked.

Céleste climbed out of bed, pulled on her bedsocks and a shawl. She said she'd cut some bread and cheese.

Downstairs Léon sat on his palliasse by the stove and rubbed his head – the cropped cut the holy brothers favoured. Léon had left the monastery following some disgrace that embarrassed his mother but only made his father laugh (not at the priests, but at his wife's and son's humiliation). When Léon came home he slept for several months in the attic, under the tiles – till the weather began to turn. He and Sobran had once shared the room Sobran and Céleste now occupied, while Sophie, their older sister, had slept in a back room now full of cellared bottles. In the year Sophie wed, Léon entered the seminary. At that time Léon was a studious boy, who was always setting himself little tests, of patience or continence – nothing remotely worldly. Perhaps, liking apples, he would deny himself apples for half a year (for the months when they were sweetest; he was no cheat). Or perhaps he'd forgo salt on his food, or wearing a wrap about his ears in the cold weather.

Sobran considered his brother a fool, and was scarcely civil to him. Léon would delight in carrying their father's messages, displeasure, nagging reminders. Before Sobran married, Léon was often sent to chase him up, loafing in the dirty, dog-crowded kitchen of Baptiste Kalmann, drinking brandy; or at the little house on the road to Aluze, which had red potted geraniums by its door, and the wood always stacked high in the lean-to by the chimney. Here Sobran kept company with the young widow Rueleau, who wore black, but had coloured ribbons braided into her hair. Léon had even, once, found his brother semi-naked and washing by the fire. Baptiste Kalmann had grinned at Léon through a gap in the curtains drawn around the widow's bed. The room smelled of brandy, soap, sweat. Sobran was completely unashamed, and took his leisure dressing. But on the way home, when Léon began to say stiffly that their father had not 'worked to build up his house, vineyard, name, to have them slowly bled of substance and honour – ' Sobran pushed him down into a ditch at the roadside, then stooped above him and shook him by the throat. Sobran said that since he didn't *pay* he wasn't robbing anyone. And Léon, slighter than his brother and half-choked, said, 'If Kalmann pays then you're as much a whore as Anne Rueleau.' Sobran called him a tick, a holy little turd, shook him some more, threw him down and walked on ahead.

Léon had never reported his brother's misdemeanours, seemed to keep quiet not in order to dominate his brother with a reserve of secrets, but because he wanted no part of his brother's *cupidity*, as he called it, those contaminating acts he, Léon, preferred not to live with.

At Sobran's wedding feast Céleste whispered to him: 'When your brother kissed me he looked at me as if he pitied me. Why is that?'

Baptiste, behind them, listening, his gunner's uniform reflecting rosily on Céleste's white gown, said, 'Léon thinks that every fart proves the world is fallen.' He raised his eyebrows, then his glass to toast them.

Léon rolled up the palliasse, tucked it by the wood box. As he bent to pull his shirt over his head his brother saw that his neck was smudged dark with dirt. Uncleanliness was so out of Léon's character that at the sight Sobran experienced a spark of shock that atomised instantly and was gone. Sobran turned away.

Their father was out by the pump, talking to Christophe Lizet, whose sister Geneviève was missing. The Jodeau men were asked to help Christophe and his cousin Jules search the far bank of the river.

They went in the Lizets' cart, the only horse the Jodeaus owned tied on behind. It was an hour after dawn when they crossed the river on the ferry that linked the road which ran past the château. There the party split. Jodeau senior went with Christophe, following the river north. Jules, Léon and Sobran went on foot, south along the riverbank. There was nothing left to ask – who saw Geneviève Lizet last, what she was wearing. But Jules spoke about Geneviève's character; she was sunny and quiet, and this disappearance was no mischief of her own making.

Léon said he knew Geneviève, they had taken their first communion together. They had been in the same class, learning their catechism with Father Lesy. 'We were children then, under ten.'

Sobran remembered Geneviève among the harvesters at the château, pressing grapes. She lost her headscarf in the vat. All the Lizet women had fine sleek hair that shucked any covering, their buns or plaits burst apart releasing slippery hair of a glossy blond. Sobran couldn't think of the Lizet girls' faces, just this hair, and the back of a head, as radiant as the moon, moving to eclipse his friend's face. In Sobran's memory Baptiste was straddling the tilted yoke pole of an unharnessed cart. He had the water bucket before him, and a dipper in one hand, his other elbow propped on his own thigh and his face rested on his fist. One finger was pressed into the corner of his mouth, like a pin on a map. He was smiling at Sobran, then the fair head of a Lizet girl eclipsed Baptiste's face as she kissed him.

It *was* Geneviève, Sobran remembered. He stopped to watch the willows across the river, their wands bent from the prevailing wind. The river was ropy over stones near Sobran's feet, but deep under the willows.

Jules said the château would send a boat to look closely at the willow roots. He spoke as though he knew she was dead, had settled it in his mind already, knew they were looking not for a girl but a corpse.

They went on. The sun, still low, lit the rolling hills, the vines across the river were nearly bare. The land behind the vineyard was in grazing, green grass coming up between dry stalks of after-grass. Thick clouds moved to cover the sky, they palmed darkness, kept the black close beneath them – the land was still sunlit. Then it wasn't, and small split-tailed birds, a kind of swallow, began to fly low over the river where insects were rising to the coming rain.

It became darker as they walked. The grass loudly scrubbed their clogs. They saw something pale on the beach of boulders where the river curved. Jules ran – Sobran followed, hurrying yet hesitant. He stopped short at the sight of the girl's bared legs and belly, puffy, bleached and bruised. Her skirts were over her head. Jules pulled them down: he was sobbing, stooped, abruptly soft in the middle, as though someone had gutted him so that his chest sagged into the gap of his gutlessness.

One side of the girl's head was black with blood, which dyed her fair hair pink to its ends. Her skull had a dent in it, and her forearms were battered and misshapen. Her jaw was askew as if she'd been caught pulling a face to frighten a child and the wind had changed as her mother warned.

Léon arrived behind them, limped up as though he had a stone in his shoe. He looked, didn't pause but came forward, took off his jacket and draped it over her face. Then he knelt beside her and began to say a rosary. Jules collapsed on the other side of the corpse, put his head between his knees, sobbed and swayed.

Sobran said he would go to the château. There was an arrangement about a gunshot to recall all the searchers.

He ran, and as he ran the heat peeled away from the land. Rain came across the surface of the river like the bristles of a broom. Sobran stopped, squatted and vomited neatly between his feet, then got up and jogged on.

Later he stood, shawled in a blanket, by the fire in the main hall of the château, the old, stone-floored, thirteenth-century hall. It was unused since midsummer and the feast of wildfowl. Sobran watched soot bloom at the back of the white-washed flue.

A crowd of men with muddy feet stood about, waiting for the return of the party sent out to fetch the body in. The Comte had given orders, was now speaking quietly to Sobran's father and the weeping Christophe Lizet. They moved Sobran's way — then he was looking down at the Comte's brown face, into his red-rimmed blue eyes. The Comte asked, 'How was it you came to find her?'

'We looked where we were told to look.' Then, 'That's a stupid question.'

The older Jodeau lunged forward and struck the side of his son's head, told him not to be insolent.

Sobran looked at the floor. He listened to his father tell the Comte that they could put something else in the river, this side, he thought he knew where, to find it on that beach.

'Of course, you know its currents,' the Comte said.

Sobran said, 'The rain is changing the river.' He glanced up, saw his father's scowl.

'Did you know Geneviève Lizet?' the Comte asked.

A little, Sobran said. He remembered her from several harvests at the château. She kissed Baptiste Kalmann.

The Comte waited.

'Baptiste is in Tyrol.' Sobran stared at the old man, trying to convey how futile he thought questions were.

'What happened when you found the body?'

'Jules wept, Léon prayed, I ran for help. We were just the right number so none of us had the same thing to do.'

The Comte put his hand around the back of Sobran's neck and held him still a moment, then nodded to his valet who brought the brandy decanter and poured Sobran a generous measure. The Comte directed Sobran to a chair. 'Sit down, and you'll be fetched something to eat.' As he turned away Sobran heard the Comte say to his father, 'He's only angry at what he's seen.'

⌒﹏

1811 **Vin tourné** *(turned wine)*

Sobran missed his friend Baptiste. Céleste gave birth to a second daughter. His father was a heavy-handed manager. Sobran was married, twenty-one, and still not a man. He'd seen nothing of the world, couldn't choose his own way, had no heir and no clear future. Yet he knew what the next years held – work, with seasonal variations; the vintages, at best bottled triumph; a life of mild, undemeaning struggle and qualified happiness. Aluze, village, farms, vineyards, all seemed dreary. And there were days when it all seemed *bad*.

Sobran was unsettled. So, despite Céleste's protests, he made a pensioner's provision, arranged to send her half his soldier's pay, and went off to look at different landscapes and faces beyond his *pays*, people he couldn't put name to.

So it was that, in high summer, in Westphalia, he stood with Baptiste in the loggia of a whorehouse, watching the privates in line outside a lamp-lit crib, for a whore to be had for copper coins. The woman he and his friend meant to share was washing in the room behind them, straddling a bowl, her skirt knotted around her waist. A leather curtain on the crib door was open a little, the next in line looking in. Sobran could see shiny-bottomed breeches and an arse, thin, fair-skinned, in motion. Baptiste passed him the third bottle of stolen Seewein, a dry, easy white the gunners had won from some cavalry officers at cards. They wouldn't have spoken, but that the towline on a river barge broke as the cavalry men, a smith, Baptiste and Sobran – artillery men with two light guns – waited to cross. As they waited they played. Baptiste for his horde of tobacco, Sobran for a miniature in a silver case that he'd taken from a corpse after a skirmish.

In the room behind them the whore called, 'All right?' Then in her own tongue, 'One at a time, or together?' She smiled, inviting with her hands.

Thirty minutes later, spent, Sobran waited for his friend to finish. For him the whore had murmured, for Baptiste she cried out. Sobran wondered why she was tender with him, or pretended tenderness. He thought about Céleste, how she liked to nurse his head against her breasts.

Sobran was abruptly sick. He leaned over the rail and regurgitated wine and bile, clung to the rail for a moment, then staggered away to the stairs, into the yard, across the straw-cushioned flagstones to the gates. He placed his hands against the gate and was sick again. It wasn't that he'd remembered Céleste – with the whore's salt, cut with soap, still in his mouth – it was the moon, a cool witness, a memory of being held, and the realisation, like an assault, that tonight an angel would wait, for however long a patient angel waited, for an appointment Sobran couldn't keep, since he was six hundred miles removed, drunk and whoring. Sobran stood with his forehead pressed against the gate.

Baptiste found Sobran, dried his eyes on a hairy forearm and gave him more wine. Later Sobran woke when the sun came in and coloured the walls of the room in which he lay, with a light as cold as aired wine full of yellow flor. The whore was beside him, and beside her Baptiste; all three lay pickled in sweat. Sobran listened for the sound he'd heard on waking to be repeated – neither cockcrow, nor a dawn enfilade, but the sound of soft multiple impacts, like a spade full of dry earth tossed on top of a coffin, or of a single downbeat of great wings. But it wasn't repeated, he'd dreamed it, and it was his dream leaving.

⁓

1812 **Vin de glacier** *(ice wine)*

A year later, despite the circumstances in which he found himself, Sobran was conscious that it was *that night*. He went to church, stood at the back while the congregation — culled of all those who had fled: the propertied, prosperous, well and whole, the well-placed and all their servants — stared at him in hostility. Poor sickly people. The priest was shabby, unused to officiating in so great a church. In the candlelight his beard looked verminous, seemed to seethe. He hadn't stinted on the incense, which flowed sluggishly from censers swung by two elderly laymen. In the darkness above the candles gilt-tiled mosaics glittered like a nest of snakes stirring. Sobran looked up and saw Christ's raised hands, the elongated flames of tapers standing in still air. His gaze found angels, in heavy brocaded gowns, and with perky, impractical wings, without sinew. Among the flock, all gold-haired and gold-gowned, was one with hands, feet and face as black as gangrene, as black as frostbite, but serene.

When he looked down, Sobran found a woman staring at him. Through the loose knit of the shawl that covered her head shone hair the colour of butter. Her skin was the watery white shade of a freshly cut raw potato, her brows and lashes as blond and glossy as straw. She didn't look away, nor did she smile, just met his eyes with a look of sober calculation, then gestured with her head toward the door.

Sobran followed her out into the day. The street was hazy with smoke from the fires in the Chinese Bazaar. The square outside the church was filled with shadow-making rubbish, a wagon with a broken wheel, a split barrel, tangled bundles of bedding or clothes, dropped by refugees, perhaps in lieu of their corpses.

She took him to her house, a first-floor room, piled with dusty luggage. She had no money, no food, and was full of child. Sobran realised this as she climbed the stairs. Until then her walk had seemed stately, her body substantial, but all her own. He couldn't understand a word she said as she stood in the middle of her chamber and pointed about her. She wasn't pleading, for her tone

17

was flat; nor defeated, for she showed not fear but pride as she let the shawl slip from her hair and began to unbutton her smock.

Her breasts were great, stiff, and veined blue. Sobran didn't touch them, but took her hands and had her step up on a box, then he turned her and lifted her skirt. She wore no drawers, and her sex was like a heavy purse, in its blond hair as dark as cured meat. Her stomach hung, enormous, full term, her navel another nipple, but pressed bloodless. Sobran unbuttoned, spat on his hand, wet her and worked himself in. He thrust his arms through the silky cascade of her hair and took her breasts, as heavy and soft as kid wineskins, pressed them against her ribs, gathered her in, close, momentous, her braced legs and arms trembling, as she supported the weight of both of them and he passed through her ghostly pallor, her slippery grip, in a fiery point like gunfire, four explosions, then a dry fire, and he began to diminish.

Sobran couldn't see, his ears rang – then a warm wave broke against his pelvis, and washed his shrinking penis out of her. Her waters had broken, and ran, glistening, down her legs.

Within a minute Sobran had pulled up his breeches, picked up his hat and coat and was on the landing outside her door. He hadn't paid. She hadn't called out, but he could hear her whimpering.

He went back, wrapped a blanket around her and got her on to the bed, told her he'd fetch a neighbour, a woman. Before going out again he pulled his purse from his tunic and dropped several coins into a wooden bowl by the bed, where they rattled among two withered pears and two dead wasps.

It was no squalid tenement. Every apartment was of a good size – several rooms, three floors and cramped attics – but all were uninhabited, only the large furniture remaining: bedsteads, wardrobes, tables and sideboards, one rolled mattress wedged hopelessly tight in a doorway.

Sobran went back out into the street. The few people there moved away from him. Soldiers around a fire, his own countrymen, laughed, told him to leave her, Russian whore. One, very sullen, asked if there was more, should he pump her up? He filled his cheeks to blow while jerking his hips a number of times. The other soldiers laughed. Sobran backed off and turned, alone, and looked at the blind windows, the littered road, near and far, the hazy sky over glossy gold bulbs of domes, gold chains strung, spire to spire, dividing the sky into high corrals for who knew what kind of cattle.

He went back to the church and spoke to one of the women at the rail, then to the shabby priest. He couldn't make himself understood till an ancient man in black hobbled from a side chapel where he was praying at the tomb of some great family. As a great man's servant he spoke French and interpreted Sobran's plea – there was a woman, alone, about to give birth. The priest asked two old women if they would be so kind as to go with him. Sobran led them across the square, through the portal, up the stairs and to the woman's door, then retreated back through them as they rushed forward to surround the bed. He saw her heavy white arm rise from the blankets. She took the priest's hand. Sobran hurried away.

He passed the soldiers at the fire, and looting Austrian infantry-men from a levied contingent, criss-crossing from building to building like bees whose hives are being moved. He went back to the encampment in the Kremlin; and to Baptiste, who was on punishment for drunkenness, and polishing tackle outside the stable that housed the colonel's horses. Sobran said he'd found a full sow of a whore and Baptiste said being in this country was as useless as fucking a pregnant whore – an imperial army that wouldn't even defend this verminous cunt of a city but was happier to go and sit in a swamp. Did Sobran know that the city was again on fire, over the river? It was like trying to catch a lizard, making Russia a subject. 'All we've got is the tail. And nothing to eat but weeks-old bread and soup of twice-boiled chicken bones.' Beneath Baptiste's hand, and the rag, the blacking and beeswax made the saddle-leather flash white.

Five months later they marched, with a wind at their backs that blew all the way from Siberia, that slowed and gripped, a freezing vice. Russia seemed to want to keep the Grand Army, after all.

Sobran marched among other gunners. They had long since abandoned their stranded cannon. Sobran's wet breath had frozen, fastening his scarf to his mouth. He let it be. There was nothing to eat and no need to speak. For days he'd coaxed Baptiste; now he supported him. He watched their feet, and the trail of muddy snow the column made. He had known men to stray, thought he'd seen them through the curtaining snow, stumbling blots that shrank and dimmed. He forgot how to shout. Days ago, when he'd seen shapes, he had thought of ambush – the harassing Cossacks – but whoever lived here had only to leave the Grand Army alone in order to secure its ruin. Sobran hadn't spoken all day, and it was a day since Baptiste had said his last coherent words, looking up at the column: 'Where are our colours?' The men around them now were a mix of three different regiments.

Sobran looked up again. The snow was brighter. There was some muttered speculation. Would it clear? Hadn't the wind relented a little? A man from the Alps said that, if it cleared, if the sky opened right up, they'd all die of cold shortly after nightfall. Better hope it keeps snowing. There was a rumour of shelter ahead. Stone walls, food and fuel, their best hope.

Baptiste stumbled and they both fell, losing their place in the line as men moved around them, till one, still capable of neighbourly behaviour, helped Sobran get Baptiste up. They walked him between them. Sobran caught sight of another straggler, a wide-shouldered phantom in the blizzard. The column curved towards the figure, which stood, immobile, solidifying slowly. It was a wayside shrine – wood, shingles, ironwork, snow feathering the iron like goosedown. There was a pulse of relief through the column: the shelter was more than a rumour. Sobran turned his head stiffly to peer into Baptiste's face. It was snow-crusted, his skin dark and ice-crisped, with raw fissures across the cheeks. Baptiste's eyes were filmed and milky.

They limped on.

At the end of that worst stretch of the longest leg of the retreat, Sobran didn't know whether they had overshot the village, the shelter, or were perhaps coming at it by a spiralling course. He walked, his arm welded to his friend's side, and didn't register the moment of his arrival at the byre, didn't see the thorn hedge, or batten fence, just stumbled over a stone lintel on to a flagstone floor strewn with straw, the lustre of summer still in it. Then his feet passed through a gory flood from the opened neck of a cow, steam boiling from the blood and creeping over the assembled soldiers like tendrils of marsh mist. Breath stood at each soldier's lips like a phantom sunning itself on the threshold of a tomb.

Sobran found a place and set Baptiste down. He was too tired to wait for the thaw to permit him to unwrap his friend's face, or his own. He went to sleep.

*

His flesh was petrified, replaced like petrified wood by brittle minerals. He warmed. The bed was warm. Its mattress had been slit and his body pushed in among the feathers, into a sleek container, a pod, or a boat, or two wings like hands cupped to catch water. A voice said, precise, a sunlit dewdrop shaking in a spider web: 'You are an animal.'

Sobran woke sobbing. The skin of his cheeks, where his beard didn't reach, had come away on the scarf as it loosened. There was no feeling in the scabbed tip of his nose, but he could smell roast beef. Someone helped him to sit up from the straw, and put a knife in his hand, spitted on its tip a thick slab of charred meat. 'You're lucky, I saved some for you,' said the gunnery sergeant; then, 'Kalmann died. We put his body outside with the others: Le Borde and Henri Tipoux.'

Sobran looked for grief but saw only the meat. He had no appetite, but the sight of the meat had meaning.

'I've seen men do that, reach safety, then die,' the sergeant said. Then, 'Eat, Jodeau.'

Sobran took the edge of the cool bloody meat into his mouth.

⟜

1813 Vinaigre *(vinegar)*

The beneficiary of his friend's will, and owner now of two south-facing slopes, a vineyard that straddled the road – for both Baptiste and the elder Jodeau were dead, one buried in the crowded churchyard three miles from his home, the other still melting into the soil of a village near Vilna – Sobran Jodeau stood, at moonrise on a night a week after midsummer, on the ridge that no longer divided his property into equal halves. He stood turned to the moon so that he could be seen – his face, and the half-mask of scars where the ice had clawed him.

When the angel came he stood between Sobran and the moon.

'Look at me,' Sobran said.

'Frostbite?' the angel asked, his voice mild and curious.

Sobran asked, 'Why didn't you counsel me to stay at home?'

'I'm not here to advise you.'

'You *did* advise me. You told me to marry Céleste.'

The angel was still for a moment, then moved his head slightly and said, 'I don't think I did.'

'You said you would toast my wedding.'

'That wasn't a prediction.'

'These past years – there were times when I thought you were with me. But they were the wrong times. Wrong for a guardian.'

The angel ignored this – didn't seem to hear – but his voice was faintly altered as he went on, calmly frank as ever, but with the merest hint of hauteur. 'I came those two nights. On one it rained. I went down into the kitchen of your house – looked at myself in the high polish on Céleste's copper pans. I saw your daughter's stable of hobby horses – all the matched blacks and browns and greys of her father's socks. Your absence afforded her many horses.'

'Why do you come here?' Sobran asked.

'I promised.'

'I release you from your promise!'

'It wasn't *you* I promised,' the angel said quietly.

Sobran, defeated, unable to raise a hand to the angel, either in anger or for help, dropped on to his knees. Then shame carried him through a barrier, and he cast himself forward to touch the warm smooth skin of the angel's feet. He said, 'I've been drunk and whoring. And a thief; I robbed the dead. My friend Baptiste is dead and I've profited by it. And Sabine forgot me. My other daughter, Nicolette, doesn't know me at all. She cried and wouldn't give up her place in bed beside her mother.'

One foot was moving under Sobran's hand, tapping. Sobran stopped sobbing and sat back on his heels. Yes, the foot was tapping. The angel was looking at it too.

'I'm making a mockery, of course,' the angel said, 'of my impatience. For me impatience would be unseemly, as if I took to wearing a timepiece. You should tell me about it. The fights in Tyrol. The battle, Borodino. How your friend died. The injuries you suffered and caused. Talk to me – I'm neither innocent nor ineducable.'

Sobran said, sulkily, 'I must say this: you *did* promise these meetings.'

'So did you, in very bad grace, then broke your promise.'

Something further occurred to Sobran. 'Did you only *suggest* that I marry Céleste?'

The angel didn't reply.

Sobran stepped up to the angel, and noticed as he did so that the angel was scarcely taller than him, and of a lighter build than he had remembered. 'You spoke as though you knew what was best for me.'

'Has what's happened not been for the best?'

'My friend is dead.'

'He went before you ...'

The angel was reminding Sobran that Baptiste was in Heaven – and Sobran wanted to hit him. He put his hands up, and the angel, by reflex, tilted his face out of reach – and into the moonlight, so that his beauty raised a glassy barrier through which Sobran couldn't touch him, a barrier through which neither violence nor tenderness could pass. The angel went on, adjusting his words, his voice full of cool scorn, 'Baptiste *went into the army* before you. He'd have died without you. And is Céleste not a good wife? Do you now not want a wife?'

Sobran stared at the angel through a minute of silent fury – it seemed to him on both their parts. Then he answered, 'I'm satisfied with my wife, and I can bear the loss of my friend. But you trouble me. Why do you come here? Why did you first come and why did you promise to meet me again?'

The angel took a deep breath then huffed out hard through his nose, like an impatient parade horse. 'I returned because *it pleased me* to promise you, and to keep my promise. I returned to see what happened about your love troubles. That first night, the night we met, I'd only stopped here to rest. The rose bush I carried was heavy. Or, to be exact, its damp roots were. It was of no great height and pruned back to dead wood, little more than a bag of roots in soil. I dropped it when I caught you – when you fainted. And I lost it. But the year it rained and I went down to your house I saw that someone had found and planted it. The pink rose I carried from Denmark and was transporting to my garden.' Sometimes the angel was vague, and the other times exhaustively informative. It made him sound unreliable. He said, 'I have a – I'm not sure what word best fits – a *collection* of earthly roses.'

'You're a botanist?' Sobran gazed at the angel in amazement. A collection of roses seemed such an ordinary thing, like the passion of a country priest. 'Aren't all flowers to be found in Heaven?'

'Everyone's a theologian,' the angel said, droll. Then, 'All things thrive in Heaven, so are unlike their earthly selves. Anyone who hoped to grow earthly roses in Heaven would be obliged to keep fetching fresh specimens.' The angel touched the young man's face, where ice had gnawed his flesh. His touch was firm, like a physician's, and his fingertips were evenly upholstered by resilient calluses, like the pads on a cat's paw. The angel was thoughtful. 'When are *you* truest, a perfect Sobran Jodeau? Is every scar or sign of age a departure? Where is your prime? How would I recognise you, thriving in Heaven?' He withdrew his hand.

'Tell me your name.'

'Why? I'm the only angel you're likely to meet in your lifetime. In your thoughts "my angel".'

'Is it a secret?'

'No. My name is Xas. Like spit and vinegar – sass. X-A-S. I'm of the lowest of the nine orders. Unmentioned in Scripture or Apocrypha.' He lifted his other hand – the one that hadn't touched – to pass Sobran a wicker-wrapped wine bottle that he'd held all the while. 'It's Yayin, from Noah's vineyard. The vintner's family tell everyone that their vines were planted by Noah. They have made this claim since before the Crusades, sometimes believing, some-times to increase the value of their wine. But Noah did plant that vineyard.'

'Vines from rootstock that came through the great flood?' Sobran asked, reverent.

Xas laughed. 'The château's cellared vintages are better. And, by the way, that's what you should do – build a bigger cellar, and stop supplying all the château's table wine. Do your best to *hoard* your best.'

'We don't have an inn, guests to entertain, a table to keep up. We are not gentlemen. And it's a terrible trouble to transport bottled vintage. The longer the road the more is spoiled.'

'I *flew* the Yayin from Palestine,' the angel said; then, slightly excited and nonsensical, 'Did you see the coalmines in the Ruhr? The machines that pump out the water?'

'I don't understand you,' Sobran said.

'Never mind, just make sure that, when the roads improve, you have good old wine to ship beyond your *pays.*'

'More advice.'

'Angelic husbandry.' The angel shrugged. 'I have time. I'll nag at you next year too. Right now, before the dawn comes, I want you to tell me about the Grand Army, and the campaign. About Baptiste and how you fared.'

Sobran gestured for the angel to sit and began to work on the waxed cork of the Palestine wine. The bottle was slippery and dewed, as though it had remained chilled while the angel held it. 'I don't suppose you have glasses too?'

'We drank out of the same bottle that first night.'

'Yes.' Sobran pulled the cork and offered the bottle. Xas swigged then passed it back. The wine was very dry, but perfumed, potent and reflective, its stored power as affecting as memory. But Sobran could recognise nothing, no remembered summer or familiar sensation of a known landscape. He did remember the moist sensation of warmth on the bottleneck – the touch of the angel's mouth. He said, 'I confessed my sins. I told Father Lesy, so I've told God. There are some things I can't tell Céleste and won't tell you. But I'll say this – I saw what I believe *you* showed me. For example, when I put the money in the bowl by the Russian woman's bed, the withered pears and dead wasps. I took note of that.'

'It's a memory, not a sign, Sobran.'

'You were with me.'

Xas shook his head. Then he said, 'Tell me what you remember, whatever you care to.'

1814 **Vin capiteux** *(a spirited, heady wine)*

Sobran was excited by what the angel knew. It seemed he had read everything. Each thread of his conversation was strong and sinuous – Sobran had only to tease it out. For hours Sobran questioned Xas about viticulture – then, sated with learning, began to wonder when and why the angel read. Did Xas read in flight, by the light of the moon, while carrying a rose bush under his arm? For that matter, how did Xas fly to Heaven? How could he carry something there? Where was Heaven?

The angel said, 'Souls go straight there, Sobran, and immediately. An angel isn't earthly, but *is* a kind of animal – as you must have realised. Roses and angels aren't souls and have to move through space. There's one way I know to get to Heaven. Have you seen lime in water – if it's deep, how blue it is? Like turquoise turned to gas. There's a place that scalds and presses and corrodes – and decontaminates. A gate through which bodies can come and go to Heaven.'

'And where is this gate – some far reach of the world, where people have never been?'

The angel changed the subject. He wanted to be told about this stonemason Sobran drank with, Antoine Laudel, his sister's husband. 'Tell me about Léon's vocation – what happened there? What does he do now? Tell me how your daughters are. And about the cellar, have you made a start on it?'

⁓

1815 **Vin brulé** *(burnt wine)*

Xas said he had flown over the battle near Waterloo.

'Since Napoleon entered Paris earlier this year, I've taken an interest. I thought you might have joined him. I wasn't sure I'd find you here.'

The angel seemed quite settled, if posed somewhat unpoetically, his body inclined against his wings, which were crossed before him on the ground. He looked a little like someone leaning across a hedge to gossip.

Sobran asked how Xas had felt, flying over the battle and imagining that he might be in the midst of it.

'I didn't plan to swoop down and save you. I wasn't darting about above the field like the dove who sees a snake crawling into its nest. I was far above the battle. I watched the cannons fire in volleys. And at each volley the smoke bloomed along their lines like brushstrokes, in simple lines and curves like the Roman alphabet. The thunder came well after the smoke. The smoke was silent. It was like watching a calligrapher at work with an invisible brush, in white ink on green paper.'

Sobran wanted to know whether Xas had made any sense of what he had seen. If he could see that Napoleon was losing.

'Yes, I could see that, though not at first. I've watched battles. This was the second greatest engagement I've seen – after the final battle of the war in Heaven, which took place on several planes and was protracted but immensely fast. By comparison this battle looked stately. At least from the air. I couldn't let myself be seen. I imagine that, on the ground, it was all din and butchery.'

The angel fell silent and watched Sobran.

Sobran shrugged. He realised that the gesture wasn't sufficiently polite *or* discouraging. 'I didn't think of joining Napoleon. My life's here. There are problems with the cellar. The cooper is waiting on our order – as though the news from Paris has some bearing on our yield. A rumour went around that I would leave to join the Emperor. After all, I hadn't bought out and wasn't discharged – you'd think people would know what that meant. But instead they choose to remember that I stayed with Napoleon when he marched on Leipzig – didn't just walk out of Russia and keep on walking. I *should* have, because when I got back here the Bourbon was on the throne and only Comte Armand was able to uphold Baptiste's will so that I could inherit Kalmann. I know that now because Father Lesy told me. I know how near I came to losing Baptiste's gift. I couldn't have followed Napoleon. That would have been to dishonour the Comte.'

Xas listened.

'Though I would have liked to be among that first thousand, to wear a little square of the flag they cut upon the deck of his ship before he landed. But I'm not much of a soldier. The battle of Lutzen finished that for me.' Then Sobran shook his head. 'None of this excuses me. It's all just treacherous self-interest.'

Xas listened.

'Napoleon will abdicate again, then the English will take him. And this time they'll put him away, far away.' Sobran was quiet for a moment then he said. '*You* could visit him, have you thought of that? Wherever they take him. That would console me. I think I'm asking you to visit him.'

Xas shook his head. 'I have nothing to say to Napoleon for myself. I could only carry the regards, apologies and excuses of a gunner from his Grand Army.'

***

1816 Le broyage *(the crushing of the grapes)*

The house was asleep and Sobran wanted the angel to look at his infant son. Besides, it was raining and he had a cold. Sobran carried a light to the cradle, his heart on the boil, so loud that he couldn't have heard if Céleste had stirred and turned in the bed.

Xas crouched, flexed his wings slowly to permit him to do so. They spanned the room, the lower pinions of the left a centimetre from the water jug, the other wing tip out in the hall, pinions as black as iron fretwork. The angel stood, stiller than a heron standing out to dry on a tree by the river. He admired the child, then looked behind him, under his arm, at Céleste's dimpled shoulder and long fringed plait. He stood to his full height again, closing his wings, and walked out of the room.

On the narrow stair Sobran heard, behind him, the harsh wash of feathers scrubbing the plaster. For a moment he worried that his angel might panic like a bird flown in to a room. He looked back as Xas came into the kitchen. The angel appeared cheerful and curious.

Sobran stoked the fire, swung the full kettle out over the flames.

He lit another candle. Of course he couldn't offer the angel a chair at the table, or even his mother's rocker ... He hesitated, then asked, 'Can you sit?' And was surprised to see Xas look about, then choose the rocker, sit and rearrange his wings so that their joints were above his head, like the high shoulders of a perching vulture. Xas folded his wing tips about his feet, pushed with both so that the rocker swayed.

Sobran said, 'I'll make an infusion of my mother's catarrh tea. Is there something I can offer you?'

'I'll have the tea too.'

Sobran, trying to hide his excitement, took the glass tower from the lamp and lit three candle ends, then replaced the brass box with its bull's-eye glass and filled the room with lamplight. Then he looked at the angel.

Xas was white-skinned, smooth. Even his mouth was pale, more blurred than coloured, like a wine stain wiped on the mouth of a statue. But Xas was no statue. Sobran could see his blood moving, a vein in the angel's neck that pulsed, and with each pulse variations of brightness in his skin, like cloud shadows passing across a wheat field, each pass of light a surprise. Where his skin was worked, the calluses on his hands, it was the same fleshy rose as the nipples of a dark-haired girl who has never suckled a child.

Xas looked amused and expectant. He turned his face to the light and Sobran's scrutiny. As Sobran stepped closer Xas said, 'The deficiencies of human eyesight – you've never had a good look at me, have you? Bring the lamp over here.'

His eyes – as it turned out – were dark blue. He sat, relaxed, open, not settling into ordinariness however long Sobran stared. 'Something seems to be moving over you, like cloud shadows across a meadow.'

Xas thought hard, then said that people were hosts to other creatures – no, he didn't mean vermin, though that too. He meant the flor in the human gut. The same kind of thing made yellow wine yellow. People are colonies, Xas said, and *time* touches them, they are in so many places permeable. Angels are inviolate. Some even seem block-headed, like armour closed in armour.

It worried Sobran, criticism of celestial beings. Xas noticed Sobran's worry and said, 'I mean, angels are unresponsive. They mind their business – which is as it should be.'

'What God intends.'

'I don't know what God intends, Sobran.'

Sobran sneezed and Xas told him to make the cold remedy. Sobran fetched the mixed herbs, spooned them into the pot and poured the water. He put the pot and two bowls on the hearth and brought another chair to the fire.

'The alterations – cloud shadows – I think have something to do with this.' Xas raised his arm and touched his side. He wasn't wearing a shirt and, Sobran thought, couldn't with those wings so complicating any possible cut. The mark on the angel's side was more tattoo than brand, but filled-in, coloured, without grain or blurring. Two twisted lines, one over the other, the vermilion one partly eclipsed the blue-green. Sobran looked away – something had frightened him. He poured the tea, passed a bowl to the angel, then had to warn, 'Careful, it's hot!' But Xas had already taken a scalding mouthful, and showed no pain.

'It tastes like dry grass.'

Sobran pointed at the mark, asked what it was.

Xas shook his head. Then he made a very unangelic gesture – bit his lip as if to check his talk and avoid trouble. 'I'm signed. I'm a signed treaty. I think what I do supplies the treaty's contents. So far its only terms are: "Xas can go freely." Not "will" or "shall" but "can". I'm a treaty signed by the leaders of both camps.' The angel said that he knew he was being coy, but he'd had a long time to think about the signatures and he remained perplexed. He spoke diffidently, but still managed to sound maddened and troubled. For a moment he was silent, sipping the tea, his face bent into the plumes of steam. 'A friend of mine – a monk and beekeeper, long since gone from the earth – said to me, concerning this – ' Xas paused, then explained that he was relinquishing his friend's very own words, which were in Gaelic, and therefore certainly incomprehensible to Sobran. 'My friend said he thought the agreement was rather more than a piece of whimsy. That's how he put it, very gentle, but telling me off. I must stop thinking of it as whimsical, he said. If it *wasn't* whimsy, it was a pact. He thought that what I did – "you curious creature", he called me – in going freely, would gradually fill up the only space between those two parties not already polluted by prophesy, policy and stony laws.'

Sobran felt thick-headed — that was the cold — but his heart seemed to be charging up and down inside him, like a dog greeting a master who has been off without it. 'But — doesn't God have everything planned?'

'You mean everything that my latitude, my "going freely", can possibly contain? Well, yes, God knows what God will make happen.'

Sobran frowned. 'Are you saying that God can change his mind?'

Xas smiled faintly. 'I might have just suggested that God's knowledge was *confined* to what He will have happen — if you *are* going to go over my words like a lawyer.'

Sobran had begun to shiver, but didn't feel afraid. 'Xas,' he said, for the first time using his angel's name, 'if your friend was right in his thinking, then what *you* do could change the last days, God's promises.'

Xas shook his head. 'How? I have harmless pursuits. It's been thousands of years since I put out my hand to catch a sword blade — and *did no good.* I go freely and, in the terms of the agreement, God shares my pains. So I try not to suffer.'

'Did it cause you pain when I didn't come for two years?'

Xas looked at Sobran for a moment then admitted, 'Some.'

Sobran raised his eyebrows and the angel looked impatient. 'Now you have the idea that even you can influence the final outcomes. But I know mortals are liable to false thinking. For example, you never think you'll leave the world until you can't get another breath or — very old — you shrink away from it like a seed dried in its pod. My friend the monk sat around saying goodbye to everything. A thin old man with thistledown hair, saying, "I'll be gone this winter." "I", he said, "I". He had humility, but the world, with its brute complacencies, had soaked him through and through, and he didn't believe he would ever leave it.'

Sobran watched the angel, his quiet vehemence. His head hurt and he felt that he was sinking slowly through warm water. 'I can change your life,' he said, 'and you could change God's mind.'

'See what I mean? What you believe in is *reprieve.* Why would anyone want to change God's mind? God is just and merciful. And time is long. Imagine ten thousand vintage years. Enough is enough. The world need not endure. And you can't change my life.'

31

'I think I have a fever,' Sobran said.

Xas stood up and over him, laid a hand on Sobran's forehead. 'Go to bed and rest.'

Sobran got up.

'I'll empty the teapot and wash both the bowls so no one will know you've been taking tea with a night visitor.' Xas stooped, took up the pot in one hand and cradled the bowls in the other.

Sobran called out to him from the foot of the stairs. Xas stopped, a silhouette in the doorway, the house wall behind him. 'What would you do if I fell sick and died?' Sobran asked.

Xas didn't answer. He turned and walked out of the house.

When Sobran had rolled himself up in a quilt beside Céleste he realised he'd just asked an absurd question. If Sobran died, Xas would find him in Heaven. Asleep, Sobran dreamed Xas was looking for him in Heaven, while he hid in a cherry tree and peered through its branches.

First came the rain, not too late, then mild weather in which the grapes ripened slowly and took in all the summer had to offer. It rained again the day after the last of Clos Jodeau's grapes were harvested, and the weather cooled. It was cool in the cuverie and the fruit fermented slowly.

The following winter when the vintner, his wife and brother transferred the wine from barrel to bottle they knew they had secured a fine vintage.

On the day of the bottling, at noon, they sat down in the cuverie to dine on bread and cheese. They sat on the pressoir and a jug of wine stood between them.

Sobran told them he was wondering how they could make it happen again, or even how to *improve* on this vintage.

'When the girls are bigger we can have them help cut off some of the stems,' Céleste said. 'Make a wine that comes to its best more slowly. And a better best.' She stretched out a leg to push the cradle in which the infant, Baptiste, lay with only his face visible in a bonnet and a nest of shawls. Sabine and Nicolette were out in the yard splashing back and forth in their pattens and trying to sweep together enough snow to build a snowman.

Léon said, 'Father used to say it was all in the fruit.'

'To press the south slope separately we would need another vat.' Sobran anticipated his brother's argument. 'But the cuverie is too small for that.'

Céleste said, 'That cool spell following the harvest was a godsend.'

'We can't reproduce those things,' Léon said. He said he thought they spent too much time nursing the vines of Kalmann. Of course Kalmann's vines should be saved, but they should sell Kalmann's grapes and concentrate on pressing only Jodeau's south slope. Why was Sobran talking about pressing Jodeau and Kalmann together? That would be like mixing wine and water and the results could hardly honour Sobran's dead friend – if that was his intention.

'There's a better income in wine. If we are taking the trouble to make wine we have to produce it in volume. That's why we are building a cellar, because we will press the crops of both vineyards.'

Léon picked up the jug. The wine flashed as it moved. 'Then why are we talking about quality? This is quality. This is the mist clearing and a mountain in our path. You can't really mean to contaminate this with Kalmann?'

Céleste laughed at her brother-in-law. She had taken off her scarf and unfastened her hair. Before putting the scarf back on again she wound her thick gold plait twice around her neck to add to the warmth of the wool. Léon watched this, distracted. Céleste looked at him as she spoke to Sobran. 'Léon is saying that we can't make a good wine by an act of will.'

Concord between his wife and brother was unusual, and annoyed Sobran. 'Do you think it's impossible to reproduce the work of luck?'

'It's either luck that makes wine like this, or the luxury of large cellars and plenty of hands,' Léon said. 'Pressing Jodeau and Kalmann together will push our luck.'

Sobran told Léon that Kalman would come right. And there *was* something they could do. They could ensure slower fermentation every year by having their sister's husband, Antoine Laudel the stonemason, build Jodeau a stone vat. 'Do away with the wood.'

Céleste took Sobran's hand, pleased with him and his idea. She said to Léon sweetly, 'Perhaps fine wine is too fine for us. And remember, Baptiste sold his grapes to Vully every year and never made enough to cover his expenses.'

'We could have the vat for the price of the stone, I suppose,' Léon said, conceding. 'But,' he added, 'you only go so far trying to outwit chance. If it had rained in August instead of June...'

Nicolette ran indoors and held out her little red fists for her mother to warm.

Sobran said to his brother that the only things he knew would happen were what he'd make happen. They had to think of the future. Some day the château would change hands, would go to someone who hadn't been raised at Vully. Hadn't Comte Armand named his niece heir? The Parisian, the convent girl. Weren't she and her invalid husband expected at Vully in the spring? Clos Jodeau must make a gift to the girl – a dozen bottles of this vintage. Yes, that was something they should do. Sobran sounded very sure of himself.

'All right, brother, we will work hard, waste nothing and woo our betters,' Léon said, as if to imply that while all these things were worth doing they weren't all worthy ideas.

Sobran felt a kind of clenching, like tearful anger. Disregarding Léon was a habit Sobran had learned when Léon was full of advice about his conduct and examples that seemed less good behaviour than petty forms of self-torture. Sobran wanted to talk to his angel, to ask was Léon wrong, and was he right? He thought of a prayer as an invocation, but trapped the words of it behind his lips, where they lay, and fermented, and slowly warmed his mouth.

1817 Vin de cru *(wine from the grapes of a single vineyard)*

The following year was very hard. Léon Jodeau took to gambling on his share of the vineyard and Sobran found he had more to pay than money to pay with. Léon swore to sign his labour over for life, a gesture that only annoyed his older brother. 'You won't turn me into your master and find a reason to resent me for ever. No, just take yourself off and earn a living – and don't speak to me again till you've given up cards, cockfights, and prize fights,' Sobran told him.

There was one black, silent, early spring night, when Sobran and his wife were in different parts of the house making an inventory of their most precious possessions – each one planning to make the whole necessary sacrifice. Céleste counted her new oak dresser, her as yet unused stores of wedding linen, her best china, the pewter tankards and platters, and the small dowry of jewellery she'd had from Aunt Agnès. There was enough.

In another orbit Sobran took stock of his guns, his mother's inlaid writing desk, his books, his grandfather's lute. There wasn't enough.

He sat at the table by the bedroom window with his head in his hands and looked through the open shutters at the hill that hid the other half of his vineyard, land he hadn't earned or inherited but which had fallen to him by default and which he somehow loved more than the family *clos* – land he wouldn't part with. He looked at Aimée, who raised her head from her paws and stared, alert and eager, but so aged now that her lower eyelids drooped to show their red lining. Sobran got up, climbed on to the chest at the bed end and felt around the top of the rafters for what he had tied there. He slipped a feather out from under the black thread and carried it back to his desk. When he held the feather to the candle its flame reached, hopeful, and wrapped readily. But there was no smoke, no scorching, the feather's colour remained as pure as the flame. Sobran watched this phenomenon and thought: here is a fortune.

Four days later came news of another murder.

Aurora de Valday saw the men from her window, a crowd on the flagged courtyard before the old château and under her window in the new wing. It wasn't an unfamiliar sight, but in this throng there were no milling dogs, or guns cradled in the men's arms – it was spring, so this was no shooting party. Some of the men belonged to the château, were servants of the Comte, and some were from Aluze, the village, farms, small *clos* this side of the river.

Aurora peered at the men over the head of her maid as the girl fastened each bow at the front of her morning gown, so that layers of ruffled silk disguised the smooth watermelon swelling of Aurora's womb. Her maid, Lucette, was not of the house, and had no idea what was up. Aurora saw her husband walk down into the crowd, following her uncle the Comte. Paul's coat looked too big for him, his head was angled back and his mouth open – the better to breathe. For a moment Aurora watched only Paul, and forgot to guess what was going on. The only evidence she had eyes for was her evident future: Paul's decline, herself alone.

She asked Lucette if she would take her tea in the kitchen this morning and bring back any news. The maid curtsied and went out.

The crowd was sorting itself into groups in consultation with the Comte. Aurora watched the men attend to her uncle, then turn to listen to one man at the back, who was wearing the smock, breeches and wooden shoes of the men of the *pays*. He was a tall man, with dark hair and a full beard cut close to his face. Aurora saw Paul bridle and begin to say something. The Comte touched Paul's lapel and he subsided. The men bowed and turned towards the gatehouse and put on their headgear as they walked beneath its arch and out of the Comte's presence.

Aurora went to wait for Paul in the morning room. Eventually he came to ask after her health. He sat beside her to catch his breath. Told her that a girl was missing. There were fears she might have been murdered. 'It isn't something you should concern yourself with.'

'I hope they find that she's run off with her lover. I've often wondered: If a girl from a cottage runs off with her lover, is she disgraced? Or rather, how great is the disgrace?'

'I don't know that they do run off. Generally. More likely get with child and are married off, or not. They don't leave their children with the holy sisters, and marry rich old men, as the ruined quality can.'

Aurora thought of the fortunes of Madame de Staël's heroine Corinne. Both Paul and Aurora were stroking her abdomen now, and both laughed as the serene geometry of her belly was interrupted by a series of heaving movements.

'Where are they looking?' Aurora asked.

'Along the river and the fields near the road. Ditches, hedgerows, copses.'

Aurora shuddered, thinking of the cold, abject secrecy of such places once a corpse was in them. She said, 'They don't hope to find her alive?'

'They remember another girl who disappeared, then appeared later, dead. Seven years ago, your uncle says.' Paul answered her original question on the matter she needn't have concerned herself with. It was always like this between them, she would have to melt his propriety in every conversation.

Paul said he thought he'd rest – later, perhaps, her uncle would need his assistance. 'With priests, bailiffs, magistrates, and what-have-you.'

He left her.

Aurora's maid, Lucette, had this report: the missing girl was fifteen years of age. Marie Pelet. Apparently her younger sister said Marie claimed to have a beau. His identity was Marie's secret, the little girl said. Perhaps Marie *had* eloped, not met the fate of the other – Geneviève Lizet – who had been found on the riverbank seven years ago, her skirts up over her head.

Lucette crossed herself.

When Marie Pelet was found the searchers would be recalled by the gun on the château's roof. 'Monsieur Paul is to light the charge,' the maid added.

The gun was fired in the late afternoon. A group of women who had gathered at the gate came into the courtyard, some already weeping.

The first of the searchers back weren't those carrying the corpse. The man who ran with the news stood in the courtyard giving his report. A Pelet, an old man, the girl's grandfather perhaps, stood among his kin, and roared with grief, till his face was as dark as a drunkard's and drool hung in clear strings from his stretched mouth. He put his head down and bulled among the other men while they closed in to hold him.

Then there was a quarrel. The women: why was Marie being brought back to the château when they wanted to take her now, wash her and lay her out by the hearth in her own mother's house? And the men: the Comte, bailiffs, the magistrate, must look on her to see how she died in order to discover who killed her. But the hour of her death was gone, said the women, and the stone long settled over Geneviève Lizet, and still no one knew who had taken *her* life.

Aurora stayed hidden, in the shadow of the heavy door to the main hall – kept still and listened till she saw Paul signal to a groom with a saddled horse. He had on his greatcoat and boots. She went out, lumbering, in her frilled draperies and satin slippers. No one seemed to see her at first, not even Paul, his back to her and foot in the stirrup.

'Paul!' she called.

The young man with the close-cut beard had seen her, had stared across the whole breadth of the courtyard then come forward at a run to stop her. 'Mind the horse, Madame,' he said, then called out to the Comte – not 'your honour' or 'your grace' but 'Vully' then 'Sir!' as an afterthought.

Paul was willing but weak, and still not in the saddle. The Comte saw and summoned him: 'Paul, come here, I need you.' And Paul, who'd meant to fetch the magistrate, desisted from his efforts to mount and went obediently to Aurora's uncle who gave him the task of settling the women.

'Madame, forgive me, I thought you were in danger,' the young man said, and let go his grip on her upper arms.

'If there was a little less confusion here,' Aurora said, 'and more mastery of emotion, the horse wouldn't be turning in nervous circles.'

The Comte came up to them. 'Aurora, normally you would be able to offer us some assistance. But in your condition, and with Paul so determined to do a well man's share – '

'I only came out to stop Paul getting on the horse.'

Aurora's uncle took her hands in his, held her there a moment exposed, underdressed, in the surgepool of hysteria the space between the château and gatehouse had become. He looked at the young man. 'Jodeau, have you ridden a horse with a saddle?'

'No. You should send your groom.'

'I want to send a man with some brains.'

'I'm sure the magistrate is sufficiently intelligent not to fish for knowledge in a pool of hay and horse liniment.'

'Do as I say,' the Comte ordered, but he didn't seem offended by Jodeau's manner.

Jodeau moved to do as he was told, but his clogs wouldn't fit into the stirrups, so he borrowed another man's leather shoes, then mounted as he'd seen cavalry men do, and rode gingerly through the gate.

The Comte told Aurora to go indoors.

The following morning Aurora found her uncle in the library, with his clerk and a copy of the magistrate's questions and answers. The clerk was blotting the pages with sand. Aurora found a candle snuff and put out the spluttering stubs.

'I'm afraid I'll go to my grave not knowing who this killer is,' the Comte said. He began to gather the pages together, turned their edges against the desk to neaten the stack. 'I'll have to add it to my list of questions to ask God.' He looked up at Aurora. 'Is Paul asleep?'

'His cough is bad. I left him tossing and turning. I asked someone to make you breakfast – with meat.'

Aurora's uncle hooked an arm at her and she came to him. They stood hip to hip and she put her head on his shoulder, felt him kiss her hair. 'I'll go to her funeral,' she said.

'We all must.'

'Who was that man, Uncle, the one who held me back?'

'Sobran Jodeau. He owns two *clos* – a vineyard that straddles the road, near Aluze. He was a gunner with the Grand Army; marched through the winter from Moscow. His wife is a beauty – great pale eyes and gold hair like a mermaid.'

'Is he an important man in Aluze?'

Her uncle looked at her. 'Did you take a dislike to him, Aurora? How like your mother you are. She disliked anyone she met when she was with child – then turned some baffled souls she had glared at in suspicion into "very good friends" as soon as her milk was dry.'

'I'm sure I don't feel the need to go so far as forming a dislike.'

'How haughty you sound. Jodeau can read and reckon-up. In his Sunday best he's what passes for a man of substance around here. Which is, of course, why I must import company for myself, like Paul, you, my hunting set.'

'You like him,' Aurora accused.

'He's a sharp-tongued, high-handed bully. He fills me with fellow-feeling,' her uncle said.

1818 Vin du clerc *(wine offered by a plaintiff to the clerk-of-the-court if the tribunal finds in the plaintiff's favour)*

Sobran had glasses and a bottle of the Jodeau wine they had drunk that first night, ten years before. 'It isn't old yet, but let's see how it fares.'

They tasted. Both were quiet, looking out over the house. The night was warm and the house walls starred with white, open flowers.

'I see that the cellar isn't finished yet,' Xas said.

'It's been a bad year. An evil year.' Sobran put his glass down on the flat-topped boundary stone he had put in – he told his family – to mark the old limit of the family vines. (Céleste thought of it as a headstone for Baptiste Kalmann – and had quietly planted marigolds about it.) Sobran took from his shirt a posy, the three feathers, and gave them to Xas. 'You must have been moulting.'

Xas tucked the feathers into the bundle he had arrived carrying – a bottle of yapincak, a turkish sémillon, and a rose bush packed in chalk and wrapped about with oilcloth.

'That first night, when the whirlwind took you, you dropped them.'

'Ah,' said Xas.

1819 Vin de veille *(vigil wine)*

Xas's offerings stood unopened, upright between the woody knees of two bared roots of a cherry tree. It was dawn and chilly, the distances were gathering distance under clouds in curtain-raiser colours.

Xas had held Sobran all night, lying against the slope, on the raft of his wings.

Sobran's daughter had died. The eight-year-old, Nicolette. Four months earlier.

Sobran had very little to say — of the fever and rash all the children had had, how they'd been afraid for the boy, Baptiste, who had been very ill. How Sobran had feared for Céleste — with child and worn out by nursing.

Sobran's sister Sophie came to help — her own children had had the disease. Nicolette seemed better, the girls had eaten a little and were sitting up in their bed, talking — then Sabine called out (Sobran remembered that, at her shout, the blood rushed to his heart and he sped up the stairs, but was sinking already, as though he knew before he saw Nicolette's blue face). She just died — Sabine said — dragged in a breath, held it, stared and fell back on the bed. 'Please God!' Céleste had shouted, but it was too late for intervention.

Before Sobran had spoken at all, he had fallen into the angel's arms, and his embrace had carried them both to the ground.

At the funeral Sobran's friends had touched him, and for weeks afterwards, laid hands on his shoulders, his arms, whenever they met. Those who had lost children did know how wounded he was. And he held Céleste — at night, when she eased her nipple into the new baby's mouth, and wept while it suckled, or when she stood in the yard, arms opening and closing at her sides in noiseless, agitated grief, watching Sabine, her bowl emptied of chicken feed and the fowl around her feet too close because she was stuck fast, her chin down on her apron bib and the knobs of her neckbones showing, a stilled child and playmate to a silence. When Sobran saw them both immobilised, his wife and daughter, he would draw Céleste back indoors so that Sabine couldn't see her mother's convulsive struggle with grief. The boy, Baptiste, grizzled and sulked and asked after his other sister and was suspicious that they had hidden her, like they would hide those fragile enchanting things he wasn't permitted to play with. The whole house was sad. Sobran's friends brought him brandy or laid their arms along his shoulders — but no one wrapped their body about his and bore him away.

41

The angel was strong and tender and as fresh as a young river. The angel wasn't tentative or impatient. For hours through tears and the painful intimacy of mourning the angel held him.

Sobran's grief lost its edge against Xas's body. He had lain quiet for a long while, they both had, till they turned their heads to watch a cart go by on the road below them. Its driver looked up, saw the man and angel and pulled up his horse. He stared, stood on the box for a better look – grew sure of what he'd first thought he could see and began to quake, then took up the traces and whipped his horse into a canter, as though he'd just heard the last wolf in Burgundy howling.

'One of your neighbours?' Xas asked.

'Yes. Jules Lizet. I hope he'll decide he was dreaming.'

'Your household will wake soon. We both must go,' Xas said, but didn't unlock his arms.

As he watched his neighbour's cart go down the road, Sobran said, 'Whenever I went away overnight, on business, I'd always bring everyone some little gift. The girls would jump up and down shouting "Papa! Papa!" Nicolette was smaller, but always seemed heavier than Sabine, getting one jump in for every three of her sister's. She would squat right down then shoot up and her feet would leave the floor about this much,' the breadth of his hand. 'I tried to teach her not to let Sabine always speak for her.' Sobran was silent for a long time. The sun broke out over the farthest eastern hill, and every tiny stone sprang a black leak away from its light.

Xas passed his palm down Sobran's face once more, his thumb a hoe weeding tears.

'I always made sure that she had her share,' Sobran said. Then, broken-hearted, 'I loved her best.' He remembered their pacts against her powerful sister. He'd ride Nicolette around on his shoulders and they'd hunt Sabine – both girls shrieking and happy. He remembered the hours he'd spent playing with her, obliged to woo her when he appeared, a stranger in her life, after his time in the army. 'I want you to find Nicolette, Xas. Find her in Heaven.'

The patient bed of Xas's body moved under Sobran at last. He was turned by hands, legs and wings, so that he lay prone on the cushion of one wing. Xas held Sobran's head in both hands and looked into his eyes. 'Do you know what you're asking me to do?' If only the angel had seemed tired he'd have looked ordinary, because there was white dust on his hair, which draped the soil, as silky as melted butter on flour.

Sobran said, 'Tell me next year how she is with God. You can do that.' He looked into Xas's eyes and felt the hands pull back in his hair as if the angel were angry. 'That's all,' Sobran said, 'no more than that. *I beg you.*'

Then Sobran was dumped on the bare earth. Xas stood above him. Sobran thought he heard Xas say, 'All right,' or, 'I will' – assent anyway. Or maybe Xas said nothing and Sobran simply knew he'd moved him. Then the great, creaturely wings came down, grit kicked up, Sobran's eyes were full of it and he opened them blinking, teary, unable to look up – but he watched the angel's long black shadow swell, dilute and slither away down the slope and across the house, as Xas swung around into the sun.

Sobran closed his eyes, coughed and hawked. He kept seeing, as he recovered and found his feet, as he opened his eyes and went down to his house, saw more clearly throughout that day and subsequent days – in a slow dawning, till months later when the vine leaves lay composting in oily drifts and the first snow came, he saw, day and night, only this – the angel's form, wings frozen at the apex of their arc, still, but in memory the angel's body was a vortex with his gaze at its centre. Sobran thought of Xas and saw him again – only this last picture, which wiped out every other so that all earlier memories melted into a warm voice talking in the darkness (when Sobran knew that, in fact, they had sometimes argued and that he'd had at least one other good look). Every day time stopped and Sobran saw Xas, the sun reflecting off his raised wings, white chest water-marked by tears dried in fine dust; bare skin and colourless nipples, as innocent as a child's; the double signature, sea-green and vermilion, awake and vivid; a white-lipped white face and eyes, abysmal, inimical, like the sea seen through holes in an icefield.

It was like being in love, this remembering, because Sobran couldn't put Xas out of his mind. And it was like shame. Because he grew so tired defending himself from the pain of this one recollection, Sobran forgot everything else he knew about the angel.

1820 Quoi-que-ce-soit *('whatever this might be' — a nineteenth-century apéritif)*

The angel was there before him, sitting on the boundary stone, his wings crossed and furled, folds of white silk up around his chin. He sat so still that, despite his clear eyes and skin, he looked ill, careful of himself.

Sobran was in his Sunday best, his hair combed and oiled. He carried two crystal glasses and the finest wine he could find. He held a glass out to Xas, who hesitated, then took it. 'Before long you'll bring chairs,' Xas observed.

Sobran blushed. 'I like our informality.'

'How old are you?'

'Thirty.' Sobran's face was hotter yet. 'The chairs won't appear till I'm fifty.'

'Plant a pepper tree. It should be big enough within twenty years to set a table under — all summer for your family, and for us, on our one night.'

Céleste, the cellar, a shade tree, thought Sobran — the changes my angel makes. He cut the lead seal, eased the cork with his thumbs, then inserted his first finger into the bottle neck to damp the foam. He filled the angel's glass and his own, drilled the bottle's base into the dirt till it stood, part buried and secure. Xas took a sip, swallowed, then spoke very quietly, 'I saw Nicolette once, and only very recently. One reason I waited was so my news would be fresh.' He paused. 'Of course it means nothing to say that she is well and happy — she's in Heaven. She hasn't forgotten you; in Heaven even infants are collected. She's all patience — can wait your lifetime to see you again — and Sabine's lifetime for Sabine. She doesn't miss you, because she has no room in her heart for pain.'

Xas spoke, measured, cool and sad. 'I don't really know how Nicolette feels — so can't convey that to you — but Heaven was like this to me: When God made me and I became conscious I wasn't conscious of *myself*, but of glory. I was in glory. Later I understood that this was *my* sensation, and I felt gratitude too. And in feeling gratitude towards God I differentiated God from my feelings — then felt consent and celebration. A human heart is formed differently. The child inside its mother learns slowly that it needs to move more, then it is born and feels loss – wants sustenance, warmth, the heartbeat it misses. It feels desire, then anticipation and curiosity. Nothing can make a human soul forget its first birth. It is made of its losses, even in Heaven, even in bliss.'

'But Nicolette was happy,' Sobran said, uncertain.

'I said that.'

'Yet she can never be as happy as an angel is,' Sobran said – trying to clarify what he was being told.

'I didn't mention happiness in connection with angels.'

Sobran said something in apology – but wasn't sure why. It was as if the angel had told him his pain was vulgar. He felt ashamed. He thanked the angel.

Xas nodded, said, 'She'll be much the same in fifty years – so don't ask me to go to her again.'

'I won't. Thank you for your trouble.'

'It's more *your* trouble, Sobran. If you start looking for news of the dead – ' Xas shrugged. 'You might want next to know about your father, or Baptiste.'

'I wouldn't know where to direct you for Baptiste. He could be in purgatory.'

'Yes, of course,' Xas said – not as though he knew but as though the possibility had slipped his mind. He drained his glass and then reached out – it seemed to Sobran – carefully, stiffly, for the bottle. As he filled his glass he made his usual request for a report on the fortunes of Sobran's family.

Sobran dutifully filled the angel in, called his attention to the grapes. It looked, God willing, to be a very good year.

Xas scarcely spoke, but to ask questions, or for elaborations on things Sobran said. Sobran missed Xas's conversation, his confidences. He felt that something had happened to divide them. He thought: 'He's angry with me still because I begged him to visit Nicolette.' And, a thought that forked: 'Where is his pity?' and 'I'll never impose on him again.' Then, because he was not a generous man, Sobran began to wonder whether Xas's awkwardness was to do with the fact he was hiding something from Sobran, something about the visit and Nicolette in Heaven. Surely the angel wouldn't say he'd seen her if he hadn't – then give such a plausible report.

Sobran stopped speaking. He tilted his glass so that the champagne spilled, in a long twisted ribbon, on to the soil where it foamed then vanished. He said, 'How did she look, my Nicolette?'

Xas sighed. 'She looked like a little fair-haired girl.'

Sobran snorted.

'You disappoint me, Sobran,' Xas said, coldly. Then he went on: 'She was with some other children. They were picking up stones, preparatory to standing under the river. Where I found her there is a narrow river, one that comes and goes and flows over grass – the preposterous valley grass of Heaven, green with a blue cast, no blade with a corroded edge, for in Heaven the insects are never hungry, no one is hungry or eats. The children were walking among some trees above the river. The ground was bare and dry and the soles of Nicolette's feet were dirty. There were a few adults, talking, reading, playing at sleep. And, if you need to know, there was the river and, a little distance away, its a course of an earlier time, a path of flowers of the flimsy sort, in red, yellow, orange and white: then drier grass and more forest, beeches with roosting birds and sparkling leaves; some friendly buildings, sandstone, a kind of town minus commerce – except conversation and music, someone was playing a violin, not very well. Then there were distances, a veritable stockpile of hills, and snowy mountains. One lake, very far away, blue-black, fringed with rushes and lilies. The other way, through the little copse, were downs, plains, a great forest where every tree is the same height, the coast, mangroves, the sea, so forth – in short, the landscapes of Paradise.

'I called Nicolette over to me. She was shy; she hadn't spoken to an angel. She was surprised to learn that her father had known one all her life – well, maybe not *so* surprised since she thinks very highly of you. She had one stone, and I helped her find another. The drowned pasture was very soft, she said. It felt nice to lie down in it – but you needed stones in order to stay under. Sometimes there were fish – always in a tearing hurry – since the river came and went, she supposed. We dug out a stone and off she ran. *She was very happy.*'

Sobran had his face in his hands.

'So, did you need to hear that? Did you really need to know more?' Xas asked.

'Yes. It's always better to know more.'

'God help you,' Xas said, with feeling.

They sat for a long time without speaking. Then Xas thanked Sobran for the champagne and suggested Sobran go to bed.

'Goodnight,' Xas said.

Sobran got up, reluctant – then held out his hand to the angel. Xas took the hand and Sobran stooped to kiss the angel's cheeks. He saw Xas's lips part and his eyes wince. He paused, his face a foot from the angel's, and asked, 'Are you hurt?' The knowledge coalesced out of several earlier moments of suspicion.

'Yes.'

Sobran knelt and, without thinking, pushed his hands into the shielding wings and parted them like curtains. His hands touched the layered silk and he felt the resilient flesh that he realised was familiar to him, then a pulpy patch – a horrible wound, mortal if in mortal flesh.

Xas drew his wings together, so that Sobran's hands were forced away.

Sobran felt faint, horrified. 'I made you break a law,' he said. 'Who punished you?'

'It wasn't punishment. An angel hurt me – what else could?'

'But you are allowed to go freely.'

'The angel thought that shouldn't include carrying private messages to and from Heaven. Besides, you mustn't imagine that angels are always obedient.'

'I'm sorry.'

'All right, enough contrition. But I'll never do it again, Sobran. I'm in fear.'

'Will you heal?' Sobran pointed through the concealing wings.

'Yes.'

'What can I do for you?'

'Go to bed.'

They stared at one another. Then Sobran obeyed, went down the slope between the vines and into his house.

He sat at the window of his bedchamber and watched. Xas didn't move, all night. At dawn a breeze lifted and the angel got up. He used his wings to stand, then beat them and flung out into the air, falling a little in the shelter of the hill – so that Sobran heard the wings crack like a sail as Xas crossed the house.

From the bed, Céleste called, 'What was that?'

Sobran got out of his chair and pretended to fasten one shutter back against the wall. 'Only the wind. Good morning, dear.'

A week later, Sobran, drinking brandy with his cronies outside the little tavern in Aluze, heard some talk. Apparently old Anne Wateau had been gathering firewood at the edge of the forest above Vully, and saw an angel asleep under a thorn bush. She said she thought at first it was a church statue someone had stolen and hidden there, and she touched it with the end of her walking stick, then discovered it was alive and looking at her. Of course she hurried away in terror, and when she came back with her two great-nephews, they found the kindling she had dropped tied in a neat bundle with a plait of willow, and the angel gone.

The men Sobran sat with listened to this with interest, but when Christophe Lizet chimed in with the story that, a year ago, his cousin Jules claimed to have seen two angels in an embrace on the southern hillside of Jodeau, they all laughed. Sobran's brother-in-law, Antoine, said, 'So that's why the harvest looks so good this year, Sobran – your luck!' Someone else said, 'Crazy old Jules.'

Sobran, alarmed for Jules Lizet's reputation, protested that every man should be entitled to one or two strange fancies in his life. 'So maybe not "crazy".'

All the men looked down at their drinks and nodded, not wanting to argue with Sobran's softening of someone's craziness. It was only to be expected, considering Céleste Jodeau's recent oddities.

⌒⌒⌒

1821 Vin d'une nuit *(the wine of one night)*

No, Xas said, true, he hadn't been fit to fly home for some time. He'd gone to ground like a hurt creature. When Dame Wateau discovered him he flew further, across the mountain to northern Spain, and slept in a forest. After a week he went to stay with a friend. Yes, Xas knew this was news to Sobran. That he had another friend whom he saw more than one night a year. But Apharah had no family – and no industry, as such. A rich widow in Damascus, Apharah was middle-aged, learned, cultivated. 'That Turkish wine, the yapincak, came from her to you. She knows a little about you – and why not? – she's your senior and, as you must imagine, sometimes I don't understand you and I ask her advice.'

The notion of a dark-skinned foreign human woman advising his angel was so preposterous Sobran refused to believe it. He felt slighted and envious. 'She nursed you, did she?'

'She sheltered me. Her house is very quiet – it has a place she never lets her servants go, the library and an adjacent roof garden, a lovely garden, with a fig, a tiled fountain, jasmine and potted peonies. Apharah and I have an untroubled friendship. *Now.* We have since she gave up Islam, fifteen years ago.'

Sobran looked away from Xas. He put out his hand to crush a cricket – only to hear, once its voice was silenced, how many there were, singing among his vines. 'I hadn't imagined that you were so incautious or full of talk.'

'You think I confine myself to collecting roses and one friend a century – the sad disciplines of a domesticated immortal?'

'I imagined you spent the balance of your time with other immortals.'

Xas made a soft noise of affirmation, then said, 'I'm at my leisure. With *my* time, what would you do?'

'I'd do *good*,' Sobran said.

The angel was silent for a moment then asked, 'Haven't I done you good?'

The blood rushing to Sobran's head seemed to close a valve in the top of his skull; it shut out a coldness. He moved closer to the angel and, without looking into Xas's face, put a hand on his bare forearm. 'Forgive me. I'm only jealous.'

'I know.'

Sobran moved his grip and took Xas's hand, lifted it to his lips and kissed. 'You're my beloved friend,' he said.

This abrupt submission appeared to trouble the angel. He

removed his hand from Sobran's and thanked him – then, putting things back on a firmer footing asked, as usual, for the news.

Wondering what Xas saw, Sobran studied himself in the mirror – his brown, scarred, handsome face. His hair was thick, with a few grey strands, sparks in its brown. It was a month after midsummer, and his face wore a look of exultant exhaustion.

Sobran had taken his troubled heart to church, had tried to pray – but his desire had sprung up, a curtain of fire, between himself and the virgin who seemed to dream behind her bank of mild candles. Years before, Sobran had taken to talking directly to God, because there was so much he couldn't say to a priest. After midsummer, when he got on his knees, he had meant to ask for God's pity and help. His desire was an imperfection. But instead of praying, Sobran remembered. The memory was a torment, of their embrace on the night of vigil, when he had been so sick with grief it was as if he'd had his skin stripped off and all the angel's touch had done was to bandage, or oil him in balm. Now Sobran relived the embrace and, while still remembering grief, he kept turning against the body he knew – *knew how it felt* – and using his hands as he hadn't to touch the skin under his own tears, touch the more-anomalous-than-a-human-male's nipples and warm fingerstall of paradoxical navel. In the dream that hatched in its incubation, a memory of warm flesh he'd touched and knew, Sobran was able to kiss the mouth that always said such interesting things.

Sobran found that he couldn't say, in prayer, 'God help me.' He didn't feel shame or fear. His desire was a triumph – Xas was so fine that of course Sobran should love him. God had made Xas beautiful, had made his clever tongue. 'What am I supposed to do?' Sobran asked God, laughing, and waving his desire up like the smoke of a sacrifice. 'This is what you get, Lord, for your great work.'

1822 Vin trouble *(hazy, cloudy wine)*

Sobran dressed for his friend, in linen fresh and pressed, but open at the neck. The shirt was untucked, as if he'd just come from hard work, his flesh bared to the cool air, but washed. He went unshod, his clean defenceless feet somehow beseeching.

Xas brought a bottle of St-Saphorin. Sobran had two of the second vintages of Jodeau-Kalmann.

'Angels don't get intoxicated,' Xas said, looking at the bounty. 'But I've told you that.'

'Then watch me get drunk and be happy.' Sobran, radiant with confidence, opened one bottle and lay back against the boundary marker. 'I have some business with you, Xas.'

'I like the way you can always think what to do with me.' Xas was smiling.

Sobran took a swig and stared, felt all the available light pouring in at his eyes as his pupils opened and opened – a sensation pleasurable in itself. The angel was so beautiful. Sobran felt no agitation – it was like basking against a stone wall in the morning light.

'We are back to drinking from bottles, I see,' Xas teased.

Sobran put the bottle neck to his mouth again, swallowed then nodded. A moment later he got up, put the bottle on the boundary stone and went to where Xas sat. Sobran crouched and, without hesitation, put his hands around Xas's wrists, to hold his arms down, and kissed the angel on the mouth. Xas's mouth opened in surprise, then against the kiss. Then Xas turned his head, so that Sobran was left with his mouth beside the angel's ear, breathing the frosty scent of his hair. Xas shook his head.

Sobran pressed his mouth against the angel's neck. There was a pulse; he remembered the pulse. 'I want you to hold me when I'm happy, too. I love you.'

A wing came between them; Xas raised it like a cold shoulder. Sobran felt the wing graze his leg, hard, and heard a pinion burst. 'I respect your wife – her rights,' Xas said, without, Sobran thought, any great conviction. 'Céleste should be sufficient for you.'

Sobran saw that the angel's mouth had colour, more than a wine stain on marble now, an internal nectar, ripe blood. The angel said, 'Besides, Sobran, do you even know what you want to do with me?'

In answering, Sobran's words were oddly broken up, not into clauses but pauses for breath. He was short of breath. He'd considered this. He knew better than the angel. It was time for him to teach the angel how to feel.

'Shut your mouth. You're acting outside your own laws.' The angel seemed to plead with him.

'What has law to do with what I want? This isn't wrong.'

'This – imposition?'

'I want you.'

'One night a year?'

'If that is all I can have.'

Xas looked angry but sounded compassionate. He began to say, 'I'm an angel – '

Sobran interrupted with his own plea or revelation. 'I love you because you're an angel.'

Xas simply erupted from where he sat, opened his wings so that they knocked Sobran back, and was upright and lifting off in a moment. The dust was like smoke. Sobran was on his feet shouting, 'Don't go!' in time to leap to catch one great wing in its second downbeat. Sobran's weight falling back to the ground, and his unrelenting grip on the wing, made a pivot on which Xas swung around, his free wing knocking down a hailstorm of cherries. He crashed on to his back. Sobran heard the breath slammed out of the angel's body. He knew only a short moment of very mixed feelings: shame, triumph, concern, amazement – then Xas was up, vaulting from the ground with hands and wingtips and feet. The angel hit Sobran in the jaw and Sobran tumbled down the slope. He lay stunned, bleeding at the mouth. As he drew his teeth from the live meat of his own tongue Xas landed on him, like an eagle with its wings arched away from the teeth or claws of prey it isn't wholly confident it has killed. Xas put his face close to Sobran's and said, soft and succinct, 'Listen, and take this in. The terms of the pact are this: "Xas shall go freely. God shall have his pains and *Lucifer his pleasures*." So, if you please yourself and me the way you want, Sobran, you will be pleasing the devil. *And I will not give you to him.*'

Xas sprang off him, straight up, and the first three wingbeats

kicked up so much earth that Sobran was partly buried. He watched
that part of the sky from which he thought the sound of wings came.
He saw a ripple against the stars, far away now. Then he closed his
eyes.

The widowed Aurora de Valday, her son and her uncle were on their
way back to Château Vully from Chagny in a cavalcade of carriages,
attended by four footmen, two grooms, the Comte's valet, Paul's
nurse, and Aurora's maid Lucette, when, within a mile and a half of
home, the Comte decided he wanted to stop and look in on Father
Lesy. Aurora couldn't imagine what her uncle was so pressed to
confess. She was alarmed by his sudden need to see a priest. Perhaps
her uncle anticipated a decline, thought he might fall ill, despite the
return of mild weather – perhaps he planned to *leave* her.

Aurora watched her uncle and his manservant go through the
low, heavily decorated arch of the church doorway. For a moment
she stared at the darkness as though it were the surface of a pond
into which someone she loved had disappeared, head to heels. Then
she seized her son by the hand and got out of her carriage, too fast
for the footman to fold down the steps. She jumped onto the road
and lifted young Paul down after her. They were pursued by the
nurse and Lucette, who broke into a run in the churchyard, to catch
up with her mistress and position a parasol between the hot sun and
Aurora's gleaming crown of dark braids.

Aurora followed her uncle into the church. Just inside Paul saw
some stairs, yanked his hand out of his mother's grasp and ran away
up them. The women followed him, calling out, 'Come back, Master
Paul', 'Be careful, please!' or, 'Where do you think you're going?' –
as the position or personality of each dictated.

Once up in the gallery, Aurora recognised, under dust, a place she
had come one Easter Sunday with her uncle and her parents to
celebrate Mass. Paul had found a carved hawk, a crest broken off the
end of one of the pews. He played with it for a moment, then he
discovered a knothole in the floor.

Paul's mother had found two views, one of the church, from font
to altar, the other, through a modest rose window, of the sunny
churchyard.

There were two girls by the font, heads together and their shawls raised to make a black tent above them. Both were in mourning. They had joined their shawls to block the light, the better to see their reflections in the font's water. As they jostled Aurora saw that one girl was dark while the other was very fair. They looked to be of a similar age, perhaps fifteen.

At the door of the sacristy Aurora's uncle had paused. Father Lesy appeared, following a woman whom Aurora recognised as Madame Jodeau. Céleste Jodeau stopped on seeing the Comte, then dropped into the kind of curtsey Aurora was taught by her dancing-master but was never able to perfect. The Comte took her hand as she came up, and held it as they exchanged a few words. Father Lesy stood by and manifested what Aurora had heard her uncle describe as his 'fussy manners', usually in statements beginning, '*Despite* Father Lesy's fussy manners . . .'

A cart had stopped at the gate to the churchyard. Three men were perched up on its seat. The one with very fair hair had to be a Lizet. The tallest, the one at the traces, was Sobran Jodeau. He no longer wore a beard, and Aurora recognised him first by his gait rather than his face. She watched him put his hand on the cart's side and vault down. A sturdy brown boy followed him. Man and boy went over to a grave near the wall – one with a wooden marker – and began to groom the weeds from among the flowers planted on its mound. The two men left in the cart sat facing away from each other as though they had quarrelled.

Aurora turned from the window to see Paul crouched by the knothole. He had been chewing a strip of paper torn from a cornet of sweets she had given him, and now pulled a spitball from his mouth and dropped it through the knothole. Below, Madame Jodeau was now alone – for Father Lesy and the Comte had gone into the sacristy. She stood completely still some distance from the girls at the font and watched them. Watched with the oddest expression, Aurora thought. She looked coldly alert like a dangerous animal keeping its eye on other dangerous animals. Just then one girl, seeing someone outside, exclaimed happily and ran out. The other was about to follow when the woman near the altar raised her voice. 'Sabine,' she called. Sabine turned, and closed her black shawl around her face. Céleste Jodeau walked along the aisle, unhurried, her eyes on her daughter. When she came near she said, 'Must you always be running after her.'

'Aline, Mama?' Sabine was confused.

Aurora faced the other way to seek out Aline Lizet who had stopped to speak to Sobran Jodeau. The sturdy boy offered her a cornflower, and then the man followed suit. He was already on his knees, so lifted the flower to Aline with teasing gallantry. She laughed and took both offerings.

Aurora met the gaze of her maid. She whispered, 'This is very diverting.' Lucette nodded.

Below, Sabine said, 'I see Uncle Léon beside Christophe Lizet.' She hesitated.

'Go on, then,' her mother said.

Aurora turned again. Beside her Lucette craned too. Framed in the rose window Sabine Jodeau joined Aline and the boy in tending the grave. Sobran Jodeau was just passing in under the feet of maid and mistress, who looked the other way, to see Jodeau step up to his wife and take her hand.

Céleste said, 'What a picture.' Then, 'Hasn't she grown beautiful?'

Sobran joined her, looked out of the shadow of the church. 'Yes,' he said.

'I mean Aline Lizet.'

'Yes, Aline has too.' There was a pause then Sobran said, 'I'm surprised you haven't remarked who's with me.'

'Oh?'

'I mean, I'm surprised at your lack of interest.'

'Why are you being so indirect, Sobran? All right, I see Léon. Have you chosen to forgive him?'

'It's only fair to offer him my trust again.'

Madame Jodeau shrugged. She followed his gaze, he was again watching the three by the grave. She seemed to weigh and measure his brief smile. And when the smile faded and the skin creased between his brows, she watched even more keenly.

Aurora also followed his gaze. She saw Aline Lizet go to her brother, saw Aline greet Léon Jodeau who might have answered her, but didn't face her. When Aurora turned, her eyes took a moment to adjust to the gloom. They had lost their point of reference, Céleste Jodeau's immaculate white lace collar. Céleste had left the church.

Sobran Jodeau was alone and walking awards the altar. He stopped beneath it, stood still, gazing with meditative penetration at the racked statue. Then he hung his head, came about, and left the church. All without the customary genuflection.

Aurora realised she had a hand on her maid's arm, and that Paul's nurse was frowning at them. She became aware that she was showing herself in a discreditable light. Calling Paul away from the knothole she led him downstairs. Her servants followed. As they emerged they met the Comte and Father Lesy. The priest was distressed to see where the women had been. He apologised. 'Countess! I'm afraid it's very grimy up there.'

Aurora reassured him, closed her hands to hide her palms, her blackened gloves.

They went out into the sunshine, where again Aurora was pursued by Lucette and a small halo of shade.

The Jodeaus had taken their cart one way, and were nearly out of sight. Christophe and Aline Lizet were on foot going in the opposite direction. The Comte took this in, said, 'Hmmm,' to himself, and looked at Aurora.

'God's architecture lends itself to eavesdropping,' Aurora explained.

'Of course,' said her uncle.

* * *

1823 Vin de goutte *(free-run wine)*

The new dog wouldn't put her head down, though Sobran had come downstairs early and petted her as she lay on her rag bed by the stove. Sobran sat still and dull for an hour while Josie blinked, then wavered. Yet as soon as he got up to go out the dog was awake, shaking herself. Her big feet hit the floor and her short, tapering tail waved.

'All right,' Sobran said. He opened the door and they went out. Josie followed him up the slope between the vines, made water beside a corner post, sniffed at this and that, pursued a toad and took it in her mouth – then dropped it, drooling and whimpering.

'Have you not yet learned?' Sobran asked the dog.

Sobran was afraid of this meeting. All year he'd been low – so that Céleste had asked, when he hadn't made love to her for weeks – what the matter was, who it was he longed for when he lay awake half the night, eyes on the ceiling and hands behind his head. She wept and he told her there was no one. He stroked her round flanks in pity, his hand busy but his body still turned away.

His wife looked about them on Sundays at church – followed his eyes, then proposed to Sobran *who* it might be. The widow Blanchard? The stonemason's sister? And, when the Jodeau family went with other local vintners, to help with the harvest at Vully, Céleste came home asking about Aurora de Valday.

'Stop it,' Sobran said when Céleste questioned him. 'It's your imagination – again. There's no one.'

In every other way it had been a good year. The Comte said, 'Jodeau, I admire your wine. You have your father's knowledge, Kalmann's vines, summer as a partner and, I swear, God as your sponsor.'

Sobran made his peace with his brother, and the whole family travelled to Nantes to see Léon off when he sailed for St Lawrence. On the return journey the family stopped at a place where the road touched the coast and went down to bargain for some fish, then lit fires and baked it. Sobran took a walk along the shore. The surf was unfamiliar to him, and the steady, unimpeded wind. Deafened by it, he expected to be ambushed, stalked, some such. Twice he turned and saw only his family at the fire. He felt as he had at midsummer in 1812, when the fires had begun to reach out to dissolve the gold stars on the blue domes of the Kremlin, when he dropped what little money he had into the bowl by the Russian woman's bed and felt – between the room, and street, church, street, room again – shadowed by his invisible, pitying, reproachful angel.

This summer's night Sobran waited, stood with the dog at his feet. He made plans. Planned to take up pipe-smoking, feeling the need of that ritual – cutting a plug, filling the bowl, striking a flint while sucking the sparks down into the tobacco. Many of Sobran's friends had the habit, he would ask them a question, or propose a bargain, then have to wait through the ritual for their reply.

When the angel arrived, the dog jumped up, barking. Sobran crouched, put his arm and all his weight across Josie's neck and muzzled her with his hands. She lunged, then subsided, trembling, her eyes starting out of her head in fury and terror.

Xas looked at the dog as if to say: 'Is this meant to protect you from me?' His eyes said this, glancing between the dog and man. He stepped closer and put a hand on the dog's brow; Josie shrank back against the ground, whined, then, when Sobran released her, she licked Xas's fingers, and the whine lifted in pitch from fear to fearful pleasure. Xas moved his hand likewise to Sobran's head, touched the hair on his crown. Sobran covered the hand with his own, took the blessing, then got up, so that they stood eye to eye. His blood reversed its flow – but he said what he had to – what he had rehearsed. 'I will never impose on you again. Please forgive me my offence. I feel that I can't live if you remain angry with me. I am your servant.'

Xas said, 'I've been angry for a year.'

'Then you should have come to see me.'

'And interrupt your journey? Don't tell me you arrived at this abject contrition three hundred and sixty-four days ago?'

'When I pulled you out of the air I felt that I could kill you – that it was possible. That alone filled me with terror.'

'You can't harm me. You felled me in the same manner Jacob brought down the angel he tackled – you are heavier than me. If I weren't light how could these wings carry me?'

Sobran remembered a tree limb bent down, as if it were a supple, unresisting sapling.

'Furthermore,' Xas said, 'I don't believe you can keep that promise. You're bound to impose on me again – though I hope not in lust.'

Sobran flinched.

'And you lie when you say, "That alone filled me with terror." I spoke Satan's name – by which I have addressed him as a familiar – and yet your eyes, sensitive anemones, shrank when I said "the devil". Your terror at *that* was the Church of your Fathers in you, as thorough as the flavour of oak in wine, and so I knew you lied when you said you had no sense of your desire as sin. Once *spent* you'd remember sin. As for not wanting to live – you remained quite healthy through twelve months of disappointing infatuation, so I can't believe you mean to die. Finally, as *my servant* you are an imposition. It didn't take you long, did it?'

'Why did you bless me? Why lay your hand on my head?'

'When you're in pain I feel tender,' Xas said. He wouldn't look at Sobran.

The man had lost his way. He wasn't sure what he had said wrong. He recognised this painful bafflement from quarrels he'd had with Baptiste as a youth and with Céleste in the early years of their marriage. He took a knife out of his pocket and gave it to the angel. 'I was going to cut my throat if you didn't forgive me.'

'And leave your wife and children? From pique, or spite?'

'Out of despair, which is a sin. But of course you've never despaired.'

'No,' Xas said. He raised the knife and moved it almost aimlessly, as a child fiddles, against the twined signature on his side. As he did so he said, with no expression, 'Is this friendship impossible?'

Sobran thought: '*He isn't speaking to me.*' He seized the hand that held the knife just as that weapon turned to dust, which settled slowly to the ground. One signature was alive – colour in the colourless gloom of a moonless night – awake against skin innocent of injury.

Xas put his forehead down on Sobran's shoulder.

Sobran put his arms around the angel. He didn't know what to say. He supposed he'd just witnessed an act of despair and an attempt at self-harm by a holy being. The dissolution of the knife was an act of God, or the pact maintaining itself, for Xas must go, not stop, in order to 'go freely'. After all these years, contemplating all possible permutations of his restricted knowledge, Sobran had learned to think like a lawyer, and test the meanings of every word. But he was slow, and things had passed him that he hadn't understood.

The dog, he saw, had draped herself on Xas's feet, wanting to comfort him too. She sighed twice, as they stood in silence, then finally gave a theatrical moan. Xas laughed.

'At least we can secure her happiness,' Sobran said. 'We could walk.'

Xas nodded.

'We could go across to Kalmann — *there's* a sight.'

And they did, the man's boots making dents in the dry soil and the angel's feet only smoother matches in the shape of a whole sole, as unshod feet do on firmly packed fine sand. The dog hared away and sped back. Xas walked as birds at the edge of the sea do when retreating before a tide, or like an owl shuffling along a limb before it swoops, not clumsy, but touchingly awkward. They came over the second ridge, and wandered down. Xas looked at the stone dust in the yard and blank tombstones stacked against the wall; the millwheel and two whetstones.

'Your sister lives here,' Xas said, 'and her husband the stonemason.'

'Antoine helps at harvest, and the remainder of the year runs his business. I meant Léon to have this house.' Sobran shrugged. 'There are a few fearful souls who won't buy Jodeau-Kalmann because of Antoine's workshop — but some more whimsical who favour Antoine's headstones because of my wine.' Sobran stroked the cool dusty face of a fresh stone. 'It's good to have them close — Sophie is hardier than Céleste, and a great help to us.'

'They keep no dogs,' Xas said, looking at the dog, who paused to hear herself referred to, her back foot at her ear. She got up, shook herself and urinated against a tombstone.

'Antoine dislikes them. And I think it might be bad for business.' Sobran scowled at his dog.

A light came behind the shutters of the second storey. Xas jumped against the wall, between the stones, and stood very still. The shutters opened and a head poked out, asked who was there.

'It's Sobran.'

'Jodeau, it's a wonder you can do a day's work, walking about half the night.'

Another head appeared, a long dark plait hanging against the sill. 'Poor Céleste, heaven help her,' Sobran's sister scolded. 'No wonder she frets — you're always abroad.'

'Mama!' a child called out. Sophie cursed and disappeared from the window.

'Go home!' Antoine said, then kinder, 'My friend – I know you don't come here to speak to either me or Sophie. But Baptiste Kalmann is *dead*.'

'Goodnight, Antoine.'

The shutter was pulled to. They waited a moment. The dog yawned and began to scratch again. Sobran took her by an ear and walked back into the vineyard. He heard the sound of wings, felt the shadow cross him and watched Xas fly to the crest of the hill, land, and wait for him. Sobran went reluctantly, knowing what Xas would ask him, but not anticipating with what eagerness.

'Is it Baptiste you miss – still?'

'I miss him.'

'He was your lover.'

Sobran glared. 'Baptiste was my elder by three years. He taught me – uses of my body. Boys do that, despite what the Church teaches. He also shared his whores with me, when I was young, before I met Céleste. And we often shared when we were campaigning. I'm ashamed of it.'

'I thought you were so troubled by Céleste because you were ambushed by desire, and didn't know how it felt when it came on.'

'It was the *love* that was new to me. I didn't love Baptiste in that way. What were you to know – how could I share my impure knowledge with a pure angel? I hoped to have time to atone for – my carnal youth.'

'And two years after you wed you followed Baptiste into the army.'

'There were things I didn't tell you – that's all. I never pretended to be better than I was. I used to believe you could see into my heart – so why bother to tell you?'

'I see,' Xas said, reasonable, and as if he thought Sobran's explanation reasonable. The angel let go of despair like a breath, was as resilient as one of those striped mountain flies which are impossible to crush. He said, 'I'll walk you back to Baptiste's headstone.'

'Fly me, angel, before I'm too fat and middle-aged for you to carry.'

'I'll fly you when you're old and your bones have shrunk.'

'And I can't hold my water, and am afraid for my life.'

'Come the day,' Xas said.

                        ⌒‿

1824 Vin tranquille *(still wine)*

Sobran waited, hat in hand, behind a butler at the door of one of the château's long dark parlours. The Comte had asked him to come at his own convenience, when the day's work was done – but meant at six, Sobran's dinner hour, yet before the château's family dined.

The butler opened the door and Sobran saw the Comte and three women – the Comte's niece, her maid, and a nurse. All four adults stood, heads bent, around a dark-haired boy in a white velvet suit, listening and smiling. Then the nurse took the child's hand and the boy offered his cheek to the Comte, to his mother and, to everyone's amusement, to the maid, who kissed him and curtsied. The butler opened both doors and the women and child walked out past Sobran, who kept his eyes down.

The Comte called Sobran in, asked him to take a seat by the fire, and poured him a glass of wine. It was very good wine and Sobran hoped he wouldn't be asked to offer his opinion on it – which would involve a description. He waited to hear the old man say, 'What do you taste?' It had been a game the Comte played with Sobran's father, and with Sobran when Sobran began to go with his father whenever Jodeau Senior had business at the château. It was a game Sobran had been led to believe he was very good at. The Comte seemed to appreciate his fanciful descriptions. Then one day, on the way home after one such session, Jodeau Senior told his son to 'stop playing the ninny' – couldn't he see that the Comte was making sport of his ignorance?

But the Comte didn't ask, instead he said, 'Five years ago you'd have turned up unwashed, to show how hard at work you had been.'

'I hope not,' Sobran said.

'Yes, you would have.' The Comte went on, 'I've lived much longer than I anticipated. Every night I climb into bed thinking I've got away with another day. God has overlooked me. But in the winter he'll be back with his beaters and will get me in the first sweep. I am seventy-seven years of age. Do you know that I was a friend of Lazare Carnot? We shared a confessor, Father Lesy. That was after Carnot voted for the death of the King. Carnot didn't like politics, he liked family life. I helped his family join him after the restoration for, you see, he liked to think he'd been some help to me in the days of the republic.' The Comte sighed. 'And I knew André Chénier. If you know who he was.'

'A poet.'

'Father Lesy said to me ten years ago that your brother Léon was the scholar but you are the reader.'

Sobran laughed. 'Poor Léon.'

'Ah yes, poor boy, never loved for his excellence. How is he?'

'Working very hard in St Lawrence, clearing land, keeping cattle. Or trying to – half the settlers live by hunting and trapping, not husbandry.'

'And your cellar is finished, I hear.'

'For now.'

'Ho!' The Comte enjoyed Sobran's answer so much he was compelled to lean forward, take up the poker and prod at the fire.

The Comte's niece came quietly back into the room, lit another branch of candles and carried them to the table by her half-finished firescreen, which stood directly behind the Comte's chair. She set a basket on her knees and began to sort thread, match it to the many greens for her hunting scene.

'Have you got Kalman's vines back in order?'

'We had three seasons of sleep in the grape, sir. And now four seasons clear. There was a recipe, a solution. We washed them as they began to fruit – changing the rags all the time. My daughters went without petticoats all summer. And we've been grafting to the three rows of gamay vines in Kalmann. I can't afford to take them up, but would prefer not to make blended wines.'

'You should press that south slope of yours separately.'

'I can't afford to, sir.'

'Very well, but don't *forget*.'

'I have twenty bottles of the 1806 to refresh my memory.'

'Do you want me to make an offer? Is that what you expect?'

Sobran shrugged. He saw the Comte's niece was watching him, her gaze quiet without being placid. He looked back at the Comte, who was smiling at him, because his attention had wandered, and because of *where* it had wandered. 'There was a matter in my mind,' the Comte said, 'I wanted to speak to you about. Something I'd like you to remember, and to assert yourself about, if and when the time comes. My niece has all the documents concerning the death of those poor girls – Geneviève Lizet and Marie Pelet – copies of everything, statements, the doctors' and magistrates' notes. If there is ever another murder, I'd like you to go over it all.'

'Yes, sir, I will.'

'Unless of course Aurora remarries and then I suppose all that will fall to her husband – or to Paul when he's sufficiently mature.'

Paul was the boy in white velvet. Sobran said, 'You are imagining quite a long career for this killer.'

'No. But I'm imagining that one day someone other than a priest will hear his confession, either as a *confession,* or as a *boast.* I imagine he'll kill again because I know he'll outlive me. It's my gloomy conviction. None of us knows who he is – but *I* will never know. If I think you will take an interest then I can have some hope justice will be done.'

'You are overestimating my wit, sir.'

'You should thank me for my confidence in you – churlish youngster. And it isn't your wit I want to employ, but your character. Aurora has enough wit for the whole province.' The Comte turned his head as far as his stiffened neck would allow, to order his niece: 'Leave off that fiddly nonsense and come closer.'

She brushed the skeins into the basket and put it down, got up and moved the little table that stood between the men. Sobran stood to fetch a chair closer to the fire for her and they did an irritable little dance around each other.

'Uncle, you shouldn't let Paul carry this table near the flames,' Aurora said. She sat down, nodded thanks to Sobran then said to him, 'The table has a wax top.' She pointed. 'Beeswax, with ferns and flowers and bees and butterflies set in it, like fruit in a cold collation. Uncle hates it – *memento mori* made to look like midsummer, he says. The beeswax is very old and hard now, but Paul carries it near the fire hoping it will melt and all the insects will be resurrected. He's persistently hopeful about that kind of thing. When we visit his father's grave he doesn't reflect dutifully – he commands, "Get up, Father! I'd like to meet you!"'

Sobran smiled. 'My second son, Martin, is like that. Imperious. And Sabine was a tyrant to her grandfather, which he enjoyed. Now she's quite a lady – for which my wife and I thank you.'

'It was Father Lesy's idea. Your daughter has written to me and says she enjoys the convent – which I find difficult to imagine.'

'And you sponsored Aline Lizet also. She and Sabine are good friends, and keep each other company. Autun does seem very far from home for such young country girls.'

'I'm sure, being a Jodeau, Sabine is quite capable of saying if she isn't content,' the Comte said, putting a stop to their conversation. He seemed amused and annoyed that they were talking over the top of him.

Sobran asked, 'Is there anything else I can do for you, sir? Or rather *promise* to do.'

'No. That will be all.'

Sobran got up. Aurora stood too and took his glass, setting it on the wax-topped table. Then she stooped to retrieve his hat, which he'd put down by his chair. She gave it to him. Sobran bowed to the Comte and his niece and took himself out the door.

'So, Uncle,' Aurora said, 'why didn't you air your theory about the mad Jules Lizet?'

'Because it isn't a theory, it's a pet suspicion.'

'You've never suspected Jodeau?'

'Do you?'

'He's secretive.'

'I thought he talked very freely to you. He's a man with easy manners. His wife has become a little mad. That's his secret. Or rather it's the commonly held knowledge that no one in the province may mention to him or any member of his family.'

'Because she's a beauty?'

'That is a remarkably murky thought, Aurora. Beauty hasn't much currency among old neighbours.'

'I suppose Monsieur Jodeau's neighbours don't defame his wife because they value his good opinion. Which is more or less the way

65

you have been treated all your life in your own circle, Uncle. People are very respectful of your feelings.'

'Hmm. The respect was never consistent enough for my liking.' Aurora laughed.

'Tell me, niece, do you still dislike Jodeau?'

'I remember that he is on your list of those I can trust.'

'Did I say that? Trust? No, dear, *employ* him. Link your fortunes. He's a very able man – and lucky. I remember I had to remind you who he was – the tall bearded one in clogs.'

'Men your age shouldn't snigger. I may have said, "Remind me", but – yes – I did know who you meant. Paul's nurse had pointed him out to me as a poor example of a mourner; she frowned on his ostentation. I watched him. I saw that in his manner of mourning Jodeau seemed to say: "Be careful, let no one forget I'm a wounded man." For the same reason his neighbours are afraid of his poor opinion. He has a manner that implies he has depths, and a temper, and untapped resources of temperament. That is why you like him, never mind his ability or his "luck". When I was a girl, Uncle, there'd be seasons we visited when everything pleased you, and others when you were disappointed with everything. Mama would read out your lettes to Papa. I remember one autumn before the hunting season Papa saying, "Oh no, not another overcast visit. I can't take this." That was the year we arrived with the two barrels of gunpowder and you and Papa spent three weeks blowing things up, and the magistrate sent a letter to the Emperor filled with silly speculations about Vully's conspiracies to revolt.'

'They were marvellous people, your mother and father.'

'Yes, I remember.'

They sat in silence for a few minutes, thinking about the typhoid in Venice. Then the Comte sighed. 'Perhaps I should employ Jodeau now – before I die. Wish him on you.'

'No, let me deal with him when you've gone, Uncle. I'd prefer him to owe me a debt of gratitude.'

'Ah yes. Offer him the bit with a handful of sugar. Very good, Aurora.'

1825 **Vin sec** *(dry wine)*

Xas gave Sobran seeds. 'Quinoa, it grows in the Andes in Spanish America. It's very tough, like heather, but in the colours of an autumn wood. Odd. Céleste will puzzle about it when it comes up.'

1826 **Vin viné** *(fortified wine)*

Sobran told Xas that Léon's letters took eight months to reach him. 'I try to have one for every ship, to time our visits to Sabine in her school to coincide with the mail from Nantes. There's a broadsheet up outside the house of the magistrate in Autun, about passages to Canada. I carry letters for two of my neighbours, write them also. It's like writing into mystery – I could be chattering on after Léon is dead of a fever, or wolves, or Indians. He's keenly aware of the difficulty – take the tone in which he asks about the children. He's thinking of Nicolette. I look at your flowers from the Andes, Xas, and I'm tormented by temptation, to ask you just to look in at him, to make a hole in his tar-paper window one night and look in. I even dreamed you were standing in the snow, and there was steam rising from your wings, and you were doing just that, pushing your finger through the paper on the window of Léon's house to make a peephole.'

Xas listened.

'I didn't forgive him graciously. I was always pompous – acted very big and generous. But really he took nothing from me – he lost his own portion of father's estate and we had to cover his debts so as not to sell. But, in effect, we bought Jodeau from Léon. Now he struggles in the Protectorate while I'm becoming a wealthy man.'

'I'll go and see how Léon is, Sobran. It isn't as if you're asking me to take another message to Heaven.'

'Bless you, Xas, you're a kind friend.'
'Oh – a demotion.'
'Pardon?'
'Never mind.'

1827 Mut *(balanced)*

'My dear friend,' the letter read, 'I am aware of the risk I take placing this letter here' (under a rock on the boundary stone). '*I* am worried that it will rain, though it seldom does at midsummer. Or that someone will find it, remove it, or that it will have slipped its stone and blown away. Don't go down to the house – I'm not there, though Sophie and the younger children, hers and ours, are. I've had to go to Nantes to meet Léon's ship. Céleste and Sabine are with me. Léon has been ill and decided to return to France. He wrote that, having survived his fever, one night he saw an angel. The angel came into his room while he was reading and assured him it wasn't yet his time but that he should take himself back to his family. "This land is too strong for you," the angel said. León wrote that it was then midwinter, with snow piled up against the door and that, in the morning, Léon saw that the angel had, like a wolf, dug the snow out to enter, not simply walked through the wall.

'I thank you again. We must be waiting when he sets foot on shore. You have sent him so far back to us we must take very good care of him. I don't know if you will consent to vary our agreement, but I hope to be back within six weeks, so please come again, my dear friend.

'I am in your debt.'

The house was a hot black cave – and full of aspiration, seven breathing bodies. The weather was overdue to break, the sky covered in melting, indistinct grey cloud. All the shutters were open. Sobran lay on his back, a sheet between his legs and sweat crawling like flies through the forest of hair in the valley of his sternum. He was asleep – or so he thought – then irritably awake. A hand touched his face. Two fingers pressed his lips and another hand clasped his shoulder. The hands were cool. Sobran opened his eyes.

Again he saw Xas, his hair stiff with frost and an accretion of pulpy ice sliding from his wings. Sobran stirred, carefully disentangled himself from the sheet. Xas backed through the door.

'Mmmm?' Céleste said.

'Shhh, go back to sleep.' Sobran picked up his nightshirt from the floor and followed Xas down the stairs, outdoors, up the slope between the vines.

Xas leaned against the shade tree, his head in the space between its first fork. He had intended only to spy, not interfere with Léon, he explained, but the winter was stored death – as he saw it – a pressing backlog of bad luck. Léon looked thin and yellow. How could he survive much more of that?

Léon was quite spent after the sea voyage, Sobran said, but they lodged at Nantes and nursed him, then took the journey home very slowly. 'From when have you looked for me?' he asked his angel.

'This is the first night. I knew that six weeks was just you being hopeful.' He passed Sobran a slender, dark green, glass bottle. 'Some cordial for your brother. Apharah sends it – my friend in Damascus.'

'Thank her for me,' Sobran said. Xas was smiling at him sweetly and he felt his heart going up like a lark, startled and silly. He began to give what he was permitted to – to talk about Léon, the journey, Sabine's suitor, things he hoped to do. He promised Xas a feast of celebration – next year, he wouldn't miss their appointment. It would be twenty years, did Xas realise? They could try the 1806 again, 'that *vin bourru* which I remember you gave the benefit of the doubt.'

'Do you remember that I said it rained in 1812, the second year you were away?'

'Yes.'

'Your father's last harvest. I want to taste that too. "It seldom rains at midsummer," you wrote, but it did when you turned your back.' Xas was smiling still, but meant something. Sobran tried not to see the remark as a reproach – then did understand it. 'You remember everything,' he said.

'Yes.'

'When will you bring me red wine, Xas?'

'I said when you were forty.'

'Three years.'

Xas nodded. 'All Spanish and Italian, I'm afraid. The best reds are on your doorstep. You might yet make them, wine like the Cîteaux monks made when they had – among other vineyards – Kalmann. Before the revolution, when Jodeau was a small *clos* and this slope was half in cherry trees and your great-great uncle – I think it was – raised cattle, made cheese and sold all his grapes to the château.'

'Yes. You can still see the old wall along by the road. How did you learn all this?'

'By speaking to the dead.'

Sobran nodded, calm. He thought and watched the fine filaments of lightning at play perhaps as far off as Autun. 'I had forgotten or maybe never fully understood, that whenever you come I have to play host to an angel. Perhaps I've insulted you with talk of debts and impositions and advice. Well, I'm older now, and more gracious, I hope – although I think I still want both dignity and wisdom.'

'I'm with you, Sobran,' Xas said, ruffling his wings in a kind of shrug, 'However you treat me.'

⁂

1828 Vin amer *(bitter wine)*

The host had set a table, had kicked away the mould-furred and fermenting windfall fruit from around its legs. He covered the table with a white cloth, brought soft cheese, peaches, pears, the bottles – Jodeau South 1806 and Jodeau 1812, plus a bottle of cognac, forty-five years of age – and a gift from his wealthy patron, Aurora de Valday. He set two chairs, at angles rather than opposite each other, facing the boundary stone on which the angel commonly perched.

Then the moon arrived, gold, dazzling and featureless. After another hour it was high in the sky, a pure wafer pressed with a holy image.

The angel came and settled, enveloped both his lower body and the boundary stone with his wings. The first bottle was over an hour uncorked, and mellow. Sobran poured it out, then proposed a toast, 'Here's to twenty years.'

They drank, passed an hour in conversation – Xas questioning and Sobran talking about Léon's health and about the child Céleste was expecting, their last to be sure, another son, he hoped. Sabine was betrothed to a vintner, from a coterie near Chalon-sur-Saône, the other side of the river. 'He has just inherited, and is a very well set up young man, though he's closer in age to me than to Sabine. Céleste, Sophie and Sabine are all very busy sewing. Sophie has only boys, you see, so she's enjoying the preparations.' Sobran told how the cellars were being extended, and how, in winter, he and Céleste had spent a month in Beaune.

'I'm prosperous, settled and very happy,' he said. He paused to slap his thigh when he saw Josie, who had slipped her rope and come up the hill. The dog ignored him and went to the angel, rolled against the bolster of his crossed wings, from which an arm with a golden wrist-guard moved to fondle her head and sides. Xas whispered endearments to the dog, in some strange, supple language that caused every hair on Sobran's body to lift and the breath in his throat to thicken. The dog writhed, delirious, mute, her ears in the dirt.

Sobran busied himself opening the second bottle. 'The Comte died last Christmas, God rest his soul. He named his niece's son as his heir, though he does have a daughter who lives in Venice – she was a lady-in-waiting to the Empress Josephine and never married. The boy is ten. His mother, Aurora de Valday, asked me to oversee Vully's winemaking.'

'Did you say yes?'

'I did. I only need to spend half the week there. Léon is here now, and Baptiste does nearly a man's share of work.'

'Good. See where the cellar got you? And cultivated knowledge.'

'And the Comte's freely given friendship.' Sobran leaned forward, offered the bottle. 'Try it, this is the year I was in Russia. The year it rained.'

They tasted. Sobran set his glass down, looked at Xas. 'I'm a very lucky man. Not wanting to tempt providence, but there are times I think I'm the luckiest man alive. I'm wealthy and healthy and have a loving family. I know you. But beneath all this, my happiness has a foundation. I mean, my luck *is* my knowledge. Whereas other men have faith, I have knowledge. Because I know you, I know that if I lead a good life, and surround myself with good people – all of us with a measure of piety – then, despite estrangements, like the quarrel that parted my brother and me, or long absences, even absences that last more than half my life, those of the dead – Baptiste Kalmann, my parents, Nicolette – no matter what my losses and my grief at them, I am certain I will be united in Heaven with those I love.'

The angel turned his head, looked towards the eastern horizon, the strip of violet sky that haloed the hills. He said, 'You won't see me in Heaven.'

There was a moment of blown silence, a rot of silence that seethed and was alive. Sobran stared at Xas, so bewildered that his body was numb.

'Not all angels come from Heaven,' Xas said. Then, 'I'm a fallen angel.'

He was the same – an angel balanced on a boundary stone – but the world blinked, or lost consciousness for a moment. A chair fell, Sobran's chair. He was standing. He held the table edge so hard that splinters lifted in stars around his fingertips. The face before him was exactly the same sober, watchful face he'd first looked into.

Xas put out a hand.

Sobran fled. He felt the flesh on his torso bouncing as his feet struck the slope, felt it as meat, mortality, age, ugliness. He ran indoors, bolted the door, then, as private as some mad men and most injured animals, he raised the hatch in the pantry floor and stumbled down into the little cellar, full of onions, potatoes, apples, bottled preserves. He sat in the dark, wept and struck his head against a beam. In the closed space he stuffed his hands into his mouth as if to smother himself.

His family found him with the marks of his fists on his own body, bruised stomach, thighs, face and chest. He didn't speak, just sat and rocked. They put him to bed, brought in more family, a physician, Father Lesy, whose hand Sobran held as he prayed. The words of the prayer were handholds in a sifting pit of sand. *'I waited patiently for the Lord; and he inclined unto me and heard my cry. He brought me up also out of an horrible pit, out of the miry clay.'* Sobran struggled, losing ground, the earth of his own grave pouring on him, waterless, the limestone at midsummer.

It was Antoine and young Baptiste who found the table set under the shade tree, the soured cheese, bird-pecked fruit, spilled bottle and two glasses – one with red tide lines and the other scarcely touched. Baptiste picked both up and turned them, saw the cheesy grease of a lower lip print he'd never thought he knew before, till he recognised it as his father's. On the other glass was the print of a smooth-skinned, full lower lip.

'Who was it?' He asked his uncle.

The stonemason thought of Aurora de Valday, the madness between some men and women. He told the boy to clear the table away.

That day Antoine searched Jodeau and Kalmann for a corpse. He thought – he scarcely knew what. Then after two days Aurora de Valday sent a letter, inquiring after Sobran's health; she'd heard he was ill. At the week's end she came herself – in her carriage, veiled, slim-waisted in her grey silk. She pulled off her gloves when she came into the house, as if she meant to set to work in the sickroom. Sophie told her it was better she didn't see him yet. He wasn't himself. The priest was with him now.

Aurora's hand went up to her mouth.

'He should live,' Sophie hurried to say, 'if he has a will to. But he hasn't eaten yet, only wants to pray.' Sophie held Aurora's gloves while the Countess retied her bonnet. Her hands were trembling. As they stood there, Sophie stolidly barring the foot of the stairs, Céleste appeared above them. Madame Jodeau offered the Countess no greeting, or any ordinary acknowledgement, but stared, and audibly ground her teeth. Aurora almost expected Madame Jodeau to begin to bark. She took her gloves from Sophie and hurried out.

A dark corridor. A long passage of horror. He couldn't bear the touch of his own thoughts. Then, one morning, he woke and looked around at the bedchamber, at Céleste by the bed in a chair, mending a stocking. Was it red? One of Martin's? Sobran found he *did* want to think about his second son, in his school clothes – but he couldn't discern the colour of the stocking. He couldn't see colour, and knew it at once, looking around himself at the dark grey of shadow and bright grey of sunlight on the quilt. Céleste started from her chair, called in a shrill voice for Sophie.

Sobran told the women he was hungry. He found his rosary in his hand.

To the sorrow of his family, and all his friends, to the secret sorrow of the aged Father Lesy, with whom he spent so much time, Sobran was a changed man. His family watched him, even in midwinter twilight, ride out to early Mass. He wore black and white, a cross buttoned in his shirt. Like a Protestant patriarch he read the Bible to his household in the evenings. He hated the hours of darkness – would call his sons to his side if the sun set while they walked from Kalmann to Jodeau. He was always shut away with lamps lit in his room at Vully – didn't take wine with Aurora in the bailiff's office, as had been their tradition in the months before his illness. He gave money to the Church. He slept with a candle lit – and Céleste learned not to quench it, no matter how its light rubbed at the lids of her closed eyes.

❧

1829 Mutage *(the process of arresting fermentation by adding alcohol)*

Because he was colour-blind, Sobran's night vision was poor. What he saw, the first time he looked through the shutters, was like a landscape through heat haze, but the swarming distortion was darkness.

Sweat ran on his body, his stomach was empty, his bowel empty, he was both fasting, and unable to eat. Sight impaired, he was slow to see what he dreaded to see – the figure waiting on the ridge. Yes, a cloud made a slight adjustment to the moonlight, and Sobran saw the white face, white shoulders, folded wings. His fingers climbed down the slats of the shutters like a ladder as he let himself down on to his knees.

Sobran prayed and the fallen angel waited, all night. Sobran's prayer had more stamina than the angel's patience. At last the hidden man observed the rising sun light the angel's black hair, whitely, though Sobran recalled the vigil after Nicolette's death, and how at *that* sunrise the sheen on the angel's hair was *robe*, the purple of wine. Here Sobran met other recollections, and crushed his testicles in one fist till tears ran down his face.

Sunrise. The angel got up, his joints as oiled, and head as steady as a person's who has paused only a moment, not camped all night. The wings spread slowly, as white as dry chalk, and he flew away. Sobran finished his prayer, then fainted with his head against the windowsill.

<hr />

1830 Jaune (*a malady of white wines when they turn yellow – not to be confused with* vin jaune)

The following year Sobran intended to be somewhere else on what he thought of now as the anniversary of his damnation. Midsummer found him at Sabine's husband's vineyard near Chalon-sur-Saône – sober Sobran Jodeau, white-haired after his illness, a handsome man of middle age, who wore only black, who was pious, but unjudging, self-denying, but generous, respected by his friends and neighbours (and mourned by all). On the day after midsummer Sobran was quiet, but peaceful, playing with his first grandchild. And another day found him, more silent, but resolute – at Mass four times (it was Sunday), fasting, retiring early. The next day he walked the roads around the town, from breakfast to supper.

The following day he set out for home.

On the night of the rendezvous he bolted the doors of the house and posted himself by the shutters of his parlour – again. Céleste called him to bed. He said he had a letter to write. She asked him whether he and Sabine had quarrelled – stood in her shawl at the door of the room – big-bellied with, really, this time, their last child.

'Of course we haven't,' he said. 'You get some rest.'

She trimmed the lamp wick for him, and the light in the room bloomed. She said goodnight, and before closing the door, looked at the desk, the letters, looked for Aurora de Valday's serpentine handwriting.

When Sobran heard the creak of Céleste's footsteps overhead he put out the lamp.

After midnight the angel alighted. He stood against the tree – the fork above his head now – the sight of which hurt Sobran, like the ellipsis in his life between the mark he'd made on the parlour door frame to measure Sabine at fourteen, before she went to school in Autun, and at seventeen, when she was home again at a time he and Céleste remembered to measure their children. In this instance it was the tree, not the angel, who had grown. Sobran was at a loss as to what part of his body to harm to stop the memory of Xas's head resting neatly against the fork – five years before?

They held their positions.

Shortly before dawn the angel got up and walked down the hill. He paused to look at the kennel, which was empty. Josie had disappeared during Sobran's illness, which caused him little sorrow. The dog was disloyal and contaminated; she had failed to warn him of danger, and had given homage to a hellish being.

Xas came up to the house and studied in turn each window that faced the hill. The ground-floor windows shuttered, as always, and those on the top floor open to whatever breezes there were. Xas turned his attention to the shutters – four windows. He stared at them, one after the other.

Sobran took a step back, and another, then a third. He stood in the middle of the room and looked at the grey bars of light. No shadow, no hands, no stealthy white fingertips. Then he heard the drum strokes of wings, the hiss of grit against the stone walls, clatter of pebbles on the shutter, a rushing sound, then every ordinary dawn noise – cockcrow, birdsong, a dog barking on a nearby farm, wind livening-up – all exact, familiar and despised.

1831 Cru *(the soil in which vine is grown)*

Sober Sobran Jodeau, in his white shirt, black waistcoat, black breeches and coat, white collar, gold collar stud, and gold crucifix, walked up between his vines to confront the fallen angel – who simply said his name, then was quiet as Sobran held up one hand. His other, a fist bunched at his side, held the blessed seeds of his rosary, hung with five holy medals from shrines he'd visited.

'I have some questions for you. You can answer them, then go and never come back.'

'Have you thought this through, Sobran?' Xas was dry. 'Which do you need more, your questions answered, or me gone?'

Sobran struck the angel with the fist that held the rosary, then looked with more satisfaction than anger on the angel's profile, the face his fist had turned. Xas said, to the ground, 'Don't do that again.'

Sobran struck him again, backhand this time, vicious, fearless and meaning business.

Xas looked up at him. 'You're striking God.'

'You're a liar.'

Xas stood up; wrapped in his wings, he was a figure as streamlined as a simple tombstone. 'Ask your questions. And please don't say you disbelieve my answers.'

Sobran felt tears, a pressing pain behind his incontinent eyes. He asked, 'Did you really see Nicolette in Heaven?'

'Of course,' Xas said, sounding as though he hadn't anticipated the question and now knew he should have. 'I saw her, yes. In the far south there is a volcano whose blue sulphurous lake is a back way into Heaven. It is a journey that takes more than human hardihood. As far as I know it's seldom used. I went through that lake. I'd

77

allowed weeks before our scheduled meeting, for troubles I anticipated – but, unfortunately, not for the trouble I was too afraid to face. I knew I'd be crippled for a time after gaining Heaven. You see, I hadn't been there for some time. I'm sorry, Sobran, to be telling you about me, not Nicolette, but I told you about her all those years ago – and didn't trouble you with my story.'

'You troubled me.'

'Where I gained access, Heaven was like the volcano – not terrible to an angel – but with winds full of ice like powdered glass. Stealing into Heaven I'd eluded everyone but God, Whom I know I've never eluded. I went down in His arms. There was ice all around me, and silence, because He didn't speak to me, just took me and held me in Heaven's ice and – terrible – His sorrow. He didn't release me, but after a time I just got up again and flew to find Nicolette. That was easy, in Heaven an angel can find whoever they want – whoever is there. I saw her and spoke to her, exactly as I told you. Heaven was how I described it – Heavenly. Then I left Nicolette and I left Heaven. Again.'

Xas fell quiet. After a long silence he asked, 'What is your second question?'

'You haven't finished your story,' Sobran said to Xas. Was the angel too proud to try for his pity? He hadn't talked about the beating. Xas flicked his wings and a glow shone forth, where the simple (the red, Sobran remembered) signature burned. To Sobran it looked grey-white, like phosphorescence in a breaking wave.

'Tell me about the beating.' Sobran's voice was rough, insubstantial – and if he'd had eyes to see he would have seen the rosiness return to Xas's mouth.

The angel said that when he came up out of the volcano, armoured in acid ice, he looked down and saw two smoother patches in the surface of the crater lake, and two wakes in the steam, two tubes where vapour eddied upward – his own and those of the archangel above him. The archangel had come through behind Xas, but was swifter and stronger. The archangel stooped on Xas as an eagle does; knocked the angel out of the air and down on to the permafrost. 'My side caved in where I hit the ground, and I had bloody icicles in my nose. He lay on me and whispered in my ear, told me to stay out of Heaven, he'd tolerate no more trespasses. I said he was striking God. And he said – while banging my head on the ice – that we were on earth now, as though earth was outside God's jurisdiction, and if I crossed his path again he would break my head and eat anything he found inside it.'

'Did he disbelieve the pact?'

'He thought it was a bad thing – I suppose – and that he was bound to ignore it. Or lodge a protest.'

'You're saying that an angel of God disagrees with and disobeys God's policy.'

'Well, if it were impossible for angels to disagree with God then there wouldn't have been a war.'

'Why did you quarrel with God?'

'Is that your third question?'

Sobran crossed himself and shook his head. 'I trust the Lord. And I'm no magistrate.'

'I'm glad to hear it,' Xas said, then, 'Is there anything else?'

'One thing.' Sobran shuddered, wrapped his arms around himself and stooped slightly. 'Because you are like a bloody murderer – one who goes from corpse to corpse – causing terror in pieces because no one can be sure the murders are the work of one hand – because I think that about you, and you have held my body, been in my house, and in my thoughts and life for all these years, I have to know: Do you torture souls in Hell? Human souls?'

Xas stared.

'Tell me,' Sobran said.

'Why won't you believe what you've learned about me yourself? Do you think I've been tender to you to win your damnation and the devil's approval like a bounty for your soul?'

Hell was horrible and scarcely habitable when fallen angels first came to it, Xas told Sobran. They were its first inmates. Since damned humans were damnable Sobran must imagine they found plenty of scope to torment each other. Sobran was a vintner, so he should imagine the angels sealed sinners in dark barrels and *let them work*. Hell wasn't crowded – half the dead of history were in purgatory, which was like the world, but without gardens or wildernesses or tools or ideas – or substance, so angels couldn't go there. 'Most souls in purgatory are there not for sins, as such, but

79

blindnesses – I say, but I'm lenient. *I* grow roses and go freely – that's what I do.'

Sobran said, 'You've caused me more pain than anyone. Go away.' The tears got out and ran down his face.

'Yes. But I'll come back.'

'No.'

'I'm still your angel, your luck. You still know there's a Heaven, after all.'

'My torment is that I know that the ones I love are there, or will go there, while I'm damned.'

'God is merciful, Sobran. He loves us both.' Xas opened his wings and went into the sky with the competent animal effort of a leopard springing from the forest floor to a branch, or a salmon leaping up a white fall in a full river.

When Sobran was at his most pious, attending Mass often on the Angelus, the six-hourly bells, Aurora de Valday told him that she didn't believe in God. She had hesitated over this confidence, but although Sobran had changed his habits, he hadn't his manners – whatever his sorrow, he had kept the good-natured canniness that had earned him her friendship despite their different stations.

When her husband was newly dead, and her uncle the Comte was ailing, Aurora looked about her at the estate, perplexed and fearful. She sought her uncle's advice and he gave her a short list of those she could depend on. The family of Château Vully, irregular in their religion, sluggish in their loyalties, but decent to their tenants, had preserved their fortunes when heads rolled, houses burned and land changed hands. A daughter had been sent, like a tithe, to Bonaparte's court; cottages were kept mended; cautious, but not fruitful, marriages were made.

'Whom can you trust?' Aurora's uncle said, then named men in Paris and Beaune, a holy mother at Autun, old Father Lesy in Aluze, 'and Jodeau, whose family is *cru* – the soil the vine stands in – who knows wine from his grandfather, who raised half of our vines from the dead after the fire in '72. Jodeau's mother's family had a knack for getting money, and making money make money, though none of them were lettered. *Her* father had two boats on the canal. Baptiste Kalmann – you wouldn't remember him, an insolent wolf – could have ruined that vineyard of his. His father was a threadbare lawyer who made himself great by conspiring to divide the monks' land. He drew up the thieving contract for the Paris timber merchant who bought Clos Vougeot – for the people, of course. Kalmann's fee was that little vineyard, till then also the monks'. A bad family – those hills were better off shot of Baptiste Kalmann. Sobran Jodeau has grown into a careful, clever, decent man, which is why I upheld Kalmann's will. Jodeau will do well by that land. And you should employ him.'

Aurora nodded, and the Comte took her hand and added, 'But don't fall in love with him.'

'Uncle, he's hardly a charmer.'

'No, dear, but despite the decency he's a bit of a free-thinker, and I know how you thirst after the company of "free-thinkers".'

It was after this, and in her new widowhood, that Aurora took to watching Jodeau. That was 1823. She didn't employ him – her uncle was often confined to bed, but still able to administer the vineyard. Besides, only a fool would seek the company of a married man if the sight of that man's face (oh, and his hands, coarse-grained, great-knuckled, disproportionately long) made the hidden saddle of her groin grow heavy and pulse in time with her breasts and her mouth and her heart. But Aurora grew tired of her desire, couldn't talk it away, because it was worthy, but wore it out, laughed it off. In 1828 the Comte died and she employed Jodeau. And while they planned, or reckoned books, or turned the tap on a barrel to taste together, they talked. They enjoyed each other's company. When Aurora heard that Sobran had fallen ill (or gone mad) she was terrified – for her who else was there in the world like-minded, forthright, *easy?* She had a son, servants, and dear old friends whose households she visited and who sent her monthly letters from as far away as Piedmont, but Jodeau was her *kind*, and losing him would mean excommunication for her mind. When she appeared at his house she was rebuffed by his sister. His wife stood at the top of the stairs glaring – shameless and strange. Aurora had to go away, get only news of him. Wait. He sent her a letter, remote, formal, just blackened paper. He was sorry for his indisposition – would so-and-so see her through this harvest after which, God-willing, he'd be able to serve her again.

Sobran reappeared one frosty morning in October, was waiting for her after her walk, standing hat in hand by the fireplace in her morning room. He had aged, his hair white, his face lined and dry and his eyes faded but, she saw, as she walked forward to take his hands, clear, and as warm as the russet stain in the coat of an ageing black cat. Her hand trembled. 'My friend,' she said.

She got used to him, his sobriety, dryness, diligence – maybe mourned the change less than many, because they had never been vulgar familiars, like the cronies with whom he had drunk brandy and gossiped under the plane trees in the square at Aluze. And she never saw him frightened, as his sons did, caught abroad in the stealthy midsummer twilight. Their conversation had never been personal. She never spoke about her husband and he spoke only with reserved respect of his wife and elder daughter – was more open about his sons, their scrapes and triumphs, their characters. And, although Sobran had become a pious man whose life was as ruled by routines as any timorously Godfearing old woman, they still talked about ideas, what was happening in the *pays*, in Paris, in the greater world. They talked about books, compared notes on the behaviour of their neighbours, what the mayor of Chalon-sur-Saône had said to the magistrate, or the priest to the seducer of young girls.

So it was that, three years after his illness, on a winter evening when they sat over letters and orders for payment in the Bailiff's room at Vully, sipping a sweet wine – not theirs, a golden Savoyard – Sobran told her about the dancing at the funeral of the ancient Wateau widow, how the combination of an enthusiastic reel and spilled beer had the widow knocked out of her coffin and draped over a chairback as if she'd been over-indulging and was ill. Aurora took in his glee, how free his tone was from tongue-clicking. The glee gave her licence to talk to him about his piety. She asked Sobran whether he knew that she didn't believe in God. He said he'd noticed she only went to church on high holy days and had assumed she wasn't a very religious woman.

. She told him about the atheists, the Rationalists she'd met at her aunt's place in Paris, before she married, when she was a girl. She had talked to and admired them, and she gave up God. 'Lazily and easily, like changing costumes. I was very young then, and untouched. I hadn't liked my convent education and was ready for another set of ideas. But I didn't believe what the Rationalists believed as an article of faith – the non-existence of God – until many years later. After my husband died I found myself running a gauntlet of consolation, "our hope in Heaven" and so on. Everybody was being kind, and I hope I wasn't ungracious. But I did have to bite my lip. Then one morning I was walking in the *allée*, alone, and still biting my lip I suppose, when suddenly it was as if the sky lifted off me – the horrible weight of my hope in Heaven. And I was filled with a feeling of reverence – oh, it was easy and ordinary, like motherliness – and I knew that *this is all there is*. It was a wonderful innocent clarity, and I've felt it ever since.'

Sobran moved some papers. The fire was behind him. He didn't look angry, and he didn't offer any argument. He just asked her what was to be done with sinners, without damnation?

'I know that I have to imagine a different world from the one I learned as a child, a world without ledgers.' She lifted the heavy leatherbound book that lay between them. 'Ledgers in the hands of a mighty judge. I think we must see to it that sinners have their recompense – or forgiveness – from *us*.'

Sobran nodded, then asked. 'And what of those losses that seem unbearable? Separations from people we feel we can't live without?'

'Perhaps our ruin honours the strength of our love.'

'Perhaps.'

'I suppose you see my atheism as a risky exercise of my free will – the Lord letting me have my head and run at His world.' She smiled as she said this, self-mocking and affectionate, and was rather startled by the vehemence of his reply.

'I think our freedom is a freedom to hear lies, and to run to the end of our leads until they throttle us. I make a point of believing only what I learned before my beard came in.'

'Why before then?' Now she was prying – now she really cared whether he answered her. Was it Céleste, then, the troubled wife he'd kept and cared for all these years, mixed his blood with again and again. Would he, finally, complain about his wife?

'Someone betrayed me,' Sobran said.

'And you took over twenty years to sicken of it?'

'Poisoned friendships are slow poison.'

*

The newest barrel room at Vully was as cool as a cave, and accessible by steps leading down from two great angled doors like storm shutters. Beyond the doors lay a closed courtyard, in the centre of which was a pool filled with waterlilies. Eleven-year-old Agnès Jodeau and thirteen-year-old Paul de Valday were squatting on the rim of the pool, hands in the water, trying to catch the carp. Paul lunged, the water flashed, splashed, darkening the stone. Both children got up, laughing – then Paul coughed. Coughing and laughing, the two walked around the pool to squat on the other side and recommence fishing. Aurora crossed herself. Sobran caught her hand before the cross was complete. She was shocked to be touched, and surprised he'd play accomplice to her convictions. He let go, but her hand caught his as it withdrew.

He squeezed her hand. 'Aurora, Paul only coughs when he's excited. When he and Martin saw the balloons crossing the river last month and ran to tell me, Paul coughed after every third word, but didn't seem conscious of it. He never holds his side.'

'I think of his father in a sedan chair, drinking ox blood in the shambles at Corbigny,' Aurora said.

'Is Paul's colour good?' Sobran said.

Aurora looked into her friend's face, puzzled by the tone and phrasing of his question.

He took his hand from hers and turned back to the table and the tall measuring glass full of wine he had just drawn from one of the barrels. He held it to the light. 'Why do you think I say "clear", then pass it to you to ask how the colour seems?'

'I thought you were inviting me to make fanciful comparisons: "It's the colour of a bishop's robe whenever he covets the cardinal's hat".'

'Since my illness I no longer see colours. That's why I ask about Paul's colour – he's stout enough.'

'Yes, you're right, he only coughs when he's excited.'

Sobran said, 'I was surprised to see you cross yourself.'

'Why? I make my curtsey at Christmas, Easter, weddings and funerals.'

'I predict that you'll call for a priest on your deathbed.'

'Since I'll outlive you, Sobran, you won't have the satisfaction.'

Aurora asked, 'Is your friend aware how she authored your illness and losses?'

'My friend isn't a woman.' He looked stern.

Aurora bowed slightly. 'Forgive my presumption. I think, because I spent a year in the salons of Paris, and because I read both novels and philosophy, that I'm a woman of the world. But my life is really rather quiet and confined.' She looked at her friend, hoping he was mollified (or moved) by this apology. She waited for a sign from him, a nod or smile – waited without anger, though what was she to think? She too had seen him glow for a year – ten years ago – glow like a man in love. Later she had loved him. And after her husband died Aurora saw that Sobran was suffering – that it was love he suffered, sullen, troubled, stuffed with spoiled blood. But he was in his thirties then, and *married for fourteen years*. Aurora had noticed this – it was observable, memorable, as fixed in her calender as an astronomical event. But she wouldn't call a friend a liar.

'Perhaps you should marry again,' Sobran said. 'You're still young.'

'I'm the age you were when we first met,' she said, perhaps to remind him of that time, remind him that she *knew*.

Outside there was a shriek and a splash. Sobran and Aurora ran out into the light. Sobran fished his daughter out of the pool with one hand while preventing Paul, who was intent on rescue, from joining her. Agnès spluttered. She was drenched and her white apron was green with pond weed.

'What will your mother say?' Sobran scolded his daughter and shook her once, sharply.

She had been crying a little, from surprise, but began now to weep hard, as if in dread. Sobran seemed dismayed at the effect his words had on her and let her go.

Aurora put an arm around the girl, told her it was all soon mended, there were plenty of clean clothes and they would hand hers over to the laundress. She walked Agnès away towards the château proper, calling for her servants as she went. Paul went with them, coughing and explaining – weak sticks, taunting carp, small girls with bad balance. Aurora glanced back at Sobran. Her look challenged him to explain a child this afraid of her mother's anger. Sobran followed, frowning.

1832 Clairet *(clear, bright, light)*

There was moonlit mist below them so that all the hilltops were islands. It was cold, and Sobran wore a greatcoat. He'd brought nothing with him but his clothes, crucifix, holy medals.

Xas had wine – white still, Sobran noticed, although he was now forty-two. 'Are there too many churches in Spain?' he asked.

'Fool.' Xas uncorked the bottle, by his magic attracting the cork into his hand. 'Blow the fog out of your sinuses and taste this.' The angel passed the bottle – they were back to that, sitting in the dirt and passing a bottle between them. The bottle's label was handwritten. Its base was chipped, so that it couldn't be stood upright. Sobran read, understanding only the date – 1828, the year of his madness.

'Go on, drink, then tell me what you taste.'

The reborn Sobran qualified everything by its lacks – so the wine wasn't great, but good, it lacked something, perhaps in its cradle, in the oak. A chablis, but not quite right, the Chardonnay grapes themselves altered. He tasted flint, then as he swallowed, woodsmoke – smoke, was it? – but no wood he knew. 'What am I tasting?' he said, as people say 'Good God!'

Xas laughed, put out his hand for the bottle. He took a mouthful, swallowed and said, 'You're tasting great heat, and strange soil.'

'That wine is a bastard,' Sobran said, disapproving.

'It comes from a valley near Botany Bay.'

Sobran didn't know where Botany Bay was. He took the bottle back when Xas held it out, but put his thumb in its neck and stood it between his crossed legs. 'I'll be stiff for days if I sit like this for more than half an hour. I'm an old man.'

'Not yet. But if you'll let me sit by you, you can lean against my wing.'

'No.'

'Then drink some more to dull your aches. I want to tell you some things, without, I hope, offending against the Scripture you hold so dear.'

'If you offend me I'll go. I'm only here now because I refuse to cower behind shutters the whole night.'

'You couldn't just close your eyes and forget all about me?'

Sobran pointed his gloved hand at the angel. 'Talk quickly.'

Xas was silent for a moment, then began: 'Of what you call the Fall – the bad end, for us, of a riot in Heaven: of the War, the chase, who I stood by, our imprisonment in a horrible sanctuary – I will not tell you. Of our engineering, our shelters, cities, governments, I will not tell you. Imagine a very long time passing – and I find my way out, following someone who already knows how to leave Hell. And God says to me, on Earth for the first time, "Xas!" in a tone of discovery, as if I'm a misplaced pair of spectacles or a stray dog. And he puts it to me that he wants me in Heaven. But Lucifer has doubled back – it was him I followed – to find me, where I am, in a forest, smitten, because the Lord has noticed me, and I'm overcome, as hopeless as your dog Josie whom you *got rid of because she loved me.*' Xas glared at Sobran. Then he drew a breath – all had been said on only three. He went on: 'Lucifer says to God that He can't have me. And at this I sit up and tell Lucifer that I didn't even think he knew my name, then say to God no thank you – very insolent this – and that Hell is endurable so long as the books keep appearing. I'll explain the books later, Sobran. Lucifer says, "Xas reads everything first, as if he's tasting my food for poison." I say that I read because I want to know how people think, not about us, but about themselves. Lucifer says, disgusted, that I should go back to heaven then, to earn human love and learn nothing. And I say, to God, although he's not asked me, "I followed him to finish hearing what he had to say." Then God says, "Xas should go freely – he has his study." Should, as though it's only a proposal. God almost always speaks as if everything is already accomplished. His manner of speaking isn't translatable. I can't even report these events in the past tense – they were momentous and feel, to me, like they're still happening. Lucifer is sneering because he thinks God means my study is humankind. I think God means that Lucifer is my study – and I decide to keep quiet about this, and have, till now.' Xas stopped and touched his own mouth. The fog had come up around them and his hair was veiled with drops of condensation.

'Then God covered my ears so that He could speak to Lucifer without my hearing Him. And when I put my own hands up to my deaf ears Lucifer knelt on the ground before me and pulled my hands down. He was shouting – though I couldn't hear him – at God, like a parent who thinks their child is being hurt. Like that, angry and protective. Or perhaps he was defending my right to hear. Whatever, it didn't last. He listened, then he put his own palms over my ears and pulled my face against his chest, so I couldn't read his lips.

'And they made their pact. Then they signed me – and one signature gave me pain and the other gave me pleasure. Then they left me to myself.'

Sobran had closed his eyes and was quietly saying the words of a psalm: 'My soul waiteth for the Lord more than they that watch for the morning: I say, more than they that watch for the morning.'

'Are you?' Xas asked.

Sobran opened his eyes and found the fog, not dead against them but soft and semi-solid, a phantom fleshiness, aquatic. Xas came closer to him, sat beside him and extended a damp wing behind Sobran's shoulders. 'Lean on me,' he invited.

Sobran got up, stiff and pained. He stamped his feet and clapped his arms against his sides. His fingertips prickled then grew heavy with chilled blood. Xas got up too, with Sobran's lamp. He lengthened its wick. They stood within a pearl, whose lustrous inner walls were the limit of the lamplight. The bottle had fallen and the wine was lost in the dirt. Xas gave Sobran the lamp.

'If you gave me time, and I knew how, I'd tell you about my millennia; my few friendships; how I went about like a botanist; or I'd tell you about my garden sheltered by a wall of black glass. I *will* tell you, next year.'

When Sobran didn't answer him and had begun to turn away, Xas said, 'I wish you believed me.'

Sobran swung back. 'That you're benign? That you are not telling lies?' He lifted the lamp between them. Xas's face was youthful, relaxed, unfathomable. 'If I could, I'd break this lamp and burn you where you stand.' Sobran was in a rage.

'Why did you shave off your beard again?' Xas asked, silencing the man. He went on: 'You grew it to cover the scars when you came home from campaigning, after you had shown me the scars as part payment for your sins, or so you thought. The beard came off again in '22 – it had gone the night you dressed so carefully for me. And you remained cleanshaven for only two years, till deciding to hide the last of your youth, perhaps. Now the handsome old man is clean- – but not freshly – shaven. I wonder why.'

Sobran waited till Xas had finished, then went on as if nothing had interrupted him: 'You are a curse I have to endure. If you said you'd never come again and I was *able* to believe you – even then I could never be a happy man. I lost all chance of happiness – for ever – the moment I took you into my confidence about Céleste...'

Xas started. It was the most wholly discomposed movement Sobran had ever seen him make.

'Any happiness I've had since was only illusion and intoxication,' Sobran added. He felt as if he'd stabbed the angel. He lowered the lamp, and as the shadow fell over Xas's face the angel said, 'I'm sorry.' He sounded stupid.

Sobran lit his own way down the hill, but looked back – *did* turn – and saw the dark vortex of clear night air strike back through the mist as the angel left the ridge.

In his office in the winery at Vully, Sobran was paying the cooper's apprentice. The young man counted, while Sobran locked the strongbox. Then the light went – Aurora de Valday was in the doorway. She dropped her hem. There was mud on her boots. The man with her touched his hat. They came into the room; Aurora stood waiting, didn't find her own chair, as usual, or put her hands to the small of her back and stretch, or step up the desk and begin turning papers to read. Instead she folded her hands together, in lace gloves, fussy and diminished by the bells of her leg-of-mutton sleeves. Sobran put his pen down and stepped over to the chair by the wall, carried it to Aurora, then went for another chair for the gentleman. Aurora sat and Sobran saw her crane her neck to look at the floor plans on his desk.

The cooper's apprentice, hat in hand, nodded to everyone in turn then went out.

Aurora introduced Baron Lettelier. The Baron did not stand, but did take Sobran's hand for a moment. (A reverse of the concessions Sobran would make in the man's position – but, of course, to the Baron, there was nothing between them *but* a difference in stations.) 'Monsieur Jodeau – my vintner,' Aurora said, 'and an old friend.' Aurora asked if Sobran could spare half an hour. She thought the Baron would enjoy a tour of the cellars.

Sobran said it would be a pleasure. And she, teasing, 'I know how you like to boast.' Then she frowned at his courteous nod.

It was warmer in the cellar. The first frost making its lacework in the angles of outside walls hadn't yet penetrated the stone. 'It's like last week in here,' Aurora said, old enough now to notice the progress of slow tides in each season, how winter came in unevenly, as the sea on a rugged coast – not yet old enough, though, no longer to bother to communicate what she'd noticed. Her remark seemed only to puzzle the Baron. He said, 'I had no idea your cellars were so extensive.' Then 'Ah!' at the fresh stonework and paler oak barrels.

'We built in from the back,' Sobran explained. He stopped on the steps under the angled doors that led to the courtyard, pond, waterlilies that Aurora so loved. She turned away, said, 'Shall we view the southern transept?'

'So, your cellar is a cathedral, Aurora?' The Baron made a point of getting her joke. 'In the worship of what?'

'Our southern transept is dedicated to Vin de Réserve. Come and choose for tonight's table.'

In their racks the bottles farthest from Sobran's lamp gave back light like eyes, with dust like cataracts or the white bloom on black grapes.

Aurora smudged her glove, wiping away dust. 'Monsieur Jodeau,' she said, 'do you remember Jodeau North and South?' Without letting him answer she turned to the Baron. 'My uncle sat me down one afternoon when I was twelve and had me taste, as he said, "anything creditable from the *pays*". He wanted me to make a distinction between Jodeau North and South. Uncle said, "It's only twenty years since they were selling us all their grapes, then the son" – meaning your father, Sobran – "began to make wine and had the wit, at once, to distinguish the difference in his vines."' She lifted a bottle, turned it to Sobran. 'Jodeau South 1808.'

Sobran felt his face stiffen.

'It's the last year the grapes were pressed separately,' she said to the Baron. Who gave a single nod of acknowledgement – all manners, no sympathy or interest. Aurora looked back at her friend. 'Why was that?'

'Father lost interest. He doted on Sabine. He was with her constantly – she had a minion: Grandpapa do this and that.'

Aurora laughed; she could imagine.

'Besides, the wine came right when we combined the north and south slopes – it was better. Especially the 1812, the year it rained at midsummer, father's final vintage.'

'I like the 1806 Jodeau South. We have two bottles left.'

'I have fifteen,' Sobran said, 'and they're yours if you want them. It never came up to our expectations.'

'It's a blessing that it's *kept*,' the Baron remarked. 'What's your best vintage?' He too was dusting bottles.

'Vully's?' Aurora and Sobran asked together.

The Baron again gave his single nod.

Sobran thought, 'He's cultivated that, probably stood before a mirror working on shades of meaning.' He said: '1810, but it's all gone from here, someone might have a bottle. 1812, 1818, 1820, 1822 ...' Sobran paused to cross himself, and even Aurora looked startled. '1822 is the very best. Then 1827, the first year I worked for the château. 1830 looks good now too.'

'Shall we have some of the '22, Aurora?' the Baron said, then to Sobran, 'Were you thanking God or warning the devil? Perhaps I need to know if I plan to drink it.'

'I was thanking God.'

The Baron took in Sobran's sober dress and silver crucifix. 'Piety is a fine thing when it secures a premier cru.'

'Henri, the influence might have been my impiety. I first came to live here in '21.' Aurora said this smiling and the Baron took her hand. He looked again at Sobran. 'And your own vintages – we've settled on your 1806 and the château's '22, so ...?'

'Jodeau-Kalmann 1820. Or the '22, or '27. They are all represented here. The château still buys a fair share of our wine.'

'And Sobran takes orders from people who have tasted it at my table – so I'm his agent as he is mine,' Aurora said.

'A happy arrangement,' the Baron said, then to Sobran, 'Have the bottles sent. And thank you for your trouble.'

Sobran and his sixteen-year-old son were strolling through the old carousel in Beaune, among the stalls, the outdoor dentists, junk shops and dog sellers. The pup Sobran picked up and tucked in his coat was a mastiff, black and tan, his hide as soft as moleskin. Baptiste took hold of his father's arm as Sobran put his hand into his pocket for his purse.

'I thought you said we'd keep no more dogs.'

Sobran lifted the pup, showed its toffee-drop eyes. 'We've room for this fellow.'

Baptiste took the pup from his father's hands and put it back in the basket. The youth led his father several steps away before Sobran dug in his heels. 'You had better explain.'

Baptiste wouldn't meet his eyes but looked to either side of his father's shoulders as if at something growing there.

'Baptiste?'

Baptiste said, 'Mother killed Josie.'

Sobran took his son by the arms. Baptiste shook himself free. 'Don't hold me. Why do you always have to take hold of people?' Baptiste continued walking and Sobran followed him.

'She said the bitch had failed you. That's what she said.'

Céleste would always send one of the boys to wring the necks of fowl. Sobran couldn't imagine how she had dispatched a lively full-grown dog – so he asked.

'She hung Josie. We all heard the sounds Josie made. But Mother wouldn't let us near. She held a hot poker at us. Antoine said to let her have her way, and Sophie took the children out. Father?' Baptiste said, for his father had stopped, his face in his hands.

The youth looked about in embarrassment as Sobran collected himself and walked on.

'I'm ashamed,' Baptiste said. 'I try very hard to feel pity, and compassion – as Léon instructed me.'

'You've spoken to Léon about this?' Sobran was appalled.

'You were unwell, father.'

'I'm not a weakling.'

Baptiste was silent and Sobran saw that the silence was embarrassed dissent. Unfortunate boy – two parents not quite sane.

⁓

1833 Arôme *(the aroma of wine)*

Sobran, on a chair under the shade tree, saw the angel first when he dropped to hover on an updraught well above the vineyard, then spiralled down over the foundations of the new house. Xas took a good look then rolled over on his back in the black air, wings out at an angle to the ground, to glide slowly to the ridge. The nearer he came the faster he seemed to move. Sobran fought the urge to close his eyes and turn his head, then Xas braked as a hawk does, stopped still in the air and fell on to his feet in front of Sobran. He was empty-handed. 'The house looks commodious,' he said.

'Two storeys, attics and stables.'

'How many servants?'

'A cook, a maid, and a nurse to help with the younger children. And one groom. A barouche, but no carriage yet. Next year.'

'Where are the family?'

'The younger children, Antoine, Aline and Bernard, are with Sabine and her family. Agnès is at the convent in Autun, Martin at school in Chalon-sur-Saône, near Sabine. Céleste has been ill and is with my sister at a bathing resort. Baptiste is with me at Vully. However, tonight I'm Antoine's guest.' Sobran looked down at the solitary end walls of his house. 'The bricklayers are camping on site. I thought it best to be here. I had to be surly to Antoine to dissuade him from accompanying me on my night walk. He was disgusted that I'd "started all *that* again".'

Xas shifted his weight and crossed his wings behind his body. In this pose he had more the appearance of a church window seraph, but he wore only supple, scaled, leather trousers with an armoured belt. Sobran saw the belt was decorated with precious stones, and one pearl, on the tip of a gold linchpin that threaded through flanges at either end and held it joined below Xas's navel. Sobran wondered how he had never noticed that this garment was both martial and lubricous. Sobran said, 'Cover yourself up.' He was too tired to feel indignant. He ran his hand over his chin. 'Beards are out of vogue for gentlemen. They have been for many years.'

Xas laughed. 'You waited a whole year for that?'

'What were you accusing me of?'

'Trying to make yourself beautiful.'

Sobran's mouth became more straight and level, but his hands left the arms of the chair and came together. He twisted his signet ring.

Xas adjusted his wings, flexed them full stretch, the light they reflected making his bare skin gleam. Then he sat on the boundary stone and cloaked himself. 'What have you there?' he asked, of the book in Sobran's lap.

'A novel, *Indiana*, by George Sand – an authoress. It was light when I came up here. Last month Aurora de Valday laughed to find me reading Caylus the antiquarian. And when I recommended that she read Charles Napoléon's *Rêveries politiques* – well,' he shrugged, then held up the book. 'She sent this from Paris, where she is on her honeymoon.'

'Oh.'

Sobran looked at Xas sharply. 'Aurora is a friend. Like Antoine, but more treasured. She is interested in books and ideas. Antoine isn't. Besides, a female friend is, not surprisingly, more tender of the friendship.'

'Is her husband interested in books and ideas?'

'Her husband is a gentleman.' Sobran pressed the book between his palms. 'I am sorry that her marriage will alter our friendship. It's been a joy and comfort to me.' After a time he looked up at the silent angel. 'Tell me something, Xas.'

'Yes?'

'Tell me *about* something.'

Xas told Sobran about his garden. He had needed something to occupy him, faced with that journey, the lethal unmarked snowfield of a treaty between God and Lucifer. Faced with his life, he needed some heroic, all-consuming task. He decided to garden in Hell.

'I found a place behind a ridge in the mountains, where the air was thin and cool – that is, only as hot as this hilltop at noon in midsummer. Then I built the ridge up, stole tools from the masons, the angels who built that dark, thick-walled citadel that is the only other bearable place in Hell. Where all the books are kept. I carried molten glass, poured and sculpted it, till I had a wall that rose between my slope and the prairies of fire, a wall of black glass, translucent for half its height, thinner towards the top. You must imagine my garden in light that arrives through imperfections, distorted, like sunshine through smoke.

'Next I made soil. I carried it from earth *and* I made it. I grew lichen, little creeping plants. I carried soil then water. Carried water every other day for a thousand years.

'Yes, it was remarked on. They came and looked. Lucifer recommended that they didn't interfere with me, either to help or hinder. They were busy anyway, herding the damned into their ghettos, shutting them away like wine in barrels to let them *express* themselves.

'My simple plants made soil, and I grew more complex plants. I closed in my garden, so that it was like a great terrarium, with its own weather. I did that till the soil was sufficiently deep and fertile, then I took everything up, opened my garden to the air, made a series of hinged hatches in the bubble, then began again. I planted flowering shrubs, creepers – but nothing thirsty. I made a fountain and kept it filled – the water burned away like drops on a hot stove if left. I began to collect roses. The plants that survived changed over the years. Everything darkened in the heat, as copper beeches darken to black at their tops in the hottest summers.

'After over a thousand years I could leave my garden for longer periods – it's six days now before trouble starts, if I close most of the hatches and let it live on its own aspired moisture. It's a sizeable garden. You can't see the back of it – the big tree – where it loses the light. Have you ever seen an annular eclipse? It has that atmosphere. My light-sensitive flowers never fully open. I add illumination for the weeks the bees are active. All the colours are saturated, plush. The light is greyish, dim, like cold water, and unsteady, as though shining off a lava flow. You expect a chill, but the air is very warm – and the water falling in the fountain sometimes sounds to me like a tongue moving in a wet mouth. The water doesn't dazzle. And there are no blues. I've brought them in – plumbago, cornflower, lavender – but they all bleach out to white. There are no pale greens, and all the rose leaves and stems are dark – the red blooms tend towards black and have that scorched look to their outer petals that some earthly roses have in the bud and lose as they unclench – open, I mean.'

Xas fell silent.

'I'll never see it,' Sobran said. 'The only hospitable place in Hell.'

'A twilit, glimmering, perfumed place.' Xas paused, then asked, ingenuous, 'Do you no longer expect to go to Hell?'

They looked at each other. Sobran blushed.

'If we can put that aside,' Xas said, 'your conviction that I've damned you, then I'm your luck again – and you're only angry that I didn't take you completely into my confidence.'

Sobran stopped grinding his teeth to say, 'All the time you've been playing with me.'

'No. But I have been entertained.' Xas came closer, leaned against the tree, made its grey grooved bark part of his finery – the palenesses of his feathers, gemstones, gold, white faultless flesh. Each contrast lent itself towards his totality – a fresh assault, the blind force of big surf. 'It hurt me when you hid from me,' he said. 'But I'd learned to be patient with your surprises. Because I've been so pointlessly busy all these years I've had but few friends, all of them good, men and women of conscience, kindness – or self-command. With the same result: they suspended their appetites, their selves, as though they were born to enact worthiness, to prove the worth of the world. They met me, and thereafter did everything for the glory of God. God being love to some, like my friend the Irish monk, truth to others, like Apharah. *You* were different. You went on being a soldier, a family man, a vintner, as though in your life I was a condiment, a salt that brought out its full flavour, not its central fact. I was part of your calendar. I think that, before, I always chose hermits, people I found alone at odd hours, or I made hermits of the ones I chose. After all, I'm a hermit in Hell. But you were different – have been different to me.'

Sobran, resisting the angel's confiding tone, told him that *of course* a fallen angel would make sure to attach himself only to hermits. Anyone whose business was damnation would need a heart like the hearts of the men who held slave auctions. A heart that heard only the sounds of commerce – plantations, mills and mines – when mothers began to wail for their lost children. How much more comfortable it must be for a fiend as half-hearted and fastidious as Xas was to keep company with people without family or land – those friends of his, those scholars and solitaries.

Xas was quiet for a minute then crouched down, brushing his wing against the tree, rubbing its feathers up the wrong way, so that they seemed to grip the trunk like flat fingers. He looked into Sobran's face. 'Tonight you said, "Tell me about something, Xas," because you were unhappy. Then you get angry and I'm a slave trader, or a murderer, or torturer.'

'I'm not unhappy,' Sobran said stiffly. He couldn't seem to turn his face away, so shut his eyes. Didn't flinch when the angel placed a warm, callused hand on his cheek.

'I'm not playing with you. I was always out of my depth. Still – your friendship helped me make sense of my other relationships. I have a better understanding of the pain of a quarrel.' Xas sighed. 'But I don't want to talk about God. Why do I? Sometimes I feel God is all over me like pollen and I go about pollinating things with God.'

Sobran opened his eyes and Xas smiled at him. Sobran said, 'I did think that you talked about God to persuade me you weren't evil. But I've decided that, for you, everything is somehow to the glory of God – whether you like it or not.'

'I feel that, yes. My imagination was first formed in God's glory. But I *think* God didn't make the world, so I think my feelings are mistaken.'

This was the heresy for which Xas was thrown out of Heaven. Sobran was happy it had finally appeared. It was like a clearing. Sobran could almost see this clearing – a silent, sunny, green space into which not a thing was falling, not even the call of a cuckoo. Xas thought the world was like this, an empty clearing into which God had wandered.

In the warm purple pre-dawn light one of the bricklayers came out of the shelter of the new house's foundation and made water against a wall. He shook himself off, yawned and looked about.

Stared at the hilltop, the seated man. Sobran lifted a hand. Xas, still crouched against the tree said, 'Does he see me?'

'I'm sure he doesn't know what he sees.'

When Aurora was a girl her father had one lame horse in his stables, an old honoured cavalry horse. The mare had been ridden near a hidden petard. The explosion had disembowelled the young viscount who rode beside Aurora's father, and felled the viscount's horse. The mare caught the blast in her flank and leg. She leapt away, prancing a quarter-mile diagonally, like a fancy parade horse, then began to limp. Aurora's father retired the horse during the battle, and told his groom not to put her down. Three days later, when he found his way back to his regiment, she was still alive and the wounds had begun to heal. The mare was good for nothing, but was kept, an equine pensioner. Years later, as he told the mare's story, Aurora's father urged his daughter to press her hand against the pocked hide on the horse's flank and feel the deeper hardnesses of shrapnel under her old scars.

At the age of thirty-three, and six months after celebrating her second marriage, Aurora discovered similar hardnesses in her own flesh. She was in her bath, soaping her underarms, without her sea-sponge, and felt – painless, myteriously sealed in under smooth skin – balls, it seemed, like buckshot.

Only days later when her maid was unlacing her bodice, Aurora noticed that her side felt stiff, not tender like an injury, but somehow wound too tightly.

She did not walk from her dressing room and into her husband's, then to his bed. She did not light another candle and write to one of her women friends. At breakfast she informed her husband that she found she tired easily. Paris was too busy; she'd like to go back to Vully. She did answer the questions he put to her about her happiness in regards to himself and their marriage. But she didn't volunteer any further information. Nor did she, on her way home, take a detour to the house of her former sister-in-law, where her son was with his cousins and in the care of his tutor – although visiting Paul was the only urge it took any strength to repress.

Her own doctor, an elderly and unambitious man, examined her first by proxy – she pointed to the site of her illness on a cloth dummy in a female form. When he looked himself he told her he couldn't say for certain it was a cancer, till he saw how quickly it grew. There were city surgeons who could operate. Paris was the best place. But such an operation would mean the loss of some measure of her womanhood, and she should consult her husband to see what he wished.

Aurora took her meals in bed for three days, sat wrapped in a lamb's-wool shawl and re-read her favourite novels. She even picked up the Bible but after an hour put it aside and shook its verses out of her head.

She got dressed and went outdoors. Ten years before, she'd reserved half an acre of flat land, part of the orchard beyond the kitchen garden. She'd had the cherry trees removed and built a trellis on which grape vines grew about evenly spaced columns twelve feet high. When the vines had leaves on them the field was a room, a green gloomy room floored with fallen leaves, in which birds hopped and pecked, through which the wind moved – the quietest, coolest place on the estate. As she walked Aurora worked her arm – felt it pull, as though lines that moored her breast to her side had tightened, and a tide was turning.

She thought about her son, how she couldn't leave him, how it wasn't possible to leave him. She was always so fearful for his health, afraid that he'd inherited his father's consumptive constitution. All his life Paul had been a hot coal in her hand, her hand in the fire.

Aurora worked her arm some more, wondered if she'd lose the use of it. She knew that this disease would make her let her son go; it was a forceful bailiff with its hands on her.

She wove her way between the columns. Two blackbirds hopped ahead of her, cocked their heads, kept her in sight. She came to the centre of the covered space – looked about at the interpenetrating passages, sun at the end of each of them.

Who could she trust not to talk about Heaven? Her husband, Henri. He would make provisions – medicine, surgeons, nursing sisters. A funeral. Henri would arrange Paul's further education, the management of the estate and, for Paul, keep a cool eye on the marriage market. Aurora could trust her husband to do everything necessary for her comfort.

She would die. She knew it.

If she left Paul in the last sunny meadow, if she watched him go away from her, into a dark wood, if she *believed* – if she believed that she'd grow wings and fly over the wood and be there when he emerged, unrecognisable, diminished by sorrow, worn by want – what good would it do? What good did it do to believe that, yet not be able to hold his hand through some of his adult life, help him up after its first falls? *Forget Heaven.* They would leave each other in terror, as Paul's father had left her, reared up in his bed, eyes fixed to follow his life, that final haemorrhage, a great gout of his own blood.

Aurora had read philosophers, poets, novelists, who talked about death as a place, an estate, the afterlife. Or as an event, of course. But she thought she was experiencing death as the knowledge of death, everything else was loss, the slipperiness of bloodied hands, and grief, about which she knew enough. Knowledge of death lodged like a bullet in her brain, somewhere above her eyes, which looked out beyond the green vistas of a room roofed with vine leaves at brightness every-which-way, looked out from under the bullet-hole, from a mind pierced by death and black in the full light of day.

Aurora wrote to her husband, her sister-in-law, and her distant friends. For now, only they need know. But in writing to her sister-in-law Aurora warned her to prepare Paul. In her letters to her friends Aurora formed her position: reserve, practicality – she would perfect her affections, thereby leave her friends with, she hoped, the feeling of nothing left undone.

She didn't tell Sobran, but did talk to him.

When they had settled all their business, Sobran poured Aurora a glass of cuvée. Jodeau-Kalmann had a champagne press, the grapes coming from Sabine's husband's vineyard near Chalon-sur-Saône. It was a good blond, aromatic, and mouth-wideningly dry.

'He doesn't trust himself,' Sobran said, and chuckled. 'And doesn't feel any shame about handing over to his wife's father.'

'To think I gave you half my authority.' Aurora was amused. 'Now you are all over the province.'

'They'll build a statue,' Sobran said, his nose in his glass.

'Of a buck rabbit.'

'Aurora!'

She laughed, savoured his shock. Then she said, 'I'll be back for the winter, whether or not Henri comes.'

They were quiet again. Aurora looking into her glass at the string of tiny bubbles rising from one speck of sediment. After a while she simply started up, asking, 'When you were on battlefields, you must have heard men, wounded men, calling out for their mothers. Did they call for their own mothers? Or superhuman mothers like Our Lady?'

'I don't know. I never called for mine. Mother was alive and with my family when I was away in the army. I imagined her where I'd always seen her. Not on battlefields. Besides, I was never badly hurt. The nearest I was to death was from freezing – when I thought I saw – '

Aurora could see that Sobran had begun to go carefully. His thoughts and words separated like a lookout and helmsman, and messages moved between them about how to go.

'I thought I saw an angel. It turned out to be only a broad-shouldered wayside shrine. Mother died the year before my daughter, Nicolette. Thank God she was spared that sorrow. She took sick suddenly, was paralysed and spent two weeks in bed, scarcely able to speak, which angered her at first. Léon wasn't there, which caused her some grief, but she settled – I don't mean into indifference, she was at peace. Her death was the best I ever saw.'

'I never met her. I came to live here after you had lost your daughter. One of the first things I heard about you was that you and Céleste had lost a child to scarlet fever.'

'Why would you learn that? Other children died that year of the fever. Two babies, one four-year-old and a girl of thirteen. The only reason I've forgotten exactly who they were is that the infants' names were used again, the living children erased the dead ones, and have grown up. The maid was the eldest Garvey, Jeanne.'

'Why was I told you'd lost a daughter? When my husband died there were those around me determined to point out other members of that secret fraternity, the recently bereaved. You wore a black armband. I remember watching you yoke a horse to a cart full of empty barrels. You took off your coat, pulled the armband from the coat sleeve, drew it up over your shirt sleeve, then rolled your sleeves up. You went about it sensitively, as if everyone was watching – which they were. My uncle had a very high opinion of you, but he said – critically, I think – "Sobran Jodeau feels his sorrows." '

'Aurora, what a memory! You've made a better study of me than – than my children have.' Sobran reached forward to touch her briefly on the back of her hand. Then he refilled his glass and held it to the light as if to appreciate its colour.

'What pleasure does it give you to stare through that glass?'

'Some. The things of the world are not drained equally. And night is better than day.' Sobran was thoughtful. Then he said, 'I know someone who remembers everything.'

'I'd love to meet her so she could remember,' Aurora said.

Sobran looked baffled, but had no chance to pursue it because Aurora went on, 'Would she remember the children dead of scarlet fever who had first use of their families' Christian names?'

'If he'd ever learned them, yes.'

The poisoned friendship. He. Aurora looked at Sobran's lowered eyelids. She felt suddenly split, her stomach dropped. Then she was whole and completely miserable, her prime gone, her breast a bag of rocks tied to her body, then swung over the lip of a grave. What good her discretion, her virtue, her self-denial when his illicit desires were for nothing remotely like her? The poison – as he put it – was just what passes between men who get too close. Hence the starch and buttoned buttons, the sobriety, the church-going. Why hadn't she guessed before?

She saw him watching her and rallied. If she'd lost colour he couldn't see it. She asked, 'Are there any books I can send from Paris?'

Rue du Bac
Paris

7th December 1833

M. Jodeau,

As you have not written to me I know that Mama *has not told you* that she is *mortally ill.* She can no longer lift her right arm. A surgeon in Paris has some hope of a palliative operation but says it must be *soon.* However Mama insists on visiting the château despite her weakness and the urgency of her situation. I think she wants to be caught by snow in the country and die beside her own bedroom fire. Recall she isn't a religious woman. Nor docile. *I am in fear.* Sir, I cannot prevent her. The Baron is angry but behaves as though he is her master and is all Madame this and Madame that. She will not heed us. She wants me to go with her, of course, has even interviewed half dozen tutors and hired a terrible German – of whom I shall not complain again if only Mama lives. I have written to my mother's aunt and to her friends the sisters Lespes in Piedmont to do as I desire you to and *implore* her to *do what she can* to save her own life.

In trust

Your friend,

Paul de Valday, Comte de Vully

Clos Jodeau
20th December

My Dear Baroness,

Paul has written to me. He tells me you are ill – mortally is the word he used – and that he believes you are avoiding an operation that may save your life. He speaks of this operation as *palliative* but I hope it is *curative*. I am sorry if anything I write seems to slight you but this is written in haste as I have the chance only of this next post – after which I think this letter and your carriage would pass each other on the road.

If you fear the operation because it is a mutilation – death is more thoroughly so. You will suffer on any course and I think your courage is equal to the suffering.

To visit the château under these circumstances is time you cannot afford – even if it is to be the last time. I beg you to stay in Paris and chance the knife. It is what everyone who loves you wishes you to do. I refuse to treat this note as my last communication with you. I hope you will take my advice. I pray you will recover. I have faith that I will see you in the spring in better health.

Your friend,

Sobran Jodeau

*

He saw her sooner, heard her arrive on the night of a thick snowfall. From his room in the château's west wing, over the cuverie, he heard an outrider, shouting voices, footsteps indoors and out, hissing pitch torches and iron carriage wheels on gravel.

They met late the next day in the château's smallest drawing room. Aurora was on a divan piled with shawls. She had her feet up and a book in her lap. Her hair was fastened in a lace bag at the back of her neck. She looked tired, pained, pale – but not thin or yellow or at death's door.

Sobran asked if she had received his last letter and she said it must have passed her on the road. But she didn't look at him when she said it; her brows were lifted but her eyes turned down. She asked if he'd got the package of books.

'Yes, thank you. But I've read only the Hugo.'

She looked up, ready to talk about Victor Hugo. Sobran said, 'Paul wrote to me. This operation isn't a hope that will keep, Aurora. You can't bottle hope and *hope* for an improvement. It's your duty to do what you can.'

He watched her eyes cool as quick as wax sets at the top of a snuffed candle. She drew her legs up, the florals on her brocaded skirt catching the light, as gorgeous as healthy plumage. She drew the cashmere shawl closer. 'It's no business of yours.'

Sobran straightened his back, sat forward on the seat, ready to leave if dismissed. He didn't realise he'd assumed this pose and that deference was deeper in his bones that his sense of entitlement. He said, 'We are friends.'

She said, 'I've never been in your confidence.'

He said that he had always respected her privacy. The two statements stood in balance a moment. Yet, although he was her servant, Sobran had the courage of a mended man. 'Write to this surgeon and ask him to travel here. Offer him a fortune.'

'He's younger than me, and almost as fearful as I am. I watched sweat bead his lip while we talked about the operation.'

'Be brave for him, Aurora. Make a better man of him.'

Aurora laughed once, dry, then tilted her head back against the curled arm of the divan. She looked a little like that painting by Jacques Louis David of Madame Récamier – but in the thick, fussy clothes of their own age. 'You are going to take me into your confidence, Sobran – now. Because any secrets you tell me I won't know for very long.'

He saw that she was angry at him, and not just because he would survive her. He saw she loved him, and not only as a friend. Hers was the gaze of an earthed fox. Any minute now she would tell him everything she felt for him – or suspected him of.

'I'll make a bargain with you, Aurora. If you write to this surgeon and fetch him here, if you have the operation and survive – then I'll tell you my secrets. I promise.'

'The things you tell no one?'

'The things I haven't told you.'

She said again, 'The things you tell no one.'

'Yes. The one thing I tell no one.'

There were no women in the room. The women she'd asked to be there stood for a time at the door as she undressed. Paul's nurse was there one moment and the next dropped the water basin she held and fled. The rug steamed – a good knotted Turkey, twice Aurora's age.

The surgeon was accompanied by another surgeon and two men. They weren't enough to hold her – one of her footmen was summoned. He lay across her legs throughout the operation, and wept.

The preparations. So much linen. Aurora climbed up on the dining-room table, which was draped with an old eiderdown. All the candles were lit in the chandelier above her, and the curtains not just open but wound in their cords so that they stood like tree trunks on either side of the windows.

Aurora felt she had come to her own execution. She looked around for an avenue of escape. The surgeon stood over her. He had no colour in his face. She didn't want to watch as he laid out the knives. Someone draped a cloth over her face. She was dead already.

Brandy backed up in her throat. She felt the air on her chest as they uncovered her. Heard them talking and felt them touch her. Then they held her arms and shoulders and began to cut.

Whenever they stopped to parley she would faint, then was roused by the pain again as they sawed and sliced. She screamed around the leather bit in her mouth. The breast was not soft, no mound of butter – the surgeon used force. She could feel where they cut, the direction and progress of the knife sawing through her flesh, a cross cut, then two circles. She felt her breast lifted piece by piece, like servings of pie, base burnt to the pan. Then she felt the knife scrape along bone.

A chasm.

Later she felt the cloth, wet, adherent, peeled from her head. The surgeon had blood on his face. And tears. Aurora found herself reassuring him. She whispered, 'It was necessary.'

They dressed the wound and carried her to her bed. To a room of blacknesses, like a blotted page. A terrible pain had torn its way into her and made its nest.

Aurora's son came into her room as her maid was spooning soup into her. A broth made of lambs' kidneys, grainy and greyish, but tasty.

Aurora put up her hand – the hand at the end of the good arm, the arm she could raise – and stopped the next spoonful. A little soup splashed her bed jacket. Hélène apologised and began to mop at her with a napkin.

'Who is it?' Aurora asked her son. The window was open a crack on the spring air and she'd heard a horse, not a carriage, so knew it wasn't the Baron, whom they expected at any hour.

'Monsieur Jodeau. Mother, he was here before, several times, but you were so very ill and then – lassitudinous.'

'Lassitudinous?' Aurora laughed.

'Floppy and dreary, Mama,' Paul said. 'Of course I spoke to him, gave him reports, sometimes daily, about your progress. And we both sat with you once, when you were very ill – I hope you don't mind.' Paul blurted, 'But Monsieur Jodeau is my friend!'

'I'm happy he's your friend, dear. And that you sat with me together.' She began to struggle up. 'Send him to my dressing room in half an hour. Hélène – ' to her maid, ' – I want a clean nightdress and robe.'

Paul went out.

Through the door between Aurora's dressing room and bedchamber Sobran watched two maids remake her bed. They did it with so much ceremony it was as if she had died; as if the room were in a convent hospital and they nuns remaking the deathbed for the next invalid. But here Aurora was, a little less thin and waxy than she'd been when he had sat all day by her bed, keeping Paul company. It had been thaw, then, and snow sliding off the château's warmed leads had splashed on the stone sills of the bedchamber's tall narrow windows. The snow splashed, Aurora breathed, and Sobran read to Paul, some of David's Psalms, he recalled.

Aurora wore a lace cap over her hair, which had been cropped during her fever. She lay on an ottoman – moved her feet to make room for him and invited him to sit.

He sat, flipped the tails of his frockcoat over her feet then put his hand down on the stiff froth of lace around the hem of her gown, clasped her ankle beneath it all. Then – he wasn't sure how it happened, but in a movement like that of a freak wave that jumps a seawall where anglers stand, safe they think, and scoops them into the sea – he stooped and she sat up and they put their arms around one another, held fast, she with only one arm, so that he could feel her halved womanhood, the bony absence on one side of her chest. He pulled back and kissed her on either cheek, then cupped her face in one hand, feeling the loose suede of the thin flesh, and her fine skull beneath.

Her servants were watching them.

Sobran sat back and Aurora lay down. For a long time they just looked into each other's eyes – from this distance – quiet, sunny looks.

Aurora ended it. Her difficulties would be his difficulties. 'Henri's first wife died of this very disease,' she said, in her husband's defence. 'It is for that reason he stayed away.'

Sobran nodded.

'But I didn't want him.' She played with the lace along her front, ran its scallops between her forefinger and thumb. 'We expect him any day now.'

Sobran nodded once more.

'I lived,' she said – met his eyes again.

'Thank God.'

She waved dismissively then asked, 'What is the one thing you tell no one?'

'Are you sure our friendship can survive my secrets?' Sobran asked. She saw that he was pale and that his back had stiffened as though his spine had fused. She reminded him that they made a bargain. And that the only secret she had bargained for was the one about the poisoned friendship.

'I hope you know it's no small thing. I hope you don't mistake my piety for preciousness.'

'Sobran, I survived this – most terrible pain.' She turned her eyes up a moment, an old trick to stop tears from falling. The memory of the operation still made her shake. She looked down again, picked at the ribbons on the front of her gown. 'I'm tired of never saying what I believe I know. I'm tired of my fear of offending you. All that delicacy and deference, because I employ you, am your better, and a woman, and ten years your junior – all these awkward inequalities – your sadness or madness, my illness.' She made a fist and pounded the striped silk cushion she lay against, three blows as firm and rhythmic as a judge's hammer.

'Insanity,' Sobran said. He laid the word between them with a look alone, no commentary, as though he played a card and they were old whist partners.

'I did say "your madness".' Aurora was weary, weak, reborn beyond decorum. But she wouldn't hurt him, so didn't say that she knew that people said Céleste Jodeau was mad, but that was a secret *everyone* knew.

'My secret is a bottomless pit,' Sobran warned.

'I always thought it was about love. Then you insisted "he" not "she" – and I still thought it was about love.'

Aurora watched the faint, involuntary rearing back of Sobran's head, and she pushed him further: 'Did you hope I'd die and you wouldn't have to tell me?'

'I wanted, I *prayed*, for you to live. So – you are alive and you're asking me to harm you.'

Aurora thought of something then. Something she hadn't considered, like a woman who opens her husband's mail, looking for the letters of his mistress, and discovers a crime. 'Why am I so frightened?' she thought – and searched her memory, her history, for a clue to the source of this terror. The terror meant to save her, she knew, for it was almost benign, like the sun shining on the back

of her head, inviting her to turn around, like a warm hand holding
her, fatherly.

Then Aurora remembered the Comte, her uncle, holding her, his
hand on the back of her head, her head bent on his shoulder. She
remembered a library full of quenched candles, one morning, a desk
covered in papers and ink-stained blotting sand. And, in the moment
Aurora remembered that morning – the morning that followed the
night when the body of a murdered girl, Marie Pelet, was carried
into the château for inspection by a physician and magistrate –
Aurora heard her old friend say, 'My secret isn't something I can
tell; I'll have to show you.'

When Aurora returned from the trip her husband insisted she take,
to a spa at St Florentin, she was well enough, to the Baron's mind, to
be allowed out on her own errands. So she went: to church, to
choose cloth for new gowns at the silk merchants in Autun, to
church – wearily – to church, till she threw the Baron off her scent
and was able to take only Paul with her the day she got in her
carriage and ordered her coachman to carry them to the workshop of
the local stonemason.

Aurora told Paul that she wanted to order her tombstone. Then
she leaned forward to close his jaw and teasingly pull the floppy bow
of his neckcloth out of his waistcoat.

Further along the road she took pity on him. 'I'm better now, but
the matter was on my mind when I was ill. I'll leave the epitaph to
you, of course, but I want a say in the decorations.' She lifted the
curtain to look out at the dusty road and vine rows and, before long,
a low stone wall and obelisk inscribed vertically: KALMANN. The
carriage turned in.

The mason had a new house, out of sight of the workshop that
now occupied the whole of the old house. The second-storey
bedrooms in which his family had grown up were now offices.
Antoine and his youngest boy were at work. The other two sons
were miles off, repairing the stonework of a château south of
Chalon-sur-Saône.

Aurora's footman folded the steps down and held the door. Paul
got out and helped his mother. Antoine appeared, slapping the dust
from his leather apron. 'Baroness,' he said. 'Come into the shade.'

They went indoors. She and Paul accepted seats, and a glass of water each.

Aurora told her son that she would like to speak to Antoine in private.

'Mother! Surely you don't need me gone in order to give Monsieur the Mason instructions about a relief of Athena and two owls.'

She looked at him, a long, level stare. After a moment he jumped up, put on his hat and said he'd walk over to visit Baptiste Jodeau, and she could pick him up there when she was finished. He stalked out.

'What is it, Baroness?' Antoine asked.

'You'll think I'm mad. But never mind. I have an arrangement to meet your brother-in-law on the hill above his house on the night 27th of June.'

Antoine blushed to the top of his tanned bald head.

Aurora hurried on, explained the bargain made when she was ill. Added, 'Sobran and I are dear old friends, and I'm a prying woman. I know this sort of rendezvous is improper, but . . .'

Antoine interrupted her: 'I thought it *was* you — forgive me, Madame — that it was *you* with Sobran that other night, six years ago. The 27th of June in '28.'

'Excuse me?' Aurora was thrown.

'The table was set, with linen and crystal glasses, cheese and fruit, wine and brandy. That morning we found him very ill.'

'Mad,' Aurora said.

'Yes, Baroness, mad. His face was covered with bruises he had made with his own fists. Sobran was always a deep one. Great for wandering about half the night. They all did that, all the Jodeaus, even my Sophie when she was younger. I'd wake up and — ' Antoine patted the air beside him ' — I'd find her outside, in her nightclothes, sitting on the swing I'd made for our sons. After *that* night Sobran was afraid, never went out after dark, for years, then two years back, when he was staying with me to keep an eye on the new house he was building, off he went wandering — ' Antoine got a strange look on his face, his mouth relaxed utterly and seemed to slip down his chin. For a moment he stared off into space then blinked and refocused on Aurora. 'It was late June, the 27th, I'm sure of it.' Then he said, 'I looked for a corpse.'

110

Aurora flinched. She asked him to please explain himself.

'Pardon me. After that night, the night he went mad, I looked for a corpse. I thought he had killed someone. The woman he had met.'

'He says it's not a woman,' Aurora said. 'I mean — he didn't say that it wasn't a woman he meets. He hasn't talked about any meetings. He says his friend, the friend of a "poisoned friendship", isn't a woman.'

'What poisoned friendship? Sophie and I thought it was you.'

They blushed at each other. Then she said, dry, 'I'm pleased to have an opportunity to clear up your confusion. Sobran and I are *friends*, and that is all. Besides, Monsieur Laudel, I'm not certain that women are Sobran's preference.'

Antoine shook his head, all set to defend his friend against this charge. 'No, no. When Sobran was young Baptiste Kalmann was a bad influence. Sophie has said that she knows they — and that's one reason Sobran followed Baptiste into the army. But that was just boyish immaturity — and his marriage wasn't all he'd hoped . . .'

They were silent a moment, trying to calm themselves. Aurora folded her shaking hands in her lap and Antoine, who had bent forward eagerly on his stool, with his elbows on his knees, straightened up and disengaged.

Aurora asked, 'When you thought of corpses did you remember Geneviève Lizet and Marie Pelet?'

The stonemason lost his colour. He shook his head.

'Sobran set the date for our rendezvous this spring. I thought about Marie Pelet even as he spoke to me. I'm not entirely sure why. Perhaps it was the first time I'd thought of his secret as a buried thing. And then, a fortnight back, this other murder occurred. In Chalon-sur-Saône, I know, so not in this province, but the Baron was asked to concern himself with the case because of the other two.'

'And because it was Geneviève Lizet's youngest sister who was killed,' Antoine said. 'Aline Lizet, Sabine Jodeau's friend.'

'A spinster, Henry told me.'

'Aline was twenty-six. In a fair way to spinsterhood, I suppose. But Sophie said Léon had spoken to her about his plan of proposing marriage to Aline. Aline stood godmother to Sabine's girls. She was close to us.'

'Henri said suspicion has fallen on her cousin, Jules, who was always a little strange.'

'He's a simpleton who sees things. Jules was in love with Geneviève – everyone knew that.' Antoine's eyes began to tear; he was clearly very upset. 'How could you suspect Sobran of murder?'

'Because, to the best of my knowledge, those murders were the only terrible, unexplained events in this province within living memory. Because Sobran says his secret is a bottomless pit. Because he once spoke to me about finding the first body, Geneviève's, and seemed, speaking of it, to be more affronted than horrified – but sometimes when he's upset Sobran is only able to show disgust. Monsieur Laudel, I don't suspect Sobran of murder, I suspect him of knowing who the murderer is. I think guilty knowledge is the poison of his poisoned friendship.'

Aurora must *know*, and she needed an ally in her investigation so that it would seem less of an intrusion. It was the kind of scheme formed by a sleepless head on a damp pillow, childish, but Aurora was tired of politeness. She recalled how she had reassured the surgeon: 'It was necessary!' So compassionate, ladylike, a saint thanking her torturers for her martyrdom. It was true, it was necessary, but she had wanted to howl, to sink her teeth into his arm. There had never been time to be civilised, Aurora knew now, and civility was dalliance.

Antoine said, 'What can I do, Baroness, to help you?'

'I want you to be there too. To conceal yourself near that hilltop, near enough to help me, if I need help. I want you to keep watch with me, secretly.'

Antoine was nodding. 'It's time Sobran was found out – whatever he is at. But, Madame, how can it be about murder? I think you must be wrong, Baroness. I think it is a lover he meets, an old lover, some great and stately person – but not you.'

Aurora called to mind everyone of her class, for thirty miles either side of the river. No one much younger than she. She remembered his glow in '22, his madness in '28. 'I'd rather you were right,' she told the stonemason.

Their faces mirrored each other's distress. Aurora said she would send a note if the arrangement was changed. Antoine took her arm when she stood. He walked her out into the sun and handed her up into her carriage.

A month from midsummer, Aurora visited Sobran's fine new house on the morning that the household was to disperse – Martin and the younger children to Sabine in Chalon-sur-Saône, Léon, Agnès and Céleste to the spa at St Florentin. Aurora brought the travellers gifts, two hampers stocked with sweet wine, dried fruit, cheeses, jellies and tins of breadcrusts baked in herbs and butter. And, of course, the society journals in which Agnès so delighted, and would spend hours studying, especially the engraved portraits of fine ladies of fashion.

Sobran saw Aurora out to her carriage. In the carriageway she paused to close her parasol and said, 'I won't be able to keep our appointment.' She hurried on: 'An aunt of Henri's is dying and I'm expected to attend.'

'Of course,' Sobran said. He watched as she fussed with the silk cord on the handle of the parasol. She settled it on her wrist and, without looking up, said, 'All women are like Pandora – avid to open locked boxes.' She was almost simpering.

'I see,' Sobran said, smoothing the path of her escape.

She glanced at him. 'I can't say when I'll return, it's all dependent on how tenacious of life Henri's aunt proves to be.' She looked past Sobran's shoulder at the ridge and the pepper tree, beneath which were the table and chairs that had become summer fixtures. Sobran and Baptiste particularly liked to sit there in the hot weather, overlooking the visible slopes of Jodeau-Kalmann, and their standing-army of vines. A triangular sail was fastened to the pepper tree and propped on two long poles, like the roofed entrance of a Bedouin tent. It provided more shade. Aurora thought she could hear the canvas from where she stood; she saw it move and heard a gulp, like the sound made by a well-trained but eager dog in a hunter's covey – waiting. She stopped fussing with her parasol and gave Sobran her hand. He paced her to the carriage door and handed her up. She called to Paul, who was in the porch talking to Agnès. Paul kissed Agnès's hand and hurried over. This made Aurora and Sobran meet each other's eyes, as if to ask, 'Did you notice that?' But Paul seemed quite unselfconscious and said to Sobran as he came up that he was pleased Baptiste was staying, he hoped they'd get in a few dawn fishing trips. He shook Sobran's hand, smiled, got in after his mother who Sobran saw watching him still, past her son's head, her eyes black and solemn.

The letter concerning the Baron's aunt was scribbled by candlelight at the aunt's bedside. It said that the old woman had faded quickly, her flow shrinking like pumpwater when the pump handle is still. Her feet were already cold, the letter said, and its writer called Henri and Aurora to attend the funeral. Aurora was gone only a week and kept her appointment – the one she had made with Antoine when her fears got the better of her. Antoine had reservations about a lady of quality out at night in secret in the company of a commoner –

'There's little difference between this and my former arrangement with Sobran. Besides, the gossip is about him and me not you and me,' Aurora reasoned.

'I don't like to deceive him.'

'What difference is there between the deception we'd be practising if I stood beside him and you stayed hidden, or if we both hide and spy?'

'You made a bargain with him.'

'*He* made it with *me*. I only bargained for him to tell me his secret.'

Antoine looked uncertain.

'What we see will be what *normally* happens,' Aurora reminded him. 'And you'll run no risk of having to rush to my rescue. Whatever we learn can remain our secret. If that's what we want.'

Antoine shivered.

'Two witnesses,' Aurora said, 'as the law requires. And nothing Sobran's rehearsed – but what *really* occurs.'

⌒⌒⌒

1834 **Boire** *(to drink)*

The house was quiet. The maid was in a deep exhausted sleep after her efforts soaping the carpets and washing the curtains, no doubt.

The cook was on holiday, and the family – except Baptiste – away, building up their strength for the long haul of harvest.

Sobran was cold from inactivity. He hadn't moved from his chair under the canvas where he sat sunk in a milk of filtered moonlight. He turned the hourglass again. It was late. He got up to pace, took off his hat and felt the moonlight. Its touch, like midwinter sun through fogged glass, was very faintly warm. He was lonely, felt Aurora's absence, and realised that he *had* wanted to share his secret. It would have been good to be alone with her, waiting into the small hours when all humans are raw and unguarded. What would they have said to each other?

As Sobran saw it, for six years his family and friends had all had the satisfaction of being gentle to a man who was stronger than them. They had practised their kindness, their distance and omissions because he wasn't in his right mind. Sabine married, but the rest of his children let themselves spoil because they thought both their parents were unstable.

Sobran knew he would never tell now. Aurora wouldn't ask again. She'd returned to her corner, cagey, self-sufficient, and proper. That embrace in her dressing room was as far as their friendship went.

Sobran stopped pacing to look out over the north-east slope, the road, the wall and rising rows of Kalmann. All was still. Yet he felt that he stood above a monstrously swollen river, watching while a whole drowned, uprooted town swept by – a fine home, a tavern, a church. *This* was the high-point of his life, the only hour with firm foundations. He could feel the moments ticking along his body, of the 27th of June for twenty-six years.

There was a noise out on the road, an explosion that Sobran identified as the momentous impact of a full glass bottle. He saw a wide dark splash on the road below the ridge, a stain and melting stars of glass. He stepped out from under the obscuring tree, turned in circles with his head thrown back.

The angel fell from the sky as though shot, plunged straight at the ground with his wings shut, then opened them at the last moment – *crack* – displaced air flattening Sobran's shirt against his chest. Xas lay on his stomach with his wings stretched out along the earth. But his head was turned and he was looking at Sobran.

Sobran dropped on to his knees. Despite the angel's bright gaze Sobran feared he was hurt.

'Lie down,' Xas said.

Sobran stretched out beside him.

'There are two people concealed, close by, between the vines. They could see us if we stood. I've circled for hours, half-a-mile up. I didn't want to go without seeing you. I dropped the bottle to draw their attention to the road, then came down as fast as I could.' The prone wings stirred like oars, made a ripple in the dirt. Xas laid his cheek down on his extended arm.

As if it was Xas who needed calming, Sobran placed a hand on his back, on the hard bands of muscle that supported his wings and made his back unlike that of any human, however powerful. Xas's skin was hot and his muscles twitching.

The angel asked, 'Do you have any idea who they are?'

'Two?' Sobran checked.

'I sensed two awake. I saw them when I came close, both are cloaked.'

Sobran guessed Paul and Baptiste. Even if they had missed Xas – had looked away when the bottle exploded – before too long Baptiste would come up the hill to see what had happened to his father. Sobran realised that he must get up and return to his chair; must be seen. Perhaps he could move the chair a little nearer to Xas, talk to but not look at him.

'I have to get up. If one of these spies is Baptiste he'll be anxious now that he can't see me. That's what I must do first – *now* – to buy us a little time.'

Xas made a harsh unhappy sound in the back of his throat. He reached out and took hold of Sobran's coat, hauled the man under his wing, which was smothering, thick, as warm as an eiderdown – but smelled of salt. Sobran felt the stiches part along the back seam of his coat.

Xas's face was against Sobran's throat. Sobran took hold of the angel's head, touched bunched jaw muscles; the angel was silent because his teeth were clenched. With many years' experience in lordly gestures of forgiveness, Sobran did to the angel what he would to Céleste whenever she came to make peace after one of her rages of suspicion or jealousy – he kissed Xas on the forehead. He said, 'You must let me go.' Xas loosened his grip and lifted his wing several inches. Sobran got up and walked away to lean against the tree. The graze on his ear stung, and one slow rivulet of blood tickled his neck. He looked at the slopes, the strips of shadow. He felt that his heart had stalled and was only blowing steadily in his ear.

'Where are they?'

'North-east.' The angel's voice was barely audible.

Sobran glanced at him; his face was turned down against his arm. Sobran decided to improvise. Since he looked like a man keeping a vigil, he must be seen to be still watching for someone. He lit the lamp, went to the boundary stone, raised it and waved it slowly back and forth. Then he came back and set it on the table, resumed his seat.

'One of them has made water, I can smell it. Pissing fear,' Xas said, then deduced, 'I *was* seen.'

'Why do you have salt in your wings?' Sobran asked.

The angel was incompletely immobile, his feathers stirring though his wings were still, as if each quill was governed by its own muscle. Xas said that the way to Hell, the only way any *body* could go, was through narrow caves of saline rock in a salt dome in Turkey. Yes, he did go into the earth to get to both Heaven and Hell, but no one could dig and find them. He couldn't draw a map, with Heaven and Hell in hollow pockets under the surface of the earth – it wasn't like that. Sobran should imagine that any map he knew he read *folded* – always folded – whole territories were hidden in the folds, and the coasts, rivers and mountain ranges of the known world crossed the edges of these pleats, crossed them as if the space in which they lay was *complete*, a whole cloth with no hidden folds.

Xas came and went through the salt, he said, a passage filled with loose salt. The tunnels changed shape over the years, often unexpectedly. There had been times when Xas had spent hours burrowing like a worm, unable to find his way in or out. Times when he'd emerged on earth breathless, burned and temporarily blind, and simply roosted in the shade of a salt pillar till the blindness passed. The salt was caustic and suffocating – like the water in the lake of the Antarctic volcano that served as a gate to Heaven – so anything he carried had to be wrapped. He veiled himself, wore silk over his eyes nose and mouth, but 'swam' with his wings so that they were always as gritty as a sparrow's after a dust-bath. The way to Hell emptied itself only once, after the earthquake at the time of the crucifixion – the Harrowing of Hell. The way was open for a dozen years. It was then Xas began to plant his garden, those twelve years of grace when it was easy to carry water.

'There's no sweet water near the passage,' Xas said, 'but I have a distillery in Hell.' Then he said, 'One of the spies is a woman. It was she made water. The fear was masking it. She has recently conceived.'

Sobran began to figure. Céleste was in St Florentin with Agnès, both under Léon's care; Aurora with her husband at the deathbed of an aunt of his. If it was Baptiste with a sweetheart why would sweethearts have posted watch near a father? It couldn't be Sophie and Antoine. Sophie had done with childbearing years since, besides she wouldn't spy on him.

'I'll face away from them,' Sobran decided. 'Give them a chance to creep off before dawn comes. There's no real cover down there other than shadows.' He looked up at the half-moon. 'I think you might have to stay put till they're gone.'

'I was seen,' Xas said. 'Why am I hiding now?'

'They're busy disbelieving their eyes. Besides, just let anyone try raising the subject with me.' Sobran was at his most autocratic.

Xas was silent for some minutes after that, and when Sobran glanced at him he couldn't make out an expression. Finally he got up and came closer, so that he stood over the angel. 'I suppose you could choose to stand up and stretch and fly away in your own good time. Let them confirm what they saw. Leave me to deal with it.'

'I want to stay secret.'

Sobran saw the glaze on Xas's cheeks. He asked, 'Have you been crying?'

'Do I do that? Do I ever?'

Despite Sobran's fear of summoning his best bet – Baptiste – he moved from view, crouched by the angel's head. 'Since the night knowledge drove me mad I haven't been able to see colours. The only thing that brightens the greys is moisture. I love the look of rain.' He touched the wet cheek.

Xas stared at Sobran, his look at an upward angle and sidelong, because of how he lay. Despite signs of tears the look was calculating. Then Xas closed his wings against his body, rolled over, relaxed them again and lay supine. Sobran could see the angel's ribs moving with each shallow breath. 'All right,' Xas said.

Suddenly Sobran was on his knees, then leaning down so that his arms trembled as they took his weight. He was too old for this. Then youth ignited where the touch first scorched. His mouth, his head, then his whole body on fire. He came to his senses to feel and taste what was really there, a firm, soft-skinned caressing mouth, spit as clean as grass sap, an ageless, inhuman body pressed against his own. For the second time in his life he was close to coming at only one touch, and that touch had been localised, exact – Baptiste Kalmann first touching him *there* when he was fourteen years of age. The angel's hands were against his face and neck and he was being kissed, and it wasn't a kiss of trouble, of crossed swords, but the kiss of a coupled harness – the present suddenly hitched to the past. Sobran remembered Baptiste, remembered so that he smelled tobacco and brandy, and felt stubble – *like* stubble, the dry stalks of after-grass that showed through the scabbed ice of the first snow that fell and lay every year he had longed for his dead friend, his eyes for that face, his ears for that voice. The angel's kiss was like a wave that washed him out of his consciousness, into his past, then came back and pulled him into itself – a mouth whose moisture was innocent of a meal, of wine, innocent even of the tang of hunger.

They both turned their mouths away, lay cheek to cheek. Sobran put his arms around Xas and held the angel.

'Don't kiss me again,' Xas said. 'I don't like what happened to you.'

'You're mine, I have you,' Sobran whispered. He didn't want to do more than hold Xas – and it wasn't fear that stopped him, but tenderness that quickly turned to a kind of tiredness. He wouldn't try to extract himself from the embrace. He felt the fatalistic torpor of an animal who has struggled for hours in quicksand.

'Your nose is bleeding,' Xas informed him.

It was, Sobran moved his head to see blood on the angel's face and a pale rind of the pre-dawn sky in each large dark eye.

Sobran made hushing sounds.

'They've gone,' Xas said. 'As soon as you couldn't see them they went stealthily, then fast. I can't sense them any more. But there's one awake in the house. I used to say that when you hid from me, Sobran. I'd stand on the ridge and say to myself, "One awake in the house." '

The blood was drying in dull scabs; the angel looked as though he'd been rolling in leaf mould.

Sobran realised that he had crossed a frontier. He was where he'd never expected to be – even twelve years back when he'd longed for Xas as a lover does. For the first time he understood that it was the angel, and not he, who was in danger. He had to be careful. The angel wasn't strong; Sobran had mistaken resilience for strength. He said, 'Don't mind what happened to me. Don't be angry. I'm a frail creature with certain crude reflexes.'

The sun showed over the hills to the east, spines bristling. The vineyard turned gold and began to exhale steam.

'The one awake in the house is either Baptiste or the maid. If Baptiste, then he'll come out before breakfast to discharge a gun between the rows to frighten the early birds.'

'Then I should fly.'

'There were things I meant to tell you – about Aurora's illness. And a murder. I never told you about the murders. And about what you just said, I mean, before. I wanted to ask you – ' Sobran stopped speaking, though his mind continued to clutch convulsively at lost time, six years of lost time. It would be another whole year till he saw the angel again. Aline's murder didn't matter. He'd kept the others from Xas, for some reason his mind shrank from it, a dread about where what he had seen and not recognised would lead him. He needed someone to command him to *think*, not shrink, *think clearly*. But all he was able to do then was pursue what interested and *moved* him most. He wanted to stand beside the angel in one of those few places in the angel's past that was illuminated – the rest unimaginable, mysterious, obscure. He asked, 'When Christ came to Hell to preach, why didn't you go with him? Did you hide?'

'We didn't hide. We hung about like a lot of bold moths, as I recall. Christ was preaching to souls, not bodies. He didn't say anything we hadn't already heard. But I remember that the resemblance frightened me. I hate this – how I've said twice tonight that one thing or another disturbs me.'

There was a gunshot by the house, and four thrushes took flight over the ridge, close to the ground, hurdled the man and angel.

'Our Lord resembled who?' Sobran was used to these shocks – almost enjoyed them – the pleasure of being unmanned as he'd been by very different things, the desire he'd felt for his friend Baptiste, his love for Céleste, then Xas, then Aurora; or the travelling he'd done with the army – the shock of strangeness, villages with shutters hinged at the top, or chimneys like upended shovels.

'Tell me,' Sobran said.

'I should go.'

Sobran released the angel, let him stand.

Xas peered warily at the house, then moved a few steps away – Sobran almost expected to see him begin to hop, as hens do when they hurry. The angel put the tree between himself and the house windows. Sobran got up, halt and sore, and joined him. He put an arm around the angel, loose and easy.

'Christ looked like me,' Xas said.

Sobran, to show he wasn't shocked, said that perhaps they looked alike because both were treaties: the Word a treaty between God and Man, and Xas between God and the Devil.

'There's a thought – of a sort,' Xas said, amused. 'Do you think there's a – ' he described a shape with his hands ' – template of my face and Christ's face, especially for treaties. As though God is forgetful, or lazy, and works to a pattern like a maker of fine bone china?'

'If it's true that there's a resemblance, then there's some reason for it.'

'The same mouth that kissed me says "*If* it's true" – when I tell you it's true. I may be a copy, but I'm not a fake. I have to go, Sobran. It's a clear day, I'll be visible for miles as I make my climb.'

'What does the Devil say about the resemblance?'

Xas looked into Sobran's eyes, said Sobran was very bold now, asking him to report Lucifer's words. 'He says, "Don't ask me." He says, "Get out of my sight."'

Xas stepped away from the tree and jumped into the air.

He was visible for miles. A shadow first, like geese in a V, then white and gold, not like a goose, or swan, or cloud, but an angel.

*

Broken lights. Trees with the sun lancing through them. The carriage jolted and Aurora raised a hand to beat the hinged clapper against the ceiling, above which her coachman sat. The carriage slowed and the coachman opened the trapdoor and looked at her, his eyes fat bags full of poached sleep. She had told him to sleep when she had left him the night before, and had only just waked him. Now his drowsy face incensed her – how dare the man still live in a reasonable world, where it was possible to doze off in the open air, when *her* world was suddenly as full of holes as the casing on a spiders' nest after a shower of hailstones. Aurora called the coach to a stop and told the stonemason to get out, forgot to thank him for his company. Antoine was still 'Dear Baroness'-ing – concerned, and burning with curiosity about what it was she had seen that had her in such a fit.

Antoine went. Aurora signalled the coachman to drive on. She rested her head against the upholstered back wall of the carriage and closed her eyes.

Something had exploded on the road. Through the vines she saw what she took for a bloodstain and broken lights. Antoine kept his gaze turned that way, puzzling it out. He said later that he'd thought someone had discharged a gun, possibly *at* them. He'd put an arm across her, pressed her into the ground. Aurora obeyed, and as she did turned back to face the ridge in time to see the result of the gunshot. Or so she thought. She saw a falling swan. Then her eyes did their duty and made faithful nonsense of the size of the wings, and of the body that fell. A second 'crack' sounded as the wings opened, great and as pale as two facing mirrors in the morning. An angel dropped onto the ground out of Aurora's line of sight. Sobran moved to stand near where it had fallen. Then he lay down; disappeared from view. Aurora's bladder gave a sharp spasm and let go, soaking her bloomers, petticoats, skirt – but stopping at the lining of her cloak. She felt the stonemason say something against her ear, grunted and pushed him away. She watched as Sobran got up again and went to stand by the pepper tree, surveying the road. He stepped up to the table, raised the lantern and waved it back and forth, signalling; after that sat, unknotted his neckcloth and dabbed the side of his face. Aurora thought she saw him speak. She was sure of it. Later he leaned forwards to listen – but turned his eyes to the eastern horizon, well over her concealed head. Aurora noticed that his coat was torn at the back; she saw a white hernia of exposed shirt. For a long time he was still. Then he turned his face from the east, and down – a glance – stood and walked slowly closer to whatever it was that lay there, till Aurora could see by his tucked chin that he gazed straight upon something at his feet. Then he stooped and vanished from sight.

Aurora seized Antoine's arm. 'We must go now.'

They ran, doubled over, between the rows and along behind the wall by the road. She looked over her shoulder once at the ridge, saw tree, table, pale awning, and the boundary marker like some large-skulled guard dog sitting on its haunches. Then she and Antoine reached the bend in the road where the long row of oaks began, and found the hidden carriage, its horses drowsing in harness.

When Antoine was gone, Aurora had her coachman stop the carriage once more before they reached the château. They stopped where the road ran beside the river. She got out and walked down to the water's edge. The river was opaque, and reflecting the morning sky with its smooth gradations of colour, from rose through gold to white, the water innocent and infantine, a child in its cradle. Aurora walked into the water. She went in to rinse her skirt, then walked faster, the water pushing in ripples before her belly, then her disfigured chest.

She was seized and struggled. The coachman carried her, sobbing and sodden, back up the bank. He held her up against the lacquered wood wall of the carriage and begged her, tears in his eyes, to consider her husband and son. His breath smelled of the sausage he had carried half the night in his great coat before breakfasting as he drove. He lifted her into the coach, took off his greatcoat and wrapped her – then climbed on the box and drove on.

That's the story the coachman told, the story that went around, as a rumour, nearly intact. The coachman said that he had waited all night for the Baroness, whose carriage stood hidden in the oaks at the north-eastern boundary of Clos Jodeau. He slept. At dawn the Baroness arrived, not alone, but with the stonemason, Antoine Laudel, whom they dropped off at the path that leads around the back of Clos Kalmann. The Baroness made the coachman stop again at the river, got out and walked into the water, without hesitation for prayer.

It was a month before the news of this suicide attempt reached Sobran, who was sequestered by a terrible event.

Sobran wound the handle on the well, hauled up a bucket and set it on the coping. He washed his face. Baptiste came across the yard from the winery, cradling his gun. Baptiste wished his father a good morning then asked if he'd been up all night – pointed with the toe of his shoe at the lamp by Sobran's feet. Sobran untucked his shirt to dry his face, then nodded. He looked searchingly at his son, whose expression matched his but was neither guilty, nor keen with knowledge. Sobran asked, 'Did you sleep well?'

'Yes.' Baptiste hesitated, then asked, 'Last night was *that* night, wasn't it? It's the same every year.'

It was time to lie. As soon as Sobran resolved to lie he realised he had finally relinquished any possibility of telling the truth. He said, 'I killed a man.' Played out a length of silence. He'd had this story ready for some years, but hadn't wanted to lie. 'When I was in the army – the night before the fires drove us from Moscow – there was an Austrian infantryman, a looter, and a Russian woman, great with child.' He paused, pushed the bucket off the coping, let the rope run and wheel spin, heard the bucket's wooden base slap the water metres below. 'I don't want to talk about it. What I did was wrong.' (The truth was worse – the truth of this story – venal, and small. Sobran vividly remembered the Russian woman, and what he did to her. He saw the woman more clearly now than he did the dead wasps and withered pears in the bowl by her bed, which he had, at the time, taken for a sign from a betrayed and blessed guardian. Now, here he was suggesting that he had taken a life to save the woman's honour. And his lie dishonoured her again.)

His son asked, 'Have you ever told anyone about this?'

'Baptiste Kalmann knew. I'm telling you now because you're a grown man.'

Baptiste held out his free hand, took his father's arm and led him in for breakfast.

They were sitting over milky coffee when the carriage came, the family's own, piled with boxes. The groom got down to open the door, but was swept aside by Léon. The groom balked a moment, then folded the steps down and handed out Céleste, then Agnès. Céleste was smiling dreamily. Agnès was so pale her eyes looked pushed back into her head.

Sobran and his son watched all this from the morning room, then went out into the hall, too late to intercept Léon. Sobran caught Céleste by her arm.

'Dear, do let me unpin my hat first,' she said, and smirked lewdly, despite the presence of her son and daughter.

Sobran released her. 'You must have been scarcely a day at St Florentin before you began back.'

'Yes, that's right. It didn't suit.'

'What's the matter with Léon?'

'He's bilious. We drove very fast.'

'And what was amiss with the spa?'

'Do you hear this, Agnès? It seems that your father doesn't want us.'

'I'm happy to have you home – but as you can see it is very hot here, and the carpets and curtains haven't been restored to their places.'

Céleste moved around Sobran to kiss Baptiste. 'I'll freshen up,' she said. 'Come, Agnès.' She began up the stairs.

'In a moment, Mother.'

Céleste turned. 'Come now, dear.' She held out her hand.

Agnès glanced at her father who said quietly that he would be in the winery. She ran upstairs.

When she was able Agnès reported that she hadn't known her mother was dissatisfied with arrangements at the spa till the morning she was told to pack. They had been there two days – Agnès was busy, she'd learned a piano piece from another girl and had bathed twice and had been into the woods with her uncle looking for glow-worms. Mother was good at the suppers to which they'd been asked, she had behaved graciously, and they'd had another invitation to a picnic. But then Agnès found herself being bundled off by Mother and Uncle Léon. Neither spoke in the carriage. Mother was sick once. They had one noisy night in the big inn at Précy-sous-Thil. People seemed to be coming and going at all hours. But, strangest of all, they stopped last night in the little inn at Aluze. The innkeeper was very surprised when they arrived, but Mother said something about the carpets and curtains being washed. No one asked why, if the house was out of order, they didn't just go on to Antoine and Sophie. Mother and Léon were fighting. Agnès could hear them half the night in the room next door – their savage muttering. They were only forty minutes on the road from Aluze and Uncle and Mother weren't speaking to each other.

Sobran found Léon at his desk, writing a letter. He looked chilled, his neckcloth wound high and hard against the line of his jaw, his ears perhaps troubling him again, as they had used to. Sobran asked him a couple of questions. Léon stood to turn his chair sideways, reseated himself as though set to listen, but said, 'May I just finish this – I have to do this. Then I'll be right with you.' He spoke while looking at his cat, who was upright and drowsing by a fire of burning papers – the rug was missing, being cleaned, and the cat was too spoiled to recline on bare boards.

'Aline's few letters,' Léon said, looking at the fire.

There were more than a few.

When Sobran was out the door and about to close it he heard his brother say, absently, 'I'm sorry, Sobran.'

Noon. Lunch was moved back to one. Agnès and Baptiste came to the table. The maid said Céleste had a headache, was going to take a bath. The maid had knocked at M. Léon's door but got no answer. Sobran asked the cook to serve; took up his spoon (in his fist first, like a peasant, then properly, as he always did to tease Agnès) but didn't eat. He watched the drifting globules of oil on the soup's surface come together to form yellow optical lenses. He was lightheaded with tiredness. He put his spoon down and pressed on the top on his head as if it were a cork he was trying to sink. 'What was that?' he said.

'Father?' Baptiste asked.

Sobran had heard nothing. Nothing – like the silence that follows cannon fire. He pulled his napkin from his collar, got up, and went back upstairs. Céleste's door was open a crack. He heard the water lap in the zinc tub; pushed the door and looked in at her – her gold hair draped on the sheet that lined the tub, her round arms steaming. She sighed and shrugged her shoulders, but didn't hear him, didn't turn. He went on to Léon's room. That door was open also. Sobran opened it further.

Léon was hanging by the rope that was used to raise and lower the bracket of candles suspended from the centre of the ceiling. Léon had cut the lamp free; it lay tilted on the floor by the fallen stool. The stool had struck one of the frosted-glass candleholders, and there was broken glass on the floor. A candle had rolled to the base of the bureau where it lay crushed as though stepped on. Sobran went into the room, closed the door and leaned against it.

One of Léon's shoes had come off. It was a new shoe: its scarcely scuffed sole was turned to Sobran. The feet, a sock down around the ankle of one, were pointed at the floor, as inert and unsupportive as the feet of a church statue portraying some levitating saint. Dye from the inner soles of the new shoes stained the heel and toe of the stockinged foot. The rope was invisible, sunk in the neckcloth that still scarfed that twisted neck. Léon faced the floor, toward which his tongue was trying to cast a mooring line of thick transparent spittle.

On the bureau lay a single sheet of writing paper. Sobran picked it up. He had to steady the paper with his other hand. Both hands trembled so badly it was as if they fought over the letter. Léon had written:

Brother –
I have tried to deserve the grace I was given although your charity has been rank misery to me without your friendship – which I know I have never deserved. I abused your hospitality and am a coward who, while wanting to confess all, cannot do so to your face. God knew what kind of man I was when He sent His angel to me in St Lawrence ten years ago. I have never understood why I was told to save my life and yet not instructed to go and sin no more. I own my carnality, the evil road that was my road. I am to blame. It was I who killed Aline's sister Geneviève because she did what I enjoyed and hated to enjoy, and later murdered Marie Pelet – my lover – because she uncovered my crime. Why did God –

Léon had crossed out 'spare' and replaced it with 'save' –

– my life when he knew I would turn traitor even after repentance and contrition? Why show me his mercy in a manner so marvellous? The angel's visit was a holy place-marker in the vile book of my life. Once I rejoiced to say: Thy Will Be Done. But for years I've been unable to see the good in God's will. Why did God make me thus? I loved dear pure Aline but I was the cause –

The latterly frugal Léon had filled both sides of the sheet of paper, but there was no more.

Sobran crumpled the paper and thrust it into his pocket. He went out of the room and shut the door. He stumbled down the first flight of stairs then had to sit on the landing – his legs wouldn't support him. Several minutes later Baptiste came into the lower hall and saw him. Baptiste vaulted up the stairs to his side. 'Father, are you ill?'

Sobran dug his fingers into Baptiste's clothes, held him close and said quietly, 'Your uncle has hanged himself. I want you to fetch Antoine and Sophie.'

Baptiste pulled his father to his feet, called out for Agnès. Together they helped Sobran downstairs and sat him in his chair at the head of the table. Sobran waved his hand at Baptiste. 'Go.'

Baptiste ran from the room. Sobran heard him stop in the hall, then start quietly upstairs, having to see for himself.

'Your hands are very cold, father,' Agnès said.

'Give me a minute.'

She sat before him, chafing his hands and peering at him anxiously. He heard Baptiste come back down the stairs and saw him look around the doorframe, his face the shade of soap, tan tallow in colour with no blood behind it.

'Go,' Sobran said again.

Baptiste went.

Sobran sat in a chair at the foot of the bed while the women washed Léon's body. Agnès, newly introduced to this traditional task, stood by holding a ewer and towels. The room was candlelit, curtains closed on a rosy midsummer sunset.

Sobran watched Céleste wring out a cloth, heard the water chime in the basin.

The maid raised Léon's head while Sophie unwound the neck-cloth. It crackled as it came free of the trench the rope had formed in his flesh. Sophie sighed, a sigh that fluttered, like a candle flame disturbed by a breeze. Sophie unbuttoned Léon's shirt and together she and the maid raised his body to strip it off. Sophie laid her younger brother back down, her arm beneath his neck. Céleste moved forward to wash his torso.

From where he sat Sobran could see that, under the entrenched purple wound by Léon's jaw, there was another ring of bruising, a line like a grubby collar, level and even. Sobran had seen this before, had recognised it before. It was the same sight that had shocked him on that remote morning when he had watched Léon dressing by the stove in the kitchen of their former house. On the morning that he, Léon and their father were fetched to search for Geneviève Lizet. Sobran's shock had, he now understood, been due *not* to seeing signs of an uncleanliness uncharacteristic of Leon, but to his recognition of evidence that someone had tried to throttle his brother. The bruises had been just like these. And Sobran had put them right out of his mind.

Sobran sat very still, watched the women gently raise a limp arm to wash the armpit. He watched them unbutton Léon's breeches and pull them off, untie the drawstring on Léon's drawers, strip him naked, then turn him tenderly on to his stomach to wash the liquid mess from his backside.

Agnès stood hugging the ewer. Tears dripped from her chin into the clean water.

The priest at Aluze would not let Léon lie in the churchyard. He said he relied on Sobran – of all people – not to prove a hypocrite by quarrelling with the laws of the Holy Church. It was simply wrong for the saved to wait out Time beside the unshriven. There were no exceptions.

Sophie pleaded with tears pouring from her eyes. Céleste stepped back from the priest and held her skirt, as though at mud or a mess of dung, then she folded her arms and looked through the priest, the whitewashed sacristy wall behind him and on, it seemed, through the little field of memorials. The priest was rocked by this look – not knowing that this was how she disengaged herself from all discussions about what was proper.

Antoine said, 'Father, Léon was with the priests for four years. He went to church all his life. To *this* church for over thirty years.'

The priest nodded, he understood this, and that the Jodeau family had paid for the new statue of Saint Barbara that stood near the altar. Nevertheless, 'It's impossible,' he said. 'I'm sorry, but I won't hear any more arguments.'

'Old Father Lesy would have known how to bend the rules.' Sobran made an enclosure of his hands, then opened them, letting something out.

'Not in this matter. There may be a place for unchristened infants within the church walls, but you must be content with – ' and the priest pointed through the side window of the sacristy and across the boundary at the back of the church, where the wall was broken by brambles. 'Your brother's casket can rest beneath the lychgate, and I will pray over him. We will ring the bells – in honour of your family, Monsieur Jodeau – but your brother will be buried outside the churchyard.'

If this was his final word, Sobran told the priest, then he must know that Léon's funeral would be the final occasion on which he, Sobran, would enter this church, alive or dead. Having said this, Sobran put his hat on and walked from the sacristy, through the church, head still covered, and out into the sun.

'If you don't let Léon rest in the churchyard Sobran won't be the only one who stays away,' Antoine said. He took Sophie's arm, then Céleste's, turned both women and followed his brother-in-law.

Léon Jodeau was interred in a dry gulf of a grave cut from among the brambles beside three listing wooden gravemarkers outside the church wall.

Three days after the funeral, Sobran, Baptiste, Martin, and Antoine arrived and began to dismantle the stone wall behind the church. Antoine's sons turned up with a cartload of stones. By noon the men were rebuilding the wall from both its back corners. They were joined by Sobran's friends from the village. All the men were stripped down to shirtsleeves and sweating profusely. Sophie,

Céleste and her elder daughters came with a lunch of bread, cheese, onions, sausage and bottles of Jodeau-Kalmann *vin bourru*. While the men rested the priest came out of the church – for the third time that day – and tried to dissuade them from their task. He became angry and cursed at them. Antoine offered him a drink.

At one o'clock the work recommenced, and by sunset a new wall stood finished. The line between consecrated and unconsecrated was now marked only by the higher level of the ground that, within the churchyard for centuries, had risen the way that water in a tub will when a body enters it, the earth slowly displaced by the mortal remains of dead generations. The flower-covered mound of Léon's grave was surrounded by more turned earth, where the men had razed the brambles.

In the last light the workers took off their heavy gloves, put picks and spades back in Antoine's cart, washed at the horse trough by the lychgate, put their jackets and hats back on, shook hands and dispersed.

Sobran saw Paul de Valday, mounted, on the road that ran by the long rolling slope to the south of Vully. He gave the sickle vine-knife back to the harvester to whom he'd been offering a lesson in cutting stems, raised his hat from his head and waved it at Paul. The Comte reined the horse in, then dismounted. In a moment one of the harvesters had put down a basket and stepped up to hold the horse's bridle. Paul met Sobran halfway along the row, uncovered his head as he came up and peered at his vintner with some trepidation.

'Why won't your mother see me?' Sobran asked, without politeness or preamble.

Paul put his hat back on and took Sobran's arm, turned him so that they walked away from the main body of the harvesters. 'You're wiser than I am,' Paul said.

'Don't butter me up.'

Paul coloured. 'I don't like to say.' He glanced about at the nearer workers who were bent over their heaped baskets of fogged red grapes. 'By the way, I hear I'm to congratulate you and your wife – '

Sobran was silent.

'*Again*,' Paul said, provoked by this lack of reaction.

Sobran's face was set and completely unreadable.

Paul pressed what he saw as an advantage, lowering his voice.

'Mother is ill because she lost a child. It was very early and, I'm told, as easy as these things ever are. But she's disappointed.'

'And this accounts for the rumour?'

'What rumour, Monsieur Jodeau?'

'That she walked into the river one morning six weeks ago, trying to drown herself.'

It was Paul's turn to be silent. He had hoped Sobran would react with more *personal* interest to the news of his mother's miscarriage.

'Did she miscarry before or after she walked into the river?'

'After,' Paul muttered. 'It was the Baron's coachman saved her. Baron Lettelier knew before *I* did. The news had to pass through the whole serving staff to my old nurse and *then* to me.' Paul stepped in front of Sobran and faced him. 'I don't know why she did it. She's said she won't see you. And she didn't send condolences to your brother's funeral. When she heard Monsieur Léon had killed himself she *laughed*. She laughed and said, "God proposes, man disposes."' It clearly distressed Paul to repeat this blasphemy, but he was making a brave show.

Sobran covered his face with both hands and rubbed vigorously.

'I knew you would know what she meant.' Paul sounded resentful and envious.

'All the more reason for her to give me an audience.'

'She left this morning for the spa at St Florentin. It's too hot here, the Baron says. The Baron is a Christian man – he dislikes the spectacle of suffering. Baptiste tells me that Madame Jodeau is at the spa in the company of your sister. You must be worried about Madame – who is some years past forty.'

'Be careful, Paul.'

But Paul went on waspishly, angry with all his elders and their secrets. 'When I told Mother you were expecting another child – in the way of good news following bad – your brother's death, I mean – she said that you must think you're Noah, with a divine charter to repopulate the *pays*.'

'All right, stop now. It's not your place to repeat your mother's insults or to remark on the age of my wife.'

Paul shut his mouth tightly, went quite white around the nostrils, then said, 'I repeat her insults to provoke you into an explanation.'

Sobran tried to put a hand on Paul's shoulder but the young man struck it aside. 'You're endangering her life!'

'Sir – ' Sobran used the honorific, hoping it would pull Paul back into line, 'your mother and I are not lovers. And we haven't quarrelled – if that's what you're thinking.'

Paul had thought the lost child was Sobran's rather than the Baron's – and that his mother was envious of Céleste Jodeau's pregnancy because of her own loss, and simply upset at evidence of the continued marital congress between M. Jodeau and his wife. Now Sobran denied the relationship. Still, Paul was sure of one thing. He said, 'You are the cause of her unhappiness.'

Sobran shook his head. 'It's only a short time since she was so near to death. And you should consider her feelings about the damage to her womanhood, the operation and then this miscarriage – one slight on top of another, so to speak.'

'No, she is unhappy about *you*, Jodeau. The whole *pays* hangs on your moods, whims and opinions. Because of you Anton Wateau has built a wine cellar and sold his cows and taken up the plum trees his great-grandfather planted and put a good flat field to vines. Because of you Saint Barbara is further forward in the church than Saint Vincent – patron of wine. A *gunner's* saint – one of your homages to Kalmann, I suppose. Because of you, the Lizet and Laudel families haven't been to church for over a month – even the women. Don't tell me you have no idea of your influence.'

'I believe I know what ails your mother – which is why I should not be prevented from seeing her.'

'Too late. And – yes – you *know*, and then you lie to me. "Damage to her womanhood"!' Paul spat. 'You might as well pat me on the head. Do you think you can make me believe that my mother would try to injure herself over a matter of a marred figure?'

Sobran saw that Paul was attracting attention. The near harvesters were looking through the vines, like fox cubs peering out of a thicket. He could feel their eyes, and appetite. 'Paul,' he said, but didn't stem the flow.

'My great-uncle was your patron, but who have I got in my pocket? Only household servants, old women, young girls, the lame old man who keeps the gardens, one or two of the grooms perhaps. You've made me a tidy fortune, but I have – what? – Latin, German, fashionable hats, a mother who won't tell me why she's in despair and – '

Sobran saw Paul had reached some decision.

' – and Agnès tells me she's going to become a nun because her uncle is a suicide and her mother is mad!'

'Well,' Sobran was droll, 'Agnès will have to go back to church first in order to find a vocation.' He waved a hand at the Comte. 'Get back on your horse and go and visit her. Pay court, by all means. Just stop shouting at me.' Sobran turned away, saying, 'I guess your mother will keep.'

Paul put his hat on, then tore it off again, threw it down and crushed it into the dry chalk. Then, much to the entertainment of the harvesters, he strode back to the road cursing. He snatched the bridle from the man who held it, mounted and galloped off.

Aurora sat on a stone seat in a sunny alcove surrounded by a yew hedge trimmed in imitation of masonry. She could hear a fountain, and see its highest tossed drops above a line of clipped peach trees. She'd been reading – Hugo again – but had turned the book down on her lap, and taken a wedge of bread out of her pocket to eat. She crumbled the crust for the birds, threw the crumbs in a fan across the gravel and on to the stone seat opposite. Aurora looked at this seat, its lustrous marble, and imagined it occupied. And, in imagining a figure there instead of air she placed the sum at the end of an equation that had pleased her more unsolved. For if there was an angel there was a God. And now, when she thought of her atheism, she took a scoop of air, as she did when she said 'my breast' of the large melted scar where her breast had been.

Aurora heard footsteps, of two walking but not talking. She recognised Sophie Laudel and Céleste Jodeau despite the bonnets that blinkered both women. They turned onto her walk and saw her. Sophie instantly smiled and raised a hand, as civil and calm as she'd been when they had met in the baths the day before. Aurora politely invited them to sit, and they did so, both tilting their parasols to keep the sun from their faces. The sun shining through the beaded fringe of Céleste's parasol made bright lacework on the heavily pleated bodice of her dress. Céleste was stately already in the loose gowns of expectant motherhood.

They had been on the river after lunch, Sophie told Aurora, but hadn't taken the waters yet today. Sophie hoped for an excursion to the salt spring tomorrow.

Céleste said she felt a little chilled. Would Sophie go back to their rooms to fetch her shawl? This sobered Sophie considerably. Her animation completely deserted her. She was neither embarrassed nor fearful, Aurora saw. She just met Aurora's eyes, and her look weighed and measured. Then she excused herself and went off on Céleste's errand.

Madame Jodeau closed her parasol, pushed its spike into the gravel and crossed her hands on its handle. Her bonnet was like the hood on a storm lamp, her eyes as bright as bull's-eye glass with a flare burning behind. She asked Aurora, 'Who is your tailor?'

Aurora named the man in Autun of whose provincial patterns the Baron complained.

'You must pass on my compliments on his art,' Céleste said, eyeing Aurora's chest.

'Yes – no lack evident,' Aurora said. 'He's highly skilled. And discreet.'

'Indeed.' Céleste inclined her head.

'Please accept my congratulations, Madame Jodeau,' Aurora said.

Céleste smiled, touched her stomach. 'A happy burden. Though it's always a bother in the hot weather.'

'When does your confinement begin?'

'February. The little thing won't see the sun till its christening.'

'How will you manage that? The christening, I mean. Paul tells me Monsieur Jodeau and the priest have fallen out.'

'We'll go to Chalon-sur-Saône for the christening. Another goddaughter for Aline.'

Aurora's hair prickled. She was cold inside her clothes, cold in the sunlight.

'Oh no – that's right – Aline is dead,' Céleste said, as placid as water shortly before it freezes. She mused for a minute, then said, 'Perhaps you would like to do us the honour?'

'Certainly, Madame. But you must know there's been, not a quarrel, but a degree of coldness between me and the Church for a number of years. Consequently I am no one's godmother.'

'You were all *but* in your generosity to Sabine when you sponsored her schooling.'

Aurora acknowledged this with a nod.

'And since you are an uncoventional woman I'm sure you won't mind that it isn't my husband's child.'

Aurora sat with her hands in her lap and felt like a jointed fowl. She caught her book as it slipped. 'Pardon?' she said.

'Well. That's settled.' Céleste touched her own stomach, smiled. 'Lucky infant.'

Aurora could feel her lips moving, but they had no muscle and no words emerged.

Céleste got up. 'Here's Sophie with my shawl.' She opened her parasol and set its handle on her shoulder. 'I know my husband shares everything with you, Baroness. So I hope you don't mind if I take the liberty of sharing this one small secret.'

Sophie arrived, settled the shawl around Céleste's shoulders. Céleste gave her sister-in-law her arm. 'Shall we walk on, dear?'

Sophie studied Aurora's pale face, said, 'Excuse us, Baroness. I'm sorry.'

Céleste, beaming and majestic, pretended not to hear. She drew her sister-in-law away along the walk.

No one communicated. Sobran told himself that Aurora could keep. Aurora composed letters, but only in her imagination. She was not on hand for questioning, though Sobran and Antoine both had questions. Aurora went from St Florentin to the Baron's estate and thence to Paris, meaning to stay all winter. Paul joined them, leaving Agnès still unkissed. Céleste burgeoned, and went with her younger daughters to Chalon-sur-Saône and Sabine. Sobran moved a third of his books and clothes to his room above the cuverie at Vully, and left his elder sons in charge all week at his own vineyard. He wasn't waiting for Aurora to return, or for domestic peace, the last child's safe birth, or his breach with the Church healed. He was waiting for summer, for the one with whom he could share Léon's letter.

On a blustery night in early December Sobran had finally fallen asleep despite the noise, snow hissing as dry as salt against the shutters, and the wind's smothered complaints. Later he was awake.

The wind was louder and a shutter came unfastened and struck not, it seemed, on the stone sill, but with a soft thump, then crashed back against the stonework. Sobran heard knocking, knuckles on the shutters. He got out of bed and went to the window. One shutter was open and beyond the glass Sobran saw the gloss of snow and midnight, then his angel, holding on to architrave and sill with one hand and two tensed bare feet, his black hair whipped every-which-way like a tattered banner. Sobran opened the window. The other shutter came loose, swung out, and knocked Xas from his perch. Xas fell into the snow in the courtyard, then sprang up again immediately, leaving a few depressions and a blur, nothing like the snow-angels children make.

Xas came in the window, brushing by Sobran, wet where his skin was warm, hair and feathers stiff with frost.

Sobran caught a window, closed it, then the other, with its two cracked panes.

Xas was already stretched on the floor, facing the hearth and blowing on the embers. Now that the shutters were closed his breath gave the only illumination, a local rosiness that came and went as he blew. Sobran found a flint and a candle. 'I'm not going to get up,' Xas said, 'and drag my wings. The ceiling is too low. I'm here because I wasn't going to wait until we were being watched again.' He began to feed the fire, did so delicately and with interest, as if it were an animal whose tastes and appetite he meant to discover. 'We should move our night. Say to the next. Even that would throw them, probably, and still fall within the weeks you customarily pack your family off to anywhere out of sight of Baptiste Kalmann's "headstone".'

Xas had compressed a good deal of casual needling into a few sentences. Sobran laughed at this and the angel looked back across his wing, hair scattering drops of water that hissed on the hot grate. 'Apharah told me that she wrote you a letter. I wondered if you had received it. I'm worried about what she might say to you.'

Xas sat up and settled his wings around him so that Sobran could only see his head and a line of bare, clean, uncallused toes. 'For the last year Apharah has nursed a crippled Russian fellmonger. I thought Kumiliev was Apharah's hobby – or a part-payment on her place in Paradise. It turned out that she had acquired him for his

French, wanting to write to you. People are so devious! Their weakness makes them astute. Think of it – it was men, not angels, who were able to discover that the planets orbit the sun.'

Sobran shook his head. He didn't believe his ears.

'Only someone with a telescope can see that planets orbit the sun. Nobody would invent *telescopes* who hadn't needed *spectacles*. Disadvantaged, needy, so *devious* – that's humanity.' As if to illustrate the differences between people and angels Xas rearranged the fire. He put his hands into the flames to shuffle burning logs, then brought them out, sooty, and wiped them on his wings.

'No letter yet,' Sobran said. Then, 'I want to embrace you, Xas – will you let me?'

'I don't like to be touched. Nor would you if your body was a two-way peephole with God's and the Devil's eyes applied to either end. For my next optical image I'll do either periscopes or kaleidoscopes.'

Sobran said with dignity, 'Very well, if you won't stand up, nor will I sit on the floor. I would like to be able to report that after my night on the ground at midsummer I wasn't able to straighten for a week. But I'm not so ancient that my aches and pains pushed themselves to the fore – given everything.' Sobran unlocked his writing case and produced Léon's suicide note, handing it to the angel.

'Do I want to read this?' Xas asked. He held the page by one corner, and seemed moved, but the paper betrayed not even the slightest tremor.

'No. But are you suddenly a coward?'

'I've never had to show courage, Sobran.' Xas began to read. Turned the paper over, read the rest then looked up. 'Is there another page?'

'No.'

'I think there is.'

'Léon lived under my roof for years and I feel I know you better than I knew him.'

'Your hospitality does seem to have been a point of contention for him.'

'Léon didn't have to deserve a place in our house. I thought he understood that. I thought I'd told him.'

'We've *all* had to deserve you, Sobran.'

Sobran sat down on the end of the bed. As he did so his bare heel bumped the chamber-pot and made its lid rattle. Sobran found himself trying to recall whether or not he'd pissed after retiring to his room and listening for the slop of cold urine. Ashamed – again – of his body, of himself, he looked down at the nightshirt over his square bony knees and his rough-skinned, roped hands. 'Léon didn't kill himself because of anything I did. It was him. He was the murderer. I can't understand it. I find I can scarcely even *think* about it.'

'The murders are news to me,' Xas said. 'Which rather diminishes the shock of discovery. You've neglected to mention these murders,' His eyes were momentarily opaque and reflective. 'Except – thinking again – that *I* seemed like a murderer to you, who "goes about causing terror piecemeal".' He held the letter out to Sobran, who didn't lift a finger, but instructed, 'Burn it.'

Xas put the page into the fire. 'It doesn't read as though he were about to confess he'd killed Aline. But her death must have made it impossible for him to put his crimes out of his mind, despite his repentance.'

'He said he sinned after repenting.' The letter was now a fragile flake of carbon and Sobran had no more need to say 'he says' rather than 'he said' of his brother, even in discussing the letter.

'Treachery he says, not murder.' Xas looked at the glossy black leaf as he said this, as though he could still read it – but of course he could remember exactly what it said, and never had cause to doubt his memory. 'Perhaps Aline's murder was just a tormenting coincidence.'

'I wouldn't have thought you believed in coincidences.'

'I do – but they don't happen to me.'

'Because you're important. Conspired against, spied on, endangered. If only by poor incontinents hidden in vineyards.' Sobran looked away from Xas and his shoulders slumped. 'You know – my whole life is a downward slope following midsummer.'

'Yes?' Xas said, mildly. He got up and came over to Sobran, who kept his head down and despondent.

'This last midsummer in particular? Or every midsummer? Sobran, the way you talk you tempt me to think I have it in my power to make you happy, which is an error, no matter what you imagine.' Xas sighed. 'But now I think I have to say to myself that this disaster is my future.'

Sobran meant to raise his face. But when his head was level he stopped, gazed at Xas's navel, the stomach, smooth and radiant above the jewelled belt. He was not surprised to be moved in the same way as he had been twelve years before, but by exactly the same thing, *that* was surprising, the exact same body, as unaltered as a treasured memory.

Xas put his hands on Sobran's shoulders and pushed, reclining with Sobran so that both their faces came clear into the light of the single candle on the chair by Sobran's bed. It was abrupt, but done smoothly. The angel had no great weight to use so did not unbalance the man. He used muscle, didn't hesitate, had decided, and nothing interrupted the impetus of his decision. If Sobran was going to talk about downward slopes the angel would increase the gradient till there was no gripping, till the slope was a cliff face without handholds and the man's only salvation was in the angel's arms.

Xas put his hands into the neck of Sobran's nightshirt so that the buttons popped out of the buttonholes. 'How old are you?' the angel said. 'Forty-five, is it? Is that old?' Sobran felt the fine fingers of the angel's callused hands touch his nipples, over his heart, his stomach, then – the nightshirt torn – his thighs on either side of his balls. Both hands, for the angel was leaning on his wings. Sobran moved his own hands, touched scaly leather, and nothing faintly moved there.

'Why would I be?' Xas read Sobran's thoughts through his touch. 'Do I need to get stiff to impregnate some female creature? No. I'm a fair copy of a man. My beauty is only armour – and to please God.'

Sobran pinched the pearl head of the lynch-pin on the jewelled belt. He drew the pin forth and the belt fell from Xas like a cut snake. Sobran pulled Xas by the hips, pulled the angel against him. He turned himself and the angel so that they lay side by side, face to face, and he looked into the angel's eyes. 'I know that you're a virgin and as bodiless as any paralytic. I know I'm old and not as handsome as I once was. But I know you love me as I love you.' And he kissed the angel.

Xas was trying to say something and Sobran was trying to listen, but was sleepy. He'd rebound into wakefulness in a moment. That was how it always was with him. No one was there but them, no peepers, sacred or profane. No past, brandy, tobacco, stubble, frostbite. He'd been weeping. The angel was an incubus – of course – thank God. The taste and scent of his body plunged Sobran into something like the thick, thickening dreams of his early manhood. Xas was saying, 'I don't – just because you do – love me. I don't, Sobran. Sobran, I want you to wake up, please, and do something you did. Again, please?'

And inexhaustible, apparently, and inspiring.

Sobran's throat was so swollen it pushed up under his ears, which were ringing. He could hear his voice, wild with exhaustion, a growl, stripped of all human expression. There was no filth in Xas, he said, though he liked to see his own flow out of the angel. But he could see no marks, only deposits, the thick pearls of his and sterile egg-white of the angel's, but not a bruise, not a red smear of rough handling, even through the angel's hair was clotted beside one ear and there were flakes dried on his face.

Xas was praising every perishable inch of him, so Sobran answered, his hands on the move, 'I still want – ' and went to sleep.

Sobran was telling Xas about the murders. How the old Comte had wanted him to look at Marie Pelet's corpse – him and Léon and Jules Lizet – the three who had found the first dead girl, Geneviève Lizet. Would they notice something they had seen before? That was what was said, though now Sobran thought they were suspected of murder. The physician was still in the room, stooped over Marie, holding a candle by her hand. It looked as if he were about to set her alight.

'The Comte stood by my shoulder and asked me if I noticed anything. I'd been away to war. I couldn't recall how Geneviève Lizet had looked, my mind was full to the brim with corpses. Both women had been choked and bashed. Léon's were the only other marks of strangling I ever saw. I noticed his on the morning of the day we found Geneviève. *There* was a connection I should have made. Yet I still don't quite understand the connection.'

'I think you do, Sobran.'

'What then?'

'Put your hands around my throat.'

'. . . .'

'Go on.'

Fingertips on vertebrae, thumbs on the soft skin over ridged cartilage of windpipe.

'How does it make you feel? Did you ever let anyone do that to you?'

'You seem to be giving me your complete trust.'

'Let me do it to you.'

'No.'

'Yes. Trust me.'

A turn about. Warm hands, faint pressure from cat-like pads. Sobran sighed. Xas moved his leg, said, 'Yes?'

'I didn't want to know that.'

'Must I remove my hands? I rather like this. But do remember, Sobran, that everything I do seems to work with you. Perhaps this is the *only* thing that worked for Léon. Those poor women discovered what he liked and he hated them for it. "It was I who killed Aline's sister Geneviève because she did what I enjoyed and hated to enjoy",' Xas quoted, then said, 'There. Don't be ashamed.'

'I'm sure that if ideas about carnal sin were out of the way, new schools of thought would flourish. About pleasure – you liking the feel of my hands around your throat. Léon's pleasures. Léon's hatred and shame. And about you and Céleste – the way you first told me about her it sounded as if you responded to her first because of her beauty and secondly for the contempt in which she held you. Or – consider this – you wanted me first *either* when I threw you to the ground, angry because you asked me to look for your daughter in Heaven, *or* when you discovered that Michael had made a pulp of my right side.'

'Saint Michael the Archangel?'

'There you go again with the inessentials. I feel as if I've discovered something to do with violence and desire – how dangerously close they can be – and you're only interested in the identity of my assailant.'

*

'I'm hungry.'

'Go and find something to eat.'

'Don't go, Xas.'

'I won't.'

'Are *you* hungry?'

'Are you joking?'

'The first time I spoke to Aurora after her illness I realised what she feels for me. We embraced in her dressing room. We both felt a great tenderness, like that between a husband and wife.'

'And now you think it was Aurora who hid and saw me. A pregnant woman, but not Céleste.'

'She had some kind of crisis. Aurora is an atheist – which you probably think is very imaginative of her. What must she think now about her beliefs? And they are beliefs, atheism isn't just a laxity. Aurora thought she knew me. What do you mean "Hmmm"? Xas, my hands can hear you being dubious deep in your chest.'

'What will you do if she continues to refuse to see you?'

'We'll have to speak soon. Paul is courting Agnès. That can hardly be allowed to pass without comment. Though I shouldn't permit it. I don't want to infect the Comte's line with the disorders of my family.'

'So you'll say "No" to Agnès, as your father said "No" to you. And beside the Jodeau disorder is the Jodeau luck. Do you no longer believe in your luck?'

'You're not my luck, fallen angel, or even my dearest friend. You're my love. My true love.'

'You've been asleep.'

'I think you've said that to me before. I go to sleep and fall into gaps when my mind stops holding court like a king on his throne. For years on waking the first thing I've thought of was you – like this – calmly watching me. Sometimes I imagine a whole future made out of the moment after I've died and you are still sitting beside me.'

'You imagine I'll be there at your deathbed?'

'Yes.'

'And if I stayed away, would you live for ever?'

*

Xas told Sobran that fallen angels were very well read. Hell was full of transcripts, one copy of anything copied. Heaven was proof against reproductions of any kind. Angels were the only copies God tolerated. 'That is, He tolerates the copies He makes. Our citadel in Hell has a static population, but keeps growing to accommodate the books. They're everywhere – stacked up against the walls, until piled books fill room after room. But though well read, angels are almost impervious to experience. They're thick. They're made that way – durable, unchanging, placid.'

'Not you.'

'Perhaps that's my garden, my communion with perishables.'

Rich men would pay fortunes for even one ounce of the angel's spit. His every secretion a potent love potion, sweet-scented, innocent as snow, fresh after days in the warmth, the proved yeast of greasy sheets.

'I knew I was in danger from the moment I proposed visiting you a second time. I knew because God warned me by sending the whirlwind that pulled a few feathers.'

'But you still came every year.'

'God is my maker but not my master. And I don't think he was saying "Thou shalt not", rather "I think you're going to regret this."'

'So, you go freely, with hints. If God made a suggestion to me I'm sure I'd take it. I mean, I assume He has, but I've misunderstood.'

Sobran found himself on the floor by the fire. He couldn't keep his eyes open – felt like a fly trying to pull its feet out of a pool of honey. Then he felt warm water and rough cloth, his limbs lifted, spread and washed. Later he was in bed, the sheets crisp and clean. Xas lay on top of the covers and touched his face. 'I have to go and water my garden. This blizzard is the only reason we've been left in peace for so long.'

Sobran freed his arms from the covers and caught the angel by his ears. He said, 'Come back soon.'

'Yes. Sleep for a week. Eat meat at every meal. Write a letter to Aurora.' He moved Sobran's hands. Stood with his wings crossed

behind him, smiled, complained again about the low ceiling, and left
by the door.

Rue du Bac

Paris

20th January 1835

Sobran,

I hardly know where to begin or what tone to take. Yes — Paul
has spoken to me about Agnès. My only reservations concern
their youth. They should not marry now, at fifteen and seventeen.
They are both patient and biddable by disposition and could
tolerate a long engagement. Their lives have been neither too
active, nor too retired — yet I think both need more experience of
the world. Paul has proposed a tour of the Alps and Piedmont
with his tutor. And I should like, and am asking for, Agnès's
company on a pilgrimage I plan to Santiago de Compostela. I will
of course write to Madame Jodeau to ask whether she can spare
Agnès.

I take your reservations about the match as they are intended, a
reminder to me of the variable stock of Paul's own line. You ask
me whether Vully would want to wed itself to a line 'mired in
dubious sanity and marred by a suicide'. Yet you know I have
professed to beliefs that find suicide an arguably rational act, and
despair no sin but simply the result of the sometimes intolerable
sorrows attendant on being human. As for Madame Jodeau — I
think there is more calculation in her frailty than you are prepared
to see. I think — and I will be daring and speak my thoughts — that
it has suited you to doubt your wife's sanity, so that she, with
whom you should be most intimate, might be sealed off behind the
glassy walls of your disappointment or distrust and muffled, as it
were.

So, you see. I don't accept your scruples as scruples. And — yes
— your scruples remind me to mention Paul's father's consump-
tion, and the fears you know I've always held for my son's health.
There — that is acknowledged. As for the differences in their
stations — thanks to your foresight, ambition and luck your
daughter has been raised as a gentlewoman — and I hope that the

society of men and women will present her with no obstacle that her character cannot overcome.

Henri raised his brows on learning the direction of Paul's affections, but, after all, he is a Baron while my son is a Comte. Besides – and by returning to it I admit it does trouble me too, but for her sake – even if Agnès doesn't suffer ostracism, she will suffer anyway. How can she be secured against suffering? You should think about your safety and see how wrong it is that you take this tone of pious fatalism regarding your daughter's life. How can someone with your privileges be so fatalistic?

I have written all this only to answer you. I have already counselled Paul to propose to Agnès. I told him not to wait, not to think it will happen tomorrow, that a better chance will present itself. Paul has not your divine charter to hesitate over right and wrong and virtue and vice and hold his tongue till his hair goes white.

On the other business – I have written to my bailiff to tell him that you may by all means occupy the old soldier's gallery over the coach-house. I think you will want to seal off those big doors at its end – through which armour was winched for storage. There is a pit of sand beneath the doors where Paul played as a child and in which, in past centuries, chain mail was cleaned, or so I believe. Still, despite the sand and soft landings I don't like to imagine you or any of your guests in peril of falling. The roof will need tiles replaced, but the beams and flooring are of oak, and sound. You'll have a great gallery to pace in, room for all your books. You need never spend another night at Clos Jodeau. I always thought the room above the cuverie too low for my vintner, but I suppose it suited his humility.

Aurora de Valday, Baroness Lettelier

Damascus
15th November 1834

My name is Apharah Al-Khirnig. I think you know who I am. For when stars glitter, and the eyes of men are closed, you are my brother.

The hand that makes its straight marks on this paper belongs to an old Russian fellmonger, a soldier too (he reminds me) and, like you, a veteran of Borodino. Isaac Kumiliev fell ill while in this city on business. Lacking money he was abandoned by his servants. I found him in a Christian hospice, a vile place with only one dry nun to every twenty suppurating inmates. I have tended Kumiliev for half a year, and in that time we have both come to understand that his illness is such that it will keep him here. And, during that period, he has taught me a little Russian and a very little French – but not enough to make me independent of his scholarship and able to write to you myself. Kumiliev has met our mutual friend – so you mustn't imagine this letter proceeding with arguments and accusations of madness.

The angel Xas has been a frequent visitor for fifty years. He came to me in my first tranquil year of widowhood. I did not enjoy the wedded state, but was, fortunately, married to an inattentive and ailing man – his eighth bride – widowed shortly thereafter and returned to my father's house to care for him in his final illness. (Writing this I realise I have spent not one half-hour of my life in the company of a young man.) As an only child, my father's death left me in possession of the portion of his fortune not tied up in trade – this house, an orchard of almond trees, and a small vineyard.

The angel enjoyed my roof gardens and told me of his own garden, not troubling himself to dissemble as to its whereabouts. When, after some ten pleasant meetings I remarked that he seemed to be a very polite and personable demon he explained to me *what* he was, indeed. He told me that demons were the native peoples of Hell, that fallen angels had colonised the demons and that the demons worked for fallen angels, cultivating sinners on vast plantations of suffering. He spoke as though to mend my childish error, not with shame, or coyness, or airs of self-excuse.

Such was our talk.

I found Xas enchanting from the moment I saw him – and was delighted to discover the scope of his reading and retention of learning. Though there were times when my faith wrapped me round with its terrors and I feared for my already lazy, vacillating soul, my heart at every meeting would say to me, quietly: This angel is a pure spirit.

Over many years I have revised that thought. Our friend *has*, rather than *is*, a pure spirit. I learned that he understood me, knew I would not preach, or even repeat, any of what he told me, because I didn't care to lose my safe place in the world. Xas understood that I was a coward of complacency, who delighted in what she knew and others did not (especially my pious cousins, from whom, when I pass them in the outer corridor of the mosque, I am obliged to turn my face). Xas beguiled me with his lovely firm face and his strange truths and I sought neither to influence him, nor the world by reporting his talk.

For many years I reserved my judgement on the verity of the matters about which he spoke. The more silent I was, silent and unaltered in my peaceful gardens, the more composed, impartial and consistent his telling became. And the less I credited his words. He was, to my mind, too calm to be honest. At some time during these years he spoke to me of the young Frenchman he had met, how he thought he might go back to see whether 'the boy had got himself married'. I told him he should cultivate more friends, and suggested he promise to visit you each year. It seemed to me you could be his first friend who was fully in the world, a family man, a man who liked commerce.

Then Xas changed. He became troubled and uncertain, puzzled and tender. He began to talk about you – brought reports of your words and actions for my wise interpretation. And I saw that his trouble was one and continuous with his former composure and I understood with a terror like (Isaac tells me he must write grace, that grace is what I mean. And I put up my hands, as one does to acknowledge marvellous calamities or fate, and say, 'God is great'). With a terror like grace I realised that I was in some ways responsible for the life of this unformed immortal.

Now, difficult Frenchman, you hope I will tell you what our friend had to say about you. Yet it seems more pressing to me that I, who was raised in the Moslem faith, could find myself in a Catholic purgatory – in the company of other hapless heretics all complaining in the thousand tongues of humankind. I'm an old woman now. Unlike you – a man of middle years who mourns his former glory because he feels it was unused – I am truly unused, intact, an untasted fruit withered around its seed. I must somehow settle my debt to the world, which I have loved, disregarding what I have learned of its Master's fastidious wastefulness.

I hope our friend has shared these thoughts with you. If so, then I offer again what we both have heard. But if, as I suspect, your talk has been loud with love and injury, and crowded with the inconsequential beauties of daily lives you felt you both must share, then attend to these scraps of testimony.

Xas is afraid of your fear. But to me he speaks about God in every shade of feeling from adoration to loathing.

Angels have cold hearts, Xas says (his head resting in my lap) and thick skulls. Hosanna is about the whole of their repertoire. That's the best God could do. He means to do better. Perhaps he means to make a world. Perhaps that is what Heaven is for; God is collecting the makings of a world. God catches and preserves what we call souls, Xas says. God has his engine of extraction. He has already built a kingdom out of our expectations of happiness, built Heaven from our hopes of Heaven.

I know I have brought much of this troublesome knowledge on myself. For instance, thinking myself very clever I asked him why he has a navel – not having had an umbilicus, a womb in which he grew, a female parent, a bloody birth and squalling infancy. Xas replied by way of a question: 'Why do men have nipples when they will never suckle a child?' Then I asked, in all mischief, whether men were made in the image of women. To which he said that all warm-blooded creatures are female first, but that this is not a heresy. Then followed with his heresy: All angels were made in the image of men.

Has he said any of these things to you? These heresies that had him follow his friend (as he calls Satan) into exile from Paradise. Am I to be forbidden Paradise for having heard these things? (And I am sure Xas's truths – as I believe they are – have not made me love God less. Indeed, I take great personal interest in God, and love him for my friend as I love King Mutamid for the poetry he composed.)

What are we to teach our friend, Frenchman? I believe we must teach him how to return to Paradise.

He says that, at a great height, on a clear day, but not in these latitudes, the air below him is like a convex lens, thick and heavy, and presses him so that it seems easier to ascend than fall. With his wings a little open he simply lies on the air, he says, till the sun goes and his breath makes ice form on his body. I believe we must teach our friend how to return to Heaven. I don't believe Xas fell – but flew downwards as a pelican pierces the water looking for fish. I believe he belongs in Heaven where he is – God tells me in my heart's voice – missed and welcome.

But, Frenchman, how can he fly to Heaven when your friendship exerts such gravity? Don't keep him any longer. He has already been detained four thousand years by having confounded God's secrecy with Satan's honesty. Please assert your influence. Drive him off. Let him go.

1835 Floraison *(the flowering of the vine)*

It was a hot night and their couch was far from the low fire, which Sobran had lit for illumination, along with the candles at the door to the staircase. That door was closed and barred. At the other end of the long gabled gallery the double doors were open on a twenty-foot drop, treetops and night sky. The room smelled of the beeswax with which its floor had been polished, the polish crusted in ancient scars made by spurs, boot nails, armour.

Sobran had just remembered Apharah's letter. It came back to him (as something to hide) after a long, fabulous convulsion of self-forgetting that had left him dry, abrased and as cleansed as old chain mail rinsed in sand. First he noticed the night, moonlight on the wands of the cherry by the open doors. Then he remembered to taste Xas's gift – Cavalierii, a sparkling wine made from white berries by the méthode champenoise. From Finland. It was like a liqueur, powerful and aromatic. It flowered in his head and he remembered the letter. Then, without thinking, he mentioned it.

'Can I read it?' Xas asked.

'No. It's between me and Apharah.'

'I'm between you and her.'

Sobran dissembled, said he didn't have the letter any more. He was destroyed, felt thinner by inches, had but one defensive reflex left to him: outright lying.

'Did you burn it?'

Sobran opened his eyes. There was something odd in Xas's tone – as though burning a letter came close to placing it in his hands.

'And if I did she and I alone would know what it said. And her Russian scribe, I suppose, the invalid Kumiliev.' It pleased Sobran to prove he'd had a letter, and insights into Apharah's household.

'If you destroyed it, it would go to Heaven.'

'So is Heaven full of laundry lists and lewd books? The sorts of things people burn.'

'Destroyed originals go to Heaven. You can find a copy of anything copied in Hell. Heaven is full of the membranes of lost manuscripts. They are like the skin a snake casts when it grows, transparent, in the shape of a snake and printed with airy scales. But these are indestructible, and lovely, like a gold leaf. There are laundry lists, yes, and love notes, totes, tavern bills, burnt verses –' and Xas quoted:

> Reputations, policies, statues, promises
> All prove with time
> My tongue is a stone and one with my mouth
> My lids never wet my eyes.

'Sappho – one of her verses lost in the fire that destroyed the library at Alexandria. I'm translating.'

'From this I deduce that you've been to Heaven more than once since the days of Pompey. I don't imagine you stopped to read when you went to see Nicolette.'

'Quick, aren't you.'

'Do you often go to Heaven? Perhaps to chase up lost correspondence?'

'I've been four times since I fell. Once to read what burned. Lucifer sent me – he thought it suited Our Father to burn the library at Alexandria. We didn't want any ideas lost to us. Human ideas. You are doing our thinking for us. I went again to ask God a question – He didn't answer me. And I went to look for a human friend – I can't say that I found him. I went for you, to see Nicolette. Don't ever ask me what question I asked my Father, Sobran, or what happened to my friend.'

'Not one of your "saints", I gather, just a "solitary" – in purgatory now, perhaps.'

Xas shook his head.

Sobran examined him, relieved to be able to disengage that much. 'So when you burnt Léon's letter you sent it to Heaven?'

'Yes.'

Sobran laughed. Apparently he couldn't rid himself of memories or evidence. 'Would you bother to look for Apharah's letter in Heaven? Are you that curious?'

'No. I'd ask her what she wrote. Or I'd make you tell me.'

'Please,' Sobran said, on a quick breath out as he was wrapped in two wings, the radiant heat of the angel's body over him now, like sunlight, but in one place a burning glass, turned to concentrate. 'You think because you can make me stiff again I'll tell you what she wrote? What a child you are.'

Xas sighed and let him go. He dropped down as heavily as he was able, in a poor approximation of a sulk. He said, 'It had occurred to me to go to Heaven to seek the other page of Léon's letter.'

'There was no other page.' Sobran went cold; he felt his cock cool and loll against his leg.

'I think there was.'

'No. He heard me come up the stairs, he – '

'Why didn't you call for help and cut him down?'

'I don't know. He was still. He was dead.'

'Where was the letter?'

'On the bureau.'

'Where was it written?'

'He was writing at his desk.'

'Was there sand on the desk? Did he have time, hearing you coming up the stairs, to blot the page, and take it to the bureau? How many drawers has that article of furniture?'

'It's tall, with a mirror at head height.'

'So, Léon didn't write his letter *at* the bureau. Must I be exhaustive? He hanged himself before you came up the stairs. Why did you go upstairs?'

'To fetch Léon for lunch.' Sobran was abruptly covered in gooseflesh which caused Xas to sigh, somewhere between pity and delight. 'No, I heard something,' Sobran said. 'Or rather I knew to listen because the house itself seemed to be listening, hard. I said something to Baptiste, then went upstairs. I looked in on Céleste, who was bathing. My first thought was that something was amiss with her. Then I went to Léon's door.'

'Céleste has the other page.'

'No,' Sobran said. He began to move to rid himself of pinpricks of terror, like biting flies in a patch of shade. But Xas held him and began to kiss him as if he enjoyed the taste of terror, and Sobran felt, for the first time, that his was not a legitimate appetite. Then he was in the big surf of pleasure, blind to everything but what was immediately before him, the congestion of this angel's deft, expressive mouth, the flushed, racked body he could not believe was his to touch.

Later Sobran gave Xas Apharah's letter. Gave it saying that she was entitled to her opinion. Xas read it, frowning.

And, while Xas read, Sobran fell asleep. When the pressure in his bladder woke him he staggered up to stand in the double doorway and piss, then stood a minute longer and, as he breathed in the summer dawn, he realised the room was empty behind him. Silent, the coals furred with ash, the angel gone.

At dusk, the day the grapes were trod at Vully, Sobran came back to the soldiers' gallery only to change his clothes – to return to the revellers, his sons and younger daughters, the château's people, the food, music, and dancing, the limbs streaked with fresh grape juice.

Sobran walked into the dim room already tugging his shirt off over his head. He was blind when he stepped into the ice-water. His feet were bare, newly washed at the pump below of grape-pulp and skins. His foot was cool, but the water cold and full of mushy ice.

Sobran freed his head and looked down at a thick bolt of water, silky on the waxed floor. Then he raised his eyes to Xas, armoured in ice from head to foot, hair like a frozen waterfall. The angel lay on his back, breathing strangely. His right hand was pressed to his side, below his left arm, where the signatures were, the arm clamped over that hand, and seams between each separate limb sealed with ice.

Sobran went to him and asked, 'What is it?' He pulled at the arm and hand. He was looking into Xas's face as he said this – saw himself recognised, saw a glimmer, relief. It was too like battlefield deaths he'd seen, and as Sobran pulled the arm and hand out of the embedded ice, blood came, black first like oil, then vivid red, in a room bright with light reflected from the green treetops at the double doors. Sobran saw it all in colour, colour that came with the blood.

Sobran tried to stem the bleeding, put his hand to the wound, and found how deep it was, the skin torn, twined signatures gone, and a hole, as though the angel had been gored by a bull. Blood poured between Sobran's fingers. The man got up, slipped and stumbled his way to the bed, pulled off a sheet, and brought it back to the angel. He began to bind the angel's chest. He raised Xas, and the angel's wings flexed once as his body, in one final convulsive act of consciousness, tried to escape. One wing knocked over a lamp, which broke, and spread oil with the blood and thawed ice.

Sobran picked Xas up, and put him on the bed. Blood formed beads on the wings, like water on a swan's back. Sobran pressed his hands against the wound and looked into Xas's face, saw something drain away behind the angel's eyes. Dark blue. Sobran had forgotten that colour, forgotten it existed. Then the eyes closed, the face composed, and the struggle for breath stopped.

Sobran moved his hand from the blood-soaked sheet. The room was very quiet. Sobran wondered what he was doing. He looked away from the angel to the treetops, sparkling, a crowd milling at the door to a room where a disaster has occurred. In a silence almost serene Sobran smelled sulphur-scented ice-water, and the blood, overpowering, not a shambles but a scent of drift and deeper drift of fresh snow. There was a moment of clean nothingness, when even time seemed gone from the room. Then Sobran stooped, wound his slick hands into the tacky ropes of Xas's bloodied hair. He raised the angel's face to his and gazed – then lay down with the angel to warm him, already in a stupor of sorrow, his lips resting lightly against the angel's own.

*

He sent Baptiste away from his door in the dark of night. Lied in his driest voice about having a guest, heard the shock in Baptiste's hesitation, but didn't care.

The following day Sobran peeled off the bloody sheet and stripped the bed beneath Xas so that the angel lay on a bare mattress smeared with dried blood, his wing tips thick with it, but unsullied at their great high joints. Sobran used the bedding to wipe up the water, gelatinous gore and lamp oil. He stuffed the bedding into the fireplace and set it alight. It smouldered, then burned, smoking thickly.

Sobran carried water, bucket by bucket, from the pump, up the stairs. He filled his bath and lifted the angel into it, sat behind Xas with the angel's head on his shoulder and washed his hair – washed till it was glossy, damp and tangled. He washed Xas's face and body, once touched the dark meat of the wound. Lastly, Sobran cleaned the angel's wings with a soapy cloth, wiped them till their fawn tips were only faintly pink.

Sobran used his last clean sheets to dry the angel, then pushed the bath to the double doors and tilted it to pour the red water slowly into the sand far below the window. He hung the sheets so they screened the window, then carried the angel into the breeze and white filtered sunlight by the double doors. He sat, Xas's head in his lap, and spread the glistening black hair in the sunlight, where it began to dry, hot across the palms of his hands.

After eighteen hours the angel's body was still warm, pliable and perfect. His skin was scarcely less radiant, lacking only that fume of lights and shade that had seemed to animate his body even when he was immobile.

Near midday Sobran took down the dry sheets and made the bed. He put the angel into it and got himself dressed. For it was Sunday and he was due at Sunday lunch in his own house. The clock chimed quarter past the hour. Xas seemed to be asleep. He looked comical, like a young man sharing his bed with two large dogs, the humps his wings made under the covers. Sobran freed one wing and laid it along the bed, stroked its inanimate softness. Then he ran a finger around the angel's mouth – as warm and resilient as ever – in a gesture that, when his grandmother performed it on her own mouth, had always meant, for she'd say it, 'Secrets stay in here.'

*

Sobran sat at the head of the table and gazed at his incomplete family. Sophie and Antoine were there, with two of their four sons, and the wife and child of one. Baptiste, the only person to look back at Sobran with any special attention, was at the other end of the table. The table lacked Sabine and her family, who were usually there at feast days; and Céleste, in Chalon-sur-Saône with her eldest daughter and her new baby, Véronique, whom Sobran had not yet troubled himself to meet. Agnès was still absent, on her way back from Spain and Aurora's pilgrimage. The other children, Martin, young Antoine, Aline, Bernard and Catherine, attended to their food. Sobran met Baptiste's eyes, but was beyond discomfort – he felt like a decorous guest at his own funeral. For, as he gazed, passed a dish when asked, salted his food, he knew he had to choose. He could feel himself choosing. It was like the sensation of overbalancing, the moment when a person knows they must stop trying to balance and somehow deal with the fall. For a fall would follow this choice.

He would turn his face to the wall. If he could choose not to use his life then he needn't use his imagination and imagine how his family would find him, what they would think, how they would feel.

He tasted his food, then put his fork down and announced, 'I have to go away on some business.'

'Where, Father?'

'Only to Autun. I think for a fortnight.'

Baptiste asked would he visit Céleste on the way – which seemed so uncharacteristic that for a moment Sobran was at a loss for an answer till he remembered that Baptiste was under the impression that Sobran had taken a lover.

'Perhaps,' he said, pacifying.

The soup, full of saffron, was the colour of marigolds, and the tomatoes, great globes, were very red. The colour was fine, even Antoine's dim and Sophie's ashy skins. Martin's hair was gold like his mother's, Baptiste's the red-brown Sobran's own had been. The colour made Sobran's family seem marvellous and unfamiliar, the table a paradise to which he didn't properly belong.

The family watched Sobran get up and go out of the room. He came back with a bottle, dusted it on his coat sleeve and began to trim the lead from the cork.

'What is it?' Antoine asked – then drained off his glass in anticipation.

'It's the 1806, Jodeau South.' Sobran poured some out for Sophie, Antoine, their sons and daughter-in-law, then for himself, Baptiste, and Martin – the other children were too young to appreciate it, he said, to which they made obligatory mutterings then went on with their lunch.

Sobran sipped. The wine's backward glance was powerful now, and came across the years.

'This was pressed the summer I was sixteen,' Sobran said to his sister.

'The third to last time South was pressed separately,' she answered. 'Father's best vintage.'

'Which I broached early. It had been in the bottle only a year. I took two bottles of the *friand* and got drunk one night because your mother – ' he addressed his children, ' – wasn't very impressed by my suit.'

'It wasn't a suit, that's why she wasn't impressed,' Sophie said. 'But you found your resolve.'

'It was only a flirt,' Sobran said, 'the wine. That little backward glance. Back then, it was ony a flirt.'

'Now it's true love,' said Antoine. 'So no one tell me off when I run my tongue around the glass.'

'What are we drinking to?' Baptiste asked.

'To our father.' Sobran nodded at his sister, who made the toast. 'To Martin Jodeau, God rest his soul.'

'Oh – I have a little difficulty with that,' said the young Martin, but complied when his uncle Antoine threatened to relieve him of his glass.

Aurora returned to the neighbourhood five days later. She stopped first at Clos Jodeau to restore Agnès to her family, and was told that Sobran was away. She had begun to miss him. Her wrath and grief had run their course. But Sobran was in Autun, not handy to her softened attitude.

The day after her return Aurora decided that, in his absence, she might go and see what Sobran had done with the soldiers' gallery.

Mid-morning she made her way from the château's new (hundred-year-old) west wing, where she lived, past the ancient keep and old 'new' wing (it had been called 'new' for two hundred years, till the newer new was built) to the sprawl of out buildings devoted to livestock (the cuverie and cellars were all in the west). These comprised a dovecot, kennel, dairy, stable, saddlery, tack room, grooms' quarters, coach house and the rooms above these last that had housed Vully's cavalrymen until the old Comte gave the remainder of them, and funds for their commissions, to the Emperor Napoleon.

As she walked, looking about her to see if she was watched, Aurora could hear the mother superior of her convent education holding forth on the curiosity and cupidity of 'the daughters of Eve'. Aurora replied to the remembered voice that it was better she took an interest in her friend's affairs than forgot him entirely and failed to forgive him.

In the heat the gravel of the walk seemed to swarm, as if each stone was hatching.

At the perimeter of the kitchen garden nearest the stables Aurora found that the vegetables had all wilted, almost *melted*, as though someone had watered them with boiling water. She would look into the matter later. She opened the gate, crossed the yard, then noticed a cat stretched out in the shadow of a horse-trough. She went closer, believing it dead. It lifted its head and looked at her then, exhausted, lay flat again. The cat had one kitten, Aurora saw, perhaps two weeks old, eyes already open, its tail a fluffy wedge. The kitten was asleep with its mouth to a nipple. Aurora recognised the cat as Léon's, knew Sobran had kept it at Vully since his brother's death. She squatted to pet the cat, then went on towards the coach house – and walked into a drift of leaves, neither yellow nor brown, but a parched green. Aurora looked up at the trees, their thinning crowns. The withered foliage and vegetables together were too oddly alike. Aurora looked about her, at weeds and moss in the shady crooks of the stone walls – all were limp and dull.

She hurried into the gloomy interior of the coach house, found the stone staircase up to the soldiers' gallery, then stopped with her foot on the first stair. Three kittens, two tortoiseshell like their mother and one black, lay huddled and still at the bottom of the stairs. The small peaks of fur on the backs of the necks of each showed where their mother had held them in her mouth to carry them downstairs and out of danger. All three were dead.

Aurora ran up the stairs. The door was barred. She was thinking of poison. She hammered on the door and called out, 'Sobran!' Then, remembering the wilted garden and trees, she stopped her hammering. For what kind of poison killed both plants and animals?

She put her ear to the door. Heard nothing but, after a moment, felt the door quiver as the bolt was drawn. When she pushed, the door gave.

Sobran stood several feet away, clothed but barefoot, his jaw dark with stubble.

Aurora stepped into the room, seized her friend's hands and took stock of him. Sobran's skin was yellowish, his eyes circled, and his breath rank – the wild onion smell of self-starvation. She looked around him and noticed first that the light shining through the open double doors, and whitely on the old oak floor, showed up a litter of – at first she thought – leaves. She saw that it was the bodies of insects – cicadas and bees, flies and moths. In the breeze that blew through the room and swept a clear, swerving path from the window to the hearth, the insect bodies tumbled and hissed.

It was the angel, on the bed, the cause of all the death and depletion. Aurora understood immediately.

She went closer to the bed to get a better look.

He was as beautiful as daylight. His beauty was somehow legitimate; it made the many human lovelinesses Aurora had seen seem like tricks of the light. The angel was as strong as daylight too – inexorable – the sun that drains silks of their lustre.

She asked, 'How long has he been like this?'

Sobran took his time answering and spoke like one who hadn't expected ever to use his voice again. 'He bled to death.'

'How long ago?'

'A week.'

Aurora looked at her friend. 'I don't know that he's dead, Sobran.'

'I saw him die. But he won't decay.' Sobran sounded exultant and horrified at once.

Aurora took a step nearer the bed. 'Everything is dying. I think because he isn't dead.' She mustered her courage, put out a finger and touched the angel's smooth shoulder. 'He's still warm.'

'I've been holding him.'

Aurora didn't try to disguise her fear, or any other feeling. 'You must not any more, my dear, I think it will kill you to stay here.'

She darted at Sobran, caught him by the shoulders – for he had moved towards the bed – and held him back. 'Please, Sobran, tell me. Or don't tell me – everything or nothing – I don't care. Just come out of here with me. He isn't dead – he's deadly – Léon's cat carried her litter out, too late, and there are three dead kittens at the foot of the stairs. He is killing everything near him. He is killing you!' She put her hands on his cheeks, rough slack skin, and turned his face down to her – but his gaze stayed on the angel.

For a moment she thought of hanging on his neck, considered tears, but she saw how he looked mad, or resolved, or both, and simply let him go.

Sobran returned to the bed, lay down and embraced the angel.

Aurora stood over them for perhaps half an hour and emptied out her store of intimacies. She talked about her illness, how fear of it made her flirt with death. She spoke about the morning she walked into the river, sought death without ever experiencing despair. She knew despair when she saw it – but Sobran should remember his loving family, and what Léon's suicide had done to them when Léon was nowhere near as loved and necessary as he.

She put her trembling fingertips into his hair, ran its glassy white strands through her hand. She touched his forearm, stroked its pelt of sun-bleached brassy hair. Although she didn't respect his desire to be on his deathbed, Aurora couldn't bring herself to rouse Sobran by repeating what Céleste had told her in at the spa. It would only sound like malice. Yet Sobran seemed beyond provocation, didn't look at her or seem to hear her. After a time Aurora stopped speaking and simply regarded them, her friend and that being – who, to preserve its toxic beauty, was using the vitality of others.

Then Aurora thought of a course of action.

The Baroness went to find her shepherd. She went out in her barouche to the sheepfold and came back with two ewes trussed by her feet. She had her footmen fit each with a collar and leash – asked very blithely for a few nannies and kids – oh, and could they please be washed? Let them think she was playing at shepherdess, as Marie Antoinette and the ladies of her court had.

Her servants were baffled, but obedient. As a young man Comte Armand had been fond of experiments, the old steward reminded them when they sat at talk over supper in the kitchens. 'Model farms and what-have-you. And this is better than the time the Baroness's father and the Comte took to playing with gunpowder. I hope we won't see any of that again.'

'Maybe the Baroness is keeping a panther,' one of the footmen said, and was quelled thoroughly by a look.

Aurora hauled the sheep one at a time up the staircase from the coach house. Their small cloven feet skated awkwardly on the waxed floor. She tethered both animals to the legs of Sobran's bed.

When she arrived an hour later with the goats, Sobran sat up.

'The firstlings of my flock and the fat thereof,' Aurora said in a droll, explanatory way – quoting Genesis on Abel's offering to God. She was out of breath.

Sobran stared at her, dull-eyed, then lay down again.

Aurora struggled upstairs with feed for the sheep and goats, then water, put all within their reach. The sheep were already on their knees, panting, a look of fever in their eyes.

Aurora went away to rest.

In the morning, after talking to her maid at breakfast, Aurora went to see for herself the strange, grey-eyed knife-grinder who had turned up before dawn with his donkey, wares and whetstone, and offered to sharpen every blade in the house. The cook and seamstress gave him work, for his feet were blood-blistered inside his shoes and his donkey's hair was pasted to its hide with sweat. Aurora asked him – as her servants had – how far he had come. He replied that he'd ridden and walked for three days just to get here, hadn't worked as he travelled, knew he'd make good money at Vully as he had after the harvest every year. And when Aurora told him it was too soon to sharpen, oil, and store the vine knives he just looked at her in incomprehension with eyes that seemed to stare through all the miles he'd come to get there.

Aurora paid him well, offered to put him up till the harvest was over. Then she went to the coach house.

All the animals were on their knees, muzzles touching the floor, not starved, but shrunken somehow.

Sobran was awake and looked at her. He seemed no worse than he had been. So Aurora went to fetch some more sheep. The shepherd wanted to know what she had done with the other two, and said that he'd heard about the goats.

'Do you like your place?' Aurora asked him.

He blushed. The Baroness had never before taken his enquiries as insolence. He did as he was told, sent a boy to drive the sheep to the courtyard by the coach house where she wanted them. She sent the boy away. Then she stood a moment and looked about her at each window in every wall that wasn't blind, the courtyard silent and hot, herself alone, for almost everyone was across the river, harvesting. One by one Aurora herded or hauled the sheep indoors and upstairs.

At dusk Aurora sat on the stairs outside Sobran's room, now and then taking a sip from a bottle of port wine. The stairs were foul with sheep droppings. Aurora had cleared a place with her boots, but the stairwell stank.

The room above was silent: flies arrives periodically, then fell. Aurora heard them come, then freeze in action, heard their stumbling buzzing against the floor, then further silence. The freshest sheep were still breathing. The first lay deflated, dead, tongues like ramps put down from their mouths to let something disembark. They had died comatose, without a struggle. The animals didn't seem afraid, and Aurora could smell snow – over the sheep shit, and wild onion stench of the animals' ketotic breath – more powerful than a range of mountains, a scent thick and narcotic, like a whole world of ice.

Sobran was conscious, unchanged, and Aurora had begun to think that the angel – that pulseless, warm corpse – was somehow making an exception of his friend while his body plundered the life of every other living thing near him.

As the light turned from bronze to blue Aurora heard dogs begin to bark. From their kennels Vully's hounds gave cry, several house dogs joining in, and the sheepdogs, all together. They ceased at once also, a moment later, as if clubbed down into whining quiet. Aurora heard the wind. A tide of insect bodies rippled across the floor, then the shit and snow smells crested like a flood breaking a levee, and came out of the door and down the stairs at her, pushed by a powerful aromatic – carnations, or cinnamon apples, something domestic, but with the force of a glacier behind its sweetness. A sensation came with the scent, as though someone were blowing lightly in both Aurora's ears. She dropped the bottle, which rolled intact to the foot of the stairs. She got up, dizzy, and slowly climbed, the ringing in her ears louder now, like a great steel hoop rolling on its edge.

Aurora saw the wings when she looked into the room. She thought, for a fraction of a second, that the angel was up, and in the air. The wings were furled, black shot with red, bronze shot with blue, iridescent white, six wings with one body between them, massive, half-armoured, and the armour gleaming with uncut stones in green and iron-black. Aurora saw white flawless skin, several thick ropes of black plaited hair. Her eyes stung, she fell to her knees and put her face against the floor.

Sobran felt himself separated from Xas. Hands sorted his fingers from his angel's, prised them apart, rolled him, then lifted him up into the air. He was dropped, then steadied and pushed away by sandalwood-scented wings. He looked up into a face, met a gaze, equitable, grave, terrible. It was like finding himself in the path of a meteor. He staggered, fell, scrambled back and huddled with Aurora.

As soon as the strange angel spoke, the noise in their heads stopped. He had seen the sheep and goats. He said, 'Someone here has been using the intelligence that God didn't give them.' He spoke in the Parisian of Aurora's peers, as if knowing to whom he should attribute this 'intelligence'. He looked at Aurora and then said, 'I need a selection of the newly sharpened knives – fruit knives with thin blades, the heavy knives used to joint fowl, a cleaver. I need fresh linen, bandages, needles, silk thread.' When she didn't move he said, 'Are you thinking of asking a question?'

Aurora got up and went to do as she was told.

The archangel – Sobran knew who it was – turned back to the bed and stripped the sheet from Xas, so that it flew out and settled neatly over four stuporous sheep. Lucifer rolled Xas on to his side to inspect the wound. Sobran stole a look at the face, saw calculation, squeezed his eyes shut, waited a moment, then looked again. Xas was face down, his wings spread so they arched off either side of the bed. Lucifer had walked to the double doors, there leaned to shake salt – Sobran supposed – out of his hair. He said something in the language Xas had once used to speak endearingly to Sobran's dog, Josie, a language of supple, complex syllabics. He spoke quietly but with great passssion. There was a multiple tiny ticking and every parched leaf on the tree tops by the double doors detached itself and fell in unison. Lucifer stopped speaking, was completely still for a moment, then stepped back, closed the doors, shot the bolt and came back into the room, the floor quivering under his tread. Sobran saw the candles and lamps ignite as the archangel approached the bed, and fire erupt in the cold coals of the fireplace.

Sobran felt that he was experiencing each instant twice – like the touch of a snowflake, first a dry, soft contact, then as the flake melts against skin a second strike of cold.

Lucifer came right up to Sobran and crouched, bent his head, face still well above Sobran's. He was very tall, nearly eight foot, but not attenuated and big-hipped as giants usually are. He was immense and perfect. His wings spread out around him on the floor, perfumed and opulent. Sobran saw the long scars on the archangel's chest, under ropes of pearl in every shade from white to blue-black. Lucifer took Sobran's face between his hands and compelled the man to meet his eyes.

He said, 'I will cut off his wings and you can keep him. He'll always have to wear a shirt – but you can keep him.' He spoke in the dialect of the Chalonnaise, his diction as crude as Sobran's grandfather the boatman's had been. He released Sobran and got up.

The man found that, although he could think, he couldn't pray. He heard the door, then saw Aurora come in with a sewing kit and knives bundled in cloth like a babe-in-arms. She went straight to the archangel and put both parcel and kit into his hands. He placed them on the foot of the bed, reached back to lift the ropes of pearl over his head, looked about for somewhere to put them – and strung them over the drooping head of the last conscious sheep.

Lucifer set to work, turned one of Xas's wings this way and that, studying its physiology, exploring the downy hollow where the wing joined a saddle of wing muscle across the angel's spine. He felt with his fingers and considered. He took a knife in hand, shrugged back the plait that slithered across his shoulder, then flattened the arching joints of his own top wings down so that they didn't obscure the light.

'No!' Sobran said. He wasn't able to find his feet so shambled across the room ape-fashion on feet and knuckles. He seized the wrist of the hand that held the knife (one of the fine fruit knives, Aurora saw, a knife with a short curved blade).

'Any display of defiance of authority will find favour with me,' the archangel said, 'but you haven't picked a good moment.'

Sobran squeezed his eyes shut, averted his face, but held on.

'I'm sure you won't love him any less,' the archangel went on in a sweet blithe tone, 'if there's a little less of him.' Then he said, in a voice that had hooks, 'I want you to help me, Jodeau. Help me hold his wing.'

Sobran didn't respond.

Lucifer flicked him off, abrupt, brutal, and Aurora saw for an instant what she thought were real feelings – a species of envy or unhappiness no more profound than human envy or unhappiness, but sharper, concentrated.

The archangel made a cut, slid the knife in under skin, leaving skin spare to seal a great wound where wing joined the body.

Aurora and Sobran crouched, near each other, but not touching. Sobran wept, his arms wrapped around his head. Aurora watched. She saw cuts through flesh so bloodless it only oozed; she saw the knives changed, but not change hands; a joint boned, blood paint the surgeon's beautiful arms. Lucifer straightened, raised a wing, one end ragged meat, and pressed his face into its feathers, stood holding it against his side, where it looked like a slight woman limply inclined against a strong man. Then he dropped it and followed it with his eyes to see it too had draped the one upright and several prone sheep. He stiffened, then stooped, pulled the wing aside and began to gather goats and sheep, the back legs of several in each hand. He held his arms out from his sides and the animals dangled in bunches, one sheep kicking faintly. The archangel went to the double doors, unbolted them and tossed the dead animals out. He wiped his hands on his own cheeks. He was speaking again, low, maddened, indecipherable.

When he came back he began, with a steady hand, on the second wing. Aurora could now see white in his eyes, which had seemed all iris. As he finished with the small knife, and went to put it down, he seemed to think again, and instead thrust it into the rounded muscle of his own shoulder, as though it was handier there. Blood, red and faintly luminescent, trickled down his arm.

He freed Xas's other wing, dropped it, surveyed his work, and began to trim the surplus of downy skin so that it could be closed in two neat seams over each wound. From the sewing kit he selected a needle and yellow silk thread, broke the thread across his teeth, as a seamstress might, and threaded a needle. He began to match cut muscle to muscle and reattach them, pinching slippery elastic ends of tendons together, then stitching.

'More candles,' he said after a time. 'Even I can't work well in this light.'

Aurora went to find more candles. She was weak and unsteady, her clothes as wet with sweat as had been that cloth with which the surgeon had covered her own face. It was raining beyond the coach house door; there was moisture dark on the flagstone floor and the ground sparkled. She found some candles in the coach house and didn't need to go out.

Lucifer had three needles in his arm alongside the knife, none sharp enough now. He let Aurora light the candles, looked into her eyes as if searching her thoughts, as if he had to look to know – just like everyone else. His eyes were black, very wide spaced, as patient as the eyes of an ox, and as cold as the river.

He made his first seam along the line of the excision. Then, as he saw what shape it took, he laughed once and bitterly – for each excised wing left a scar that curved six inches below and parallel to the top of Xas's shoulder, then straight down beside his spine, then curved again shallowly, under his shoulder blade towards his side. A capital J on the one side and, on the other, a mirror image of a capital J.

The last thread cut, knife and needles pulled from his shoulder, Lucifer gathered Xas in his arms and lay down with him, his bloody arms crossed behind Xas's head and wings encasing them both so that together they were a great chrysalis.

Hours passed. Aurora fell asleep.

Lucifer got up after dawn, opened the other leaf of the double doors, and came back to look at Xas in the morning light. He bent his fair, blood-mottled face down to Xas's and kissed him once, beside his mouth, as though deflected at the last moment by some prohibition. He went to the windows, thought of flight, but looked down and jumped instead.

Aurora went to see what he was doing, found him relieving the dead sheep of his strings of pearls. Apparently an archangel could be as forgetful as any human in the thick of things. He looked up at her, in the daylight as colourful as the dusky, jewelled tropical moths in her husband's butterfly collection. Selecting one strand of pearls he tossed them up to her. She caught them – and he smiled at her, sad and charming and reprehensible, then took off. The wind his wings made knocked her over.

***

1836 Cep *(vine stock)*

'This time he breaks his promise,' Sobran said.

It was dawn and the distances were back with a vengeance, no heat pulling the air into transparent gathers. It was clear to all points of the compass; the east an open furnace, the west blue air.

Aurora nestled under Sobran's arm, held one of his hands with both hers, his little finger closed in one fist, thumb in the other.

'He won't come back. Once he breaks his promise there'll be no promise.'

Aurora asked Sobran to recall how they had feared Xas would never move again. 'He had the patience to stay backed into that corner for a century.'

They were quiet, remembering.

Xas had said he'd been 'out of time'. When he came back into time

– came to – he'd tried to fly, had lunged at the open windows as a trapped bird might, awkward, powerful, unbalanced. Then he caught himself – came into knowledge as some come into money and it wrecks their lives. He'd backed into a corner, hiding his back – the sutures and downy skin – not his uncovered genitals.

Half a week after Xas woke, the sheep and goats were bloated and stinking. Xas still hadn't moved, spoken or let Sobran near him. Aurora put on a headscarf and went to ask the angel to help her bury the dead animals. 'I don't want to call on Antoine or Baptiste,' she had said. 'Or involve my servants. After all, you're responsible for the deaths of these creatures. You know that, don't you? I am not merely in an awkward position – my servants will think Sobran and I mad, or monstrous, if they see these corpses. If they haven't already seen them.' She said, 'Help me now then go back to whatever it is you're doing.'

The angel looked at her. 'I'm not doing anything.'

'Are you in pain?'

'Yes. It's strange. The pain – strange to me.'

Aurora didn't know what to expect from him so wasn't inhibited by her expectations. She just kept on asking for what she wanted. 'Sobran can't help me. He's ill – as am I.' She pulled the scarf from her hair and watched the strands settle gently on and around the angel's feet. Her hair had come out in horsetails in her comb. To Aurora, Xas seemed whole. She looked at his feet, hands, hair – could see nothing missing. The wings were wrapped and hidden under the bed. She and Sobran had done that before Xas woke.

'I've been out of time,' the angel said. 'Tell me what happened.'

Aurora had him put on one of Sobran's nightshirts – and clogs, so he could stand on the edge of the spade. When it was full dark they went out. She watched him learn to walk. He learned very quickly, like a foal, as though winglessness was a contingency for which his nature had provided. He was clumsy to the foot of the stairs. Then awkward. And by the time they'd fetched spades and had begun to dig beside the piled animals, Aurora saw how deft he'd become – still an angel in every competent particle of his maimed body. But she could see it took all the angel's self-discipline not to turn and turn, looking for causes, the slight, horrible pressure of the cloth against his back. In the end she had to stop digging and just watch him

work. She sat by the side of the pit and told him what had happened
– what she thought had happened.

Xas didn't sweat, didn't tire, never used his weight, never stood
on the edge of the spade. He didn't look at her but once said, in
warning, 'Opinion,' when she offered her interpretation of one of
Lucifer's actions before describing the action. He didn't want
interpretations, only evidence.

She thought he had been in despair. Then she thought him cold
and methodical.

When the corpses were in the pit he paused, looked down at them.
'Where are the wings?' he asked. 'Perhaps I should bury the wings.'
He was ghostly in the grubby nightshirt and she couldn't see his
face.

She corrected him. '*Your* wings.'

'My wings.'

Aurora looked at the jumble of bodies, bloated, mottled bellies
from which the hair was beginning to moult – balding like worn
velvet – a dozen stiff legs, a pouting vulva. 'You can't put them in
there,' she said.

Xas was quiet, then made a sudden impatient movement of legs
and shoulders, a gesture that didn't make sense without wings. 'Are
they relics or rubbish?'

'My breast wasn't rubbish.'

'Did you keep your breast?'

Aurora began to cry. She pressed her hands to her face and
swayed above the stink.

The angel came around the pit. He apologised.

Aurora said, 'I want you at least to speak to Sobran when he
recovers. I have to help *him*.'

'Sobran wants to touch me. I don't want to be touched.'

'He wants to comfort you.'

Xas didn't say anything further, but began to fill in the pit.
Aurora dried her tears.

When Xas had finished she took him to the pump, cranked the
handle for him while he stripped off and washed.

'Those sutures need removing, will you at least let me do that
much?'

They went upstairs. He sat hugging his knees, a branch of candles behind him. She knelt and snipped, then pulled each cut stitch free. 'They're completely regular, these stitches, the same distance apart and same size.'

'Complete symmetry is an insult to God. Lucifer does everything as perfectly as he can.'

'What he did to you was an insult to God.'

'God let him. Or colluded. I don't care to know. I'm putting them both behind me.'

Her hands were shaking. There was one stitch left. The scissors caught his skin but couldn't cut it. Or *she* couldn't. 'I've finished,' she told him.

He sighed and unfolded. For a moment she imagined he'd lie back in her lap, but he got up and went to the wall of the room, further from the window, put his back to it and sat down.

'You'll need clothes,' she said, 'and shoes.'

'Do you remember his first shoes?' Aurora asked Sobran.

What Sobran remembered was that Xas apparently had been afraid of space. He tolerated daylight, but didn't like to be out in it. It gave him no satisfaction to shade his eyes and measure distances. He stayed indoors, still by the wall, wouldn't look at Sobran's face, but at his feet if the man came within two metres. It was as though he'd drawn a line and let the man know by a look that his feet had breached its bounds.

'I have no prospects,' he said to Sobran and Aurora. He showed them what he meant by making blinkers with his hands to hide the view through the open windows.

He wasn't afraid of space, but of distance. Everywhere was too far. He couldn't tire – but why cross the room, descend the stairs, cross the courtyard, why walk out under the trees? Covering the ground seemed foreign and futile. He *was* above all that.

'I know you feel vulnerable and unsightly,' Sobran said, on just one occasion when he tried to coax the angel back to life. 'But you can't spend your life with your back to the wall.'

'I could find another wall,' Xas said, angry – which was good.

'Here are your shoes,' Sobran said, and pushed the pair forward with one of his feet. 'They are made to a tracing, but are very fine.

The best. Aurora has a shirt, breeches, a jacket and stock. Come out and look at the vines. The workers are burning the prunings now.'

'Come out at night and look at the river,' Aurora said. 'You could swim. You would be weightless in the water.'

'She has more imagination than you,' Xas said to Sobran, not looking at him.

'Here are your shoes, Xas, your first shoes.'

The angel hated not to feel cocooned. At first he'd sit with his arms wrapped around himself, but later took to winding himself in a blanket. Autumn turned to winter, but he wasn't cold. Sobran spent his Sundays at Clos Jodeau – then Mondays, Tuesdays, Wednesdays too, till work called him back to Vully. The first time he saw Xas he had mistaken the angel for a statue; now Xas had turned himself into a statue, who did not need to eat or drink or eliminate waste, and was indifferent to time passing.

Aurora visited him every day.

Some days she noticed that his clothes seemed to have been immersed and then to have dried on his body. Then, on a Sunday night, Aurora went to the soldiers' gallery and found the doors hooked back and snow blowing in. She wrapped herself in the angel's abandoned blanket – wool freshened, it seemed, by contact with his body. She waited by the window. When a couple of hours had passed she saw him come around the side of the coach house in his shirts, trousers and shoes. She moved back against the wall but he saw her as soon as he looked up, his gaze penetrating the shadow where she hid. They looked at each other. His hair blew around his face like black smoke mixed with the white vapour of his breath – breath, warm like that of any other mammal. He crouched and sprang up twenty feet, caught the doorsill by his hands and came inside.

Aurora stood and surrendered his blanket. She could see that his clothes were wet through, but he didn't shed them, just wrapped himself, not for the warmth but the sensation of constriction.

'Sobran thinks you never move,' Aurora accused.

'I don't care what he thinks.'

Aurora knelt near him. He was like a wild animal, his sulking, his leap, and his resentful wariness. 'I know that you must feel unclean now, and not want him to touch you. I know that you and he were lovers – though Sobran and I haven't spoken about it. Have you noticed that he's never here now?'

Xas didn't answer her, so she changed tack. 'When I had recovered from my surgery, when I could be touched – ' she touched her chest, not now padded by her prosthetic corset, for she had come out in her nightdress and an old greatcoat of Paul's – 'the Baron wanted to resume relations. He was at pains to reassure me that I was still beautiful to him. But I didn't want him to find me beautiful – it was like an insult to my loss.'

'You think I imagine I'm ugly?'

Aurora opened her mouth to say that wasn't what she'd said – but then thought that she didn't need to be understood, she just wanted him to talk to her. His imperfect comprehension made her feel protective – for inside his smooth cocoon of grief this ancient, intelligent being *wasn't thinking right.*

Xas said, 'I don't want him to touch me. The touching was a mistake. I should have stayed chaste. I shouldn't have gone to Heaven unchaste.'

Aurora nodded. 'Perhaps. God didn't save you – true – except that you're alive. But it was Lucifer who cut off your wings and I don't think that had anything to do with rules about chastity. I told you what he said to Sobran: "You can keep him. He'll always have to wear a shirt, but you can keep him."'

Xas's hands crept up from under the edge of the blanket and covered his own ears. 'Yes,' he said.

'What do you think?'

'Yes. I see.'

'Who wounded you?'

'Michael. He warned me before about trespassing.'

'I think Lucifer spoke to God about you – when he was standing here, where we are sitting. God answered him by all the leaves falling from these trees. Or, at least, I think that's what happened. That's what Sobran told me. Lucifer shut those doors and came back angry and cut off your wings. Do you think he acted on instructions, or to spite God?'

Xas shook his head.

'Don't you have any idea?'

'I was sure they both loved me.'

Aurora, fishing for information, ventured an opinion. Since the God who made the world had a plan, Xas's punishment must be part of that plan.

Xas said, 'God didn't make the world.'

'I've tried to make my peace with my idea of God – but I'm always using my imagination,' Aurora said. 'Besides, I prefer facts to faith, I always have. When I was an atheist I didn't have faith in God's non-existence – I knew it, it was a fact to me. But then I suppose I was trying to imagine my *creator*, not some almighty plagiarist, someone who puts His name on another's work, or nature's work. Lucifer scared me half to death with his six wings and terrible gaze, but there were several times when he looked into my eyes as though I was real and we were somehow equal – equally miserably *there* – and he knew I was making some sense of his actions.'

Aurora listened to Sobran use Lucifer's words. 'I didn't let him know I wanted to keep him. He won't come back.'

The sun was up. The night of the 27th of June had passed, and the darkness of the morning of the 28th. Aurora saw Baptiste and Martin Jodeau come out of the house with their guns. The young men were dressed in the leather hunting coats they wore to keep gunpowder from their clothes. They began up the slope. A maid opened the curtains in one upstairs bedroom.

'Did I tell you what I did to him?'

'You told me you threw him out the window.'

'Worse than that.'

Sobran had come in one evening after a day balancing the books. He was tired of the winter, of his work, and his fingertips were dry from paperwork and shrunk against the bone. He was tired of his anger, more angry now than ever, and out of patience. There was Xas, bundled up by the open double doors. The room was cold, the one other window filmed with frost on the inside. Sobran strode over to the angel, took the blanket by one corner and pulled so that the angel sprawled and lay for a moment looking faintly surprised and very grubby, his clothes muddy, and hair matted. Sobran began to shout at him, then to kick, then fell on his knees to work with his fists. Xas presented no guard, his face pushed and turned by each blow but showing no sign of damage. Then the man picked the angel up by his armpits and pushed him out the window. He saw Xas fall, rolled up, as light as a spider, then uncoil in the snow and raise his face. Sobran slammed the doors, bolted them and leaned, saying perhaps, 'Go away. Get out of my sight.'

'I'll never see him again.' Sobran mourned. Aurora cradled his head against her shoulder. She looked up as Martin and Baptiste came into sight again out of the switchback of the slope. They stopped and stared. She heard Baptiste say to his younger brother, 'Leave this to me. You go on.'

Baptiste stood above them, then, leaning his gun against the boundary marker, he crouched beside them. 'Baroness. Father. It's *that* anniversary.' He looked unconvinced. Aurora knew what he was thinking – how could his father confine guilt or grief so neatly to one night a year. 'He told me about the Russian woman and Austrian infantryman,' Baptiste said to Aurora. 'But, Baroness, I must say I'm surprised to find you here.'

'Why? Considering all the conjecture about me and your father over the last ten years.'

Baptiste said, spiteful, 'But you were on your pilgrimage to Compostela when I discovered a woman in Father's room.'

Sobran laughed at that, told Aurora, who had turned to him in indignation, that he'd told Baptiste, through a closed door, that he had a guest, Baptiste hadn't 'discovered' anything.

'Oh,' Aurora said.

'I'm sick of this,' Baptiste said. 'I worry about you, Father. You're not always strong.'

Sobran got up, shook himself, set his clothes in order then gave Aurora his hand and helped her to her feet. 'It's all over now,' he told his son, and patted his shoulder in a reassuring way. When he offered Aurora his arm she waved him on down the hill and said, 'Baptiste will escort me to my horse – I've not kept the coachman out this year.'

Baptiste blushed. She held out her arm and he was obliged to take it. He left his gun and they started down the slope to the road.

'Careful,' Sobran called after them.

'He means I should keep my mouth shut,' she said.

'Baroness –'

'Shhh. You want to know everything but are appalled by what you already know. How Antoine Laudel and I hid here once to spy on your father. How I walked into the river. You know all that.' She sighed. 'I'm not going to tell you everything. Your father has his secrets.'

'Was it a man in his room?'

Aurora paused a beat, then said, 'No.'

'Who is she then? And what can it have to do with the dead sheep and goats?'

'Nothing. The animals died as the result of an experiment.'

Baptiste was outraged. 'What kind of experiment?'

'A scientific experiment.'

'Splendid! You and father conduct scientific experiments. He has a mistress who no one has ever seen. He does penance one night each year for a twenty-five-year-old murder – he says. Now you've joined him.'

'It was *my* experiment, Baptiste. Your father was in Autun. When he returned he helped me clean up.'

Poor Baptiste – he must think every woman a creature of sweet surfaces covering rank lunacy. He let go of her arm. 'I won't stay here and run his vineyard. I won't watch this – Paul and Agnès will walk up to the altar on a path of flowers strewn over who-knows-what pits of sin and madness. You are all mad.'

'Well then, you should certainly go somewhere else to find a wife,' Aurora said, in a tone of great reasonableness – mischief on her part, but she couldn't help herself, he was so like his father, haughty, excitable, distressed. 'Come now, dear, bring me to my horse.'

After a minute in which all he did was glare and grind his teeth Baptiste took her arm again. He opened the iron gate in the wall of the *clos* and they went through.

'Your father has a broken heart, Baptiste.'

He let out a loud nasal breath but refrained from comment.

'And if he's right that it's all over, then there isn't any need for you to know more. You have to consider that, although you've been ready to share his trouble for years now, he's still in the habit of thinking of you as a child – who mustn't be troubled.'

'So it was never you – pardon, Baroness, but it made sense.'

'It does make sense. I love your father. But I can't compete.'

They reached her horse, tethered to an apple tree that grew against the wall.

'What about now? If "it's all over"?' Baptiste asked, and to avoid her eyes he stooped and made a stirrup with his hands.

'I'm a married woman.'

Baptiste boosted her into the saddle. 'I forget that.'

'So do I.' She smiled at him. 'Dear – I'll look after your father. You should go and seek your fortune. Shall I send you to Paris on business? Shall I foist you on Paul? Would you like that?'

Baptiste nodded, the colour gone from his face. It wasn't any one thing she had said, he was just worn out by the conversation. He was forward – just like his father – but hadn't Sobran's nerve.

'He won't – hang himself, will he?' Baptiste asked.

'Oh, I can see that – Sobran charging wrathfully into Hell. No, he wouldn't take his own life. I think despair has had its moment with both of us.'

The horse was dancing and Baptiste moved back. 'That animal isn't sufficiently gentle for you. Baroness.' He was gallantly disapproving – trying for some reason to get the upper hand.

'Child – I am not an old woman. I'm the same age as the century and my father was a cavalryman.' With that she rode off.

⌒

1837 Casse *(an unhealthy haze or deposit in wines)*

A year of blankness. Nature was an engine, the vines, unattended by the vintner, grew flowers, fruit, thicker shade. Sobran was tired all day, every day, and irritably wakeful all night. When Paul asked to press the grapes of the south slope, Sobran was lockjawed and unresponsive. Letters went unanswered – Baptiste's from Paris, Aurora's and Agnès's from Dijon.

On their anniversary Sobran took out what he had hidden, the wings, still fresh and supple. From them Sobran made, on his bed, a bier or boat in which he lay and – somehow – caught the tide of grief and sailed away from his blankness. Day by day, week by week, the pains and itches, taste and warmth of the world came back at his eyes, into his ears, and against his skin.

⌒⌒⌒

1838 Buvable *(drinkable)*

On the morning of the 27th of June Paul de Valday married Agnès Jodeau in the Chapel at Vully. The marriage was conducted with great, high ceremony. Afterwards the bride removed her veil – Brussels lace, fifteen feet in length and fifty years of age – and went out to the celebrations, the trestle tables on the terrace in front of the château. All the well-to-do peasant families of the *pays* were at the feast – the Laudels, Lizets, Wateaus, Pelets, Garveys, Tipoux. Among these were some who had done a little better, climbed a little higher, like Sabine and her vintner from Chalon-sur-Saône. Here were Paul's aristocratic godparents, the old Comte's surviving cousins, Paul's Parisian friends, some of Agnès's schoolmates from the convent at Autun. The bride was a bit too thin for her dress – nerves, of course. The groom seemed rather limp, but pleased. The bride's mother was dazzling with happiness.

The bride's father kept close to the groom's mother. All the locals were past remarking on this – everyone knew that the Baroness and Sobran Jodeau were the best of friends. And the Baron, Henri Lettelier, seemed to accept this figure on his wife's far flank as though it was quite natural – a gracious man, all agreed. And, after all, at the high table the usual protocol sorted them all out, sat bride by groom, bride's father by bride's mother, groom's mother by her husband.

Baptiste leaned around Céleste's back and whispered in his father's ear that he, too, was married – he'd beaten Paul to it – and no, he thought parental consent an outdated imposition. Anne was sixteen, a Parisian milliner's apprentice. Anne had her older sister's consent. He would bring Anne home before winter came.

Sobran inclined the other way, towards his daughter. Did Agnès know that Baptiste had wed?

Her eyes went wide. 'No!'

Beyond her, 'Yes,' said Paul.

'What's this? What's this?' Aurora, beside Paul.

'What? What?' Paul mimicked, affectionately. 'Before long she'll be jabbing me with an ear-trumpet. Mother, there was no *good* time Baptiste could pick to tell his father he's married.'

'You didn't tell *me*,' Agnès said. She couldn't believe it.

Paul put his mouth to her ear. 'I don't approve. But I was waiting for him to introduce the girl to you so that you could form your own opinion.'

Agnès nodded. They gazed at each other, very pleased with their understanding.

'I look forward to making Anne's acquaintance,' Sobran said to Baptiste. Then, 'Please inform your mother of your good news.'

After dark Baptiste found his father nursing a glass of brandy and looking from the terrace down the avenue that approached the house, towards the road and along it to the first four folded slopes, one of which was Jodeau.

'Don't go up there,' Baptiste said.

'What?'

'I've come to tell you about Anne.'

Sobran shrugged. 'A fine girl, but you were careless. I suppose that's what you have to say.'

'No. It wasn't like that. She laughs at me and I like her.'

'That sounds good.'

A large branch tumbled out of one of the bonfires and the wedding guests shrieked.

'Have Paul and Agnès gone?'

'Yes. But they're all still toasting at the high table. I think Baron Lettelier and Uncle Antoine are in competition.'

'Antoine always thinks he can hold his drink.'

Baptiste smiled. He put out a hand when his father shifted his weight and stumbled, but didn't touch Sobran – who, on the other hand, usually held his drink well, just slowed down.

'One more toast,' Sobran said, very deliberate, and raised his glass to that distant slope. 'Here's to thirty years.'

After the harvest Jodeau South was pressed separately for the first year since Martin Jodeau died. The grapes were crushed by the great stone presses in the winery at Château Vully, fermented in the vats of the cuverie for six days, Sobran's older two sons climbing in twice a day to break up the 'hat' of pips and skins that formed on the surface of the fermenting juice. After six days the 'free-run wine' was put up in the two new barrels named by the vintner and his employer Angel One and Two, names that, within one season, where contracted by other interested parties – Comte Paul, the Baron, the cellarmen – simply to 'the angels'.

1839 Délayer *(to dilute)*

Paul and Agnès produced a girl, born in Paris and christened Iris. Baptiste's wife Anne gave birth to a boy, christened Paul.

Aurora and Sobran became lovers almost by accident, or, at least, she hadn't foreseen anything that night, the night they sat up late – as they often did, regardless of whether Henri was in Paris or Vully. Aurora and Sobran were having an argument about the newly published *Idées napoléoniennes*. Aurora's calves were aching, so she slipped off her shoes and, to interrupt a particularly pompous speech her friend was making, put her stockinged feet in his lap. He stopped talking and stared at her. She grinned. Then they were in each other's arms. Following this were weeks of discovery, warmth, laughter, natural intimacy, confidences like trapdoors giving way, turn by turn, on hitherto hidden places in their lives, conversations where they lay face to face in his bed in the soldiers' gallery, her hand under his cheek.

⁕

1840 Pique *(a pickled, vinegary wine)*

The days were gone when people would hint, or accuse, or ask them privately to please be careful, or good to each other. They were friends; he had the freedom of her house – though he was never to be seen upstairs in the château. He never came to her. When she came to him, Aurora walked in her night attire through the library doors, down from the terrace and around through the shrubbery, the walled orchard, the kitchen garden, to the courtyard by the coach house. There were sixty servants in her household and she was seen, but her servants thought Aurora and Sobran both deserved better than the spouses they'd chosen – they deserved each other, and were both grandparents, so why trouble to tell. Sure, they both had their demonic side, she with all her books, even the banned *Corinne*, he with his night walks, strange turns, and their experimenting, the mass grave of sheep and goats in the deep sand by the coach house. And the elaborate secretive orders the cooper had received for the construction of 'the angels' – in which, it was rumoured, something had been sealed. Yet the Baroness and M. Jodeau were fine people, in whose service one could prosper. Let them be.

Besides, inevitably, one widow whispered to another at Easter as Céleste Jodeau went by with her younger children and their nurse – it was on one of those rare occasions when the Jodeau and Laudel women at least deigned to come to church – 'How like her father's dead brother that child is,' pointing a crooked finger at little Véronique. Then the old women looked at each other, eyes wide, having innocently surprised a scandal and an explanation for Léon Jodeau's suicide. Soon the whole village of Aluze had something new to say behind Sobran's back. *Oh, and be careful of the mad woman herself, don't let her hear you, or Sophie Laudel, or the Comte and his dear little wife, or that fiery eldest Jodeau son . . .*

Jules Lizet heard it, though, in the asylum at Autun, and wept in his cell, because Léon Jodeau had loved Aline, and only Aline, whose innocent head he had not broken, he had not, he, Jules, had not . . .

⁓

1841 **Grume** *(a single grape berry)*

Iris de Valday, the little countess, thrived, and had her portrait painted by a great Parisian artist, fat-armed in a foam of lace on her nineteen-year-old mother's knee.

Baptiste and Anne's son was never well. He was large, but had rough, dark hairy skin and a terrible thirst, never seemed to keep enough water in his body. He died at eighteen months. The only words he ever learned were what he craved: 'water', 'salt'.

The priest followed Sobran away from the grave. 'Monsieur Jodeau?' he said, hesitated, then took Sobran's arm. 'My son.'

Sobran said, 'Christophe Lizet has just reminded me that it is only the fifth Jodeau family funeral in over thirty years. He's keeping a tally, working up some figures on our luck.' Sobran then laid the names between himself and the priest in order to keep the conversation polite. 'Mother and Father, Nicolette, Léon, little Paul.'

'God rest, and have mercy on, their souls. Will you come back to the Church now?'

'Are you asking me whether I can forgive you for forbidding my brother the churchyard?' Sobran loomed over the priest, but smiled. The priest scowled. Jodeau had just buried a grandchild but was standing there in his power, proud man, an affront to the place and the occasion. The priest bit his lip so that his face became all chin, a whiskery shovel.

'The Church is no place for me,' Sobran said.

'Are you magnifying your sins against God's mercy? No sin is greater than God's mercy.'

'I don't know what God intends, or what qualifies Him to forgive me –' Sobran said, which puzzled the priest – 'so won't vote for Him by attending church.' He watched the priest cross himself. 'I'm sorry, Father, penance and prayer are of no use to me. But please do offer every comfort you can to my son and his wife. Can I ask you for that? I'm not bargaining – but if you can bring them any comfort I'll send my family back to your church.'

'Do you think your sons will go where you won't?'

Sobran was surprised. 'My sons will do what I tell them.'

The letter read:

I couldn't tell you where I've been. I don't mean that I could tell you but won't – I mean I don't know. When people spoke to me I replied in whatever language they used. I had to invent things – like names. That was difficult for me and sometimes I said I was you. My feet became hard. I went around pretending there was nothing behind me – it was that conceit, or not move at all. After I was overpowered once I decided it was better to pretend to be someone and acknowledge the world at my back. It's a shame about lepers, that there are no lepers now wandering around the landscape with their bells and wooden clappers and people leaping out of their paths. That would have suited me. I stole a Franciscan habit and played the begging friar but people kept giving me food and money I didn't need. It was easier to accept the invitations of wealthy men and women and have a little conversation and contact – with the rest of it. What they wanted. And I came to like warmth and being clean.

This is my first letter. The first time I've put pen to paper. I've only ever read, and I thought writing would be like reading. I find it hard to believe I can alter a piece of paper in this way – like any other person.

'Other people' – I've learned that lie. I use the phrase because it is indispensable. We can't live without 'other people'. 'Other people', I say to distinguish myself when explaining myself. When *lying*. Before, when I was honest, I seemed simple, an idiot and madman. Typical conversations used to go like this: A carriage stops where I'm walking along the roadside barefoot in the snow and someone says, through a scarf or veil, 'You must be famished.'

And I agree that I must be – too heartily, because I want company but am not at all cold. Now I say, 'God bless you,' and knock my teeth together.

I borrowed his pen. He writes poetry. I think he thinks he's another Lord Byron. He's on the move all the time but with nothing whatsoever to run away from. He came back and was surprised to find me still in one of his rented villas, in dim rooms filled with shrouded furniture where the light comes through waterfalls of rain on the windows. He says he almost expects me to build a big web in the corner of the ballroom. Mirrors. I'm there now. He calls me his 'fey'. I keep my back to the bottom sheet so that, without having laid eyes on the J's and feathers, he doesn't know how right he is.

I know you'll mind this. I go through soap like nobody's business. That's his English expression and I like it. 'Who are you?' 'I am who I am' – which is to say 'That's none of your business.' I hope to learn that – how to repel by reflection. The scars on my back, the J and mirrored J, are Yahweh's reply to Moses's 'Who are you?' – the words of a God who will not explain himself, who won't be questioned, who wants to be obeyed, not understood, who blinds people with their own light, their own world's loveliness. I go through soap just thinking about soap – in my bath, rolling it between my hands, so smooth and pale and I keep hoping to be used up by handling as soap is.

I've learned too much about unhappiness. I have it now, a permanent condition, like deafness. When I go out and watch the creamy surf pouring into the cove I can't hear it – I'm not *here* to hear – or something is crushing the sense out of me all the time.

I love you, Sobran, but I'm not coming near you until I stop wanting to burn away this pain with pain.

1842 L'Épluchage *(the picking out of rotten and black grapes from the picked bunch)*

Sobran did not show the letter to Aurora. Nor the next:

I found work as a gardener, promised the Head to work all day and that I could tell a weed from a cultivar. He laughed but did employ me. We've been grafting plum to peach. He says, 'Who did you kill?' That finding me is like finding a stray thoroughbred in the orchard, I have all the skills, I'm *somebody's* gardener, he says. I invent a parent with whom I've quarrelled. That isn't difficult. He's offered to indenture me, and all the other undergardeners are bitterly jealous. 'Other undergardeners' – that's more applicable than 'other people', I am not a person but am an undergardener.

I won't stay here – before I got out of the last carriage in which I begged a ride I saw from its window a long ramp built on a bluff and, I think, some contraption intended for flight. I'll go back there. I'll have to walk or pay my way since I can't stand any more to play Venus to various Tannhäusers in frockcoats or farthingales. I must be stronger, because the dark ones who used to find me when I was first wandering leave me alone now. I don't know where they are. Maybe there are none in Germany. No one punishes me and I'm numb to all sensations without the sensation of pain.

Garmisch
5th March 1843

This Prussian count – he is forty-five – has lost one leg to cannon-fire and talks of having a surgeon take the other one off so that he can pilot his heavier-than-air machine. He says he's not after a substitute for a man's gait – he just needs to know if it can be done.

I'm working for him. I had no credentials of course and no one to make an introduction. I did take care to appear before him in something better than the shabby clothes I usually wander about in. 'Usually' – there's a strange word. I usually haul water through the salt to my distillery. I usually lie on a rooftop, shaded by the palace's bulk from the fires below, and read. I usually fly up where the air is thin and the horizon has a curve.

I got a new coat and shoes. I went and introduced myself, by another name. I told a truth – that I'd sat on a bench by the door of an inn in Bruges and watched a Scotsman sketch a glider. I told the Count that, if he wished, I could reproduce the Scots engineer's drawing. The Count had his own plan book fetched, and I drew. I said I saw his glider when I passed in a coach last year. 'Why didn't you come then?' the Count asked. I was about my father's business, I said, then that I had thought by the look of it that it wouldn't fly. 'They won't fly, young man,' the count said, 'they'll glide, these machines.'

I asked if I could assist him – for board and food alone and he took me in.

Early on I told him that I have no ideas, so he talks to me, theory and diagram – chalkdust sprinkling down from his messy calculations like the paint flaking from a painting of a divinity.

I like this man. Just now he saw me smiling at him and asked me what I was writing. I said a letter to a friend and he said he didn't know I had any friends, he thought I'd just fallen out of the sky.

There are two contenders for the honour of the flight. One is an eager and unimaginative boy of fifteen. 'You might break a bone,' the other fellow tells him and the boy looks as if he's never considered before that he has bones to break. He just can't see it. The other fellow is a starved whippet of a man, the Count's manservant, long ago infected by his master's obsession. *I* want to be the one. I show how a man can make himself weigh less. I walk on a soft swatch of river sand leaving the slightest marks. I talk about balancing between each foot, and carrying my weight over the whole sole, and how softly to set each foot down. The Count gets fed up listening to me and roars that we'll find out once and for all – he'll weigh me himself. He's as scientific as a bull when annoyed. He picks me up and his wooden leg is mired to a depth of nine inches. His eyes pop not from effort but surprise, and he drops me, declares that I'm as light as a feather and that I can fly the glider.

We sat in a draughty attic for three weeks watching the

pigeons come in to land. 'What is its tail doing?' I'd ask, or, 'Do you see how it isn't the wings that fly? It's the bird, the whole bird.' We made models and, eventually, a wing, one wing, because he wanted to glide, not to fly. A wing of five fine bent bamboo wands sewn into silk. The struts are braced by diagonal wires. The glider has a harness with a pulley system that will haul a man's body parallel to the wing after the launch so that he can use his legs like a rudder as birds do.

For years the Count has ruminated on the problem of what *materials*, then what *shapes*, offer the least resistance to air. Now he has directed his thoughts to how to make that resistance work for him, how the pressure of air lifts a wing. (Much easier to learn this by its sensation than from observation. I have had him watch birds and whispered to him, 'It looks as if there is more air under its wings. I don't mean the action of the wings — forget their action — think about their shape.' This prompted him to spend weeks in his laboratory, which began to look like a game pantry, with feathered bodies stinking of methanol heaped high on long benches. We dissected wings, made cross-sections of the wings of doves, swift, waterfowl. He finds me crying in the corridor and compliments me on my soft heart but warns me that nature favours brutes. Then, at last, he sees it, and says to me, 'There *is* more air under the bird's wings, because *the air is moving faster above than under its wings.*')

The test flight is in two days. He has me eating only honeycomb — every ounce counts, he says. And when I ask whether every count counts ounces he winces. And he says, 'Have a little more, you're light-headed.' 'Light all over,' I say, then, 'The light of the world.' (The thought of flight has melted me, I am less solid than liquid, then I'm going up and going invisible like steam.) The Count wants the boy to go, or that sleepy, thirsty, starved manservant of his. 'You're an educated man,' he says, 'and I haven't even begun to put you to work.' Then he pays me. I give the gold back — too heavy, I say, 'Carry it for me till after the flight.' Then I tell him that what he is saying is it's too great a risk, that he doesn't like to think of my educated brains dashed out on ineducable rocks. 'The boy and man want the pay they'll get, and the boy wants to please you,' I say. 'But I want to

be airborne. That's why you'll let me – you believe my desire will
help elevate me.'

He's full of peach brandy now, talking about seeing a man
running on some English downlands hanging on to some winged
contraption, kicking off and being borne along yards at a time.
And I want to tell him that, however fine flight was, the arrested
fall was most thrilling – to close your wings and go face down
into the haze over seas or hills or into a mountainous chasm
where you can judge the speed of a fall – a blur, then clarity, a full
stop in the air, wings open, sky abruptly overhead and gravity
grabbing at your body like a hungry flame reaching for fuel just
out of its reach.

But you know how I liked that, Sobran, I so often did it right
over your head.

Despair is gravity. What an appetite it has, hotter than hellfire.
'Here, let me have you,' it says.

1843 L'Émondage *(pruning dead twigs and suckers off the vine)*

June 1843

I hate the connective tissue in a story. I think of the time I've
spent silent or speaking secretively and it seems impossible to me
to describe even a short journey, for every step depends on other
earlier steps and my whys and wherefores are as infinitesimal as
atoms in the scent trails we leave in the air – negligible, not
evidence, but *there.*

I am obliged to write what happened before telling you where I
am. Yet I wish I could ignore the formalities and not say anything
about the glider.

About the glider. We had a good day for it and were all up at
dawn when the air was still. I'd persuaded the Count to launch
from the ramp on the escarpment where his family's former keep

stands and from which he'd launched earlier, unmanned machines. The crag looks out over several forested miles.

The assistants strapped me to the glider. I could see that, finally, the boy was glad it wasn't him going. He was pale and staring at me with blurry worshipful stupidity, as though I was doing this thing to save his life. The Count wrapped cords around my gloved hands, the cords that crossed the pulleys and would raise my legs once the glider was level in the air. He asked me why he felt that this was an act of faith on my part, that whatever faith he had in his machine was irrelevant – and he must have, for he wouldn't let me go if he hadn't. 'Do you think this glider will fly?' I asked him. 'I don't know. I think *you* will. I'm mesmerised by your conviction – you must be the one to fly the glider because without you the glider won't fly. That's what you've made me believe. How did you do that, make me think something so unscientific?' Then he took my arm. 'If you fly it's because the glider stays in the air.' He said he shouldn't let me do this – make my leap of faith. 'I didn't take your money,' I reminded him, 'I'm not your servant. I'm a scientist, like you. But lighter. That's the whole point – I'm the least substantial person here.'

The boy knelt at my feet and unbuttoned my boots, removed them, rolled the stockings off. I was ready. The assistants licked their fingers to test the wind, the Count held up his silk handkerchief. Then they wished me good luck and got out of the way. I could feel an updraught through the boards under my feet. I ran the few steps to the edge and leapt far to make sure I cleared the end of the ramp with the glider's tail. I wound the cords swiftly and smoothly to haul my legs up, then quickly moved my legs left to avoid too steep a bank, and felt the first shiver of a stall. The scars were writhing on my back because my brain wouldn't stop trying to adjust the angle of wings – phantom wings. The shiver stopped and I looked down on fir trees the way they *should* look, like a bed of nails. I could hear the shouting behind me on the crag, faint, exultant.

Something came over me then. The moment contracted into stillness. I think it was despair. When I tried to cut my own side and the offensive signatures with the knife I took from you – do you remember? This was the same. But whereas that was the stillness in the spindle behind a body moving through the air, or the smooth water at the stern of a ship with the wake banked up beside it, this stillness had been spun by the forces about it into a hardness, a solidity. I solidified. I knew I'd flown out there to fall. So I reached with one hand and pulled the slip knot that unfastened first one then the other foot. The glider banked and I let go.

I lay on the air.

Then I fell through the trees, breaking branches, and landed on rocks. A rock split. For a time I lay still and looked at the raw red of the broken branches above me. Then I picked up my wretched, indestructible body and walked away.

An hour later, from the crest of the next hill, I heard them searching for me. I could hear the Count calling your name – I'd used your name again – I could distinguish his voice from the others by the tears in his voice. I could see the glider, or a big piece of it, pierced by trees. I kept on walking.

Where am I now? With gypsies at the border near Strasbourg. When I arrived at their campfire in my torn clothes they let me sit down. They just stared at me. Then the oldest there took the pipe out of her mouth and said – in Romany, a language in which I am not very proficient – that I'd do better if only I'd cut my hair. 'Do better?' I asked. 'Pass better,' she said. She offered to cut it for me, she'd help direct the scissors, but I'd have to work them myself. We did that, cut it off at shoulder length, as neatly as we were able. The other women had put their children to bed under the wagons and had their backs to us, shawls over their heads. The men sat and watched and sweated. The old woman began to make a plait with the cut hair, then another – one each for the chief and his son, she said. To ward off evil, my hair was the very best thing, she explained. She promised to show me how to make up my face with rice flour, pale to hide my pallor, so I'd be able to play the carnivals at night – wire-walk perhaps, she was sure I could do that. 'And you can ride in the wagon, with the shutters closed all day, so long as you don't prey on my people.' Then she signalled to one of the men and he produced a sharpened stick which she showed to me. 'We all have to be careful,' she said. I told her that her stick couldn't hurt me – whatever was she thinking? And she poked it through a tear in my shirt and scratched at my skin – then, seeing no mark and very annoyed, put her gnarled old hands against my chest. She exclaimed, 'His heart is beating and his skin is warm!' And someone sniggered – I saw her authority waver for an instant – then she put her face into mine and demanded to know what I was if I wasn't what she thought I was. I said, 'I'm a man.' She laughed, 'If memory serves –' and they all laughed at that – 'no man is as fair as you are.' But she didn't pester me any more. I went with them, slept in her wagon, in her bed to keep her warm. She paints my face with rice flour every morning and evening, and dresses me in a big sleeved shirt, black velvet trousers and red velvet jacket, and I wire-walk or juggle, as the girls do (the men don't perform for money, it's beneath their dignity). The gypsies are going to Paris. The old woman says she'll leave me at the Funambules – that if I'm going to go around saying I'm a man I belong in the theatre.

Late morning, market day, Sobran took a cab to the street of the Funambules and strolled among the crowds. He stood before stages decorated with flags of cotton bunting, their cut edges starched so they wouldn't fray – makeshift, grimy decorations. The costumes were better, their removable collars washed every night of grease-paint, in the sunlight sewn spangles glittered like armour. Sobran watched the tumblers till they were still. Any who were lithe and of his height he peered at – falsely identified their fluent movements for half a minute at the most – but the feet always came down too hard and the stage would shake. There was one Pierrot, his limbs covered with white silk and face in a sad fugue. But no.

Sobran went into tents to look at novelties, freaks, or fair girls posed emblematically as Beauty or Truth or Beauteous Truth. He collected hand bills for all the shows. He went back to his peaceful room at Paul and Agnès's townhouse and lay on his bed with a wet cloth over his eyes. He slept a while, woke with the impression there was someone in the room – but it was only Iris's nurse tapping at the door because her charge insisted on seeing Grandpapa. Sobran sat in the big nursery at the top of the house and talked to Iris about all her dolls. Agnès arrived, then half an hour later Paul – all the adults filling the furniture by the nursery fire, Iris leaning between the knees of father or grandfather then against her mother's side.

In the morning Sobran and Agnès went to watch the couples and children at the skating rink glide about while they sat in an iron pavilion and fed Iris ice-cream.

Sobran went by himself to the afternoon matinées. He claimed to be walking to this or that famous church. And Agnès said to Paul, 'This interest in architecture is a little suspicious.'

'You Jodeaus always suspect your father of God-knows-what kind of errors or double-dealing. Baptiste used to – '

'Oh – Baptiste! Baptiste is a sourpuss.'

'Your father was never temperamentally a peasant. Why shouldn't he take an interest in the finer points of the Chapelle de l'Hôtel-Dieu?'

'He reads books, Paul, that's his only cultivation. He made his Grand Tour with an artillery piece, remember. Besides, what makes a "peasant temperament"? A degree of tolerance to having wet feet?'

Paul, exasperated, would say, 'You are so like him.'

Sobran watched the streets outside the shows – the gypsy jugglers and comic singers. He took a seat in the gallery and watched the influx of bodies when the seats were reduced to half-price, the workers, shabby students, shop girls. At evening the streets filled with the city's poor. In the Chalonnaise the poor wore peasant clothes, clogs, smocks – their own clothes. These people wore cast-offs, fashionable coats, dresses, bonnets of ten years back, their decorations bedraggled, filthy flattened silk flowers.

Sobran walked the streets. Ragged boys offered to black his boots. Open doorways breathed the stink of shit, spoiled meat, candle smoke. He haunted the low theatres, saw mime, tumblers, farce. There was commerce of every kind in the hallways that backed on to the galleries. Hard-faced dirty men with their wares, whores, women with their bare breasts bound by only a little gauze. Sobran walked into palatial 'finishes' dazzled by gas lamps where rich men drank themselves into bestiality and watched the high whores, the whores in finery, parade enticingly along elevated tables. Sobran looked at each of them: the men sprawled on sofas; the parade of women; the servants in rich liveries, bustling and obsequious. No one he knew.

Sobran had a week of this, then saw a handbill for the man who walked on the points of swords and recognised Xas balanced with smug nonchalance on a fence of old-fashioned flat blades.

He went to the show.

Xas's hair was shorter, thick and ragged, with a slight wave that made it curl into flat hooks along his jaw as he bent his head to watch his feet. He was stitched into clothes, the front panel of his shirt was the finest grade of pale blue silk through which showed the rose of his nipples. He stepped along the ranks of polished sword blades, some on edge, some braced point up. Stepped from level to level with his arms out, careful as a child climbing on slippery rocks near the edge of the sea. The audience was hushed. In the pit before the stage the musicians played a flute, a drum, and chanter – something vaguely eastern. Xas acted as though there were an art to it. Once he paused on one foot and waited as someone passed a powder puff on a stick with which he thickly dusted first one sole then the other. At the end he made a turn before he started back – just after the dusting this was, so it must have been then he applied the little skinful of bogus blood that ran down the sword blade as he made his turn. His lips parted, his shoulders dropped, not sagged, but back so that his neck arched, just a little, and his chin tilted back, just a little, all signs of pain – like pleasure – and a woman in the audience fainted. Xas walked back with his bloodied foot to where he begun, stepped on to a platform, bowed from the waist, sprang upright with the hooks of hair clinging to the sweat on his throat. The audience roared and stamped and Xas bounded offstage favouring the bloodied foot in a way that made his gait –

'Why am I looking for this devil?' Sobran muttered. He was amused and moved, although he felt weary, as if he had spent the last hour arguing with one of his sons (Baptiste – it was always Baptiste who argued with him).

He bribed the man at the stage door, went through into the cramped corridors backstage – and false corridors formed by stored scenery, thunder machines, racks of costumes. He asked for 'Sobran the sword walker'. A girl of perhaps thirteen – a tumbler – took it on herself to go before him and announce at the door to a room stuffed to bursting with bright costumes, candles, powdered bodies, most of

whom were hurrying out on their way to the stage, 'There's a
gentleman here to see you, Sobran.'

'No! Tell him to clear off!' ordered Xas. Sobran couldn't see him.
As the room emptied Sobran could only see a mirror and
candelabrum coated in melted wax, flames that seemed to float
between the candles and the surface of the mirror. The girl began to
close the door, saying to Sobran, 'He cut his foot.'

'Nonsense. He faked cutting his foot in order to swoon prettily.'
He stopped, remembering the girl's youth. Her eyes were wide with
delight and she was laughing at him, liked either his show of temper
or the indelicacy.

'Pardon,' he said, then, as she danced away from him laughing,
'You know too much.'

He pushed the door open, went in, shut it and leaned against it.
He said, 'Sobran the sword walker.'

'Oh – Sobran the vintner.' Xas had his feet up on another chair,
one sole pinker than other, with blood dried between the powdered
toes. He had removed his shirt and was shaking it from his arm. It
floated to the floor like a cast snakeskin. His face was whiter than his
chest and coated with a cracked paste of rice powder.

'I'm surprised to find you alone,' Sobran said. 'Sobran the sword
walker, scientist, slut –'

'I'm not alone. Here you are.' Xas got up and came to Sobran. He
took the man's hat off and put a hand on his hair, stroking it back
from his brow. This close Sobran could see the disguise of powder
flaking away on one cheek; the skin that showed through was firm
and radiant. Sobran could also see that Xas was assessing the
ground his looks had lost to age over the seven years. Sobran must
have said that, to himself: 'Seven years.' Because Xas said, quietly, 'Is
it that long?'

Sobran caught the angel's hands and held them. 'I've found you,'
he said, then, 'I have an idea. Listen.'

1844 **Délicat** *(delicate)*

Of the six who replied to his advertisement for a tutor, only one was suitable, Sobran told his family at the Sunday lunch table. He asked Céleste if she'd like to see the tutor's references.

'I'll leave the whole business in your capable hands,' Céleste said.

'What about us? Are we invited to look over this fellow's references?' Bernard said. 'After all, Antoine and I are to be his pupils.'

'I liked Father André. And enough is enough,' Antoine said.

'I need you to know German and English.'

'I've had enough of books.'

'Antoine, I don't want to argue this again. Paul has employment for someone with English.'

Antoine subsided. He liked Paul de Valday and didn't like having no real employment. Martin was with Sobran in the winery at Vully, and Baptiste – in charge at Jodeau-Kalmann – was not easy to work with. Sobran had expected this slight resistance: Antoine thought education unmanly, and teased his 'finished' sisters – though Aline was scarcely ever home to be teased, busy being seen chaperoned by Sabine in Chalon-sur-Saône, or by her mother and aunt at various fashionable spas, the desired result of all this exposure being some advantageous match. All this was none of Sobran's business, and it suited him to let Céleste and Sophie manage marriages for his unmarried daughters.

'Has the tutor any science? Botany or Chemistry?' Bernard asked.

'Yes. And Astronomy, Anatomy, Physiology, Physics – quite a list.'

'And languages!' Bernard blushed. Sobran could see that his youngest son was already anxious to please this prodigious tutor.

'We've only just made enough room for everybody,' Céleste said. 'Don't tell me we'll have to build-on again this summer?'

'Anne wrote to me to say that her sister has been told to keep to her bed for eight weeks. The fever weakened her,' Baptiste said.

No one knew he'd had a letter. Anne had departed two weeks back – her sister had puerperal fever after the birth of her third child. Anne went not knowing whether it was to nurse her sister and the child, or to bury either one or both of them.

'Was this Anne's first letter?' Céleste didn't like her daughter-in-law, regarded her as a bit of a failure where it mattered, the production of children (a second child had died, thirsty and dark-skinned, in its first year of life).

Baptiste didn't respond to his mother, didn't even look at her. He refilled his wineglass – for the fourth time. 'So,' he said, 'our room is free for any necessary juggling of sleeping arrangements. I'll make my bed in the cellar at harvest. But first I'm off to Paris to see my wife. I'll stay with Paul and Agnès.'

'Lucky Paul and Agnès,' Antoine muttered.

'Well, that's convenient, at least,' Céleste said.

Bernard asked, 'What's his name?'

'The tutor? Niall Cayley. He's Irish.'

'A foreigner?' Antoine the stonemason blinked in amazement. All the family were staring at Sobran.

'Admiral Lord Nelson was Irish too, wasn't he?' Baptiste added, idly, looking out from under his brows at his father who said, 'Don't stir them up.'

Antoine the stonemason asked, 'Do we know any foreigners?'

They thought about it. Finally remembered Jean Wateau's Spanish wife.

'I have dealings with two English wine brokers,' Sobran said.

'You do not,' Martin interrupted. 'I do all the dealing. You refuse to speak to anyone English. The Emperor's downfall – all that.'

Sobran scowled. 'Besides, Bernard was quite specific about his requirements. I required a teacher of German and English, Bernard wanted a man of science – and that's what we have.'

'When does he come?' Bernard seemed eager.

Sobran said the tutor was expected on the first of the month.

'So you have three weeks to get your grammar up to scratch,' Baptiste told his younger brother, 'for that essay on pond life Monsieur Cayley is bound to have you write.'

1845 Équilibré *(harmonious, well-balanced)*

The village of Aluze named the Jodeaus' new tutor Le Beau Cayley, and took him to its heart. Sobran was rather startled by this, and offended, which amused Aurora. 'All these years you've been thinking you chose him – but he chose you. He'd be anyone's choice.'

M. Cayley was a sunny, hard-working, astute young man, who always looked people in the eye, remembered everyone's names from one meeting to the next, would always recall a person's preoccupations and ask for an update. Despite his beauty and good diction the tutor never put on airs. He'd roll up his sleeves to help raise the mired cart with a broken wheel which he met on the road; would collar the runaway toddler at the fair; or he would walk out of his way to carry an old woman's kindling. The men drinking brandy or cassis under the plane trees by the inn at Aluze would never simply let him pass them by – even when he was with his pupils. They'd call out and wave him over, and often enough he'd sit a while, take a glass, set his timepiece open on the table so as not to always be fishing impolitely in his waistcoat. The Jodeau women (or their female servants if their mistresses weren't about), when Niall was on hand, would ask his opinion on this sash or that bit of bonnet trim, regardless of the fact his stock was in a snarl and he had his hair tucked behind his ears again. He gave the same careful consideration to any question above the class of, 'Do you want some more potato?' – but was bad with *those* questions and ate like a bird. The only exception he made was for questions about himself. 'There's not much to tell,' he'd say, and relate the same sparse facts. He was the youngest of nineteen. His parents were dead and his brothers and sisters scattered now between Ireland and the port of Sydney. Because he'd shown promise his way was paid through school by a maiden lady of the county. He had given the Church some serious thought, but it wasn't for him.

A group of old women gathered around the trestle tables on which a meal was spread, at Vully during the pressing at the end of the harvest, wanted to know if Niall had ever been in love. Their age entitled them to ask anything – their age and the singing, Niall's loose hair, his white shirt wringing wet with grape juice.

'Yes, but I had nothing to offer.'

'No money he means!' They laughed. Then, among themselves, 'And he spends his pay on books which he then lends to his employer or the Baroness.' The women were in fits, then the one who had spoken last suddenly threw her apron over her head because she'd seen that the Baroness had walked up behind them.

'Monsieur Cayley?' Aurora touched his arm and he followed her.

'They're the women who say you're Baptiste Kalmann's son for whom Sobran has found a place in his house. They argue that you are quite a lot older than you look and cite your learning as proof,' Aurora told him. 'Others say you are mine and Sobran's, and are younger than you claim to be.'

'I have another book for you, Aurora. But it's in my jacket pocket.'

'You're not telling me that you've mislaid your jacket?'

'No. It's just a way over there. Did you like the Esquirol?' Xas had given her *Des Maladies mentales*.

'It was interesting – quite revolutionary. I think I take your point. You were making a point, weren't you?'

'You said to me –'

Aurora braced herself for a perfect portrait. Xas would quote her word for word and reproduce the tone in which she'd spoken.

'– that I feel pity without effort, that it's in my nature. But, Aurora, I'd read *Des Maladies*, and I don't think it is pity I feel for Céleste. I hope it's understanding.'

Xas hoped Esquirol's book would give his behaviour some authority. Esquirol argued that insanity involved not only disordered understanding, but a disturbance of the feelings, the passions. Aurora told Xas that she shouldn't have accused him of never having to make an effort. 'What I want to make you see is that others don't find it as easy as you do to be kind and patient. But I did notice that you had folded the page corner where that term first appears, *lypemania*, from the Greek *lupo*: "I grieve or make sad". I think that when you look at Céleste you see extreme sadness – you see your own sadness. Whereas I see robust, hard-hearted madness.'

'Are you right, then? Am I wrong?' Xas asked, turning to peer into her face as they walked. It looked a little odd, anyone else would stumble, but Xas had an extra ten degrees of peripheral vision and could watch her *and* watch his step.

'Are you serious?' Aurora hated that kind of question.

'Why have you fetched me?'

'I *rescued* you, Niall, from that interrogation. And I hope you'll rescue Paul.'

For here was Paul, with Bernard and Antoine, who were both bending his ears, Bernard about birds' eggs and Antoine practising his German.

'I'm sure Monsieur le Comte has business to be about,' Xas said. Then he pointed. 'Yes. Here is Monsieur Jodeau and Messieurs Baptiste and Martin with the grapes from Jodeau South. I'm sure you'll both be expected in the vat with your sisters.' And he offered to hold their shoes.

Paul hurried to meet his vintner. It was his greatest coup, that Clos Jodeau sold Vully its best grapes for pressing – and one for which he hadn't to work. Sobran and Aurora had built the two new barrels and – of course – they had to make a new wine. Château Vully l'Ange du Cru Jodeau. Its eighth vintage. The wine was a triumph. The 1838 had already made eyebrows fly up the foreheads of the vintners at a gathering of the commune of Gevrey-Chambertin. Though these gentlemen said to themselves out of the hearing of the Comte, his mother and vintner, 'It won't last though, it can't last.' There could be no Grand Cru in the Chalonnaise, no process, no secret use of the wood, could supply the greatness the soil lacked.

The cart was tilted and the grapes raked in armloads into the vat. The family encircled it and all the workers hushed for the vintner's prayer to Saint Vincent. Then all the light and tender-footed youths and maidens of the *pays* climbed into the vat and began to tread the grapes.

The only opinion Céleste Jodeau ever volunteered about the tutor was that she liked his manners. From his arrival Niall Cayley was demure and pacifying towards the lady of the house. When she was bad in company, the rest of the family would walk out of the room, or squirm, or stare at their feet – all but Sophie whose place it was to take Céleste's hand and say something soothing, or to distract as one did a fractious infant. But the tutor would meet Céleste's eyes, mild, attentive, and she would begin explaining to him, steering herself slowly into the kind of pretence that sounded like everyone else's 'reason'. Céleste would hear herself sounding unlike herself and be reassured. Like Baron Lettelier, M. Cayley was a gentleman. There were days when the tutor was the only one who didn't irritate her.

Bernard and M. Cayley made a garden for their experiments in propagation. They read Lamarck. Bernard struggled through the English of Erasmus Darwin, then they both read its neighbouring title in their bookseller's catalogue, Charles Darwin's journal of his voyage on the HMS *Beagle*. Whatever they studied, the tutor would interrupt the lesson with 'by-the-way' and spread the net of relevance to catch other facts, theories, stories or, as he referred to them, 'ancient rumours'. When Bernard would set off into a meadow of waist-high grass with his butterfly net, Cayley would talk to Antoine, teaching German by conversation, not the endless conjugation of verbs. Cayley might say, 'Those butterflies are going about the world's real business. Bernard is not. He wants to *know* about them. The *nature* of grammar, all those conjugations, those couplings, that is real business too, but conversation is wanting to know.' Then he would ask, in German, 'What interests you?'

'Another nice little conceit,' said Baptiste, on hearing Antoine enthuse about his tutor's methods, 'from the whimsical Monsieur Cayley.'

Antoine said, 'Well – I know now that I was never right to be impatient with books. Books can be the people we never get to meet, ancestors or far neighbours.'

'Far neighbours?' Baptiste mocked. 'That's a very poetical way of saying "foreigners".'

Baptiste made no effort to hide his dislike of the new tutor. He spoke as though the four moves of room that the family made to accommodate a servant they couldn't just house in the attic had discouraged his wife Anne's return. For Anne never came back from Paris – not even when Baptiste went to fetch her. There was no one to blame but the blameless, yet Baptiste always averted his face from those two graves when he rode past the churchyard. He couldn't even speak about his dead sons, let alone acknowledge that their deaths had wrecked his marriage. Sobran suggested that Baptiste divorce Anne and marry again – start another family. The weakness that darkened each child's skin and made them die of thirst was new to the Jodeau line, after all. Iris, and Sabine's five children, were thriving.

'No,' Baptiste said, 'I should have cut off my hair and put it in their little hands before they were buried, as widows still do in the *pays*. I'd promise *them* never to marry again.'

'I did that,' said Aurora, who had only listened to this conversation till now. They were in her carriage. She and Sobran had found Baptiste sitting on a milestone between Chalon-sur-Saône and Aluze, thrown by his horse and still drunk. 'When my first husband was laid out beside his coffin I asked for scissors to cut my hair off. My uncle stopped me. He said that you never know what will happen to change your mind. And that's true.'

'Henri Lettelier,' Baptiste said, with profound scorn. He heard his father's little snort of laughter and doubled back to his original complaint. 'If it hadn't been so convenient that Anne went –'

'You can't blame your mother –'

'Why not?'

'Because that's just the sort of self-righteous thinking that she practises.'

Aurora touched Sobran's arm, said, warning, 'Sobran.'

'Besides, I'm not blaming Mother. Anne obviously just wasn't fine enough for a family connected to a comte. A family that is bettering itself from the bottom up.'

'Father Lesy taught you,' Sobran said, hurt. 'You couldn't have had a finer teacher.'

'Till I was twelve. There was no refining *me*. Now all my sisters are ladies, and my younger brothers are being transformed into gentlemen by a scholar with his suit out at the elbows.'

This was such an odd mixture of resentment and snobbery that Aurora simply stared at Baptiste in admiration.

'Is it already?' Sobran said, side-stepping everything. 'Out at the elbows. Can't have that.'

'You'll have to advance him the price of another suit,' Aurora said. They smiled at each other. The angel, his oddities, his needs, something sweet they passed between them.

They were still lovers. Aurora and Sobran. Sobran and Xas. There were dawns when Aurora got out of Sobran's bed to creep through the château's grounds and corridors to her own room. Sobran would wake up enough to feel her kiss his brow. Then the warmth she had moved out of would be invaded by a hotter body, Xas – the rain-on-dust scent of angel sweat – pleased because he'd timed it so he didn't have to wait. He had even spoken to Aurora on the stairs and she'd said, 'Have pity on him, Xas, for heaven's sake.' And Xas would arch over him asking, 'Do you want me to, you know, go easy on you?'

He would leave when the sun was up, with only forty minutes to spare before breakfast. 'I run fast,' he'd say. Sobran watched the angel, in his haste, mismatch button to buttonhole so he was left puzzling for a moment over a hole spare at the tail of his shirt. 'I go across country and I don't slow down on the hills.'

'Yes, yes, you're the salmon and the river both,' Sobran said, his eyes closed already so he didn't see Xas look back from the double doors, then step out and drop.

When Baron Lettelier came down to the country, Niall Cayley was always very pleased to see him. 'Delighted to see you again, Baron,' he'd say, utterly sincere, so warm that even the Baron would smile. Then, as an excuse for his pleasure he'd pick the Baron's brain about politics – for instance, what would this Louis-Napoleon do next?

Aurora hung back as she and the Baron were seen to their carriage. 'You are like a dog,' she said to Xas, sidelong, 'you are corrupt and writhing.'

'Say that with your teeth clenched and you'll sound like Sobran,' Xas whispered.

'I'm not saying it appreciatively,' she hissed. Then Céleste was there and took her hand, gloating too. 'Well, Baroness, I expect we won't see you for a while.' Céleste looked up coquettishly at the Baron, who was sitting inside the carriage already.

'I'm afraid not. I hope you continue well, Madame.' Aurora got into the carriage beside the Baron, glancing once at Sobran, who looked calmly sympathetic. Then Xas, the rat, behind all of them now, playing *commedia*, a sentimental Pantaloon, supporting one hand with the other to make her a small fatigued wave.

1846 La Tête de cuvée *(the best growth)*

The schoolroom was quiet, the late afternoon sun muted through its closed windows. Xas was washing the blackboard. Sobran sat turning a piece of chalk in his fingers, its fine tractive dust made his fingertips sticky. They had been discussing Antoine and Bernard, their progress. Xas was still talking, offering further reasons why Bernard should be encouraged to try for the Sorbonne. He was interested in the boy's future. More interested than Sobran – and, at that moment, than he was *in* Sobran. Xas finished washing the board and began to fold maps. His was quiet now and Sobran supposed he was waiting for a respose.

The angel hadn't buttoned his shirtsleeves, as an employee should in the presence of his master, hadn't brushed the chalk dust off his waistcoast, but he was waiting deferentially – Sobran thought – till he thought again. Xas was making his thoughts known, then, not forcing his hand, but managing Sobran in exactly the same manner all those reasonable women could – Aurora and Sophie, Sabine and Agnès – and Sobran supposed that the angel had been watching them. Or perhaps – Sobran noticed the angel's patient, diligent map-folding and the hair lifted on the back of his neck – perhaps Xas's mind was somewhere else, on other places he had lived, that he had once asked Sobran to imagine lay in hidden folds in the maps Sobran knew.

Sobran went to open the window, watched two sparrows pursue a small white moth over the roof of the dormer window below them. 'I suppose I can spare one son to science, since I have none in the army.'

A cloud covered the sun, but Sobran could still feel warmth radiating up from the roof tiles. 'It's this time I'll forget,' he said.

Xas came and leaned on the window sill, his ankles crossed.

'Your visits are like stepping stones back into my past. I remember each of them. This time, when you're living under my roof and I see you every day, this I won't remember so well. When I was ill – mad – my behaviour was so cold and impassable that my doctor diagnosed "nostalgia". His recommended treatment was this: I had to learn to forget the past.'

'And you said – I am guessing – "Please see the Doctor out and fetch Father Lesy." '

'More or less. I was thinking of my salvation, my future. It is *now* I'm nostalgic.'

Xas said, 'Aurora said to me the other day how surprised she was to find herself spending more time looking back than forward. She clearly remembers lying in the grass in Vully's orchard when she was thirteen, full of self-satisfied wonder, mostly wonder at herself. "In no time at all it's over," she said. "That sense of endless possibility. Or perhaps it's all the time in the world, but because you remember it so well it seems very immediate. But the power is gone." That's what she said. The power and the possibility she thought were her birthright.'

'She speaks to you like that?'

'Aurora doesn't feel responsible for what happened to me. There are things I can say to her I can't to you. Not that I do. But she speaks to me like that to show me that the invitation is always open.'

Sobran picked up the angel's hand and kissed his knuckles. 'Thank you for your patience.'

'I'm not, Sobran. Patient. When I feel your time passing me it makes my palms itch.'

'I'm fifty-six.'

'You're always counting.'

'I'm a vain man.'

The only thing that troubled Aurora and Sobran that summer was his expectation that his happiness would end. He could contemplate, in a sentimental way, the idea of his wife, children and grandchildren arranged, well-dressed and weeping decorously, around his grave. His lovers, she ten years his junior and a handsome woman, and the lovely immortal, he imagined *them* disentangling their feet from his ribcage and walking on.

It was the region's best summer, its finest vintage. Vully and Jodeau-Kalmann were paradise. The vineyards kept them all busy every day but Sunday, and on Sundays they entertained themselves like pagans – as Father André complained to the Bishop at Beaune.

One Sunday they picnicked on the bank of the Saône, by the château's boathouse. Martin and his sweetheart lay in a moored boat, the oars pulled up through its jug-eared rowlocks. The inflexible elders and corseted young women were in chairs while the rest of the family sprawled on rugs, all the children in white, the women wearing striped silks and holding ruffled parasols. Baptiste and Paul lay a little further off − with a bottle apiece and, in Baptiste's case, drinking from the bottle. Both were laughing. Aurora watched Sobran watching Antoine and Bernard trying to entice their tutor into the water − it was so hot, why wouldn't he? He shook his head, threw his jacket down on the grass and lay on it looking up at the sky. And Aurora and Sobran said simultaneously, like parents, 'I *think* he's happy.'

They had both seen that he could hold his own with the only person he hadn't conquered. Over lunch, Baptiste, trying to discomfort the tutor, told him how one of his father's protests against what the English had done to Napoleon was to pay the pensions of the four other local veterans. The rest of the family looked embarrassed. Céleste said, 'We don't talk about that, Baptiste.' And Niall Cayley said, 'The Irish are not the English, Monsieur Baptiste.' Very mild. Antoine, amused at his older brother's humiliation, reported to Sobran that when Baptiste, he and M. Cayley were helping Martin launch the boat Baptiste said something insulting about tutors as servants with pretensions, to which M. Cayley replied, 'Our citizen king was a tutor in Switzerland, did you know that? It is a gentlemanly profession.'

'I laughed,' Antoine said. 'Then Baptiste made a sneer and said did Monsieur Cayley hope his fortunes would change as dramatically as Louis-Philippe's? And Monsieur Cayley said, "God forbid. I've had enough of that."'

'He's happy because his needs are simple,' Aurora said. 'He likes people and to be busy. If only he'd put his mind to some plan to disarm Baptiste. I don't have any ideas. Do you?'

'Don't argue with Baptiste,' Sobran told Xas when they were next alone. 'Please.'

Xas stopped feigning sleep and made a noise of irritation.

'You could just nod your head, coldly, as women do when they don't like what a man says but don't want to do anything as ill-bred and fatiguing as contradict him. A few signs of dignified concession would be better than this sparring. Besides, he's drunk too often. I wish I knew what to do about his drinking. He's a good worker. I can't pack him off like I did Léon.'

'No,' Xas said.

'He's very unhappy.'

'Yes,' Xas said.

'And you're not.'

'No,' Xas said.

<hr>

1847 Cellier *(cellar)*

The family came out of La Madeleine in Vézelay, where they had gone among tourists to admire the beautiful capitals, and to visit Antoine the stonemason's sons, who were all employed on the restoration. When they came out only Bernard was talking. Sobran stopped to draw on his gloves. Céleste looked down the long straight street and sighed languidly at the distance she had to walk back to the hotel. Sobran took her arm.

Bernard was saying to his tutor how he liked best the giants and pygmies and men with pigs' snouts.

From the street a man called out Sobran's name. He turned to see a gentleman he didn't recognise walking towards him with the sideways walk of one whose feet are always too long for steps. But at a second glance Sobran saw the man wasn't moving towards him, but at an angle up the steps to where Bernard and his tutor stood. Sobran called to his daughter Aline, 'Take your mother down to that café.' Then said to the rest of the party, 'Go on. I'll follow you.'

He wasn't able to intercept the man, but arrived a moment later and put out an arm between the man, and Bernard and his tutor. 'Yes?' he said, 'I'm Sobran Jodeau. Do I know you?'

'Did I address you, sir?' The man spoke in accented French. He was taller than Sobran, and heavier, younger, wealthier – judging by his beringed hands. 'Sobran,' he said again, and preceeded to speak to Xas in English. Sobran couldn't understand what he said, but he saw Bernard's eyes widen and jaw drop. He looked down the street to see most of his family receding towards the café – but Antoine had turned back. Only the women would be spared, Sobran thought. He knew what was happening, and that he wouldn't be able to explain. He didn't know how to save himself. He said, 'Xas,' once, meaning, 'Do something.'

Xas didn't speak. He moved his friend and his pupil aside and then took the Englishman by the wrist in a grip so hard the man lost all his colour. The angel walked the man backwards, his arm straight and adamant between them. The Englishman staggered back one step at a time till they were on the street.

Antoine went to help. It was all clear to him: this fellow had attacked his father, and M. Cayley was seeing him off.

Sobran called Antoine to heel. The young man paused, quivering like a dog, then came reluctantly up the steps. 'Are you all right, Father?'

'Yes.' Sobran put an arm around each son. 'Let's join the family.'

Antoine objected. 'We can't abandon Monsieur Cayley!'

'Monsieur Cayley can look after himself.'

Antoine shook off Sobran's hand and Sobran had to recapture him, shake him, hold him hard.

Bernard said, 'I don't understand. Did Monsieur Cayley give that man your name as his own?'

Sobran deflected Bernard's good guess with exasperation. 'How should I know?'

'Then it wasn't *you* the fellow assaulted?' Antoine asked, and began to comply, letting himself be led along, led away.

'But,' said Bernard, 'the Englishman said, "I've been looking for you for ten years."'

'You can't have heard him right.'

Antoine stalled again. 'I can't just leave him. It's all very improper.'

'Do you think I care about propriety? I'll begin to think Baptiste is right and your education has unmanned you.' Sobran was furious.

'Who are we to worry about a scene on the steps of a church in a town where nobody knows us?'

'You're wrong, Father. You're beside the point, and just *wrong*.' Antoine turned back in time to greet Monsieur Cayley who hurried up to them.

'I'm sorry,' Xas said.

'Are you hurt?' Antoine was concerned, then indignant. 'What was all that?'

'I have to make my explanation to your father,' Xas said. 'I'm well. Go on.' He made shooing motions at Antoine and Bernard who both looked at Sobran to convey their opinion that the matter wasn't settled with them, then they walked away down the street.

Xas said, 'I have his flesh under my fingernails. I said I'd kill him if he came near me again.' He seemed stunned by what he'd said.

Sobran saw the angel's throat work and his eyes get a faraway look. He put a hand on Xas's arm. 'Come back into the church.'

In the church there were dark corners.

'I can't stay with you. I can't be with people. I should live in a cave.'

Sobran turned Xas, led him back up the street – keeping an eye out for the Englishman. But the Englishman had fled. They entered the church through its southern door, and stopped by Slander and Avarice. Sobran put his arms around Xas, who whispered, 'I could have killed him. I thought he'd take me away from all of you.'

'All of us?'

'Yes. The family.'

Sobran saw they were in the line of sight of two old women in black who, naturally, were scandalised. He wondered how they knew Xas wasn't his son. He let go of the angel and led him further along the side aisle. They stopped under Jacob Wrestles with an Angel.

'Which angel was it?' Sobran asked, looking up at the capital. Xas could always be distracted by a question.

'That was Yahweh, I think,' Xas said, 'being obtuse.'

'Are you feeling calmer?'

'I'm afraid.'

'Yes. When we get back to Jodeau shall we make you a list of names we know are nobody's? For future use? You can use them by rotation, a new one every twenty-five years.' Sobran straightened Xas's collar and brushed off his coat.

'What will you tell Antoine and Bernard?'

'It's none of their business.'

'Treat me coldly for the rest of the trip. And I'll be nervous and contrite. Otherwise they'll think I've got off without a warning.'

'That will be enough, probably.'

Xas nodded, submitted to Sobran's kiss on either cheek. He said, 'This can't last, Sobran.'

And Sobran, with a kind of derisive triumph, said. 'This will outlast me.'

The quiet months were, for Xas, a long reprieve, when it seemed he belonged, was necessary, would never leave.

1848 Ha *(the French hectare, an abbreviation)*

On a hot Sunday night in early September, at suppertime, when the light had gone but the family were all still up, it began to hail. They heard it first in the vineyard, then came a cry from one of the outbuildings.

The first wave hit the tiles, and a windowpane in the parlour cracked. Sobran hurried into the hall. The door was open, Antoine outside already, without a coat. There was a crush in the hall as coats and hats were snatched from a cupboard, and the men rushed out into the vines that began at the very edge of the narrow carriageway. Sobran's daughters stayed in the porch but Céleste came up beside him with her fine silk shawl held above her head. Baptiste, who had been in the winery, was already halfway up the slope, turning and turning with his head raised and bare but his hands over his face. Antoine was on his knees at the beginning of the rows, crying in frustration.

The ripe fruit was knocked into pulp, the ground whitened by

heaps of jagged hailstones. The hail thickened. Sobran covered his
head with his jacket and Céleste called out to her sons, 'Come in!'
She ran back herself, cried out as a large chunk of ice struck her
shoulder.

Xas passed Sobran and went to Bernard, stood stooped over
Bernard with the hail striking his back, bare neck and head.
Suddenly he stood straight and shouted in that terrifying and
compelling foreign tongue. Sobran watched the hail part in a wedge
along the precious south-facing slope, perhaps five rows wide, hail
still falling in walls either side of still emptiness where leaves
glistened and wounded grapes glowed and dripped. Then the wedge
filled with a wave of the same hard hail. Xas flinched, put his hand to
his face then hauled Bernard up and led him back to the house.
Sobran went with them into the porch. Then Antoine arrived and
lastly Baptiste, bloodied, cursing, in tears.

Xas had a streak of blood on either cheek, like two fraternal
kisses.

'As soon as the hail stops, go and see Martin,' Sobran told
Baptiste. 'If the storm crossed Vully, ask Aurora what she intends to
do. If Vully was spared, come back and tell us. If not, bring Martin
back with you and we'll harvest tonight – here – see what we can
do.'

Aline came out with a cloth for Baptiste to wipe his face. 'There'll
be warm water in a few minutes,' she said to her father.

'Good girl.'

Baptiste wiped his face, then looked over the cloth, his mouth
muffled, and said, 'There'll be a few economies next year, I expect.'
Pointedly, he didn't look at the tutor.

'One lost year won't ruin us, Baptiste. Look, now it's only rain,
why don't you get on your way.'

Baptiste went.

The women led Antoine and Bernard inside to wash. And Sobran
was able to ask Xas what he'd said to God.

'I wasn't talking to God, I was talking to the hail. God heard me,
though.' Xas touched his own cheek, and his hand came away bloody
and he put it to Sobran's mouth. Sobran put out his tongue – and it
was as though he made a childishly defiant gesture towards God –

to taste, in the blood, the flavour that lay behind the grapes and before the oak in Vully's best wine.

~~~~~

1849 Taché *(stained; a malady of white wine)*

On a cold March dawn, when the light was watery and sky a white like sheets washed threadbare, Paul and Agnès arrived at Jodeau. They'd been looking for Baptiste along the road between Jodeau and Vully. Baptiste had left them, very drunk and scarcely able to stand. He had refused a bed for the night, and hadn't waited for the carriage to be readied. He'd pushed Paul, Agnès said. Paul and he had scarcely argued before, and had never come to blows. The couple had gone to bed, but got up after an hour and sent for the carriage to go and find him. 'There wasn't any sleep to be had, so we went ourselves, didn't send a servant.'

They both seemed very distressed.

'We couldn't find him and it's cold,' Agnès said.

Bernard appeared at the library door. 'Why is Paul's carriage – oh, good morning, Paul, good morning, Agnès.'

'Bernard, could you send in the maid to light the fire here, and then get dressed.'

Bernard went to do as he was asked. When he reappeared it was with his tutor, also dressed.

'Has something happened to Baptiste?' Bernard asked.

Sobran thought with some exasperation that Bernard really was the shrewdest of his children. He said, 'Baptiste has probably fallen into a ditch somewhere between here and Vully. Could you two please help look for him?'

'Shall we go on foot?' Xas asked.

'Perhaps you should. Wrap up warmly, Bernard.'

They left. Agnès was chafing Paul's hand between her own. 'We'll get you both some breakfast,' Sobran said, 'and, if you wish, you can tell me what you and Baptiste argued about.'

'His drinking,' said Agnès.

'Of course.'

Two hours later Bernard appeared in the parlour, blushing and pop-eyed and said Baptiste was being put to bed by Aunt Sophie and Aline.

'Should I go to him?' Céleste asked, with no real interest.

'He's not sober enough to tell off.'

Sobran wondered what Baptiste had said. Then he felt a small spurt of anxiety. 'Where is Monsieur Cayley?'

Bernard's face grew so red that his eyes appeared feverish. 'I don't know.'

'He was with you when you found Baptiste?'

'Yes. I'm cold and wet, Father. Can I go and change my shoes?'

Sobran waved him away. He waited for some time, during which his family tried to involve him in a discussion about what was to be done about Baptiste's drinking. He was silent and could see they thought he was about to do something heavy-handed and ineffectual. After five minutes he said he'd just go ask Sophie for a report on Baptiste, then he went up to Bernard's room – and pounced.

He closed Bernard's door and leaned against it. 'What happened?'

Bernard shook his head.

'Forget your embarrassment. Just tell me.'

'I'll tell you if you sit down and I can stand up.'

Sobran found a chair, he sat and looked up at his son in what he supposed was a calm and reassuring manner.

In a rush Bernard told all. Baptiste had kissed Monsieur Cayley. He and Monsieur Cayley were supporting Baptiste between them, his arms over their shoulders, when Baptiste swung off Bernard and embraced the tutor.

'And then what happened?'

'They kissed. I mean they *both* did.'

Sobran looked down at his feet, shuffled them. Yes, those were his feet. 'Will I dismiss him,' he said. Then, 'Why aren't you asking me will I dismiss him?'

'It's too late. Monsieur Cayley said something to Baptiste. I don't know what because he spoke softly. Then he walked away up the road.'

'And?'

'And we stood and looked after him. Baptiste called out a couple of times, the second time like he was sorry and it was all ridiculous. Then I chased Cayley.'

'Did he stop?'

'For a minute. But he didn't say anything. He shook my hand.'

'And walked off.' Sobran wasn't really asking.

Bernard nodded. 'Then I got Baptiste home. By myself it was hard, cold going. Baptiste acted as if he thought it was all very funny. He kept laughing. So I dropped him a few times, or let him down hard, rather. But he only laughed more.'

Sobran nodded.

'I don't understand what happened, Father. I saw it all happen and I can't make any sense of it.'

'No,' Sobran agreed. He thanked Bernard for his frankness, and left the room. He had his groom ready his calèche and drove himself to Aluze. There he discovered that Monsieur Cayley had been seen, without baggage, waiting at the coach stop.

Baptiste was in the winery early the following day. He and Antoine had out spades and hods and were about to put in some hours carrying the soil which had washed down the south slope that winter back up to the ridge so that it could lend its essences to the next crop. Baptiste regarded his father in a wary, sidelong way. He was red-eyed and pale. When Antoine saw Sobran he picked up his hod and went out, leaving them alone. Baptiste sat down on the step of the *pressoir* and met his father's eyes.

'Bernard told me what happened,' Sobran said. 'It appears that Monsieur Cayley has departed without his possessions – though it's to be hoped he'll send for them – and his wages.'

'How maidenly he is,' Baptiste said.

Sobran waited.

'I thought I'd offended him. In as much as I was thinking at all. But then he said he was your lover.'

'Bernard told me he whispered in your ear.'

'He didn't whisper in my ear. He looked me in the eye and said he was your lover.'

'I'm an old man, Baptiste.'

'You've professed old age since you were forty, Father.' Baptiste shrugged. 'I don't know what came over me.'

'Oh? So it came over you all at once?'

Baptiste admitted that it had been coming over him for some time. 'I'd decided he was your son. The son of your lover, whoever she was, the lover people have speculated about for years. From Chagny to Chalon-sur-Saône they say it's the Baroness – but *she* told me it wasn't. When Mother is bad she goes on about Aline Lizet. Perhaps there are other possible candidates.'

'So, you had decided he was your brother, and that was what stopped you from kissing him sooner – or when sober?'

Baptiste looked scornful. He muttered something and Sobran asked him to speak up.

'I don't know how you could bring your lover into your home as a tutor to your sons.'

'You believed him?'

For a time Baptiste just sat, with folded arms and clenched teeth, then he said that although it wasn't very clear in his mind, and he couldn't work it out logically, with evidence, still he thought he believed Cayley's mouth, his kiss, and that he thought Cayley gave him the only reason why he wouldn't *continue* kissing him – apart from that Bernard was watching. 'Why would he lie when there were so many reasonable objections he could make? He could have just said, "Have you gone mad?" That would be sufficiently discouraging – once I sobered up.'

They were silent for a minute. Then Baptiste said that – well – after all, Antoine had finished his education and Bernard could probably manage the Sorbonne's examination of entrance without Cayley's coaching. And Cayley couldn't be expected to teach the girls, Catherine and Véronique had their governess. Besides, it had always been rather like Aristotle teaching Alexander the Great, except Antoine and Bernard weren't that great.

It was clear that Baptiste thought the tutor was good at his job, even too good for his brothers. Baptiste said he had hated Cayley because he was sure Cayley was Sobran's son and that it was obvious Sobran loved Cayley more than he loved his other sons. 'Anyone could see that. Everyone cared for him, but you looked at him as though he'd been given to you, the miracle of life itself – the same way Paul and Agnès gaze at Iris. And then – ' Baptiste spread his hands, the same hard, hairy, roped hands Sobran had at Baptiste's age. Baptiste was thirty-three, as Sobran had been in the year of what he used to think of as 'his trouble'. If Xas couldn't have Sobran's future, knew the fifty-nine-year-old intended, at sixty-five, to abstain from making love to his youthful angel, perhaps that angel thought he could take back what he'd first refused, the young man, the old man's son.

'Maybe I misheard him,' Baptiste said. 'I was very drunk.'

'You have to drink less. Pull yourself together. Try to find yourself another wife.'

'No.'

'You're a refuser, like me. Fortunately I always had your mother bringing me back to life.'

'Not the Baroness?'

'Aurora has too much respect for my feelings. Your mother carried on regardless. I could be secretive and full of sorrow but so long as I was physically sound I could be persuaded to father another child.'

'Until the end,' Baptiste said, held his father's gaze.

'Even then. I didn't realise that Véronique was not my daughter till Aurora warned me what people were saying. Véronique *could* have been my daughter.'

Another lengthy silence. Baptiste stood, picked up the hod and spade. He said, rather mournfully, 'I only wanted to kiss him. That's all.'

'Ha!' Sobran said.

⌒⤳

1850 Charnu *(full-bodied)*

I'll visit you [the letter promised] not, at first, on our night or in our place because even Baptiste has sufficient wit to post himself there and wait. I'll come to you. Do you remember how you told me about your cat? When you were a boy your bed was by the stove because your cough kept the household awake. You had a cat. You liked that cat to settle on your bed but never knew when it would arrive. Some nights you'd lie awake with your heart pounding waiting for that cat to jump on to your bed. It'll be summer, one of the big doors at the end of the soldiers' gallery ajar. I'll come in like the cat did, soundless, blocking the light, then landing heavy on the cool side of your bed. If you want you can say, 'Stop this.' If you think you should. I only want to hold you.

Another letter said:

I won't send any return addresses. Now you listen to me. Baptiste was your image. I've known other angels to lose their heads a little over a good likeness. I kept thinking, 'What does this likeness signify?' regardless of everything I know and believe about nature. It had disturbed me that he disliked me, and I didn't like him, but as soon as he was breathing against my face I thought he was made for me – wasn't *born*, didn't *grow* that way. But it's you I love. I loved you since the night I held you after your daughter died. It wasn't only pity, or only your body. It was what I knew – the shame of what I knew. I had to give myself up to you for your lifetime. What is faith when you feel you've lost something forever? I had to have you – someone I could lose forever.

1851 Marc de Bourgogne *(a Burgundian digestif)*

Xas wrote from Damascus, where he'd found Apharah's house occupied by her heirs, remote relatives. He hadn't expected to find her, but to visit her grave, lay flowers there. He was pleased to think she'd died imagining she had helped him back to Heaven.

Sobran, reading this letter, swore to himself that he would never tell Xas how, on the receipt of Xas's first tormented letter to him, he had written to Apharah to tell her what had happened – Xas's injury, death, resurrection, mutilation, wanderings. Sobran didn't know if the letter had reached her before she died. But if it had he could imagine how she felt.

Agnès and Paul had a son, christened Armand after the old Comte. Because Agnès had chosen to confine herself at Vully rather than in Paris she wasn't with Paul in December during the *coup d'état*, when Louis-Napoleon's soldiers marched into the city in an orderly and jaunty way, camped at the Hôtel de Ville and began to drink. Like many other citizens, Paul sat tight through the days of drinking, of silent drills, when gunners stood by their cannons on street corners, with smoking slow-matches in their hands.

When the killing began Paul followed the soldiers, unmolested, a gentleman. He picked up a man shot in the courtyard of his own house. 'They came in here,' the man said. 'What did I have to do to offer no offence, hide under my bed?' Paul saw an officer with his hands over his ears order his men to use their bayonets because powder and shot were too noisy. He saw a woman shot. The child she carried as she ran fell from her arms and unfolded, shocked and bruised by the cobblestones – then it was knocked flat by bullets from *more than one gun*. Paul followed the soldiers into Montmartre and saw all the dead. Then he went back to the townhouse, lay low for two days, and left Paris for Vully.

'Stay at home for a year,' Aurora said to him. 'You are Burgundian. You can leave Paris alone. We don't need Paris.' She thought to herself how like her uncle she sounded.

There was nothing much in the papers about the coup, then the Bishop at Autun had, in his New Year Sermon, some words of praise for the Emperor. Aurora came home from the service saying, 'This ruler of ours knows whom to seduce – the Church, for instance. A murderer who knows how to be moderate. I think we had better get used to him.'

1852 **Liqueur d'expédition** *(sweetened liquor used to dose champagne)*

'How did you go unseen in Aluze?'
  'I came by the canal.'

~~~~~~

1853 **Vin de garde** *(the good vintages, for laying down)*

Xas sent a photograph from Glasgow. It was taken in a studio – he was leaning on a marble plinth against a backdrop of misty crags. He'd kept still, was wholly in focus, even the saturated blacks of his eyes. But his feet weren't quite flat to the floor and he seemed about to step out of his boots and ascend something he could see before him, a stairway of air.

In the letter that came with the photo he wrote, 'I'm impressed by this city's necropolis. I've never seen a burial ground so clearly imagined as a silent and civil community – the plinth tombs like chimney stacks without houses, for the houses are underground. When did you all begin to think this way about death? What happened to the solemnity and the horror?

'I went to visit George Cayley, whose name I stole from his treatise on flight. I saw his famous glider, which was larger, heavier and less responsive than my count's. I mentioned the count's name but Cayley had never heard of him or his experiments, which leaves me to suppose that my "death" discouraged him from further experimentation.'

~~~~~~

1854 Dosage *(the dosing of champagne with sweetened liquor to make up the volume after the dégorgement of sediments)*

'I came by train.'

<hr>

1855 Plein *(frank, forward, full-bodied)*

Baptiste went to Dijon for a year, and when he returned to his forewarned family he brought his second wife, a widow, and her seven-year-old daughter. He also brought for his father a white clay pipe, whose bowl bore a likeness, a human head, most would say, a fair serene face with flat hooks of hair, like wings, against either cheek.

<hr>

1856 Journal *(a land measure used in Burgundy: earth that can be worked in a day)*

Sobran told Aurora that, on that night every year, he waited alone. Sometimes it was simply a vigil he kept with his past.

Then he changed the subject. He asked about the broker who'd been to Vully while he was in bed with a cold. Martin hadn't reported what the broker had said about the Vin de l'Ange. Aurora repeated the price offered for the 1850 vintage.

'I said no,' Aurora told him. 'I said it's a sacrament. He said the sacraments have had two thousand years of advertisement.'

'And Paul? Martin?'

'They were with me.'

'Good. Even a doubting Thomas could believe the evidence of his senses – these people, all they can believe is the soil.'

Sobran had taken laudanum because his legs pained him. He was disgorged by sleep in the late morning, his pain gone but his body fizzing with drowsiness, a slow aspiration of unconsciousness. He found Xas beside him, asleep too.

Sobran reached for the angel. Against that lustrous shoulder he saw his own arm – thin, its tan fogged by white hair, his elbow a dry knot. Fine feathers overlapped the red and white gathers of scar tissue on Xas's back, filling them in as moss fills the cracks between paving stones. Sobran touched the angel, whispered, 'Are you really asleep?'

Xas rolled over, stretched, breathed deeply then opened his eyes. He had learned how to sleep, he said, and sometimes dreamed. He had dreams about flying, still felt the shame of not having wings, even among the wingless. And when he was sad he still sat with his back to a wall. 'But you, you're happy now aren't you, most of the time?' Xas asked, and touched the wedge of hair on Sobran's high, bare forehead.

'I'm never fully at ease in my mind till I see you. Fortunately, at least in this matter, the years pass very quickly now. Do they for you?'

'I'm patient, so they pass. But I'm not waiting for anything, and so much happens to me.'

'You're young.'

Xas laughed.

'I mean, you're alive to everything. Whereas I'm becoming a little like your friend the monk.'

'Niall.'

'Oh, it was his name you used. Niall, the bee-keeping Irish monk, your friend, whom I recall you described as shrinking away from the world like a kernel dried in a peach pit. I'm beginning to feel like that.'

'How? How does it feel?'

Sobran wondered whether the angel was trying to follow *his* feelings about age or those of humans in general. He felt that he had to get his answer right so thought for a time before he told Xas, 'It's as if I can no longer fit the space I've made for myself in the world. Yes – I've shrunk inside the space I've made.'

⁓

1857 **Domaine** *(privately owned vineyard, estate, field)*

Mid-morning, early autumn before the harvest. Sobran brought in the breakfast that a servant had left for him, as usual, on a tray by the door. As he paused with the tray in his hands and back against the door he saw Aurora coming up the coach house stairs. He wished her a good morning.

'How did you sleep, dear?'

'Brokenly,' Sobran smiled. He kept the door open and she edged past. She stopped at the sight of Xas, who was sitting on the floor laughing over Bernard's letters. He looked up, jumped to his feet and came to embrace her.

Aurora pushed him away to study him. 'You,' she said, 'have given me a great deal of trouble. Both the Baron and Paul want to know who this perpetual traveller is who sends me all the views. Sir Walter Scott's memorial, a steamer on the Côte d'Azur, the Vendôme column, the Piazza della Signoria in Florence. Men in canvas trousers sitting on stone benches . . .'

'I have considered getting my own camera. But then I'm discouraged because I see things no photograph can reproduce – like the way the sky looked to me one day over the flat land at Amiens, like fair impermeable skin, as if it was asleep and about to be rudely awakened. Signs. How can I photograph signs?'

'If you do get a camera, Xas, all I ask is you send the photos in packets. All this mail! And no return addresses. I tell the Baron that I've met a lot of people on my pilgrimages and he says, "Enthusiasts, no doubt." Fortunately, some of the nonsensical things you send confirm this opinion. Like the playbills: *Christ heads the Praetorians.* Frankly I'm puzzled. And postage is so costly.'

'I don't eat.'

'You don't earn.'

'Yes I do. I worked as a stoker some of this year. For the passage. And I'm making maps in my head, the kind that consist of sentences, descriptions of what I see at the end of streets, of shrines, milestones, old trees. Cartographers are like angels, they imagine everything from the air. I enjoy learning how to get around, it's an inexhaustible project.' Xas sat on the floor again among the letters; he picked up another page as he spoke to Aurora, as though he was reading Bernard's words by touch.

Aurora told him that, while nothing much changed at Vully, the railway was a boon, and their wine travelled well.

'I told you so,' Xas said to Sobran. 'I had a feeling about those pumps that drained the mines in Mülheim. I first heard them as something huge hammering to get into the world.' The angel reached out and encircled the ankle of the old man who stood beside him in his nightshirt.

Aurora and Sobran exchanged looks, in the sorry warning way of parents who have to tackle telling their child some bad news.

'Xas,' Aurora said, 'I imagine you've noticed that Sobran is – isn't the man he once was.'

The angel got up, fast and fluid and moved away from them. 'Do you think I pretend not to notice he's old? I notice. But Sobran is so familiar to me that his age isn't an otherness, a mist gradually obscuring the body I know, or something that stands in opposition to my "youth" like some vulgar emblem. His age is as much himself as his youth.'

Aurora sighed.

'Thank you,' Sobran said. 'You're very gallant, but not quite right in your thinking. You've adapted to my ageing in the same way as you've learned to find your way around on foot. I think *you* were more yourself when you would fly off leaving me blinking the dust out of my eyes, and I was more myself in my prime. Nothing matters to me as much as it once did. My feelings are not tenacious or energetic.'

'Do you mean you don't love me,' Xas said.

Sobran said, 'Now you sound like a young man.'

Xas crouched to gather the scattered pages of Bernard's letters. He said to Aurora without looking at her, 'Why did you start this? Are you hoping to have him to yourself in his declining years?'

'I do have him. And his family has him. You come and go, Xas.'

'And you are saying I should just go.'

Aurora was unhappy. She told Xas that she would never suggest that. They were speaking at cross-purposes. Did Xas think she was trying to tell him that it was unseemly for him sometimes to climb into bed with the old man? They *both* did that.

Sobran protested that the ten years Aurora had on him didn't entitle her to keep calling him old.

'You be quiet. Xas – what Sobran and I are trying to do is prepare you somehow, as good parents do. When Sobran is gone and you are grieving for him, he won't be able to comfort you.'

Xas approached Sobran to give him the letters, but Sobran took the angel's other hand and drew him against him. For a moment Xas pressed his forehead against Sobran's shoulder, then looked him in the face. 'We still see eye-to-eye. You haven't lost any height. Don't send me away, Sobran. Don't do me any fatherly services. I have all the time in the world to live with your absence. I'd be with you more often except everyone in the province remembers me too well.'

'And you're restless.'

'Yes. I find places I want to stay because of the people I meet. But I shouldn't stay anywhere till I learn how to – not trouble anyone.'

1858 Le Parfum *(the fragrance of a wine)*

The pearls were in a box that stood between Sobran's brushes and cologne on the dresser in his room at Clos Jodeau. Aurora had given him the pearls, saying, 'I've never worn these, of course. But Iris saw them the other day and asked if she could wear them. I don't want her wearing them. Give them to Xas when next you see him.' Sobran forgot to bring them to the coach house and, when he did next see Xas, he had to ask him to stay put for a while, not to go quite yet, till he fetched the Archangel's pearls.

Sobran was delayed at Clos Jodeau by his youngest daughter who didn't see why he hadn't sent someone else – he shouldn't be running errands, riding to the château and back in one day. Why didn't he take a carriage? What would mother say!

He came away again at evening with the pearls in his coat pocket. Véronique wouldn't let him turn around without a meal, and Antoine said he should stay put because Baptiste had said this morning that he wanted to speak to Sobran about something – Baptiste was over at Kalmann – if Sobran would just stay put Antoine would walk over and get him.

Sobran said he would see Baptiste on his way, and left them.

It was twilight when he handed his horse to a Vully groom and walked around to the coach house, squaring his shoulders and smoothing his hair.

He saw Baptiste at the coach house door. Yes, it was his eldest son – in work clothes, and carrying a soft-brimmed hat – who vanished into the black square of the coach house doorway.

Sobran quickened his step. At the foot of the stairs he looked up to see the light grow on the landing as someone opened the door above, the door to the lit room, the soldiers' gallery. He was short of breath but called out 'Baptiste' and saw the light steady, not increase. Sobran hurried up the flight, stopped on the landing, saw his son looking back at him, Baptiste's hand flat on the door to the soldiers' gallery and that door half open.

Sobran began up the second flight, talking as he went: 'You wanted to see me?' Then, 'Wait.' He could hear the tense conniving note in his own voice. Baptiste tilted his head, frowned, then his face cleared into a look of triumph and, just as Sobran reached him breathing hard, his hand grappling at his son's sleeve, Baptiste pushed the door wide and stepped into the room.

Where Xas stood in the lamplight, bare of chest but for the black straps of his trouser braces, barefoot, and apparently calm.

Sobran rested against the doorframe.

'You,' Baptiste said.

'Me,' Xas answered. Then to Sobran, 'Are you all right?'

'Just catching my breath,' Sobran said, catching his breath.

'Cayley,' Baptiste said.

Xas made a polite, non-committal sound, then held out his hand to Sobran.

Baptiste moved aside and looked at his father. The look was wary but not hostile.

Sobran came forward, took the pearls out of his pocket and coiled them into Xas's cupped palm. 'Aurora stored them in a bank vault in Paris for twenty years. She was afraid they would bring Vully bad luck. She's still afraid.'

Xas looped the pearls over his head. Greenish black, their colour in deep, oily layers of lustre, the pearls made the angel's beauty more lordly. Or perhaps it was his expression. 'I suppose you kept my belt?'

'The belt with the topaz, tiger's-eyes, lapis lazuli? I recall I took it off to wash you. I didn't see it after that. It's all so long ago now. I suppose he removed it. Aurora followed him to the window and he tossed her those pearls. She didn't tell me he carried anything away with him.'

'He must have. As a souvenir.'

'Or it was buried.'

Xas put the pearls to his mouth and rolled them against his lips. He glanced briefly at Baptiste. 'It seems we are tying up loose ends. As if I'm collecting what's mine. Perhaps I shouldn't come back. Sobran?' The last rather plaintive.

'Why shouldn't you come back?'

'He looks like you –' Xas said, without looking again at Baptiste, who was quite still, listening carefully – 'at forty. When you came back up to the boundary stone after the three years we didn't speak, and you were decorated with all your sorrows and reverses, frostbite, white hair, the walking stick – a bit of an affectation, that – your white collar and crucifix. All that icy indignation. You said, "I have some questions for you. You can answer them, then go and never come back."'

'What did you say to *me*, Xas?' Sobran asked. He didn't remember, scarcely remembered his anger. He *did* recall how Xas had looked, perched on the boundary stone and cloaked by his wings.

'I asked you whether you had thought it through.'

'How could I?' Sobran took another step and put his hand on Xas's cheek. 'You're not going to leave me and not come back, are you? Just because Baptiste looks like me. I doubt you'll encounter him again. He can't stand watch over me. I'm not yet an invalid or an imbecile.'

'I think I must,' Xas said, and Sobran was surprised by the hot streak of a tear on the back of his hand. 'Why does he have to look like you? I'd be still in one piece if I hadn't resembled someone else. Likeness is a sin. It's a sin.'

Xas broke away from Sobran, turned his back to search for his shirt, coat, boots. Sobran saw Baptiste's jaw drop at the sight of the white down, flush to the contours of the angel's back.

Xas found his shirt and coat. He put them on. He picked up his boots, said to Sobran, 'Don't tell him anything. It's my history too and I don't want him to share it.'

This, and the former speech, were so wounded and irrational that Sobran felt a kind of tender terror for the angel that he didn't know how to act on. He said, as calmly as he could, 'I'll see you again.' Watched Xas stride to the open double doors, called out, 'I'll see you again!'

'Yes,' Xas said. And jumped.

Baptiste was reeling. Sobran took his son by the arm and led him to a chair near the fireplace, sat him down.

'He has feathers,' Baptiste said, his teeth chattering.

'If you had seen the wings you would have fainted,' Sobran told him, soothing and conversational. 'Aurora only saw them in action once – like two mirrors facing each other, she said. God's fearful symmetry.'

1859 **Servir frais** *(serve chilled)*

... This winter I went to the salt dome in Turkey. In the last twenty-five years they've increased production by several thousand tons a year. The evaporation ponds cover acres and are marked out at night by lights at each huge, clawed-together heap of dirty salt. I went to the place where I always hid my copper water vessels and found a pipe that vanished into the salt. I followed it back to the lake and asked some of the workers what it was for. A foreman told me that the Bey who owns the land employed an English engineer to build the pipe to siphon off the lake near the spring. Yes, this had exposed more salt pans. No, he didn't have any idea where the water went. Somewhere underground...

1860 **Sleepiness** *(grapes attacked by* Botrytis cinerea*)*

In May, Sobran was at Chalon-sur-Saône for the christening of his third great-grandchild and first great-grandson. He felt ill and took to his bed in Sabine's house. Céleste, Sabine, and Sabine's last unmarried daughter all nursed him. He was never alone – from this he divined how ill he was. When the worst of the pain passed, he drifted, was between times disturbed by females plumping pillows or sliding bedpans under his bony backside, or sitting him up to the tiresome task of swallowing soup. In his periods of consciousness he'd forget anyone who wasn't in the room – but never lost sight of that triumvirate of wife, eldest daughter, granddaughter. His sons seemed to appear in a parade. Martin – of all people – knelt by his bed and wept. Baptiste came and poured out a glass of Château Vully l'Ange du Cru Jodeau. He held it to his father's lips and Sobran tasted the wintry richness behind the grape, before the wood. Then he sensed a change, as though of air pressure; he was pulled out of himself and saw curtains drawn around his sight, then the blackness turned turquoise and he surfaced from a lake to look for a minute at mountains, snow veined by wet black rock, and glassy green ice with light shining through it. But it wasn't him this landscape wanted and he sank back into his own substance, not just his sick body, but his memories, preferences, hard-held loves.

Aurora sat by Sobran for more than an hour. The noise in the street increased as people hurried home to dinner. She thought the bustle might wake him. The house, on the clock of the conscious, began to quicken. Lessons had finished, the front door opened and closed as Sabine's youngest came in from his day school, and then her husband from his place of business. Aurora heard Paul's voice – he and Agnès had arrived from their hotel and were to dine with Sabine and family.

In rehearsal for his own funeral her friend didn't stir. The light faded. Aurora turned her head to the window, and her earrings tickled her neck, lively, a little momentous, on an afternoon that was like a stilled pendulum. The twilight caught whitely in small dishes of the patient's urine that, for some reason unknown to Aurora, Sobran's physician had left drying along the windowsill.

Céleste came in with a lamp. Its pink, frosted glass chimney lit her face, which was serene, smooth-skinned for a woman nearly seventy. Sobran looked ten years her senior now, a mottled, desiccated old man, and so still.

Céleste set the lamp down and came to the bed.

'Our children are here with Iris,' Céleste said, and it was the first thing she had ever said to Aurora that acknowledged the connection between them as a connection rather than as an area of dispute. 'Antoine has come and the house is bursting at the seams. Sabine's boy has collected his clothes and books and has gone to stay at a friend's house. Baroness, you should go down. If my husband wakes up while I'm watching I'll send for you.'

Aurora got up. 'How is he? I can't tell how he is.'

'He has spoken twice today, each time asked a question. I nursed his father and, shortly after we married, the uncle everyone says died too young. These Jodeaus don't go till they stop asking questions.'

Downstairs Paul kissed Aurora. There weren't enough chairs in the parlour, and Baptiste, Martin and Antoine were leaning on the mantelpiece, their bodies forming a fence that kept the heat from the room. Aurora told them to move.

'Thoughtless lumps,' Agnès said, but when Antoine sat on the floor by her chair she put her hand in his hair.

'Couldn't possibly eat,' Iris said at the sound of the dinner bell.

'You could,' Paul told her.

Sabine appeared. 'Please come through. What a crush.'

'Sabine tells me Father has improved,' Agnès said to Aurora.

'Yes, your mother thinks so too.' Aurora didn't want to move. She felt paralysed by the bustle, the brittle cheerfulness around her. She shook her head at Paul, who had Agnès on one arm and the other held out to her.

'You feel bad because you need to eat,' Antoine said, with an intrusive simple frankness that he had picked up from his tutor.

'I'll bring her in,' Baptiste said. 'Tell Sabine to start. The Baroness is composing herself, or collecting her wits — whatever seems the more dignified excuse.'

Baptiste and Aurora were left alone.

'He won't die this time,' Baptiste said.

'When he does I'll be widowed, without a widow's claims.'

'We all know that, Baroness.'

'Our friendship was all on his terms.'

Baptiste smiled. 'His children have similar complaints. He was always either preoccupied, or pushing us about. That's the kind of man he is. Whenever any of us did something unexpected he would look at us as though we'd just jumped out on him, as if we were playing that game children play after dark — actually, we did play that game, when I was very small, before my *other* older sister died. Anyway, Father looks at us as if to say he is *most definitely not* playing.'

'You put it well, Baptiste. He was frosty to me whenever I trespassed. It was as if I was presuming on my title and wealth. And, whenever Sobran "fell ill" he would carry all his power, intact, into either impenetrable sorrow, or silence. Now it's fever and sleep.'

Baptiste leaned a little closer, said in the tone of a conspirator, 'Shall we go upstairs and pull his beard?'

Aurora considered. 'I think I'd rather have something to eat.'

*

The following day Aurora was able to reassure the invalid, who wanted to know whether he looked like a corpse.

'No,' she told him.

His eyes brightened, but only with shrewd humour. 'Do I look like a yellowed, withered old man?'

Aurora hesitated, then told him yes, he did. And watched him laugh, laughed with him – conservative, close-mouthed laughter, but carefree, because something that Sobran had held on to tightly and jealously had finally been taken out of his tired grip.

Sobran was at Vully again for the harvest, on his feet with the aid of a stick. Xas reappeared and showed every sign of winding himself around Sobran permanently, like – Sobran complained – some parasitic vine. 'I won't die,' Sobran promised. 'You are breaking your own heart. Go away for a while. Come back soon.'

And, of course, there was no love-making.

1861 Vin diable *(a bottle of champagne that bursts through too much pressure)*

When Bernard visited in the new year he brought with him a copy of *The Origin of Species.* Bernard had heard of Charles Darwin's heretical work and had ordered a copy upon publication. Two arrived. One from his German bookseller, and another from Leeds in the north of England.

'Look at the address on the wrapper. I know that hand. It was Niall Cayley sent me this. I know it. But there was no letter. I wish I hadn't lost sight of him, Father, he really was a wonderful teacher. And an original. When I matriculated at the Sorbonne I thought I'd enter a wide world of fine and unusual minds, more people like my tutor. I have met men, and several women, with fine minds, but no one like Cayley.'

Sobran put out his hand for the book. 'I suppose I should read it.'

1862 **Vin des Dieux** *(wine of the Gods, sweet botrytised wine)*

For a whole year Xas didn't visit or write. In that year Antoine the stonemason was carried off by a series of strokes, and Christophe Lizet finally succumbed to a tumour that stopped up his stomach so he wasn't able to keep down what he was able to swallow. Sobran didn't visit his neighbour as he lay dying, although his wife, sons and daughters did. Sobran did not want to hear Lizet voice his lifelong regret – that no one had discovered who it was murdered his sisters, Geneviève and Aline.

Aurora was in Rome for the Easter Benediction, 1863.

She sat in a cab that had its glossy black leather top raised against the fine rain. The cab was in the first of four circles of cabs at the edge of the square, parked facing Saint Peter's. The square was packed with soldiers, priests, seated officials and the populace, their heads already bare, though the Pontiff had not appeared. Between the huge statues of saints on the Vatican roof people leaned, arms slung in a friendly fashion about stone knees.

Someone who passed paused to look into Aurora's cab, then got into it and sat beside her.

She asked Xas, 'Where have you been?'

He shook his head. He wore shabby clothes and was carrying a string bag of carrots and onions. His neck was grey with dirt, and grime defined all the whorls of the skin on his wrists. Inside his open shirt Aurora saw the gleam of the pearls, as alien and acute as the eyes of a live octopus she had once seen in an aquarium in a fancy Parisian restaurant. The angel was too unexpected and too lovely; for a moment Aurora had to shut her eyes.

'You don't believe in return addresses.' She was scolding again.

'Protestant by temperament.' With a wry look around the field of the faithful. 'What I don't believe in is intermediaries.'

'You're tiresome.' Aurora was tired, so got down to business. 'Sobran is very old and ill.'

'I suppose he must be.'

It was a hard-hearted reply, but his voice was edgy, close to panic. He took Aurora's hand and caressed it with his thumb, rolled the tendons inside her loose skin. Through her lace glove she could feel that the angel's hand was colder than hers. He said, 'I'll come. I have to make some provisions. There's a woman I'm keeping.' He smiled at Aurora's expression. 'I'm working as a public scribe. I come home from my place of work, in the Piazza Montana, with a bag of vegetables or ham bones and this old woman cooks me soup, which I don't eat, so she "finishes it up" for me. She lives in a small room under the stairs. I pay her to cook and clean my room. I'm not sure she'd make do without doing for me. I suppose I can leave her my writing desk and pens and other possessions to pawn or sell.'

'I'm pleased to hear you are making new friends. But Sobran – ' Aurora stopped speaking because the angel's lips had lost their colour.

'This woman is more like a pet,' he said, coldly. 'But among the poor and weak and old my strength is obscene. How can I live without a commitment to help at least some poor creature? It's pity someone or pity everyone. And, because it is impossible to act on universal pity, my pity is liable to evaporate. I keep the stopper in. For without pity, and among you, what would I be?'

'Forgive me,' Aurora said. To her he had become just the one whose absence caused her friend pain. She had forgotten *him* – his moments of awful swooping certainty.

Xas got down from the cab and held up his own hand in a quick mockery of a benediction, and she saw the lines from the handle of the string bag red on his pale palm before the blessing became a closed fist which he lowered slowly. 'I'll come on the 27th of June,' he said, and walked away through the crowd.

1863 Vinifié *(made into wine)*

Sobran got what he had bargained and bullied and begged for. At sunset, despite the fact that movement tended to shake him out of consciousness, three men and a youth – his sons Baptiste, Martin and Antoine, and Martin's son – carried him out of his house on a stretcher. He saw the stars, clear in a cooling sky, clamped his mouth in a lipless line when the stretcher tilted and his feet, fat with fluid, pressed against the tight package of covers. The sheets of his makeshift bed were so secure it was as if his sons had him already sewn into half his shroud.

Sobran thought, 'I'll feel let down if I'm alive tomorrow.' That struck him as amusing, but he hadn't the energy to report his thought to Antoine, whose arm he held as the stretcher jostled. A joke would be gallant. A joke would help them. But he couldn't speak.

The procession passed through the rows of vines up Jodeau South and stopped on the ridge, where Sobran got one look at the far hills, outlined by a rind of gold light.

Céleste said, 'Now you must all go. Get to bed early, please.'

Martin's son set down the chair he'd carried up the hill for his grandmother, and Céleste posted herself by Sobran. She rearranged her shawl, nodded at the men, dismissed them.

Martin pulled the blanket up around his father's neck. Sobran shook his head slowly. He wanted to sit up, and began to cough. He required help to lean forward and clear his windpipe. Martin and Baptiste raised him, and he trembled against their strength as though he fought them. He coughed, pulled in enough air to expel the phlegm. Baptiste held a cloth under Sobran's mouth, then wiped the thick mucus that dripped from his lower lip; refolded the cloth, dabbed again, till Sobran's mouth was clean. They laid him back down. Martin restored his nightcap and pulled the blanket up again. 'You know what I think, Father? That this is sheer folly with your cough.'

'You are not going to die tonight,' said Baptiste. 'However tidy that would be. Only last week you were offering us all your opinions about – I don't even remember what it was about. Uncle Antoine was silent in company for half a year before he died, he only spoke when spoken to, and without any show of emotion.'

'Yes. Yes.' Sobran didn't want to be lectured. His sons were having their revenge – but he would rather they were abusive than nagged.

'Go now,' Céleste told them.

One by one they kissed him – his grandson dutiful, a little fastidious, which let Sobran know how unappealing he was.

He slept for a time, woke as Céleste lit a lamp. He watched her strike a match, stoop, keeping her balance, remove the chimney on the lamp, hold the flame to the wick, replace the chimney. In the yellow lamplight she looked girlish and untouched and her hair had the sheen of spun sugar. As she sat down again Sobran asked her if she had the laudanum.

Céleste fished for the bottle in her pocket – held it to the light and shook it. The resinous brown liquid clung to the glass as it slopped.

Again Sobran slept, was roused in the dark of night by the urge to cough. He tried to roll on to his side, was prevented by the barrier of his own arm, like the side of a cot. Someone came to his aid. He coughed, hacked, cleared the blockage, spat on to the ground. It was one of his sons returned – and dressed for a town outing, in a suit, hair short and oiled. Once Sobran's throat opened he could smell the scent of the pomade – and something else. Snow. Sobran kept the hand that held his own, closed his hand on it.

Céleste was saying to Xas, as though she was at the end of a long and involving confidence, '*My* angel had wings fledged with feathers like those marigolds.' She pointed at the lava flow of marigolds surrounding the boundary stone. Then she slapped her knees once and got up. 'I'll leave you for a little while. I'll just sit over there, if you'll carry my chair.'

Xas took Céleste's chair and carried it to the flat spur where cherry trees once grew.

'She chose not to recognise me as Niall,' Xas told Sobran when he came back. 'She seemed to be expecting an angel.'

The branches of the shade tree stirred and dropped a confetti of leaves on Sobran's bed.

'You smell fruity and sweet,' the angel said. 'Your breath.'

Sobran said, 'Let me look at you.'

Xas put his face near to Sobran's and they gazed at each other. Then the man drifted. He began to make a slow inventory of the people who he expected to receive him in Heaven. Nicolette and Aline Lizet, his mother and father, Baptiste's infant sons, his brother-in-law Antoine. Baptiste Kalmann would be in purgatory, unless Sobran's prayers had bought him out. And where would Aurora go?

'You're dying and you fuss about it as if it's travel arrangements,' Xas said.

'Fetch me my wife,' Sobran told him.

Xas went to get Céleste who, as they came, explained that her husband was really too tired to talk. Yesterday he had said that nothing he thought seemed worth repeating. 'Baroness Lettelier came out of his room crying because all he'd said to her was that his mouth was dry and could she help him with that glass of water.'

Sobran had freed a hand from the covers. He twitched his fingers at Céleste. 'The bottle, the bottle.'

'What part of you isn't in pain?' Xas asked. His eyes glimmered. Then he said to Céleste, 'It's often like this – they go away to get ready for Heaven.' His voice was rough; he sounded like a boy.

'Too much,' Sobran said. 'What's the point.' He made them wait, held their words back with his eyes, held Xas's gaze. 'Of shaking off this cough.' Then a breath. It was an airless midsummer night. The sky should open a crack, or the great thick fans of wings he remembered propel the air into his lungs as hard as the sea pushes air through a blowhole.

Céleste gave him the bottle of laudanum.

'I see,' Xas said.

Sobran said, 'I wanted you with me.'

He made the angel unstop the bottle, leaned back against the angel's warm, resilient chest as he sipped the laudanum.

'It's not enough,' Céleste said. 'Pardon me for being so practical.'

'Thank you, Céleste. *You*,' Sobran said to Xas. 'You finish it later. Finish me. You haven't anything to lose.'

He watched Xas, then angry, said, 'Show that you give your consent.'

'Yes,' Xas said.

After a moment Sobran told them that he couldn't keep his eyes open. 'I want you to put my hand on your mouth.' He saw his hand lifted, his clawed fingers and one damaged nail like a chip of agate. He felt the kiss, the smooth, plump mouth.

'It wasn't possible,' he said. What he had wanted, with all his heart, was to match this being stride for stride over the miles. But a crippled angel will outstrip a man.

His eyes were closed. The bones in his neck were wax, melting, his head settled like a flower on a withered stalk, his throat began to occlude itself, never mind the thick liquids that crept up it from his lungs. He felt a hand on his mouth. They made a mirror, hand to mouth, and for a moment weren't anywhere particular in their lives, but were together.

Sobran roused himself one last time. He was exhausted, but love was never finished, it had its rights, it had the right of prophesy. He said, 'I'll see you on the day beyond days.' For a long second, like the shock of falling, he waited for the answer he deserved, the aspiration of 'yes' on his fingertips.

The angel let Sobran's hand fall from his closed lips.

'He's as good as dead,' Céleste said. She sounded as though she had been holding her breath. 'I have something I want you to carry to my husband in Heaven,' she said.

Xas opened his eyes in time to take the folded page she offered him.

'When I found Léon hanging I took only what accused me. I defied Sobran to speak to me about my unfaithfulness — *he* wasn't faithful to me. I've forgiven him that. Léon Jodeau was another kind of traitor. He couldn't be true to what he knew about himself.' Céleste brushed at her dress. Her tone, phrase by phrase, was self-excusing, remote, gloating. 'He liked me to put my hands around his throat and choke him.' She put up her hands to show the angel, clenched and flexed them in the air. 'Aline Lizet had taken my husband once when she was only a girl — bewitched him. I know that. Then she meant to have Léon. She — ' Céleste's voice was now stiff with pride — 'wouldn't have known how to handle him. Even after Aline was dead I was able to have Léon. Even when he said he hated me.'

She took a deep breath and stared into Xas's eyes. 'Angel of God,

I didn't show Léon's letter to Sobran not because I was afraid of what he would do to punish me, or to spare him pain, but because I didn't want him to share his trouble, or *halve* it, with the Baroness.' She nodded slowly, as though expecting him to join her by saying, 'I understand.' Then she gave herself a little shake, pursed her lips, stretched her eyelids in a girlish expression of I'm-all-innocence. 'Now, you should do what you promised him you would,' Céleste reminded Xas.

The angel put his face down to feel for breath – thought he felt something steamy stir the small hairs on his cheek. He placed one hand over Sobran's mouth and pinched his nose closed.

There was no sign, no struggle. After several minutes Xas let go and saw that Sobran's nostrils had retained the white pressure marks of his pinching fingers.

Céleste stood, pressed her hands into the small of her back and arched. 'There is plenty of light to see by. He'd better have the lamp – he and you. You watch. I'll go and sit in the house till five, then wake my sons.'

Madame Jodeau went down the slope, made her way carefully, but unassisted by a stick. She came out of the vineyard and went into the house. The low light in one room brightened. Xas turned to the lost page of Léon's letter.

– and the inspiration of her death. God help me. For five years under your roof and your protection I have betrayed you with your wife. There was a time when as any other indecent but ordinary erring man I would have pleaded clemency for Céleste for her betrayal of your mutual vow. I cannot beg for her now though I must acknowledge that there were times when she seemed to know me so thoroughly and be so easy in her mind that I allowed myself to imagine that you had guessed everything and permitted everything. This is my worst sin – the sinuous hypocrisy of my reasoning. Céleste isn't sane, so I am doubly to blame for the suffering she still struggles against so strenuously and so murderously. I meant to finish with Céleste as my love for Aline Lizet grew. But she would not let me. Aline was murdered in the same manner as the poor girls I killed. I supposed like a madman that this was some judgement of God. Céleste meant to be a consolation to me after Aline's death. I tried to resist renewing our affair and last night in the Inn at Aluze, Céleste, in a rage with me, told me that it was she who killed Aline. I cannot tell you any of this and live. It doesn't please me to have her hurt me any more. She guessed my guilt because she knew my weakness. I can't live with my life in her hands. I am sorry, Sobran.

Xas closed his hand on the hot glass chimney of the lamp. He took it off and held the page to the flame. The ink flared green and iridescent, as the page was consumed. The angel dropped the black flake as its last corner caught fire. He wiped his hand before putting his palm down to smooth his friend's thin, white hair.

After a minute he got up and turned to face the road. He stood under the shade tree and listened to a dog bark and a train whistle.

~~~~~~~

1997 Château Vully l'Ange du Cru Jodeau

It's a lovely day, at the height of the tourist season, and the three English who have come by car eye the group gathered in a strip of shade beside an air-conditioned bus. Some wine tour from the South Pacific — beefy, tanned, expansive people who seem to have a clue or two about the vineyard. Their driver talks to the tour guide, an employee of the château. They are expected, she'll take them through now, first the tour, then the tasting, and then they can carry some wine away to Lateron, the restaurant at Aluze.

The Englishman asks whether he and his friends can join the New Zealanders. 'Yes, all at once, why not?' the tour guide says, then flicks her eyebrows and gestures, 'You too, come here,' at the young man in dark glasses leaning against the door of his dusty Renault — a rental. He is another tourist, she thinks, so keeps her foot light on the gas of her French.

On the walled walk the finest grade of gravel is loud underfoot, but when the tourists pause they can hear the bees in the lavender and flowering thyme. The arched gates in the walls give onto the vine rows, shallow slopes that rise on either side of the château's buildings, like furled wings. A picture of order in ancient cultivation.

As they go, the tour guide tells them about *Phylloxera vastatrix*, the vine louse that devastated the vineyards of Europe between 1863 and 1890. The vines here were grafted onto American root stock in the 1870s. Only the vine stock of its Grand Cru was spared – just one walled vineyard between Macon and Chagny, Clos Jodeau, which lies three miles south of Vully.

She conducts the tourists into the cool cuverie to show them the old oak presses and copper fermentation vats. One tourist, used to the stainless fermentation cellars of his own vineyard in Hawke's Bay, points at the grape-pulp, caked and dry like wasps' nests, above one vat.

'Since when was wine all about hygiene?' the tour guide tells him, light as a wasp. 'Remember those bare feet treading the grapes.' She is annoyed to see that the young man in dark glasses – still in dark glasses indoors – has his head back to peer at the ceiling above the vat. A health-inspector type. American, perhaps.

I am looking up at the panels of the high ceiling of the cuverie that I know form the floor of another room above, a room with a low ceiling. I am looking at everything. There is a work in the Pompidou Centre entitled just that: Everything. *Tutto*, by Alighiero Boetti. A meticulously embroidered mosaic of animals and artefacts in many colours, where the border of every shape meets that of another, and all the spaces are shapes, each recognisable: lamp stands, guitars, traffic lights, deer, trains, swallows, hammers – everything. A perfect puzzle, a jigsaw of the world with each thing beside another, nothing beside itself, and not one thing broken.

We walk into the cellars through a new door, an enlargement of a hole used to hide Allied airmen during the war, the tour guide tells us. She takes us along the long ranks of barrels, where Vully's two Premiers Crus mature, as still as sphinxes. The barrels, she says, are not new, for Vully doesn't hold with over-oaked wine. Some were new in 1970, but 'the angels' of the château's Grand Cru are original.

In 1931 I was working in Germany. I was in charge of the fire in the film *Kameradschaft.* An explosion in the mine – a fire that broke through a mortared stone wall, dragon's breath, its steady, muffled roar going on after the engineer's quenched screams. Well – that's how it plays. Of course, there was no one in the flame-filled shaft but me, in a protective suit, pumping kerosene. For almost three decades I'd watched films, but *Kameradschaft* was the first time I'd looked at anything over the camera's shoulder, looked at artifice in its true colours; then through the camera's eye, when my first shot was set up; then afterwards, at a screening. And, despite my faithful and unfading memory, I found myself regretting you – your voice, face, gestures – as lost evidence. Why remember, when I had nothing to show for it? Now, my fire is as grey as the faces of the actors and extras I knew. That monochrome radiance, the fire's speedy, repeating tumescence, was the best we could do – the most I could want.

There were two things I didn't tell you.

When my beekeeper monk died, I discovered I couldn't do without him. I sat by his hives in the humpy meadow and ached with sorrow. I wondered whether angels got ill, I found myself rocking out stiffness I couldn't possibly feel. Then I flew to Heaven and found him. Or – I found his soul, and it wasn't the same thing. Niall's soul had his liveliness, the vitality that had been worn away in the remote old man he had become. But Niall's soul wasn't Niall. Lucifer wanted to know why I thought this was. He'd never troubled himself to get to know a human, so had no basis for comparison. When I said I didn't understand or have any ideas he tried a theory. Lucifer has theories. What God makes are copies and distillations. A soul is a distilled human. Earth and purgatory are distilleries. My Niall and your Nicolette became blissful distillations, not themselves, if Lucifer is to be believed.

I believe him. I'll never see you again.

We walk out of the fermentation cellar and around, the easy way, the tour guide says, to the new cellar. 'New, 1770 or so.' The women sigh at a stand of hollyhocks in a sheltered corner. Where Aurora had a lily pond is a rectangular flowerbed, and a pump smothered in red clematis. We go down the steps into the cool cellar. The tour guide poses between 'the angels' and tells her tales of the only Grand Cru of the Chalonnaise, legends of its provenance, and of the bundles the cooper claimed M. Jodeau, Vully's vintner, hid in each barrel.

I lied about my other visit to Heaven. God did answer my question. I asked why I looked like Christ and God answered, 'Because you are a copy of Him.'

How could I be, wasn't I older than Him?

'I knew about Him from the beginning,' God said. 'I made my copy before He was born – wanting to see what He would do if He didn't do His duty.'

'Did Lucifer know?'

'Not until he came to Earth to – as he puts it – *reason* with my Son. Lucifer was thrown by the likeness and made a poor job of his pitch. That was also my intention. My Son needed an element of surprise. By that time I had some knowledge of His susceptibilities – I'd been watching you. After this encounter Lucifer told me, in a great rage, that he was going to kill you, and that our bargain was off. But when he went to kill you he found you planting your garden.'

I remember. Lucifer found me in my open black glass dome, standing in a paste of sand, and covered with the spores of various mosses. I hadn't spoken to the archangel since he'd 'signed' me. I said to him, nervously, that I was going to make a garden. He seemed perplexed and stared at me for a long time in silence. Finally, sounding amused, he said, 'Don't you mean rather that you are going to *try* to make a garden.'

'Yes, try,' I said.

'All right,' he said.

God and His copies and extractions, His improved editions, His finer things. In His world it is as though there are no particular things – or the particularity of each thing depends upon another. So hollyhocks smell like watermelon or watermelon like hollyhocks. And there is a taste in some good but perishable sparkling wine that is like the bindings of books printed between 1890 and 1920, perhaps some chemical in the glue. This hateful phenomenon of likeness is more than the meanings made by human minds – that old conspiracy of significance – it is evidence, the pollution of God's plan.

If I hadn't withheld these thoughts from you, would you have gone to Heaven carrying your knowledge like an infection, one of those improving infections, like the flor that makes yellow wine yellow?

The tour guide walks away from 'the angels'. She turns her body into a signpost, directs us into 'the eastern transept'. That old joke. 'Monsieur, s'il vous plaît ... ' She tells me not to lean on the barrel. A wing at my back, a wing behind the wood. 'If you please,' she says. I move on.

You fainted and I caught you. It was the first time I'd supported a human. You had such heavy bones. I put myself between you and gravity.

Impossible.